HER ROAD FROM WAR

ALLY McCORMICK

ESSEX COUNTY
COUNCIL LIBRARY

Disclaimer:
As the story is based in various British colonies, the spelling used is British English that was common shortly before WW2, such as Hongkong and Tokio. Sexist and racial generalisations and terminology are also faithful to those expressed in that era. They neither reflect the opinion of the author nor publisher. Although this story is based on true events, the characters have been fictionalised.

Acklowledgements:
I wish to thank my major sources
The Knights of Bushido, by Lord Russell of Liverpool, reprinted 2002 Greenhill Books. Although these extracts from the Military War Tribunal of the Far East made for gruesome reading, they were invaluable to my research.
The web sites and contributors of COFEPOW and FEPOW for sharing real life stories and photographs. These are wonderful resources which I hope will continue to educate new generations, as they did me.
The National Archives of Singapore who allowed me unhindered access and help with microfiche files.
The National Library Board, Singapore who have marvellously digitized the old newspapers of Singapore, giving so much detail into daily life and more than a glimpse into the mindset of the day.
The National Library of New Zealand, and finally, Auckland Libraries.

Cover Design by: Instagram@matyan90

Copyright © 2016 Ally McCormick

All rights reserved.

ISBN: 047337076X
ISBN-13: 978-0-473-37076-3

Totara Books, New Zealand
www.totarabooks.nz

*For Mum, who entrusted me with her story,
and who encouraged me to sculpt it into a novel.*

ALLY MCCORMICK

Sometimes our biggest mistakes have the best of consequences.

PREFACE

If Japan had not invaded Singapore, I would never have been born.

And who was I?

I was an innocent toddler with soft dark ringlets, glistening blue eyes and rosy cheeks—a confused little girl whose crime was simply being herself. My punishment for being born was to requisition my natural identity and at 18 months of age, replace it with a new one. I was collateral damage; no more, no less. Naturally, I grew into a woman with an intrinsic need to make sense of my very being.

In my heart, I know that I cannot be blamed for any of the devastation that both preceded my birth and came after. But if I was not to blame, then who was? My mother perhaps? My father? Lt-General Percival? The Imperial Japanese Army? God, even?

I discovered that the list of possible people to blame is long and eventually realised it is cruel and pointless to blame anyone for the events that happen after one is blindsided on the *Road of Life*.

Someone once told me that there are no U-turns in life. Undoubtedly, my mother's journey through life took a wrong turn from which she could never fully recover. The road she was born to was a privileged and relatively happy one in the British Far Eastern Colonies. The disastrous crossroads was the War in the Pacific where she inadvertently collided with the Japanese invasion. And the unexpected direction was my illegitimate birth.

I started investigating my birth story in an effort to make sense of it. I began with my mother's recollections, but before she passed away, her memory faded and many questions were left unanswered. So I spent years researching. I was able to verify most of her story; however, I discovered that my mother had concocted several minor details. I can only guess why; perhaps to protect herself, to keep her secrets, to protect the ones she loved...

I've given the story a life of its own in this book. In order to respect her wish to protect innocent family members, I've changed the names of many of the characters. Obviously, all conversations are fictionalised and I've used my imagination wherever necessary to join the dots. But at its core, it is as close to the truth as possible. As much as this is her story, it is also my story. It is the story of my birth. My beginning.

During my research I realised that, while many women in WW2 had illegitimate children, my mother's journey was quite a remarkable one. Despite her failings, she was a courageous person, and faced unenviable dilemmas. When the War was *done and dusted* and finally relegated to the pages of history, she had left behind a tapestry of broken hearts, not least her own.

Perhaps you'll have little sympathy for either her plight or my search for answers. Some readers might conclude that a good grounding in morals, a dose of common-sense and a sprinkling of humility should be enough to keep us on the straight and narrow. They might even think that I should be thankful I received a good upbringing.

In my opinion those views are both inflexible and smug. They neither resolve my inner conflict nor do they compensate me for what I have lost.

If the path is straightforward, then yes, virtuous personal qualities should suffice in life. But when we reach a critical crossroad only to find our road map is full of incorrect information, or when a thoughtless motorist clips our rear end sending us spiralling out of control ... can we be blamed for losing our sense of direction?

And when the road behind us is completely demolished, how do we right our wrong-turns?

How does one traverse the *Road From War?*

Christina Whitlock

1
NORFOLK ISLAND 1937

HUNTER WHITLOCK

Down on the shoreline, Hunter felt an angry change in the wind. He paused, sandpaper in hand, listening. Distant voices, jarring voices, drifted in on waves, lapping at the edge of his audible range. The shouting was coming from the direction of Burnt Pine.

Still kneeling beside the slim gunwales of his little sailing boat, he bent his head and closed his eyes, allowing himself a brief moment of concentration. There was something wrong, he knew that instinctively. He thought perhaps it was a fire, but then again the voices were fierce rather than panicked. While he listened, intently trying to get a feel for the nature of the crisis, his mind also ran over his plan of action if he was to go to help. He would need to gather his tools and stow them quickly into the tiny iron tool shed he had built on the shoreline. He could tidy them later. His little yacht would stay as she was sitting on the hard packed earth in front of it. It shouldn't matter if he left her uncovered for a few hours.

Another sound came rushing in at him. A galloping horse, perhaps? Yes, almost immediately he discerned the noise of hooves thudding on the clay road above. Hunter stood waiting for the horseman to rein in. He soon saw it was Wally, both a friend and the most trusted man on his banana plantation. In fact, Wally was the only man, other than family, who had been kept on since the collapse in the banana market a few years earlier.

"There's trouble. It's yer wife. You'd better come," he said in between laboured breath while struggling to hold his wild-eyed heavily panting horse.

Hunter didn't have to ask what was up with his wife. He could guess more or less. Truth be told, he had been expecting this day for some time.

Instead, he asked, "How many?"

"Half the village and then some gathered out front of Young's House. It be an angry mob. Yer father-in-law and the boys are up at the farm. They be expecting trouble."

Just like Hunter and his in-laws, Wally was not a native of Norfolk Island. But his speech was littered with sprinklings of borrowed pigeon English from the local islanders and a heavily accented Cornish that would have been as foreign sounding in Cornwall as it was here.

"They be getting quite savage like," he reiterated. "They's talk o' lynching an' such."

Hunter sucked in his breath. Already while Wally was focussed on explaining, Hunter had straightened his precious tools and whistled to his pony who was at his side in an instant. He'd left the solid beast grazing in the field beyond and hadn't noticed that she had very recently come in to stand beside the tool shed where she was currently shifting her weight uneasily from one leg to another. Hunter allowed himself the extravagance of considering whether the beast had heard the angry voices on the wind as well. He had a knack of processing several unrelated strands of thought at once, and his next sentence reflected that perfectly.

"Will you back me up, if I try to explain to them about her illness?"

Wally gave a snort. "Of course! If you want to call it an illness. Personally, I think shez just lost her marbles. Nothing a good holy shag would'na fix and a belt on the back-side. If ye asked me, I'd say she needs a wee bebe to look out for. Then she'd have sommat else to think aboot asides he'self. Not that ye did ask me mind."

Hunter manoeuvred his pony through the gate before responding harshly.

"I'd not inflict that woman on any baby of mine. What is it this time: a dead rooster or a sow's heart perhaps?"

"Nay. This time be different. She be naked and performin' atop the roof of the packing shed. She won't come down and she has drawn the attention of yer neighbours."

The news surprised Hunter and his mare hesitated when Hunter exhaled heavily, sinking into his seat. "Completely naked?"

"Aye. That she is. Seems to be enacting some sort of satanic ritual; chanting and the like."

Hunter kicked his pony into a gallop. The little beauty had no trouble keeping up with Wally's great ugly nag.

He couldn't help wondering what his wife looked like nude. It had been almost a decade since he had shared her bed and even then he doubted that he had ever seen her completely unclothed. Since her mother had died, she had taken to dressing entirely in black, from the spidery shawl tightly pulled around her bony shoulders to the narrow boots that encased her miserable feet. He was just the tiniest bit scared of the woman he had once loved. She was all but a stranger these days; not only to himself but also to her father and her brothers who all lived in the big house at the other end of the plantation.

He was well aware that Joseph treated him more like a son than the son-in-law that he actually was. He was equally aware that Joseph and his daughter Hester seldom spoke. Heck, Hester seldom spoke to a single person on the island. She had long since stopped attending church. Hunter knew by the account books that she had not visited the village shops for at least three months. She refused to cook and did no housework. Hunter had taken to eating at the big house with his in-laws. He'd seen her picking at wild beans and eating raw eggs and goodness knows what else. Bread loaves that Joseph's housekeeper gave Hunter to take home were eaten secretively when he wasn't there. When he was home she persistently ignored him, sleeping in the front room on the sofa and wearing the same clothes day in and day out. Certainly she never washed herself when Hunter was around though he assumed she did so while he was out on the plantation. Her hair was constantly wrapped inside a turban-like scarf. He hadn't seen it in years.

As they galloped towards the small island centre at Burnt Pine, he wondered what he had ever done to deserve a wife like Hester.

Soon they reached the turnoff to the hill road leading to the plantation. The angry mob had already passed through here. They could hear it ahead. With less than a mile to the family plantation, the mob must be nearly there. Wordlessly, Hunter and Wally kicked their horses with renewed energy, but only caught up to the tail end of the crowd as it reached its destination.

The mob parted to allow Hunter and Wally to pass through their ranks. Unkind murmurs and whispers about his ineffectiveness as a husband followed their passage.

Finally, Hunter's horse came to a standstill in front of the packaging shed where he gazed at his wife upon the roof. For the briefest moment, he was entranced by what he witnessed and a great swelling of emotion began to build in the pit of his gut.

For there she was. Her white skin glowing with reflected sunset. Her arms outstretched, the tips of her pert breasts, as yet never suckled, pointing towards the sky. Her hollow hips thrust forward, back arched, eyes closed. The dark mound beneath her belly exposed for all to see and her thin lips pursed into a never-ending chant.

In most marriages, there are moments of doubt and even regret. Moments when either or both participants wonder what on earth possessed them to marry in the first place.

For Hunter, this wasn't a moment of doubt, rather it was one of sudden clarity. The strong emotion surging through him was not lust. No, far from it. This emotion he knew was dread. It was the realisation that his life on Norfolk Island was over.

He dropped his eyes towards Joseph who was being harangued by several neighbours and the village wheelwright. Joseph's housekeeper was standing resolutely beside him, her arms folded and disapproving lips pursed.

Hunter caught Joseph's eye and tried unsuccessfully to call him over before sliding from his horse to the top of the fence.

"People! Friends, neighbours, all please listen. I know you are upset at Hester's behaviour."

"Shis mard, insane!" someone cried out in the Norfolk language.

"Shi giwe me dar bloomen willies."

"Shi esa witch!" someone else yelled.

"Witch! Witch! Witch!" a chanting began.

"Please, hear me out!" Hunter pleaded uneasily above the din. He had begun to notice the rocks that many held in their fists.

"My wife is ill. She has been ill for many months, years even. I had been hoping she would get better on her own, but now, I think it is best if I take her back to New Zealand. So that she can receive hospital treatment. She's no witch. She has lost her grasp on what is real and what is not. That is all. She is a good Christian woman, from a good Christian family. A family that has been respected in these parts for many years."

"Hear, hear!" Wally spoke up.

There was a brief moment of silence and Hunter hoped that someone else, someone more local and respected than Wally might also support him. He looked around anxiously.

The auctioneer spoke first, his deep voice booming across the yard, though Hunter could not at first see where he was standing.

"Yoosa guden, Maister Whitlock. Sos Joseph, gehl's faada. Nun'es har'ses an'thin tuther. But in ar illy ailen ye Ken nort baid efluens be wis dem sen emuns en ooah waawaha en pontoo. Mebe daunle mebe nor. Tis baid nuf wi'oot thus pouri. Aye, nay stoen t'bang hir en yer haus, ais ful ve yus vamoose Nyuu Ziilan."

Despite the tension in the air, Hunter looked to Wally with a slightly bemused expression, lifting one eyebrow in question to this strongly worded Norf'k dialect.

Wally knew that Hunter's grasp of the local language was very limited, so he gave a loud translation.

"They say the island is too small to have people who don't contribute, who keep to themselves and who are a bad influence with her unkempt appearance and uncleanliness. He says whether or not she is ill and whether or not she is practicing witchcraft, her suggestive erotic behaviour is a bad influence on the young people of the island and is going too far. And essentially he is saying if you and your in-laws don't have the balls to sort her out yourselves then he'd be happy if the entire family would decamp to New Zealand as quickly as possible."

Hunter addressed both the auctioneer and Wally, his impromptu translator.

"And would they be happy to leave it at that? No harm to come to her today, no stoning?"

Before either could answer, the crowd simmered and Hunter's attention was drawn to the roof. Hester had turned to the crowd and for the first time looked as if she was aware of her surroundings. She had a sneer on her face.

"Balls? He doesn't have any balls. That is the problem. This be all *his* fault." She pointed to her husband before returning her arms skyward. "Feast yer eyes, go on, leastways someone appreciates me. That one of you be man enough to give me a child. Come on up and fill meh cup."

"Silence child!" roared her father.

There were cruel jeers from the crowd of "*baswargus,*" and "*hue hue*" and "*inkerdus,*" all of which meant things like ugly beyond description, dirty and unclean and not likely missy.

Then the first rock was thrown. It fell wide and bounced off the corner of the roof, narrowly missing Joseph below. A second rock was already mid-air, when the auctioneer called, "Enuf!"

"*What a way dem musa shame,*" he said to the islanders when they had returned their attention to him. And then in his best English he said, "Yer family mus'bus be ashamed. Ail vouch fer yers safety. But I warn ye t'be gunna from des plais afore nixt Sabbeth. Tek the plantan bowat and be gon – alla ye," he said indicating Hester's two younger brothers.

"He wants us to catch the banana boat which leaves next Saturday..." Wally began.

"I heard him," Hunter interrupted annoyed. His brow furrowed while he stared at his feet considering the whole deal. How would they uproot themselves in just four days? There was his little sailboat he had worked on so hard for months for one thing. What would he do with that? Nobody knew anything about sailing on this island. There would be no one to buy his pony or indeed the farm. No one was buying banana plantations these days. It would mean walking away and leaving behind his capital investment. Joseph would be furious; he did not dare to look over towards him at that minute.

When Hunter did finally look up, it was to see that all of the villagers had turned to go and many had already begun the trip back down the hill.

He glanced back up at Hester, but she was no longer on the pitched roof and looking around he could see no sign of her. No doubt, she had climbed down to the back of the shed where the large bean frames abutted the side. These had once produced runner beans in export quantities, but now only grew wild and unkempt. When the family had emigrated from New Zealand, they had purchased this bean farm and immediately planted a grove of bananas, riding the wave of success that the abundant crop had brought right across the island.

The current banana crises, caused by the Australian and New Zealand government's unfair embargo on imports, meant that Hunter and Joseph had been contemplating leaving the island for some time. Given the current family crises, Hunter felt an urgent need to talk to Joseph but first he needed to deal with his wayward wife.

He found her standing in amongst the beans, attempting to wrap the vines around herself.

"Come inside now," he commanded as gently as his simmering heart rate would allow him.

She showed no sign of having heard him.

For a moment, he stood undecided as to how to approach her. He felt like slapping some sense into her, but then violence towards women was something he could not abide.

Finally, he attempted to seize her around her middle and drag her towards their cottage.

Hester immediately gave a blood-curdling shriek and raked his face with cat like claws.

He promptly released his feral wife and reached up to press the smarting wounds, which already oozed with blood. Staggering back, he found his shoulders gripped hard by his father-in-law. Joseph's housekeeper, never far from her employer's side, immediately pressed her apron to Hunter's wound. From the corner of his eye, Hunter could see Hester's younger brothers, Bert and Del, looking confused and upset, while Hester fled back to the cottage.

"You cannot go on with this marriage son," Joseph said softly.

And with those words, Hunter suddenly realised how strange it was that not once before had he ever entertained the notion of simply walking away from Hester and her family. Certainly he often regretted his marriage, but ending it in divorce had never occurred to him before now. He wasn't entirely sure of the law, but he had heard the phrase "divorce by reason of insanity" before, so he suddenly wondered whether her behaviour would constitute a legal argument towards that end. This startling revelation stung more than the scratch on his face and yet at the same time he felt like a candle had been lit in a very dark passage. For the first time in as long as he could remember, he felt a glimpse of optimism—a life without Hester.

It was true too that he was nearing his middle age and starting anew with very little capital would not be easy.

He would be abandoning Hester to her madness. Expecting her family to pick up the pieces and face the return to New Zealand. It was more than cowardly to leave the responsibility to them.

The housekeeper let go of his wounded face. The sting had turned to an aching throb but he could still feel blood dripping slowly off his chin. Hell, the woman needed to trim her nails.

Anger surged up inside of him. Yes, it would be difficult starting again, but surely, it would be easier than staying married. When he returned to Auckland, he could evict the tenants on his father's citrus farm and live there. Or, with all his previous Territorial experience, he could join the Army or even the Royal Navy. The idea appealed to him. Why not join up, while he was still young enough to be accepted? There was talk of war in the New Zealand newspapers, which always arrived several weeks late now that the regular banana boats no longer plied the seas between the two countries. For all he knew, war may already have started in Europe. If not, he could always head over to Spain to join the Spanish Foreign Legion. He had heard that *they'd* take anybody.

2
HONGKONG 1938

RUTH WARNER

"*CHINESE Trained Fleas Executed!*" Henry read loudly and then chuckled. "Listen to this, my dear. *Honolulu Customs Authorities seized and gassed to death ten trained fleas belonging to Tong Shong-Chang, when he arrived aboard the steamship President Hoover from Hongkong today. An official remarked, 'if he wants to run a flea circus he will have to use American fleas.' Tong is angered by this remark because he conducts his flea act in Cantonese and he is fearful that American fleas will not understand him.*"

Henry gave a loud belly laugh but stopped abruptly when he noted Ruth sitting hunched and scowling in the deep club chair across from him. "Come on, where's that beautiful smile? You can't convince me you're not amused."

"Yes, it's a hoot father. But I don't see how you can be reading The Straits Times, of all newspapers, when my life is hanging in the balance."

"Don't be dramatic dear. It's a marriage not a death sentence. And I happen to be interested in Singapore news since my only daughter may well reside there before long."

Ruth twisted away from her father so that she could watch the far end of the room. She made a feeble attempt to hide her face behind the tortured handkerchief balled in her hand, all the while furtively scrutinising the small group of officers standing at the bar. One in particular held her attention.

From just behind her ear, her father's voice purred gently.

"He's a good lad, I swear it. You'll live a comfortable life with all the same privileges as a navy wife. The base at Singapore is brand new, new houses, plenty to do …"

Ruth noticed her father's sanctioning of the mad idea falter. She wondered why he wanted this so much. He owed nothing, as far as she knew, to this young suitor. She turned back to her father with a face strung with anguish, but still unable to verbalise the confused feelings she held in check.

"Well I am surprised," he began, "I thought you were very keen on him. Is there something wrong with him? Perhaps he's not tall enough for you?"

"Dad, honestly he's well over six foot or the Pope's not Catholic."

"Well, what then? Do you find him repellent?"

"No, he's very agreeable. It's just that, well, I was hoping that now I'd finished with school I could come back home and we would finally live as a family. You and Jeffrey and me. You need looking after, Father."

"Home? This is not our home. England is home, you should never lose sight of that. Besides my dear, you've been back in Hongkong for what—three months? You must see what's going on out here; we're all on high alert. It's not just the communists over the border; we now have the Japanese throwing their weight around too. Look lovey, whether you like it or not, the reality of living in Hongkong is no longer like some of the carefree holidays you've known in previous years. To my mind, you're well out of it. Singapore, on the other hand, is a safe haven and knowing you'd be there was reason enough for me to give the lad my blessing."

"But ... I don't ... love him," she eventually managed to mumble.

"What's that? Love you say? Do you think I loved your mother when we were first married? I hardly knew her. I may have told myself I loved her, but as our love grew, I realised that my initial feelings hadn't been love. No, not really old girl, not by a long shot."

"You hardly ever talk about Mother," Ruth said softly.

"Truth is, it doesn't hurt so much now. I've gotten used to being a widower. It suits me, I'm finding." Henry Warner drained the last of his stengah and continued. "I'm going to find a place for Jeffrey in the Dockyard Defence Corp. He'll live in barracks and I'll return to bachelor's quarters."

"Jeffrey! But he's only twelve," Ruth nearly shrieked in shock.

"They'll take him on as a cadet. I've already asked about it."

Ruth was stunned into silence for a while.

"You realise he's not a catholic?" she managed eventually in a slightly timid voice.

Henry, who had been absently twisting his empty short glass on its little rattan coaster, appeared to be choosing his next words carefully.

"Look my darling, I won't force you to marry him. But my advice is grab this opportunity with both hands. I don't think you'll ... well to put it plainly, I don't think I'll find you a better match."

"He's taking me dancing later," Ruth said morosely. "So I expect he'll pop the question then. I'll have to act surprised, I dare say."

"Yes and perhaps you could make your voice sound a little brighter too. No sense scaring him off, what?" Henry watched her features darken slightly. "Well, think on what I've said. I might be an old sock, but I do know a thing or two. Drink up; I expect that boy is coming over to tell us our table is ready, and about time too."

Ruth negotiated a twelve-month engagement to Sergeant Charlie Cole. Initially, the plan was to allow her time to get to know Cole before she tied the proverbial knot. As an additional incentive, she also wanted to spend more time with her father. This idea was born from years of separation from her immediate family. When her mother died of cholera ten years earlier Ruth had been sent to board at the Holy Child Convent School in London. Her father was stationed with the Royal Navy in the Far East. For an inexplicable reason, he deemed the local school in Hongkong adequate for a boy but not appropriate for a daughter. So while Ruth was sent away to a life of strict moral routine, her young brother was looked after day to day by their kindly Chinese amah. From what Ruth had seen, he spent his weekends running free around the dockyards. As a family, they hardly knew each other. The travelling distance was such that the majority of Ruth's holidays were spent with her mother's spinster sisters in England. If it were not for summer hols at the British naval base in Hongkong, Ruth's father and brother would be strangers to her. Nevertheless, she had grown to love the eastern way of life during those precious short breaks.

Ruth should have detected the fault in her extended term of engagement because a few weeks after the announcement was made, Sergeant Cole's planned transfer to Singapore took place. He was to join the Admiralty Police Force, which was tasked with guarding the big new naval dockyards on the island. Ruth discovered that if she wanted to get to know her future husband, she would need to live in Singapore too.

The only person Ruth knew in Singapore was Irene Ardern, a school friend from the Convent. So she wrote to ask Irene if her family would allow her to board with them. When a response arrived by cablegram, Ruth was almost too frightened to read it.

YOU ARE VERY WELCOME DEAR ADVISE DATES LETTER FOLLOWING Mrs Ardern

By the next afternoon, Ruth had replied with her dates and ship. She eagerly awaited the promised letter, which arrived three days later.

"Dear Ruth, how excited I was to receive your letter. Mother is sending a wire to you today, which you should have by the time this letter reaches you. There is no need for you to worry about whether you will be welcome. You can stay for as long as you need, so long as you don't mind sharing my modest bedroom with me. Mother and Papa are genuinely pleased that I will have company, as they tell me that I mope around too much. It can be monotonous on my own and I don't always feel like going out with mother's circle. I think I shall scream if I have to play another round of badminton. But don't fret, there is ever so much to do here to fill in our time and with a companion it won't be nearly so dull. Do tell me what your fiancé looks like, so I can try to get a glimpse of him before you arrive. There are so many handsome men floating around, but the white APF dress uniforms are easy to spot. Mother says that we shall meet you on the wharf, so do wire or write back with your dates. Now I am so excited I expect I shan't be able to sleep until you arrive. So don't be long.

Yours in expectation, Irene."

3
SINGAPORE 1939

CHARLIE COLE

Thirty-eight and most of thirty-nine passed in an epoch of sultry distractions.

It would be fair to say that the majority of Colonials living in Singapore at that time were unaware that their hedonistic way of life had reached its pinnacle. With the Great Depression of '29 behind them, they had been busy getting on with a particular kind of artificial existence that most of them would not have known had they never ventured from Europe.

Were they not poised to join the War, which had already begun in Europe then, perhaps, they might have continued in this luxurious manner. The most observant amongst them may have already recognised that the Straits Settlement was gradually metamorphosing from one of the greatest trading post crossroads in the history of humankind to a military stronghold of significance.

Sergeant Charles Ivory Cole was one such person. He was already turning a wary eye towards the events unfolding in China. Having lived a while up in Hongkong he was more suspicious of Japan's expansionist policies than most in Singapore.

"Sergeant!" Lance Corporal Ajmer Singh saluted. "I have your cycle out front."

"Thank you Corporal. I will be along presently," Sergeant Cole replied. He closed the duty book with a snap and went to retrieve his gloves and helmet. Then, nodding goodbye to another Constable who would remain in sole charge of HQ until daybreak, he went to join the Punjabi police officer who would second him during his night rounds.

"Fuelled up?" he asked routinely, knowing that the answer would be affirmative.

"Oh, I do enjoy working nights," Cole said conversationally. "Wouldn't want it that way all the time mind, but I like the gentle heat; the warmth without the humidity."

"Not for me Sarg. I count the hours before I can go back on days."

"Ah well, let's get it over with, shall we? We'll start at Sembawang Gate and mark our way back to Woodlands. You can drive."

Lance Corporal Ajmer Singh suppressed a smile as he gunned the motorcycle into life. He always found it comical to see the tall sergeant squeeze himself into the sidecar.

At each stop, their task was to check-in with the constable on duty at the guardhouses, ensuring nothing untoward had occurred and check off the visitors' book.

When they arrived at the Canberra Gate, there was no sign of the guard, who surely would have heard their vehicle and should have been approaching to challenge them.

Dismounting the bike, the two men unclipped their pistols and cautiously ducked under the barrier. A few steps further in, a strange noise greeted them, and Cole dashed his arm out to halt the Corporal. Almost immediately, it became clear that the noise was a man's snoring. The Corporal looked at Cole with eyes wide in disbelief. Meanwhile, Cole's eyes creased in anger. He indicated to the Corporal to remain silent.

They took a few steps towards the back of the guardhouse where on the verandah they could clearly see a pair of legs sticking out in the lantern light. One was properly attired and the other leg was bare, with the puttee unwound and the boot and baton laying to the side.

"How do you credit that?" the Sergeant asked the Corporal, in a conversational tone.

"That's no good Sarg," Corporal Singh agreed just as loudly.

Still the man slept on.

"Constable," Corporal Singh called loudly.

There was no reply.

"Constable!" Cole roared.

The sleeping policeman jerked awake, swallowing a snore, causing him to choke a little on his spittle. He jumped up and withdrew his bayonetted rifle. His eyes widened when he saw his superior glaring at him.

"Sir!" he responded quickly lowering his weapon.

"Name?" Cole demanded.

Although he had already visited the guard once that night and knew his name, protocol followed that he had to be certain to whom he was speaking.

"Constable Ude Singh, Sir!"

It was no coincidence that it was another Singh. The Naval Police

Force had been drawn from the 2nd and 5th Punjab Regiments and many of them were Singhs. It was unlikely that the two Singhs were related.

"Why were you sleeping on duty?"

"Sleeping? No Sir, I wasn't sleeping. I just closed my eyes for a second to rest them."

Cole was livid at the barefaced lie.

"Why are you half undressed?"

"I've got an ulcer on my leg and it's giving me some gyp."

"Don't you realise that you are the Naval Base's only defence against any Fifth Column that might want to snoop around? Don't you know that the red army are only a hop, skip and a jump away from Malaya?"

The Constable shrugged like a sullen schoolboy.

"I'll have to default you for sleeping on duty. That's a Court Marshall offence man. Write it up Corporal."

RUTH WARNER

Mr Ardern, Irene's father, was a merchant and didn't have a lot to do with the military on the island. His home was a fifteen-minute drive away from the Naval Base, but this didn't stop Ruth and Charlie from finding time to fraternise. It often seemed to Ruth that the navy only worked mornings, so while she and Irene spent these planning and shopping for the impending wedding, the afternoons were free for socialising. More often than not, they would meet Sergeant Cole and his friends at the Swimming Club and then join them again later for a dance, a play, or a myriad of other amusements.

During the term of their engagement, Ruth learned that Cole's Scottish parents, who had first immigrated to Hongkong and now Western Australia, would definitely be attending the wedding. Of course, her own father would be unable to leave Hongkong. The current military conflict between Japan and China meant that the naval base at Hongkong was on high alert. Henry Warner was a specialised engineer who worked in turns either at the floating graving dock or away on-board a Parthion-class boat such as HMS Pandorra, or perhaps a rainbow class sub like HMS Rover. Approval of unnecessary leave requests were near impossible to obtain.

Ruth was therefore in a quandary as to who would give her away at the wedding. She wondered if she should ask Mr Ardern and broached the subject with Cole one day during a game of whist at the Admiralty Club.

"Do you know that is a pickle I hadn't considered," he said earnestly putting his black cheroot down to give her his full attention.

"I don't mind Mr Ardern giving me away, but I'm not sure if he would want to. I don't want to put him to too much trouble. Not after everything he has done for me and it wouldn't be fair to expect Mrs Ardern to sit by herself in the cathedral. After all, Irene will not be able to sit with her since she is to be my bridesmaid."

"Do you mind if I make a suggestion?" asked Sergeant McGregor who occupied the place opposite Cole at the whist table. "Why not ask Armstrong? It's the first wedding for any of the APF lads and he will be the senior officer attending, won't he?"

Ruth was mortified when Cole immediately turned and loudly called Captain Armstrong over, explaining the situation with, Ruth thought, a lot of exaggeration.

"By Jove, I'd be honoured to give her away," Armstrong answered without hesitation and personally signed a chit for drinks all round to toast the fact.

During the toast, Ruth looked sideways at her fiancé. He was very debonair sometimes and didn't seem to have the same social fears that she herself held. Her scalp prickled and she knew her cheeks were flaming as she fretted over the horrifying fact that he had casually tossed the idea at Armstrong in front of the room full of people they knew. It made her feel like a penniless orphan. She would have appreciated being consulted first and then she would have approached the matter in an entirely more delicate manner.

Ruth knew well enough that Captain Giles Armstrong was quite the heartthrob. His father was the younger son of an Earl and he was irrefutably the centrepiece of the NBG Amateur Dramatics Society where he regularly walked the boards at both the naval base and in theatres all around Singapore. Ruth was well aware that the mere fact that he would attend the wedding was reason enough to make it one of the season's not-to-be-missed events. Therefore, she was flabbergasted that he had so readily agreed to give her away.

She blinked back her resistance as reality kicked in. Having Armstrong give her away was a social coup if ever there was one. She knew that any boost was desirable in the claustrophobic society that was late-1930s Singapore, especially since her family connections were limited to the Arderns.

As the toast came to a conclusion, Ruth reflected that Cole often acted the clown, bringing himself to the centre of attention. It was in stark contrast to the serious way he undertook his police duties. She didn't like it when he became loud and excessive, but she was beginning to wonder if the pressures of his workload meant that he needed this coping mechanism.

Although Ruth still couldn't honestly say she was in love with Cole, she certainly respected him and so she silently chided herself. The sentiment behind his impetuous request of Armstrong was nothing but a kindness.

In fact, the moment when she finally fell in love with Cole didn't come for another few weeks. It was precisely nine days before the wedding. The couple were meeting with the Reverend Hodge when he asked them if they truly loved each other. Charlie gently took her hand and held it to his cheek. His tone of voice, when he openly declared his love, made her heart melt. Ruth knew in that moment that she'd follow him anywhere: whether it be through the steamiest jungles of Malaya, the driest deserts of Western Australia or the foggiest days in Portsmouth.

CHARLIE COLE

But well before that meeting, when the wedding was still over a month away, something else of significance happened. It began when Ruth proposed a night out in town to see the remake of the Sherlock Holmes film, "The Hound of the Baskervilles." The film was due to begin screening at the Cathay cinema on the last day of October.

Charlie was keen, as he had yet to visit the Cathay, which had only just opened earlier that month. The theatre was situated in the unfinished, 16 storey building on Dhoby Ghaut, just off Orchard Road. It was reportedly very modern with lush upholstered seats and the new Mirrophonic Master sound system.

He knew that Ruth and Irene were desperate to see the film in which the leading lady, Miss Barrie, had been an old-girl at their convent school and had coincidentally grown up in Hongkong.

Although Irene was not officially seeing any particular young man, she was always popular with the APF lads and Charlie knew he'd have no trouble finding a suitable partner to escort her. So in the late afternoon, when the skies were dark and brooding in that characteristic stillness that always proceeds a thunderstorm, Charlie and Sergeant Bill Sutton collected the two girls in the sidecars of their motorcycles for the drive into Singapore.

It was half past eight when the picture ended and the lights came on. Charlie stretched out his legs and turned to smile at Ruth.

"What happened to those people sitting beside you?" she asked him.

"Oh, they left during the séance scene. Perhaps it was too frightening."

"I'll bet they didn't think it proper," Ruth retorted. "Not Christian, probably."

"It would be fun though," Irene said leaning forward from Ruth's other side and eager to join the conversation. "I've always wondered what it would be like to hold a séance."

"What do you think Sutton?" Cole called over to his colleague in a bemused tone.

"Load of old codswallop," came the reply with a yawn.

"I guess you need someone versed in the occult," Ruth ventured.

"Like one of those fortune tellers in Buffalo Road?" Irene suggested.

"Ooh, rather! I've never had the courage to visit one, but I'd love to have my fortune read. Could we do that tonight Charlie? Oh, do please say yes," Ruth pleaded earnestly.

Cole smiled. Not so much because he liked the idea, but more because Ruth had just addressed him by his first name in front of their friends, which seemed quite forward for his prim fiancé. All too late, he realised that Ruth had misunderstood his smile to him being agreeable to the idea and he thought she would be disappointed if he tried to back out now. The question was where to find a blasted fortune-teller at that time of night. He did not intend to drag the ladies around the depths of Little India and he said as much to the group.

"There'll be fortune tellers at the New World," Sutton suggested.

"That's settled then," Ruth said jumping up. "Oh, I say. Look!"

Ruth pointed down at the empty seat beside her fiancé, where a dainty petite point evening purse lay unattended.

Cole reached over and flicked up the purse, catching it neatly in his other hand. "I suppose she was in such a hurry to leave she left it behind," he suggested. "I'll drop it off to the cloakroom on the way out."

"Better to take it to the ticket booth," Sutton said. "An unregistered item at the cloakroom is bound to go missing."

"I wonder if there's a name inside," Cole said attempting to work the clasp and looking for all the world as if the item in his hands was as technical as the tuning dials on an autoradiogram.

"Oh, let me," Ruth said sounding exasperated and practically ripped it out of his hands. With a simple flick of her fingers, she unsnapped the clasp and then with one last glance around the theatre as if at any moment she might see the object's owner come running up, she pulled the purse open.

Her head knocked against Cole's as they both peered in at the same moment. He was quicker, pulling out a set of cards, all with the same name and address printed on them.

"What's that? Calling cards?" Irene asked trying to see over Ruth's shoulder.

"Mr and Mrs Theodorus Ohlrich," Cole read out. "641 Holland Road, Tel 5616. Oh well, I'd better go and sort this out, if you don't mind escorting the ladies Sutton?"

While Cole headed to the ticket booth, Sutton led the two girls to the lounge to wait. Leaning casually against one of the many shiny black marble pillars he asked conversationally, "were you friends with the actress then?"

"Not really," Irene answered. "She was in her last year when we were in our first year."

"We do remember her," Ruth added. "But of course she wasn't famous then, and her name was different. Barrie is just her stage name. But around Hongkong everyone knows her. Her father was shot dead, you know."

"He was a bigwig lawyer," Irene added.

"King's Counsel," Ruth agreed, just as Cole re-joined the group.

"All set?" Sutton asked him.

"No darn it all. The boy at the counter seemed very uninterested and I didn't like to leave it with him. Perhaps we ought to drop it out to her residence. I haven't been out to Bukit Timah for a while, and it's what, only six miles at a guess? Only we'd have to give the New World a miss because by the time we get back it would be too late to start in there. I hate to disappoint you though. What do you all say?"

"Yes, of course we shall," the other three agreed almost simultaneously. They all appeared eager for an adventure of sorts.

A short while later, the two young men had brought their cycles around to the entrance and helped the girls climb into the sidecars. As a precaution, the girls tied pretty rayon scarves over their hair in readiness for the inevitable drops from the bulging cumulonimbus hovering above.

The upper end of Holland Road was relatively undeveloped with 50 year old bungalows interspersed amongst virgin bush and swamp. The thin beams from the two headlights did little to illuminate the eerie shadows and Ruth glanced up at Charlie to see if he was as anxious as she was. She couldn't really see his expression under his leather cap, but he was peering ahead intently, no doubt concentrating on the various potholes. This did nothing to allay Ruth's formless apprehension.

Eventually, Charlie pulled in to a driveway, where the number 641 was clearly displayed on a brick wall supporting a pair of iron gates. These were closed with no sign of any servants. Turning off their engines, the two men dismounted their motorcycles. Sutton rattled the gates and hallooed loudly. There was no response.

"Looks like the gates are locked. Shall we climb over and walk in?" he suggested.

At that moment, a bolt of lightning shot through the clouds, causing

Ruth to yelp slightly. Fortunately, the rain was still holding off.

"Blast, I don't like to leave the girls here. Best if just one of us goes," Charlie answered.

"We can climb over too," Irene immediately countered. She had climbed out of the bike and was standing beside them.

"Hang about, there's a side gate in the wall," Ruth said, pointing the torch that she had released from its little holder in her sidecar. "Let's try that."

"Well done old girl!" Sutton said. "Come on."

With virgin jungle hugging one side and tropical plantings on the other they set off silently along the neatly raked driveway. It was not especially long, but it curved somewhat, so that they had walked a half minute or so before they could see the house. When it did come into view, there was a lantern lit at the front door, and another inside a front room, but little other lighting visible from the drive.

"I'd say they've either not returned home yet or they've retired to bed early," Irene murmured.

"Well I should think they'd be thankful even if we have to wake them, and if they are still out we'll just leave it with their head boy," Charlie replied just as quietly.

They continued their walk in silence. Each of them feeling that something was not right with the situation, yet not quite able to identify exactly what was wrong. None of them voiced their concerns.

Soon they were at a small covered portico where the driveway rounded past a wooden front door, which was impressive in both its size and bronze detailing. Still there was nobody in sight and the absolute stillness made the little group feel as though they were trespassing. The hour wasn't particularly late, but Cole didn't feel inclined to knock at the door. A stone path led to the foot of an arched verandah where the single lantern splashed its light, and Cole's instincts made him turn towards it. The others followed him without question. A wide set of stone steps lead to French doors, which appeared to be open. It was the only illuminated room and Cole thought it odd that the verandah chicks and nets were not drawn down, because obviously with the lights on and the door open, such protection from mosquitos would be the norm.

He began to lead the way up the stairs, and was about to call out a hello, when his nostrils caught a waft of an alarming smell. Blood! The redolent warning came to his brain just in time, allowing him to recognise the crime scene at his feet efficiently. He flung up his arm to stop the others barging past him, but a small cry from behind told him that Ruth had seen the body too.

Lying just inside the doors, the thin man on the floor was dressed in the typical starched white *tutup* jacket of a house boy—in this case an elderly servant. A modest red stain on the front of the tunic indicated a stab or possibly bullet wound, and his too-pale skin was obviously drained of life.

Instincts and training stepped in. Charlie Cole had to assume that the perpetrator could still be around. He knew he should probably check for any sign of life, but as that was unlikely, he felt it more urgent to both protect the women and secure the scene. Wordlessly, he blasted himself for leaving his non-issue pistol locked in his bedside cabinet. He doubted whether Sutton had any weapon either.

Using just a flick of his eyes, he indicated to Sutton to take the girls away. Sutton took the torch from Ruth's shaking hands and pushed it at Cole, nodding agreement.

Cole waited while Sutton pulled both the women back into the shadows of the driveway, and saw him furtively glancing around, no doubt looking for any sign out of the ordinary.

"Blast it all," Cole thought to himself. He knew it was precisely the lack of any signs that should have warned him. There was none of the usual rustlings and noises in the shrubberies. The house itself was too quiet when normally there should have at least been servants bustling about, the odd voice, a radiogram programme perhaps—something.

He slipped into the sitting room beyond the doors and played his flashlight across the cluttered layout. Empty. Negotiating a path through the furniture, he silently turned into the hallway and saw candlelight coming from a room at the back of the house.

It appeared to be an empty scullery leading into the kitchen proper. A second flash of lightning illuminated the larger room beyond. In a sickening pool of blood another lifeless body, probably the kitchen amah, lay on her side near the back door. Perhaps she had been trying to escape. He played his torch over her body. She seemed to have had her throat cut. Cole had to assume the perpetrator was armed with at least a knife.

He briefly considered checking outside the back door but then decided it best to secure the house first. He headed for the remaining rooms on the ground floor, which were all empty, but just inside the closed front door was the body of another Malaysian houseboy. There was no obvious sign of injury, but his crumpled form and blotchy skin seemed lifeless. Cole decided to check back on the others outside, before he attempted the stairs.

Sutton was hard to spot at first, but Cole's torchlight brought him out of the shadows slightly. He motioned to Cole who hurried down to him, switching off his torch as he went. He began to feel the odd fat raindrop hit his face.

In hurried whispers, Cole told him about the three bodies.

"I haven't checked upstairs..." he began but stopped suddenly when a silhouette shot out the front door crossing the lawn in front of them. Both men bolted towards it at a neat angle and took the surprised figure down in a rugby tackle of which even the famous Dougal Harper would have been proud.

It was in that precise moment that the skies decided to open and buckets of rain soaked them all as quickly as if they had been standing in a shower box.

After a short wrestle on the lawn, the two sergeants had restrained the Chinese assailant. They frog-marched him back to the house, where they could telephone the local police.

Meanwhile, Ruth and Irene inexpertly checked the bodies for any signs of life but were unable to determine if any were still breathing. The woman's neck was gruesomely severed and they could not see any way she could still be alive with those injuries.

Unexpected shouts were heard from outside. The family syce, holding an umbrella over his middle-aged employer, trotted up onto the terrace. As they came upon the first body, their shouts grew angrier.

"In here," Cole called out.

"What's going on? Whose motorcycles are blocking the driveway? By god, you'd better explain yourself, man."

"Sergeant Cole, A.P.F.," Cole introduced himself without getting up off the criminal. "This is Sergeant Sutton, and yes those are our motorcycles."

"What's happened to my man here, and who is that?" he asked pointing to the squirming man being pinned forcibly to the floor by the two sergeants.

Behind the older man, the syce was examining the elderly servant and asking where the other servants were in his broken Malay, though nobody was answering him.

"Well, we caught this man running out of your front door. You must be Mr Ohlrich. Do you know him?"

"No! Certainly not! Has he done this? Why are you here? What's this got to do with the dockyard?"

Cole briefly explained what was going on as far as he knew. The Dutchman was worried that his wife was sitting in the car unprotected at the front gate.

"If your syce can help me restrain this man, Sergeant Sutton will accompany you to retrieve your wife and move our motorcycles. The regular police are on their way," Cole reassured him. "Miss Warner, be a good girl and pull my keys out of my coat pocket."

Mr Ohlrich seemed to notice the two young women in their soaking wet dresses for the first time, but flustered, he followed Sutton out without fully acknowledging them.

While he was gone, the big Tamil syce helped Cole tie the Chinaman's wrists and legs together. Soon Mrs Ohlrich arrived and wordlessly dashed from room to room looking for her servants. She returned moments later looking pale. Irene and Ruth moved quickly to her side, offering assistance.

"But I don't understand what brought you here in the first place," the woman finally blurted trying hard to keep her tears at bay.

"We found your purse at the cinema tonight on the seats beside us," Ruth answered. "I looked inside and found your address on your cards, so we wanted to return it but we ran into this right to-do. It's been terribly frightening. Oh! Of course, my fiancé still has the purse in his coat pocket. I must get it for you."

"Can I make a pot of tea for anybody?" Irene asked.

"No, don't do that," Sutton called out. "In fact it would be best if we all stay in this one room until the police arrive."

"I need something stiffer than tea anyway," Mr Ohlrich said heading for the drinks cabinet across the room.

The regular police arrived not long after while he was still dithering with the drinks. They took charge of the prisoner and the crime scene. Cole and Sutton gave their names and a quick outline of events as they had seen it. Then, seeing that there was nothing more they could do, the four young people took their leave.

"Gosh that was an exciting evening," Irene said when they arrived back at her house on Orange Grove Road.

Her three companions groaned and looked as though they thought Irene had lost all common sense.

"I for one could easily do without that sort of excitement. I don't think I'll ever get that image of that poor cook out of my mind," Ruth blurted in protest.

"But what about that splendid tackle? You boys ought to try out for the Navy Rugger team," Irene persisted.

"That part was rather impressive," agreed Ruth reaching up on tiptoe to plant a rewarding kiss directly on Charlie's lips.

Perhaps she had only meant it to be a quick affectionate peck, but Charlie caught her around the waist and pulled her into a deep passionate embrace. For a moment he was sure his fiancé enjoyed the kiss and she relaxed in his arms, but then a long low whistle from Sutton and an embarrassed cough from Irene seemed to bring her back to her senses and she struggled free of Charlie's teasing grasp.

"You're not married yet Mr Cole," Irene admonished, but Charlie saw she was smiling. It was probably the first real sign of affection she'd seen between them, he realised and he hoped it would go a long way towards allaying any fears that she may have held about her friend's impending marriage.

4
SINGAPORE DECEMBER 1939

RUTH WARNER

The day of the wedding finally arrived. Ruth and her bridesmaid Irene were nearly dressed, but still Irene's mother fussed over them happily.

A Chinese housemaid sidled into the bedroom and announced the arrival of Captain Armstrong. Mrs Ardern left the room to go and greet the guest.

Despite him pledging to give her away, Ruth had still only ever held brief exchanges with the man at various social functions. His popularity was such that he always seemed to be pulled away mid-conversation to speak to someone or other. At the wedding rehearsal, he had sent a stand-in with the message that he'd "wing it" on the day. Ruth supposed it would be up to her to prompt him when needed. Still she refused to let it put a damper on the day. After all, he didn't have a lot to do and only one line to remember.

The thought that he was actually in her house caused Irene to make eyes at Ruth, resulting in the two girls to dissolve into fits of giggling.

"Oh, he is so dreamy," Irene said spying through the gap in the semi-opened door.

"Let me look," Ruth said standing on tiptoes to peer over her friend's head. But then finding she couldn't see, she ducked her head below Irene's instead. "I'm so pleased he is wearing a morning suit rather than matching Charlie and his best man."

"Yes, it would have been a very white wedding otherwise," Irene observed dryly, "what with the naval uniforms and your white slipper satin."

"Not to mention my crown," Ruth said wryly.

"It's a coronet," Irene corrected, looking at her friend in exasperation. They had argued over whether she needed this affectation many times until Irene had gotten her way. "And it *is* beautiful. Those white blossoms. You are going to both look and smell gorgeous, old girl."

"If you say so," said Ruth, feeling a little nauseous. They turned back to watch Armstrong accepting a short drink offered by Mr Ardern. Suddenly he seemed to look directly at the door to the bedroom and both girls jerked back. Ruth's head smacked into Irene's chin with a hard thud and the girls peeled apart to separate corners of the room each holding their battered heads and moaning.

Glancing at each other, they got the giggles again, which soon brought Irene's mother marching back in.

"I think it's time dearie. Are you ready? Goodness, we still haven't attached the veil. Chop, chop Irene."

A few minutes later, they emerged to the sitting room, where Armstrong jumped up and after an appreciative appraisal, gave the girls a deep bow.

"If I didn't consider your fiancé a friend Miss Warner, I'd ask for your hand myself. You look simply exquisite."

"And what about Irene? Doesn't she look beautiful captain?" Ruth tried her best to promote her best friend's interests.

Captain Armstrong turned to Irene and pretended to mop his brow. "Well, how am I to behave when I'm surrounded by such beauties," he said.

"You had better behave, young man," Irene's mother said sternly, but only because, feeling a little thrilled herself, she thought she ought to add her two pennies worth.

"Shall we?" Armstrong offered Ruth his arm.

In a brief moment of panic, Ruth wondered if there was still time to reconsider, but then she remembered those new feelings of love that had blossomed during the past few days and swallowing away her nervousness, she accompanied the captain out to the waiting motor car.

The wedding was certainly going to live up to its reputation as a social event of note. Despite Ruth being Catholic, she had had her banns read in the beautiful Anglican cathedral, St Andrews, which had received its unusual name from the original Scottish architect. As well as securing St Andrew's, the girls had also managed to book none other than Raffles Hotel for the reception. This was certainly due to the pulling power of Irene's father because both the bride and groom were more military than money; although the initial suggestion had unexpectedly come from Henry Warner, Ruth's father. Some months earlier, he had sent Charlie a hefty banker's draft along with a missive to give Ruth the fairy-tale wedding of her dreams. In a rare moment of candidness, his note had contained the admission that he had spent precious little on her during her life thus far.

Every moment of the next few hours became etched into Ruth's memory. There was the worrisome beginning, where she knew she had several impediments to negotiate in her awkward wedding attire before she could properly begin the wedding march. She remembered gripping the back of Armstrong's hand as she gamely left the north transept to enter the cathedral via the north portico. Her long train, trimmed with Brussels lace, floated behind her as she swept towards the main entrance to the nave. Irene bumbled behind her, doing her level best to prevent it catching on anything. Next, she wound past the marble baptismal font oddly placed in the centre of the blue carpet just inside the main doors. Once past that obstacle, she paused while Irene rearranged her train, and looked across the pews toward her guests.

It was a very lopsided congregation with only the Arderns and one or two of their friends sitting on the left side of the church.

Ruth had sent an invitation to her aging aunts to come out from England for the occasion, but she had never dreamt for one moment that they'd actually accept. So she wasn't surprised and only slightly disappointed when she received their blustering letter declining the invitation and citing the restrictions in travel as the reason. Ruth knew that even if there hadn't been a war brewing, they would find a reason to decline. Not because they didn't want to celebrate her wedding; nor because they disapproved of an Anglican service. It would simply be because the thought of travelling halfway across the globe was far too frightening for either of them to contemplate seriously.

The organist heralded her arrival and all the guests stood to turn and greet her. More than a few titters and some loud giggling reached her ears, causing her to stiffen and shake. She couldn't understand why they were laughing at her and it was all she could do to stop from running back to the safety of the transept.

Perhaps recognising her stage fright, Armstrong whispered in her ear, "they love the dog."

And then she felt able to breathe with the realisation that the laughter & smiles were in support of her, rather than against. For in her left hand, she held not a bouquet but the flower trimmed lead of her little black dog named Mack who trotted obediently at her side. Not having any family of her own at the wedding, Ruth was determined to have her little dog accompany her. She had especially ringed one of his eyes in white chalk to match her outfit. Only the vicar and Irene had known she would be bringing him before that morning and Irene's mother had given her blessing to the idea when she'd discovered the plan.

"Breathe," Armstrong reminded her as the mighty pipe organs began

Mendelssohn's Wedding March.

She was more than half way up the nave's central aisle, before she saw her intended and his best man, Sergeant Sutton, turn to await her. His face held no smile and he looked more nervous than she felt. Ruth took her place beside her groom feeling a little lost and not willing at first to let go of Armstrong's secure hand. The captain lifted her hand off his own and placed it on top of her groom's hand. Ruth stole a glance at Cole's chin which was at her eye level.

The vicar began his service in his usual ambling voice. There were readings from the lectern behind the great golden eagle, which dominated the cathedral. The vicar spoke from up in the octagonal pulpit of the sacrament of marriage and the effort required to build a Christian life together. The congregation sang two hymns.

Ruth and Charlie obediently sat and stood and knelt all the while with their heads bent before the man of God, not daring to so much as glance at each other. Finally, when the vicar placed Ruth's hand into Charlie's, she could feel Charlie's thumb secretly stroke her palm. Heat surged from her palm throughout her body, as she became encouraged to look up at him. From then on, she was completely alert to her husband's every tingling movement. His deep voice nourished her heart with his fulfilling pledge, and in return, she felt that every word of her own steadfast vows were accompanied by his eyes penetrating deeply into her soul. Her voice croaked out the last quiet words, "until death do us part," for it suddenly seemed sacrilegious to speak of his death.

Trembling, almost as much as she was, he lifted her veil and his lips pressed onto hers to the sound of clapping and hurrahs from the congregation. They had done it. The newlyweds emerged from the cool building out into the steamy afternoon to stand beneath the West Entrance, a confection of neo-gothic archways. Naturally, Irene was first in line to congratulate them. Charlie thanked her for helping Ruth organise the day and jokingly congratulated both women for even managing to arrange for the monsoon rains to hold off.

But if the weather was to be a metaphor for their married life, then it was well that they could not see the rolling black clouds that were building on the far side of the massive cathedral.

There was no time to hang around after the Raffles reception. They needed to board their train for the honeymoon at the Lakehouse in the Cameron Highlands.

The guests followed them out to the wide entrance steps of the luxury hotel where Ruth thanked Mrs Ardern for being such a wonderful surrogate mother the past year. She clung to Irene, who literally had tears spilling down her face as the reality hit her that she was in many ways losing her best friend. No more would they share a bedroom and every moment of every day. Ruth would be responsible for her own home and it would be a brick and concrete bungalow some distance away on the Sembawang Navy Base.

The hotel's Sikh jagah, dressed spectacularly in an immaculate white badjhu, black sash, red cuffs, tan cowboy boots and an immense white silk pugree on his head, indicated for a specially decorated ricksha to pull up. The guests watched, entranced, as the tall, imposing Peshwari doorman held Mack completely under his spell, ordering him onto the rickshaw with nothing more than a series of vivacious hand movements.

Finally, he helped Ruth and Charlie climb aboard the traditional contraption, which would take them to the station where their luggage was waiting.

Charlie finished shaking hands with each officer of the APF. He kissed his mother and patted his father on the back. Then he joined Mrs Cole in the ricksha and the wallah pedalled away grinning like an incarcerated idiot as several long strings of tin cans clattered along behind them.

At long last, Mr and Mrs Cole were shown to their sleeper compartment for the thirteen-hour journey to Ipoh. From there they would transfer into a bus for a further three-hour winding trip up into the mountains. Charlie wedged Mack's rattan basket into a corner and the little dog immediately fell asleep. It had been a big day for him too.

"What a beautiful wedding. You did well, Mrs Cole," Charlie said earnestly.

"It was good wasn't it?" Ruth's eyes creased into a smile before changing into a more wistful pose. "The only thing that would have made it 100% perfect is if Captain Armstrong had shown the slightest bit of interest in Irene. I really think they'd make a lovely couple."

"Ah. I believe the captain already has his eye on one Miss Victoria Wainhouse."

"Her!"

"Yes, is that a problem?"

"Oh, she's alright I suppose. Irene can't stand her though."

"Why?"

"Well, I don't really know precisely. I'm sure there's nothing wrong with her as such. I believe it's their mothers that do not get along, or some such thing. In any case, Irene has nothing to do with her."

"Sounds like nonsense to me," Charlie commented. "But, a word of warning my dear: if anything comes of their romance, this Miss Wainhouse would be the only other woman in the APF family and the most senior to boot. You could end up being neighbours. So you'd do well to keep on her good side, just in case."

At the mention of their new home, Ruth's attention was diverted.

"Ooh! It's so exciting. I love the little bungalow we've been assigned and I can't wait to start making it my own."

Falling into silence while lost in images of new curtains and lampshades, Ruth busied herself with a jar of cold-cream, wiping away her powder and lipstick, and removing pins from her thick dark brown hair. The rocking rhythm of the moving train and the repetitive action of her hairbrush calmed her nerves until she had almost forgotten Charlie who was patiently waiting. Sitting on the narrow bed he quietly watched her preparations.

She was jolted out of her reverie by a singe of static electricity snaking down her spine. The touch of his fingers lightly traced first the line of her neck and then came to rest at the top of her modern primrose *going away* dress. She held her breath as she felt the snagging sensation of the zipper being lowered inch by inch. His cool fingers ran along the edge of her rayon slip and he gently pushed the thin straps off her shoulders dropping the silky garment to her waist. Something wet ran down her spine to her brasserie. She wondered in surprise if he was kissing her or actually licking her and questioned in her mind whether it was the act of a normal rational man.

Then he pulled her up from the seat and her clothing dropped away to the floor.

She turned to face him wearing only her sheer French knickers and lacy brasserie, both of which were designed to hide very little. A sudden memory flashed through her mind of a giggling shopping excursion where she and Irene had chosen these intimate items. It had seemed funny then, but now she wished she wasn't so exposed. Charlie stood seemingly mesmerised by the vision of her, until Ruth felt so self-conscious that she had the urge to apologise and cover herself awkwardly with her arms.

Hushing away her apology and giving her a reassuring smile, Charlie began to undress—right there in front of her! First, his shirt was casually tossed aside. A light covering of chestnut hair did nothing to hide his attractive muscular torso. Then he began to unbutton his trousers while Ruth looked wildly around for a place in which to discreetly retreat. Save leaving the cabin, there was no escape. Sensing her begin to lose interest, Charlie shoved the trousers off his hips in a rush sending them, together with his undergarments to the floor.

Blood rushed to Ruth's face as she caught a glimpse of his male member, which was pointing up towards the ceiling. Funny! She had always imagined it would hang downwards, as they did with a horse. She concentrated on maintaining eye contact and slowing her breathing. Charlie put cool hands gently over her flaming cheeks. She wondered what he was up to, until he pulled her head down, forcing her to look at his throbbing phallus. Then he took her hand and wrapped her fingers around it. She obliged him by giving it a quick squeeze.

Charlie moaned slightly, and the tip of the thing glistened.

Timidly at first, Ruth ran a fingertip along the length. The smooth skin felt like the soft muzzle of a horse, but underneath there was an unyieldingly hardness that both resisted and quivered with her touch. Daringly she even ran a finger lightly over the tip spreading the bead of liquid forming at the top around in a little circle. It was fascinating and she almost forgot herself.

"Stop!" Charlie commanded in a quiet yet fierce voice.

Ruth dropped the whole ensemble in fright, knowing he must despise her. She drew in her breath sharply and glanced towards the door, on the verge of making a run for it. But he took hold of her wrists firmly and pulled them up to his shoulders. Confused, she dared to look at his face, but his hungry eyes were on her chest and he didn't appear to be disgusted with her at all—quite the opposite in fact. He reached forward and gently undid her brasserie buttons releasing her bosom.

"You are so beautiful, my dear, dear wife," he groaned. His husky voice gave her a fraction more confidence. His fingertips lightly played across her nipples causing them to harden in a way that she was certain they never had before. Still with her arms around his neck, he took a step back towards the cot where he perched on its edge and pulled her between his knees. Then without warning, he took her whole nipple into his mouth and sucked it hard. She was about to protest, and would have if only she could think what to say. But as she paused, delightful sensations danced through her nether regions.

At that moment, Ruth decided to just let him do with her what he would. After all, a girl had to assume that a man had more experience and knowledge in this area.

Well before dawn, Ruth awoke with a start when the train noisily pulled into a station somewhere along the line. She could not remember when sleep had finally caught up with them, but her skin felt sticky with sweat and Lord only knew what else. She was currently cocooned tightly inside her husband's very naked embrace in an unseemly but glorious way.

Charlie stirred and nuzzled in closer to Ruth's pale neck.

"It's not quite morning yet," he murmured. "We still have time before we have to be up and dressed."

It was true, Ruth realised. The inadequate blind on the window, showed only grey pre-dawn light around its edges.

"If only our entire honeymoon were to be spent in this cabin on the train, I would be in heaven," he told her earnestly.

5
SINGAPORE DECEMBER 1941

RUTH COLE

Jean Daisy Cole's first birthday party was nearly over. Inexplicably, her favourite present was a beautifully painted wooden truck presented to her by her adoring father. Its front windows were painted to look like eyes and its engine hood & grille was the nose, while the bumper was the smiling mouth. She hadn't let go of it since she had first set eyes on it at breakfast that morning. Quite why this rather boyish toy fascinated her so, nobody knew.

Although every British child whose parents worked at the naval base had been invited to the party, not all had attended. Every other day, it seemed, another family left Singapore. They left behind their rented homes with the gardens they had carefully created. They left behind many of their possessions and discharged their servants. In most cases, they also left behind the husbands and fathers who were bonded to the navy or naval police. It was the same over at the air force and in the land forces. In fact families all over the Straits Settlement, whether military or not, were quietly leaving, first by ship to Europe but lately more often by air to Australia. Ruth had begun to notice this trend over a year ago, before the war in Europe had really come to anything, but in the last few months, it seemed to be escalating.

The trend went against all official advice in the daily newspapers and radio reports, which insisted that there was no danger to the general population in Singapore.

The official media releases from the Straits Government and the Army HQ were contradictory which didn't help matters. At the same time as being told they were safe, some coastal communities were being told to be ready to evacuate into the city on two hours' notice. Nobody knew where they were to be accommodated or why they might need to be evacuated.

Despite worried whispers circulating around the women's circles, there was also a band of influential long-time residents who would not hear any talk of this sort at all. If you were to bring it up in conversation, you would be immediately shut down. Those that were brave enough to suggest that Singapore could be in danger from the Japanese threat, would be rounded on by several senior women and made to feel unpatriotic.

Jeans' amah picked the sleepy girl up and brought her over to her mother to say goodbye. Ruth pecked her daughter on the forehead and sent her home. It was the indication to the other guests that the party was drawing to a close.

Ruth's best friend Irene had returned to England with her parents shortly after Jean had been born. So Ruth's circle of friends now consisted solely of other women on the naval base, including Captain Armstrong's new wife. Just as Charlie Cole had predicted, the captain had married Victoria Wainhouse several months earlier and just as Charlie had anticipated, Victoria and Ruth had become friends simply because of the fact that their husbands were the only two married men in the APF, and because they now lived in an identical bungalow next door. Even though she had no children yet, Mrs Armstrong was here helping Ruth with the party.

Another young woman whose husband was based at Sembawang, Mrs Marion Trimble, offered to take down the paper streamers. Soon a band of willing women joined in as each of their children left with their amahs for their afternoon naps. It was a happy group but the atmosphere changed when Mrs Trimble tentatively brought up the subject of Pearl Harbour.

Up until the previous week, Pearl Harbour had been an impregnable American naval base in Hawaii. Newspaper reports had been filtering in over the past two days that the Japanese had attacked it, but so far, little real knowledge as to the extent of the damage was known. The big news overnight was that both Britain and the US had declared war on Japan. Britain was already at war in Europe of course.

Mrs Trimble, however, had more details about Pearl Harbour. Her Australian parents had made a special long distance telephone call that morning to tell her that the Japanese had totally incapacitated the Hawaiian base. They urged her to return to Australia, but she had yet to speak to her husband, who was a wireless mechanic assigned to the dockyard. Marion asked the other women if they thought it would be safer in Australia or Singapore.

It was a dangerous discussion, but fortunately, there were mainly only young mothers around and the old biddies who disliked this sort of talk had been largely absent from the event.

Suddenly, a British Navy mem ran into the room and cried out the news.

"The *Prince of Wales* had been torpedoed. They think that she is sunk! Oh god, it's true, I tell you there is no doubt!"

Several gasps and cries of "no" went around the group.

"How did you hear?" someone asked.

"But what of the *Repulse*?" someone else asked quickly.

"*HMS Repulse* will pick up any survivors," an authoritative mem said.

"How do you know? She could be miles away," Captain Armstrong's new wife said.

"No, they were in convoy. Don't worry. She won't leave those men behind."

The room fell into silence for a moment, as the reality of the news sunk in. The two warships had only been docked at the base a couple of days earlier. They all knew that the *Prince of Wales* was a beautifully modern battleship, a jewel in the Navy's crown. On board was none other than Admiral Sir Thomas Phillips himself. Furthermore, many of their husbands had socialised with the crew. They themselves had all played their usual part in entertaining the visitors. There was going to be deaths; there always was when a ship was sunk.

For some of the women, it became urgent to get home, to turn on their wireless sets. Others grouped together, thinking that they could find out more here on the base, than back in their individual bungalows.

Ruth peeled off from the group, her brain reeling. She had never really expected Charlie to attend the birthday. It was meant to be a party for the children and women, but he had said he would look in if he had time. Now she reflected that his absence could well be because he was waiting for news of the stricken warship. She desperately wanted to get over to the APF station, but as the Host her responsibility was to leave the Admiralty Club in the same condition as she found it. She began sweeping up, leaving the wrapping of the leftover food to the other women. The navy cleaners would do a proper clean later, but she needed to sweep up the bulk of the streamers and general litter.

When tears began dripping down her face, Ruth was surprised with herself. Of course, she was sorry to hear the news, but she had no reason to be particularly upset about the *Prince of Wales*. After all, other than having once met the Admiral, she didn't personally know anyone on the ship, or on any of the other ships that were in the convoy. Busying herself away from the other women so they would not see her weeping, she tried to blink the tears away and attempted to identify precisely why the news had affected her so. Perhaps it reminded her how close the danger was to home. Or more likely, she thought, it was because she had been counting on the convoy of ships to relieve poor old besieged Hongkong. She had not heard from her father or brother for some weeks. As far as she knew they hadn't yet been evacuated, and now it looked like the British settlement would be left to the mercy of the Japanese on their doorstep. If one was to believe the newspapers, mercy was not a concept with which the Japanese were familiar.

It was too much: the build up to her daughter's first party; the declaration of war just the night before; and the realisation that Hongkong was more in danger now than ever before.

She did not realise her husband had even entered the room until strong hairy arms wrapped themselves around her shoulders. She recognised Charlie's short-sleeved khaki working uniform and turned to face him.

"I see you've heard the news, then?" he stated gently. Ruth nodded. He wiped her moist cheek with his finger. "Come on. Leave this, let's just get home."

Later in the afternoon, Sergeant McGregor dropped by with more news. It hardly seemed credible but apparently, both the Prince of Wales *and* the Repulse had been sunk by Japanese aviators. It was thought that there would be survivors who would be pulled from the sea by the two old destroyers that were accompanying the big ships. That was provided they weren't sunk as well.

"It might be time to face facts," Charlie told her. "We've lost the only two battleships that Britain could spare us. Pearl Harbour may be out of action, Hongkong is besieged. And if Singapore can no longer depend on naval support from either the Americans or the British, then we'll be cut off from Europe and the Pacific. Every day now, we're getting reports that Japan is marching out this way and that. Japan is as relentless as voracious pangolin sucking up every nook and cranny before moving on to the next undefended community. Half of our Asiatic neighbours seem to be rolling over like 'possums playing dead. Maybe our only safety is south to Australia."

"What about Father and Jeffrey, and your sister in Hongkong?"

"I'm still waiting on news from Hongkong. Nobody will tell me anything there."

"The papers mentioned that the volunteers have been called up and that means that Jeffrey may be in the thick of things."

"Well if we are going to believe the papers, the Governor says Hongkong can hold out for nine months, even without help from us."

"Do you think that's true?" Ruth asked.

"I think we have to assume that we'll get more information from the naval base rumours than from the papers. My point is I'm beginning to think it's high time you both went to my parents."

"But surely it can't be that bad. Couldn't we wait until they reach the causeway? Our boys will hold them there for months, just as they're doing at the Hongkong border. We know they've only just landed in Malaya. Surely they will still have to fight and win every town the length of the peninsula before they can get anywhere near us? Any old rubber farmer will tell you that won't be easy. Remember how rugged the country was when we went to the Highlands for our honeymoon? And they wouldn't dare come by sea. We're too well protected on that score."

"I'm sure you think you've thought this all through my darling. But tell me, what if they attack by air? Are you willing to put up with air raids every night like last night? Waking Jeanie up at 4am? Not even being allowed to light a lantern?"

Charlie fiddled with the dials on the wireless, trying to bring in the 6:30 *News In English*.

"But do I really have to go to your parents? What about your other sister in New South Wales? Couldn't you write to her and see what she thinks?"

Charlie's answer was drowned by the clear voice of the broadcaster. The news was followed by the War Report, which allayed their fears somewhat. Apparently, the Japs were busy fighting sea battles in Guam and near the Philippines. There was no mention about the warships. As usual, most of the news centred on Africa and Europe though there had been some damage in downtown Honolulu. It was unclear what had become of the naval base up there but there were reports of some 350 land forces killed in the Hawaiian attack.

The most astonishing news of the evening was that in the previous night's air raid, a bomb had dropped in Singapore's Chinatown. Chinese were being evacuated to the suburbs apparently. This was somewhat ironic, as during the previous several months, the residents of the coastal areas had been repeatedly warned that they might have to evacuate at any time with minimal notice to the city or interior. The thought of living in some of the attap huts like a native Malayan was eclipsed only by the horror of having to bunk in with the Chinese in their rabbit-like warrens in Chinatown. But all of this was a civil matter and didn't really affect those living on the naval estates.

It was a couple more days before the full horror of both Pearl Harbour and the local naval battle played out in the media. With both warships sunk, the surviving sailors returned to land aboard not two, but three destroyers who had managed to evade the enemy. Admiral Sir Tom Phillips, the highest-ranking Naval officer, was reported to have gone down with his ship. Every new snippet of information reinforced the fact that this was a comprehensive disaster for Britain's Far Eastern outposts.

Each new day brought declarations of war from foreign nations towards either the Axis or the Allies as the world scrambled to take sides.

The air sirens played regularly and people dug trenches in their gardens. But since most warnings were inevitably false alarms, people seldom bothered to get up in the night to use their trenches. Hardly anyone had an Anderson bomb shelter installed in their garden and nobody had the more modern Morrison indoor shelter. The local ARP did hand out gas masks, which the civilian population were supposed to take everywhere, just in case. They were such a jolly nuisance, that this order soon got boring.

The Straits Settlement officially became governed by martial law. Civilian citizens were continually requested to register themselves and wear a little metal ID tag at all times. These tags were to enable officials to identify bodies who succumbed to bombing raids.

Those Japanese civilians who had not been repatriated to Japan were required to report to Government House for arrest. The APF's prison guard duties at Changi increased to accommodate them. Charlie hated garrison duty. After a much delayed court case, the constable he had reported for sleeping on duty had been both sent to Changi Gaol and subsequently released from it. Now the sullen man's duties seemed to keep him out there and Charlie privately dreaded having to cross paths with him. Fortunately, Charlie's usual assignment was to guard Navy House and Rear Admiral Spooner's staff and family, which meant he was rarely out at Changi.

Blackouts and curfew conditions were enforced by wardens every evening. Brown-outs now affected driving with covers over headlights reducing the light to narrow beams. Businesses that relied heavily on electricity, such as the cold storages, struggled. Shops were forced to restructure their opening hours to accommodate the reduction in voltage.

The Navy mems, including Ruth, were disappointed when Government House postponed the Servicemen's Christmas dance. Otherwise, regular evening entertainment continued as usual. Because entertaining at home had become next to impossible during blackouts, the multitude of clubs provided a welcome alternative. The majority of these did a thriving business, despite being unable to use their open terraces.

Everyone adjusted to the new conditions and continued to plan for a subdued Christmas. Ruth and Victoria joined the other mems from the Naval Base in making Christmas packages for the surviving sailors from the two battleships. The Admiralty Club held its usual Children's Christmas Party and the King gave his usual Christmas speech, though it was a rather stern one calling on his empire to give a little more. The Coles had a particularly low-key Christmas. They were keeping a keen eye on the daily developments in Hongkong, limited though the reports were, since they both had family members living there.

On Boxing Day, they heard the horrifying news that contrary to earlier boasts, Hongkong had surrendered to the Japanese. To Charlie, it felt like there was nothing standing between Japan and Singapore. He felt like the umpire had called "Game, Set" and they were only waiting for the words "Match" to complete their downfall. He couldn't understand why nobody else seemed to be unduly concerned. Armstrong tried to assure him that there was no sense in running around like a headless chook. Rather they'd be better served if everyone stuck to their guns and went about daily business as usual.

"It gives the natives a sense of assurance. We don't want them switching their allegiances, which they might if they think we aren't on top of the situation." He said this in full hearing of his household staff, and Charlie couldn't help thinking that now was not the time to be quite so arrogant.

A driving party of mems were finally heading to the Wardens Office for the compulsory registration of citizens. While there, Ruth enquired about her family in Hongkong. They told her they had already put out several enquiries on behalf of other anxious citizens, but so far, the Red Cross had not been able to access the State.

New Year's Eve approached and the senior APF boys booked a table at the Adelphi Hotel for a modest celebration. Ruth and Charlie left the party early because Charlie was to go on duty at five the following morning. He was back at the family bungalow by midday and they were able to attend a New Year's Day luncheon at the Sea View Hotel. It was the second year that they had come to this place for a New Year's Day function. Although the Palm Court orchestra played the patriotic sing-a-longs faithfully, Ruth noticed a few anomalies. For instance, the snake charmer was absent from his habitual position on the front entrance steps. The grand old building possessed a faded look without him.

During the dinner, Ruth found out that Captain Armstrong's wife was leaving for Ceylon.

"I'm expecting," she confided to Ruth. "Captain Armstrong wants me out. So I'm to go to his family in Colombo."

"I suppose Ceylon is safely behind British lines," Ruth commented, but her voice betrayed her lack of conviction in that statement.

"To be honest, I'm rather worried about it, and not just because it's a risky journey. The thing is, we've been married such a short time that we haven't made an official visit there yet. They are very well to do."

"But you must be used to all that pomp. I remember your mother's outfit at your wedding. She seemed very swanky."

"Ah yes, but the Armstrongs are a different level again," Mrs Armstrong whispered conspiratorially. "Their Colombo estate is palatial. In fact, I believe it used to be a Raja's palace. It is situated right on the harbour's edge with the water lapping up to fortress walls that surround it." She raised her eyes at Ruth meaningfully.

"Oh. Well at least you'll be able to barricade yourself in, if the Japanese ever reach it."

"20 servants," Mrs Armstrong added, nodding her head as if Ruth would know what she meant by that.

Ruth just blinked at her, wondering if she was meant to be favourably impressed, when in fact she was more bewildered. She knew the Captain came from an aristocratic family, but she had been reliably informed that his father was only a third or fourth son.

"So, what about you," Mrs Armstrong asked casually, seeming to change the subject. "Are you staying in Singapore?"

"Probably not. There's nothing been decided. Charlie has written to his sister in Australia, but as yet, we've had nothing back."

"Captain Armstrong was saying that the police may be able to get away earlier than the navy. You know, if the worst happens and we go the way of Hongkong."

"It'll never get that bad," retorted Ruth. "I mean, the Japs are not that well organised. They don't really know how to fight properly."

"Do you really believe that?"

"Well, it's what one reads in the papers," Ruth said defensively. In fact, Ruth didn't believe it one bit. She had only the day before had the exact opposite argument with another neighbour who had visited while she was watering her hanging orchids underneath her bungalow.

"If they are no good at flying and bombing and all that, then how did they sink our two best ships?" Victoria Armstrong whispered even more softly. One didn't want to be overheard talking about that in such a manner, or one might be labelled a renegade. Despite being newly married, Victoria was at least five years older than Ruth. She watched Ruth's reaction to her statement carefully.

Ruth merely nodded dejectedly. After all, she had had the same thoughts.

There was a moment's pause, and then she asked, "Why don't you come with me to Colombo—you and your little girl?"

Ruth realised that this was what the other woman had been building up to all along. "But …"

"We'll pay for your fares," Victoria interrupted quickly.

"I don't know. I'm not certain I could leave Sergeant Cole."

"But you just said that you were thinking of going anyway. Look, don't make up your mind yet. Talk it over with your husband tonight. But don't take too long. Armstrong has already made enquiries at P&O. I'm hoping to get a passage this month or early next month."

"But will I be welcome? What will your husband's family say if I turn up with a baby?"

"Oh, don't worry about that. For starters, his grandparents relocated to Wiltshire months ago and his parents have never lived there as far as I'm aware. There may not be any family in residence, or there may be a brother or two."

"Well, if they are not there, then what are you worried about?"

"I would very much like the company that is all—especially if there are no family out there. I'm not sure how accommodating the servants will be. I thought if I had someone else to back me up. Well, you know, there is always security in numbers."

"Have you mentioned this to Armstrong?"

"Yes, of course, it was as much his idea as mine. He is very fond of you, you know. In fact, unless I'm very much mistaken, he is discussing this very thing with your husband right at the minute."

Ruth looked over towards her husband who was indeed, head bent in a serious discussion with Armstrong.

6
SINGAPORE JANUARY 1941

RUTH COLE

Jean teetered over to Charlie. She was only just walking and her proud father was encouraging her to show off her new skills to their visitors who were fast approaching the front door.

Giles and Victoria Armstrong were giving the Cole family a lift into Singapore. The four of them were going to try the P&O office once again after the two women had been turned away the day before.

They were hoping to make a sailing to India, which was leaving on the 17th January. There had been no ships going to Colombo, so the closest they could manage was to get to India and transfer from there.

Now that 'running away' from Singapore was no longer frowned upon, the entire population of women and children were being encouraged to evacuate if they had the means to do so. Unfortunately, this meant that passages were becoming harder to come by. As it was, there was no regular timetable. Sailings could only go ahead when there was both a boat and an escort to go with it. Unfortunately, most of these convoys seemed to be heading to Australia.

On top of this, the struggle to get their paperwork in order had continually frustrated them.

A few days earlier the three women had gone to get a passport for Jean's baby amah and proof that Victoria was pregnant, as passages were only available for women with children. Neither problem was easily sorted.

The hospitals were flat out busy with casualties from the bombings. The doctor who had seen Victoria told her he didn't have time for paperwork right then. He would try to attend to it at the end of his shift. If she wanted a certified document, he'd leave it at the desk and she'd have to drop back in the following morning to collect it. Of course the following morning nobody knew anything about the matter and the doctor was not in. Frustrated, they were about to leave the hospital when a volunteer came running after them waving a piece of paper that had been entrusted to her.

Getting the amah's passport at the Chinese Protectorate took even longer. The queue to get the forms took a half hour, but when they saw the queue for the finished paperwork they realised it had no chance of clearing before closing time. Anyway they realised amah would also have to source a photograph as the one on her Malaysian Identity Card had been stamped and was therefore no good. It was common knowledge that there were few photographers left in Singapore since most of them had been Japanese and therefore had either fled or been interned. Ruth reminded them that there was a Japanese photographer adjacent to the Naval Base Pass Office. There was always a chance that he was still there.

So they all trooped back to Sembawang only to be told the man had left on the evacuation ship that the Japanese government had sent for its citizens last November.

Trying to stay positive, amah had an inspired idea. She explained that anyone who wanted to access the naval base had to carry either a Naval Base Pass or a Visitor's Pass. All day-workers had to include a photograph with their pass. She herself had been no exception. Her work application would have had to include a photograph when she was originally employed by her first naval family, prior to Mrs Cole hiring her. Perhaps all they really needed to do was ask nicely at the base if they could have it back.

At first, Victoria laughed at her suggestion. But since neither Victoria nor Ruth had a better solution, they drove along to the HQ records office.

The young officer that took their enquiry looked embarrassed by their request.

"Ah, it's not that I have a problem with you having it Mrs Cole. It's just that, ah…" his voice trailed off and he looked nervously behind him.

At that moment, the door to an office behind the man opened and the three women were given a glimpse of the scene beyond. Boxes of files had been loaded onto a wheeled pallet that was now being rolled out into the hallway.

"Those are the personnel records," the officer said forlornly.

"What are they doing with them?" Mrs Armstrong demanded.

"They're taking them down to the basement to be burned in the incinerator."

"What on earth for? No wait! Yoohoo! Stop that man. Stop," Ruth called out and hurried after him as he rolled the pallet along the corridor.

The group at the desk trailed behind her.

"They're looking for documents for a Chinese amah employed by an

APF family," the officer told his colleague over Ruth's head.

"Oh right, just a tick, let me check. No these boxes are all Boyanese. Go and check the records room. You might still be in luck. We've only taken down one other load so far."

The women hurried back to the records room and explained to another secretary what they wanted, giving him their amah's full name, Lee Jion-hu.

"Well, as you can see everything is in boxes," the secretary began, waving at the stacked shelves behind him. "They are organised by race, then by department, then type of servant, and then date. So we need to go to the Chinese section, which is mostly in these three rows. Then we need to find the boxes for the APF—I think they are right here on the end. Yes, here we go. There aren't many since the APF has only been around a few years. And I should think there won't be many amahs in it and even less baby amahs."

"Ours is the only one," Ruth agreed.

They congregated around the man while he flicked through the box.

"Hmm, I don't see any APF baby amahs in here. There are about a half dozen cookie amahs and two wash amahs; strangely few of those," he muttered.

"The naval dhobis do most of the laundry," Victoria explained.

"Oh, of course. I guess very few of the men have their own quarters."

"But what does it mean? Do you think you've burned her records already?" Ruth interrupted.

"No, we are burning them row by row. We haven't got near this part yet. It's not just a matter of throwing the boxes into the fire, they have to be fed in slowly or they won't catch."

"I work at Tuan Prebble three year," amah spoke up.

"That's right, she did. We got her from the Prebble family when they returned to England. He was a civilian engineer I believe, not navy at all. I think he advised on the floating wharf project."

"In that case, it is possible ... hmm," he pulled out a few other boxes, looking for the right one.

Meanwhile Victoria wanted to know why they were burning the personnel files in the first place.

"If the base falls into enemy hands, anybody who worked for the British Navy will likely be punished."

This was greeted with silence while the three women mulled the idea over in their minds. Nobody came out and said it, but the overriding thought for each of them was that if the Navy was going to this extreme, then they must think that the possibility of Japanese occupation was an imminent likelihood.

Noticing the sudden silence, the naval rating reassured them, "merely a precaution ladies."

Eventually, they pulled the correct file and of course, the photograph matched amah's round face. Thanking the young man who had stopped his work to help them, they left.

7
SINGAPORE JANUARY 1942

CHARLIE COLE

At dawn the following day, both Sergeant Cole and Captain Armstrong took baby amah down to the Chinese Protectorate to wait in the queue. Ruth remained at the bungalow with Jean who wasn't good at queueing.

Even though the office would not open until 9am, the line was already ten deep. By opening time, it stretched right around the corner of Havelock Street and it was nearly midday before they were seen by a clerk. Apparently, two photographs were required: one for the passport and another for the Indian entry visa. The women's savvy actions the day before had only garnered one.

"Not my problem officer," the clerk said handing the finished passport document to amah as the air raid siren began to wail. He motioned for the two men and amah to leave his office, as he himself strode to the door. "Look, take yourself down to the India office anyway. In the current situation, they might overlook the problem. Stranger things have been known to happen," his voice disappeared amongst the crowd.

Back out on the street, they followed the large group of mainly Chinese workers to the closest storm drain while they waited for the all clear. Soon the nearby sound of breaking glass accompanying the thud, thud, thud of an explosion told them that it hadn't been a false alarm, though the planes themselves were too high to see or hear.

Getting up out of the drain, they eventually found their car, which their Malayan syce had prudently moved around the corner. As they drove the short distance through the heart of Chinatown to Anson Road, the sound of wailing fire trucks could be heard getting closer. Several buildings here were in bits, and for the first time they began to see the destructive impact the aerial bombings were having.

They found the Indian office had also been interrupted by the most recent air raid but was undamaged. Now people scrambled to retake their places in the queue. The line instinctively parted for the two uniformed APF officers unaware that they were on personal business. This was a boon, to which the two men took full advantage without any qualms. Armstrong's face was written with irritation and Charlie knew he must be frustrated at spending his valuable time on a seemingly never-ending mission for somebody else's servant instead of with his own wife who was soon to leave.

Perhaps it was because the amah was accompanied by police officers or perhaps they just got a friendly clerk, but they were surprised when her entry permit was authorised immediately.

"You may have problems getting in to Ceylon, but they won't be able to send you back, so my advice is take the chance. Frankly, I'm beyond caring," he said pocketing 50 of the 350 British pounds, which Armstrong had generously provided for the woman's bond. "Next!"

A road blockage due to a broken water pipe caused a detour on the way home. In the end, they didn't arrive back until just before tiffin was being served.

As more and more refugees flooded into Singapore, and as more and more Asiatic workers were seeking to leave for mainland Malaya, queues, including traffic queues, were getting longer by the day. Collyer Quay, where the P&O office was located, was becoming a real bottleneck. A big part of the bombing had been aimed near the godowns lining the river, and rubble lay where it fell on the roads and the five-foot-ways. Those government workers who hadn't already abandoned the Settlement were too busy elsewhere to remove it.

RUTH COLE

Now that the Ruth and Victoria had their paperwork in order, they needed to head to the shipping office to collect their tickets. It was not necessary for baby amah to be there in person, so she stayed with Jean. Likewise, the men were both working that morning, so the ladies requested a navy driver to accompany them.

The queue at the P&O office was much shorter than the nearby Blue

Funnel office. Apparently, Blue Funnel had several ships leaving for Batavia and Perth, whereas P&O only had the one sailing planned for India.

"Aren't you glad you're not going to Cole's parents?" Victoria Armstrong commented when she saw the queues next door.

"Not that I had a choice," Ruth muttered.

"I beg your pardon?" Victoria exclaimed misunderstanding her. "It's not as though I am forcing you to come with me."

"No, no. Oh, please don't think I meant that. It's just that, er, it's terribly embarrassing. It's just that we still haven't heard from my husband's sister."

"But didn't you also write to his parents? What did they say?"

"Well that's the thing," Ruth replied morosely. "You won't believe it, but they wrote and said that *things* were difficult for them right now. Apparently, there is a war going on, as if we didn't know. They have already been coerced into billeting a serviceman, so they have no spare room and not enough food to feed another two mouths."

"Oh, I see." Victoria was visibly shocked.

"Yes, well I wouldn't go to them now if it was the only option available to me."

"Quite right! To think they would turn away their own grandchild. It isn't natural."

"Charlie was livid; though of course he tried to defend them. He would have put a trunk call through to them, but then your offer came along and so he hasn't bothered to call at all as far as I'm aware."

"Next!" came the response from the desk.

The women handed over their documentation, naively expecting the issuing of their tickets to be merely a formality. They were shocked to the core when Mrs Armstrong was told that being pregnant did not count as having children and she therefore did not qualify for evacuee status. The man was emphatic and would not listen to a word more, pushing them aside for the next in the queue. Of course, the Coles would not go without Mrs Armstrong, so they all headed back home.

Later the men decided that there was no other alternative than to keep trying. It was agreed that the men would go with the ladies the following morning for added support.

So it was here that the Armstrongs arrived at the Cole's house to collect them in their car and found themselves greeted at the door by little Jean proudly showing that she could toddle all on her own with no help other than her father lightly clasping one finger held above her head.

They all trooped into the city only to find the end of Collyer Quay lying under a blanket of thick oily smoke that issued from a burning godown bombed the night before. The rubber warehouse appeared to be beyond saving and blackened Fire Auxiliary Volunteers were leaving it to burn in a controlled manner.

There was a new man at the desk, who didn't even mention Mrs Armstrong's pregnancy. He attached their tickets to their travelling documents immediately.

But to their dismay, they were told that luggage was to be limited to only one small trunk and an attaché case each. No pets would be allowed on board, and furthermore, there were no state cabins available. He also informed them that it was futile to argue the point as P&O's hands were tied. These instructions had been issued by the Head of the Evacuation Committee who they knew to be the Rear Admiral—a very busy man. Everybody else was apparently in the same situation.

The SS Islam was due to leave two days later at 1030 hours and they were required to be on the pier no later than 0900.

The following day they all had to get their second of two typhoid inoculations. This was both because the water supply in Singapore had become unreliable due to the incessant aerial bombings and because typhoid was reported to be rampant in Ceylon. The travelling inoculation nurses were not due at Selangor until the following week, which would be too late, so another trip into Singapore became necessary. Jean required hers at a special centre for infants in New Market Road. Ruth and Charlie took her on their own so that their amah could have the day off. She needed to say her goodbyes to her own family and make her own typhoid arrangements. The Armstrongs also wanted to spend the day together and Ruth understood they planned to go to a more local inoculation centre.

The countdown to departure continued and increasingly Ruth felt a sense of surreality. It seemed quite impossible to believe that she'd have to say goodbye to Charlie, or that Charlie would have to say goodbye to his darling little girl. The couple had discussed the feasibility of the men coming with the ladies and while that was improbable, it did seem quite likely that they would be able to follow before long.

It was a strange set of circumstances which led them to this understanding. With martial law in place, the general Singapore police were now under the control of the Malayan Defence Force led by Lt General Percival. The APF, on the other hand, were still annexed to the Navy. However, there was talk that the land forces might soon be taking command of the naval base as well. Charlie had explained to Ruth that with the Japanese approaching from the north, the naval base would conceivably be on the front line and they didn't have the staff for that type of combat.

He thought that troopships would, in the near future, be directed to disembark at the Harbour Board's wharfs on the south side of the island instead of at the Naval Base. Of course, the Harbour Board had its own police force to guard it.

Ruth secretly felt that there was hardly any point in having a naval base when there was no battleships to speak of, but she knew better than to voice that opinion for fear of being ridiculed. If the naval base ceased operations, the APF would very probably be out of work with just the exception of the Changi jail to guard. Charlie told her that if it got to that stage, the likely plan was for the APF officers to make their escape by police launch for Batavia. From there they could make private plans to get to Australia, New Zealand, India or South Africa. It was thought that the rest of the APF, that is the Indian police constables and lower ranks, would be treated favourably by the invading force considering that they were neither British nor Chinese.

The latest intelligence was that the Japanese were moving at a rate of 20 miles a day down the Malayan Peninsula. At that speed, it would be well into March before they reached Johore Bahru, the southern-most town on the Malayan mainland. And, at that point the naval base would be within their grasp, being situated less than a mile across the Johore Straits directly beside the Causeway that linked the island to the mainland.

So Ruth wasn't really thinking along the lines of a long-term farewell, but rather a short break apart of perhaps a month. Even so, she knew it was still a foreboding circumstance when an awful lot could happen in a few short weeks in these uncertain times.

The two families rose with the sun on the day of departure. Ruth walked around the rooms of her little bungalow, thinking about her furnishings and belongings that she would have to leave behind. There was nothing of real value, but everything was a tribute to her ability as a homemaker.

Mack was tucked under her arm. For some time now, he had been a changed dog. The regular sirens and the change in the tempo of their lifestyle with the curfews and blackouts had caused a noticeable impact on his temperament. Gone was his puppy-like qualities. He was a mature dog now and had a morose air about him. He continually sniffed Ruth's nose, but the wag in his tail was absent. Charlie had promised to try to take him when he eventually evacuated, if circumstance would permit.

In her heart, Ruth knew that the possibility was Mack would be abandoned. She just couldn't bear to dwell on it, any more than she could dwell on the sure knowledge that her home might be ransacked during the hostilities. Mack was a dog, and as such, he would have to learn how to fossick for himself.

"Amah should be here by now," Charlie commented restively to no-one in particular, while taking a cup of coffee from cookie.

"I suppose she has her own farewells to make. Give her a chance," Ruth answered looking nervously at the door to Jean's bedroom where her daughter was still fast asleep.

A half hour later, Ruth had woken and fed Jean herself. Charlie was keeping an eye out the window for baby amah, but there had still been no sign of her when he spotted the Armstrongs getting into their car to drive over and collect them.

There was still time to spare so they invited their neighbours in to wait. Everyone agreed that even though it was not yet midday, the situation justified a break in tradition and a farewell glass of sherry was in order. The thimble-sized glasses were soon drained and still there was no sign of amah.

"Do you know where she lives?" Captain Armstrong asked.

"Well, no. Not exactly. Well hang about; it'll be on her paperwork which we have got with our tickets."

"We are going to have to pick her up, or they'll miss the sailing," Armstrong decided.

Everyone agreed that they would have to go and find her. Cole left instructions for baby amah to make her own way to the wharf if she arrived. Then with the suitcases on the roof, the foursome plus the baby and the dog piled into Armstrong's car. They drove towards Chong Pang village where it seemed the amah lived.

Soon enough they found the correct street. They had driven through the village regularly without realising that amah lived in the row of two-storied shop houses adjacent to an intersection. They stopped to ask an older woman sitting on the steps for directions. She didn't speak English, but she led them to her neighbour who did.

The neighbour knew Lee Jion-hu and even knew of the Coles and all about Jean. She walked them along to the correct house where she didn't stop to knock before opening the door and calling out in a rapid Hokkien dialect.

A voice coming from a room beyond the stairwell rang back towards them in similar spurts of Chinese.

"Ah, she left here. She go over Causeway with her sister."

"What? When did she leave?"

"Last night, last night. I sorry, she not live here now."

Ruth looked at her husband in despair, unable to put her thoughts into words.

"Of all the ungrateful…" Captain Armstrong began.

"Mr Armstrong, don't!" his wife reprimanded him.

"You'll just have to cope without her. Plenty of woman go without a baby amah. My little sister doesn't have one," Charlie tried to reassure his wife, though it didn't really help much. It just made Ruth feel all the more useless.

The group trooped back to their car and continued on to the waterfront.

All the while Ruth desperately wanted to have a good old howl, but she knew her husband wouldn't approve of such a display. She also didn't want to appear pathetically tear-stained in front of the others. Instead, she cuddled Mack on her lap and listened to the nervous superficial small talk going on around her.

With not a moment to spare they arrived in Singapore. Parking was no longer allowed directly on the waterfront so they had to pick their way through the city streets. They struggled along past abandoned household goods and vehicles, some with their doors still open, all the while carrying the bags, the attaché cases and Jean in her pram. It was a long way to the pier where they were to catch a launch out to the ship. Ruth checked her wristwatch. They still had five minutes to go until nine.

When they arrived, there was no activity on P&O's private passenger pier and the little pilot's booth was closed with just an attendant sitting inside.

Armstrong rapped on the window to get his attention.

"The Islam has departed," was the response.

"No, she hasn't. I can clearly see her in the roads."

"The boarding launch left two minutes ago."

"But we've got tickets," Ruth said holding her tickets up to the window.

The man opened his window. "Sorry, she was fully loaded. The departure time was strictly 0900 hours and your tickets were resold. Demand is outstripping availability."

"But it is only just gone nine o'clock now," Mrs Armstrong complained.

"Not by my clock," the man tapped the clock on the wall beside him.

"I say, this is not on. We've spent a lot of coin on these passages. You can't just resell them," Cole blustered.

"Look fella, you'll be able to exchange your tickets for the next sailing," the man replied.

"When's that?" Ruth asked.

"I haven't the foggiest, madam. You'll have to enquire at the P&O office."

"Can't we put them on another launch out to the ship?" Armstrong asked.

"There are no other launches."

"Well what if we hire one. We could ask one of the coolies to take us out on a sampan," Mrs Armstrong said stubbornly.

"Good luck with that," the man said and closed his window.

"Well, of all the nerve. Come on, we'll have to find another way out to the ship," Ruth began.

"Sweetheart, it's no good. Didn't you hear him say he has sold your tickets to someone else? Even if we could find transport out to the ship, even if the captain would allow you to embark, there is nowhere on board for you to sleep."

"Are you saying it's hopeless then?" Ruth asked.

"This time it is. Look on the bright side. You get another day at home with me. Come on, let's walk across to P&O and light a fire under them."

After listening to their story with a bland look on his face, the manager at the Peninsular and Orient Line office was unsympathetic.

"Do you want me to spell it out to you people? We – have – no – ships! None! Nada! Zip! Nothing at all. The whole god-be-damned lot of them have been requisitioned. We've been told that we are the only agents for India and we are doing our best with last minute information. Officially, we have no future sailings scheduled. Unofficially, I have heard that there is a big convoy leaving together in a week or so. The Rear Admiral is in charge of all evacuation ships, as I'm sure you well know and I have no idea where the convoy is coming from or going to. Don't ask me if we'll even be handling any of the ships in it. But if there is something going out towards India, certainly your tickets can be transferred. Until we know what is going where our hands are tied."

"Is there another shipping agent we can use then?"

"There's us, and there's Blue Funnel, handling all Australian ports, next door. All other shipping lines are being directed back through either of us."

"I suggest you check back each day," he finished by saying. "You can telephone if you prefer not to come down."

The following day, Ruth and Charlie walked across to the Armstrongs early with the intention of putting a call through to the shipping office for news.

"There are no sailings today," a clerk's response came back.

"Can you tell me when the next ship leaves to either India or Ceylon?"

"There's a troopship coming in soon, we hope. I heard that it might be requisitioned for evacuees. But that is just a rumour. I can't guarantee it and I can't guarantee you'll get a berth on it. Try again tomorrow."

The day was promising to be the hottest day ever experienced. Since he wasn't on duty, Charlie decided to take his wife and daughter to the seaside for a dip. They hadn't been out to the Swimming Club in months and he wasn't sure whether it was still operating or not. Yet most places seemed to be still open for business albeit a slightly modified operation in many cases. Singaporeans were nothing if not business-minded.

The little family had just gathered their swimming togs and rustled up a picnic when an urgent order was hand delivered.

"Orders to evacuate the bungalow," Charlie said after reading it through. "Apparently the entire naval base and neighbouring estates are evacuating. All naval families, civilian staff and any animals are to leave immediately and go south towards the city. All uniformed men are ordered to return to the HQ to standby for emergency service instructions."

"But the city is where the worst of the bombing seems to be happening," Ruth said shocked. She took the sheet of paper her husband handed to her. "Surely we'd be safer up here?"

"We have to be gone by 1700 hours today," she read dismayed and looked up at her husband's worried face. "Oh well," she surprised herself by saying in a semi-cheerful voice, "we were leaving anyway."

"I guess the question is: where will you go? Blast that woman, leaving without warning us," he said referring to baby amah for the umpteenth time. "What the devil she thought she was doing going up to the mainland anyway. It defies logic."

Charlie left Ruth in turmoil as he obeyed his orders to return to the base immediately, but promised to return before five if possible or send a note with instructions.

He had no sooner left when a chorus of '*yoohoos!*' came from the front fence.

Ruth and Jean barrelled out onto the verandah and found a trio of navy wives assembled below them. Ruth recognised them all, though none were particularly close friends.

"You've heard the evacuation news then?" one of the women called. She was smartly dressed in a navy linen frock with white piping.

Ruth nodded half raising the paper order which she still clutched in her hand.

"Mrs Spooner has arranged for us to camp at the Sepoy Lines Golf Club," one said, referring to the wife of the dockyard's Admiral Superintendent, Rear Admiral Spooner. "We're going house to house to see who wants to join us, dear. Are you interested?"

"Oh!" Ruth said, too surprised to say anything else.

"The plan is to meet at the Club at midday," a second mem said, obviously referring to the Navy social clubrooms, rather than the distant golf club. "We'll see who we've got and what our transport options are and go from there."

"Don't bring anything you can't carry," the third woman said. "We may have to walk."

"Or better still, if you have a car, load it up with blankets, pillows and food," the first woman corrected.

Ruth stood there blinking, tears threatening at the corners of her eyes.

"Well ta-ra then. We've got to get around everybody on the Base and get ourselves organised too."

"Thank you ladies," Ruth remembered to call out as the trio disappeared back out through the garden gate.

Ruth rounded up cookie and told her the news.

"There is a crate under the house. Ask the boy to bring it up and help you pack it full of linen please. Strip all the beds."

Since she was planning on leaving anyway, Ruth had already packed crates full of good china and crystal and other wedding presents that they didn't use on a daily basis. She also had a locked sea trunk half full of personal items like photograph albums and such. This she pulled out and unlocked. She wandered around the house, collecting anything and everything that she hadn't already packed.

Secretly Ruth wondered what she'd do with the trunk once it was full. When she took down the last remaining family portrait that she kept on top of the drinks cabinet, she suddenly felt inspired to pull it from the frame, tucking it into her purse.

"At least one keepsake of happier times," she said turning to Jean who she found was busy unpacking everything out of the trunk.

A little while later Ruth heard Charlie return and anxiously stepped out onto the verandah steps to meet him.

"Well, the APF have been ordered to ensure every navy house is being evacuated. We're to take around the evacuation orders today to the outlaying most residences and tomorrow we need to ensure that the properties are empty and secured. Apparently the navy wives are to go to Sepoy Lines Golf Club."

"Yes, I've heard."

"So, I guess it's time to pull chocks my dear," Charlie said wistfully as they stepped indoors.

"It's all happening so fast," Ruth breathed. "I don't like it. I don't like just walking away from everything. I don't like being separated from you."

"Come on now, you're a big girl. You've got Jean to think of. Besides, you won't be there long without me. I'll take the first opportunity to get down to you. It won't be tonight, mind. Perhaps tomorrow and in the mean time you need to see to your passage. If you hear of any boat coming in, then go down to the shipping offices; walk if you have to. You know how to get to Collyer Quay from Outram Road, but for heaven's sake, don't go on your own if you can help it. I think we should forget about Ceylon and just concentrate on getting the first boat, whether it be to Australia, Batavia or even direct to South Africa. Take three tickets, just in case I can join you."

At that moment, the telephone rang and Charlie spoke briefly to the caller, while Ruth hovered anxiously.

"That was Armstrong," Charlie said as he replaced the receiver.

"Mrs Armstrong is going to join you at the Club, but she can't take their car. Since I've got the bike, I offered our car. You're to collect her on the way to the Admiralty Club."

"I guess we'd better send off the servants," Ruth said, motioning to cookie who was hovering at the door, having heard most of the goings on.

Ruth regained her inner strength as she gripped her cook in a sad farewell. The poor woman looked bewildered and Ruth hardly knew how she would fare without employment. Charlie gave the woman $10 and Ruth insisted she pack a suitcase full of preserves, which she soon hauled awkwardly down the garden path.

"Wait!" Ruth called before the woman left the property. Dashing inside, she grabbed the silver teapot that had been a wedding gift. She ran towards the Malay woman and presented it to her. The amah's eyes took on an even greater look of fright, as she tried to deny the gift.

"No mem, no. I cannot take," she said as she looked at the item that she had spent the past two years proudly polishing and brewing endless cups of tea with.

Ruth insisted fervently that she take it and pushed the item at her. I'd rather you have it than the Japanese dear. You should get good money for it if you need to sell it. It might help you get through. Charlie came down to add his blessing to the gift. At that moment, a bullock cart approached carrying two Malay families. Charlie ran out onto the street to halt them asking if Cookie Amah could be taken towards Changi, where she lived. A moment later, Cookie was aboard the cart with her case of preserves and her teapot safely hidden inside her jacket and soon was out of sight.

Turning back towards the house, Ruth caught sight of her hanging orchid garden and the houseboy standing uncertainly beneath it. All at once she felt the weight of reality crushing her. A whirlwind of questions spun through her brain. What were they to do with all their possessions? Was she really expected to just lock the door and walk away from everything? Should she try to bury the crates of china in the garden? Hide the trunk in the walls perhaps? What should she take with her?

Charlie must have read her mind, because he said, "We'll have to leave all this behind sweetheart. Try to keep in mind what is important. You. Me.

Jean. None of this matters; the house, the garden, the furniture—none of it belongs to us anyway."

"But the china, mother's album! Jean's toys, all the rest. Oh Charlie, we were having such a lovely time."

"I know my dear. Look, take your pearls and brooch, as much cash as we can put together, your papers and just the essentials for Jean."

"Clothes, I'll need clothes and toiletries."

"Yes, a change of clothes. Sensible shoes. The dog. Napkins for Jean. Take her carriage. It'll be easier than carrying her back and forth to the P&O office. I've got to keep going my dear. You'll have to manage on your own. I'll ask the boy to tie a mattress onto the roof of the car and then have him stay with you until you go. I'll come by later and try to secure the place."

"Can you bury the sea trunk? It's in the front room. I've filled it with photos and such."

"I've heard there is storage available in a godown along the river. I'll try to drop it all off there, but if I run out of time I'll look at burying it and we'll just have to hope it survives its interment."

By the time Ruth had packed the car there was barely any room for Victoria Armstrong's belongings. She drew up outside the neighbouring bungalow where a very flustered Victoria came out to her. "I'll go ahead and unload and then come back for you," Ruth called through the driver's window. She was worried about the scattered sun showers damaging the mattress, although in the extreme heat, it would have dried quickly enough.

A half hour later as Ruth helped Victoria unpack the car at the Club, she overheard one of the navy mems saying, "Mrs Spooner has arranged for lorries to take us all down to Sepoy Lines,"

"Good. Some women had been talking about walking," another woman said.

"By god! All the way to Outram Road in this heat?" Victoria exclaimed. "They must be touched by the sun."

By six pm, the women had settled into the main dining room of the golf club. Each found an area of floor for their mattresses and the mood was jovial. A late tiffin was rustled up from the kitchens and someone got on the piano. Later, a group of ladies went for a walk across to the General Hospital beyond the 7th fairway. They came back with news that any help from the women would be appreciated and donations of blood were still desperately needed. The hospital was overrun with patients. There were burns victims, lacerations, broken bones and head wounds. Patients were even being treated on the verandahs.

Ruth resolved that she would be better off helping with meals at the club. She couldn't take a toddler across to the hospital, so that was that. Although her cooking skills were rudimentary, Ruth, with the help of a few others, was able to produce edible food even if not exactly gourmet.

Charlie didn't show at all that first evening. Ruth tried not to worry. After all, the other women were in the same situation, though the majority did not have children. None of the women slept well that night. Jean, overtired from all the excitement, had been grumpy and unsettled. Air raid sirens, fire sirens and the ack ack guns from nearby Fort Canning meant it was impossible to snatch more than two hours of decent sleep at a time, although once Jean had finally fallen asleep she slept deeply. Ruth even managed to bundle her out to the Club's crude bomb shelter both times the sirens went off without waking her.

The following morning the big news at the hospital was that many of the nurses were to be evacuated in a few days' time. Two large troop ships were coming in, the *Duchess of Bedford* and the *USS Wakefield*. These would take the nurses away on their return journey. Ruth was determined to get down to the ships office to secure a passage for her family too.

Another air raid sounded just as Ruth and Victoria were about to leave in their car. They only just made it to the shelter before they heard the thud of bombs, which sounded awfully close. Soon the all clear sounded and they hurried on their way. It was so late in the morning, they dreaded the inevitable queues. It had only been a few days since they were last in the Commercial district, but the state of affairs had deteriorated considerably. As they drove down through the Chinatown, they could see a commotion up ahead. Across the street lay debris from the most recent bombing. Dreadful cries carried clearly across to them and getting out of their car, they could see an elderly grief-stricken woman sitting amongst the bricks and dust. The small body of a child lay sprawled beside the broken axel of a rickshaw. Already the ARP were dousing flames while more fire sirens could be heard approaching. The two women were asked to move their car. They drove on past what appeared to be the remains of a basket weaving shop and turned into Church Street. Due to restrictions, they could not park on Collyer Quay, so they parked at the end of Church Street and putting Jean into the carriage, braved the queues.

As it turned out they weren't taking bookings for the *Duchess of Bedford* until possibly late afternoon, but since they already had unused tickets, which only needed to be transferred, the kind man at the desk agreed to endorse their tickets there and then. They also registered their husbands need for a berth and paid a deposit, though they were told that the chances of the men actually getting aboard was very unlikely since the Governor had ordered that all men under 55 were to remain in Singapore and offer assistance where required. Still the women insisted on registering their request for a passage. The departure point, they were told was Clifford Pier downtown, rather than P&O's usual private wharf on the waterfront.

Having spent their cash, a trip to the bank was in order next. Ruth changed a hundred dollars into pounds and she thought that Victoria had taken out considerably more. Jean needed her napkin changed and Victoria was feeling decidedly green with morning sickness. Ruth suggested they pop into Robinsons, which had moved into brand new premises just around the corner. There they knew they'd find decent facilities for Jean and a reasonably priced scone or cake to keep going on. The enormous department store was still trading happily enough and meals were still being served although the cafeteria had moved to the basement due to minor bomb damage on the 2nd floor.

"May I?" Victoria pointed at a copy of the *Free Press* which a couple vacating a nearby table seemed to be leaving behind.

"By all means," the man said passing the newspaper to her. She smiled in return and laid it down on the table between herself and Ruth.

"God, it's all war, war and more war."

"At least it seems to be about our war and not all Europe this and Europe that," Ruth responded trying to read it upside down.

"How ghastly! Look here. The Japs are breaking the International Treaty for warfare and treatment of prisoners of war."

"Why, what have they done?"

"A dead Philippine scout has been found. His hands have been bound behind his back and then he was bayoneted and left to die."

"So they killed him," Ruth asked, trying to make sense of it, "even though they had already captured him?"

"Precisely. Well they wouldn't dare do that to a British soldier," Victoria sniffed, turning the page.

"Here we go, back to European news. Hitler Must Be Bled To Death. Where do they think up these headlines?"

"Look, Hongkong Refugees Arrive in Free China," Ruth interrupted her.

Both women quickly scanned the brief article.

Victoria was well aware of Ruth's concern about her brother and father, but the report didn't give much hope. "It could be good news," she told her friend cautiously. "Although it does rather sound like they are talking about native refugees. There is no specific mention of British citizens there. You can only hope my dear."

"Yes, I can hope," Ruth repeated cheerlessly.

After that they ate their morning tea quickly with an unspoken desire to return to the golf club. They were both aware that their husbands could return at any time. Victoria tucked the paper into her handbag and Ruth pushed Jean's carriage as they walked back across Raffles Square to their parked car.

The sound of Charlie's motorbike later that afternoon saw both women rushing out onto the Club's verandah. Giles Armstrong was riding in the sidecar and the news they brought with them was terrific. They were to be released from duty the day after the next. In fact, they had only one more job to do and many of the other APF officers were already being relieved of their duties. They had all been firmly "invited" to join the volunteer land army or become air raid wardens if they wished, and some of the other officers intended to do just that.

"Not that I'm ungrateful, but it does seem silly that you're being released from duties just at the moment that you're needed most," Victoria commented.

"No you're wrong love. You wouldn't recognise the naval base. It's nothing like it was before. It's no longer a job for either police or military police. The base is expected to become the front line. Naval personnel are being shipped out and it's all the land forces now."

"But who is policing the causeway? Who is guarding the prison, and the Admiral's family?" she asked.

"Don't worry about the any of that—the Admiral says he only wants bachelors guarding his family. He reckons we have our own families to worry about. And the G.O.C. is now in charge of the entire coastline, the causeway, everything," Armstrong said. As for the prisoners, many have been moved, deported or released. In fact the reason we are here, is that we have just accompanied a truck full of prisoners who were being transferred to Outram Road."

"And that brings us to another reason we are here," Cole added, before pausing and looking guiltily at his colleague.

"Tell us," Ruth urged noticing the look the men shared.

"Well, we've been promised crew positions on an evacuee boat if we just do one last thing for the navy. We just have to dash across to Johor. I expect we'll be back tomorrow night."

"But the Japanese are on the mainland," both women wailed almost simultaneously.

"Yes, but they're not quite that far down the coast yet. We won't be anywhere near them. Look, at the very latest, we'll be back early on Friday," Armstrong assured them.

"Mr Armstrong, what on earth are you needed over there for?" Victoria asked her husband angrily.

"Well, you know many of the navy personnel live in Johore Bahru. And so I'm sure you can understand that we have to visit every household and ensure each is empty and secure," her husband said. "Look my darling, just be grateful that we will be free to go after that. Take a look at the women around you and remember that they aren't so lucky. Many of their husbands are being redeployed without them."

"Which reminds me," Charlie said. "How are you getting on securing a passage?"

Ruth told him their news, and that the two troopships were due into Keppel Harbour on Thursday.

"They plan to leave on Friday and we have to be on Clifford Pier by mid-afternoon for a 5pm departure. They will be loading up with nurses but we were able to transfer our tickets and we have put your names down. You might be able to get on with us."

"Oh we will try sweetheart, don't you worry. If we don't see you here, we'll meet you on the pier. Don't panic if we are late, we'll definitely be there," Charlie said.

"If you have to go down to the pier without us, take a yellow-top cab, or a rickshaw if you can get one. Leave the car keys here. We might need to use it," Armstrong added.

"It's a dreadful state of affairs in the Chinatown and the Quay is a complete shambles," Ruth told them. "Dead bodies in the street, fires, burning rubber. It's awfully tricky to negotiate, so be sure to give yourself enough time to get through."

"I know love," Charlie replied, taking Jean into his arms. "And how's my beautiful wee sweetheart? Are you being good for mummy?"

Jean just dribbled in reply, while her father bounced her on his khaki clad thigh.

8
MAINLAND MALAYA 1942

CHARLIE COLE

The causeway that separated the island of Singapore from the Malayan Peninsula was full of traffic travelling in both directions. Native Malayans were heading back to their families in Malaya whereas soldiers plus the last of the plantation managers and miscellaneous Asiatics were moving south into the supposed safety of Singapore. Most of the British women and children had left the peninsula days, if not weeks, before.

A pair of ARP bikes, ridden by Captain Armstrong and Crown Sergeant Day with Cole and Sergeant McGregor in the respective sidecars, pulled up alongside the Woodlands Military Checkpoint on the Singapore side. The two police officers wore civilian clothing and carried only their personal side arms. Their official navy dog tags were replaced with the civilian registration tag. The bikes were no longer army green but had been painted matt black.

Naturally, the checkpoint soldier was suspicious of the four British men and had no intention of allowing them to go north. Warily he took the official letter of authority handed to him and his demeanour changed immediately. Still he hesitated, worried for their safety.

"How long do you think we can hold out here?" Armstrong asked indicating the bridge that straddled the Johore Straits.

"Officially, I couldn't say, even if I knew," the uniformed man said. "Unofficially, my advice is don't take too long over there. When they make the decision to take her down, they won't be waiting for the likes of you to come back first."

And by this, the men knew he was talking about the possibility of destroying the mile long causeway in order to prevent the enemy from advancing across it. It would be a last ditch option once the enemy were all but upon them.

"Got you. Rest assured we'll not be spending longer than we need to. We've got wives and kiddies waiting for us back here."

"On you go then and God be with you," the soldier said waving them through the checkpoint.

Once over to Johore, Armstrong turned his bike left, hugging the coast towards the Sultan's palace for the start of his journey while Day and McGregor went straight ahead. Armstrong and Cole had lost a coin toss which meant they had only to check on 15-odd properties but these were further out in more affluent areas, whereas Day and McGregor had nearly 40 properties to check, but these were all neatly contained within an urban area of only 5 square miles and situated close to the causeway.

The decision to live in Johore Bahru, rather than Woodlands, was a personal one for each navy family. Some families just felt that the cheaper, larger properties were more desirable than the rat race of Singapore. Very few navy families actually lived in Navy-owned houses like the Coles and the Armstrongs. Most were required to rent privately owned houses and were subsequently reimbursed by the Navy. The ARP were assigned two family bungalows for married officers within the Naval Base close to the Admiral's Navy House. As a fairly senior officer, Armstrong was allocated one of these but Cole had always known that he had only secured the other bungalow because there were no other married officers in the ARP more senior than himself. It had always been a possibility that one day he might have to relinquish it and rent something else privately in a nearby locale.

Part of the ARP jurisdiction was to ensure safe lodgings for all navy personnel whether they were in navy owned homes or navy approved private homes on either side of the causeway. Armstrong and Cole expected the job to take about two hours, all going well. As it turned out, it was never going to be quite that easy. There was a full on retreat in progress of the entire British contingent on the Peninsular. This often meant pulling over and waiting for long trains of vehicles and foot soldiers to pass.

Then there was a tyre puncture to deal with. The dirt roads were littered with debris from aerial bombardments. These attacks in themselves caused several holdups where they were forced to swiftly drive their bike under the cover of jungle, to hide from rogue aircraft.

Although progress was slow, they were in fact getting through the properties on their list and had found nothing untoward other than: an open front door; a few Malay houseboys staying behind to guard properties, which they were entitled to do if they were inclined to; and a forlorn looking dog that had been left behind. This they took with them, but then dropped it off to the first English-speaking Malayan they could find with assurances that it would be cared for. It was the best they could do for it under the circumstances. They estimated that once they reached the furthest out property, they could probably zip back to the causeway in 15 minutes making them only slightly later than the other crew.

DAY and McGREGOR

Meanwhile the other two APF men, Sergeants Day and McGregor, finished their rounds and returned to the causeway. They soon found they had arrived at the rendezvous point first. So they parked their vehicle on the siding beside the checkpoint and settled in for the wait. Trevor McGregor took the opportunity to doze but Harlow Day, elected to periodically scan the far side of the causeway with his field glasses. He opened his second packet of cigarettes for the day and smoked in silence.

A quarter hour later, both men were startled into alertness by the ack ack sound of nearby anti-aircraft guns. Even as the first rounds of flak burst into the sky, a belated siren sounded and suddenly Day pointed out towards the late afternoon sun.

"Tally-ho, ten o'clock and heading this way," he said to McGregor, who turned to see a black speck that was fast materialising into a relatively low flying single engine aircraft.

People were scrambling off the causeway and taking cover from both the possibility of being hit either by spent flak or from the evil that the aircraft no doubt intended to inflict upon the adjacent naval base.

Day flung the glasses at his passenger and roared the bike into reverse, completing a messy turn that would nevertheless take them to the cover of the nearest row of trees.

He manoeuvred the bike 50 or so metres down the road in between two Asian bullock carts that were also taking cover. The aircraft was very close now but swerved away from the line of flak keeping it on the Malaysian side of the causeway. It seemed to be doing a wide circle alternating its altitude.

All eyes were on the sky, watching this brazen pilot. All except McGregor who had his glasses trained on the far bank. From this angle, he could better see the road leading up to the Johore-checkpoint where hundreds of troops were like sitting ducks as they either scrambled to take what little cover was available or make a run for the causeway. Suddenly, Trevor McGregor gave a low whistle.

"There they are!"

"Who?" Day asked.

"I see a matt black bike hurtling down the road. Hang on, there's no-one in the side-car. No wait, he just sat up, he must have been laying down. Taking cover no doubt. Here you have squiz."

"They seem to be wearing army issue helmets. Must have picked them up along the way," Day pointed out as soon as he picked out the bike.

"Look out, the plane is coming back directly towards us."

The two men dove out of their bike and crouched behind it. Day retrained his field glasses on the bike. McGregor was watching skyward. Bombs were leaving the aircraft directly over the causeway.

"What on earth are they bombing the causeway for? They'll need that if they want to take Singapore."

The black bike containing their colleagues and friends had stopped. The road ahead looked to be blocked by abandoned vehicles.

Like a slow motion horror film, the two men watched the bombs drop. At first they had seemed to be directly above the causeway, but they lazily sank over the Johore Road instead. A split second before they found their targets, both Day and McGregor knew the outcome wasn't going to be good. In the late afternoon haze all along the road leading to the causeway, a row of flashes marked the spots which, in the next instant, became great clouds of dust and smoke. A succession of booms sounded a moment later.

A change in the sound of the aircraft's engine made both men suddenly shift their focus back up. The invader was climbing steeply, but smoke trailing from its rear indicated that it had suffered a slight hit at least. Soon it had flown out of sight and the men's eyes returned to the scene across the water.

Where the APF bike had been, there was now a crater. A broken front wheel, clearly visible through the glasses, lay on the edge of it.

Even before the all-clear siren sounded, both men emerged to mount their bike. They had one thought on their minds that didn't need communicating. They had to get over to try to find and help their friends.

Back on the causeway, the scene had changed. The checkpoint guard now had orders to close the mile long bridge to all northbound traffic. Only retreating troops and citizens, if there were any, were to be allowed to come south across it, thereby freeing up both sides of the road.

There was nothing the two men could say which would induce the guard to let them cross. All they could do was wait for news.

It wasn't good news when it came. As the injured started to flood across, eyewitness accounts told them that there had been nothing left of the two men on the black bike. Their bodies were scattered and in part buried. The bike had apparently suffered the same fate, ending in a thousand pieces.

Feeling hopeless, Day gunned his bike and sped away from the scene, weaving in and out of the traffic and onto Woodlands Road. His dangerous driving caused several loud shouts and angry gestures, which he ignored. He turned off at Butik Batok Road and slowed until the bike simply puttered to a stop in the middle of the empty lane. McGregor, lost in thoughts of his own, seemed oblivious to their surroundings.

A few moments of silence passed before Day cried out, "We'll have to tell the ladies."

"I can't face it," McGregor whispered. "That poor wee kiddie."

"No, come on. Buck up. People are losing their lives and making children orphans every day in this damnable war. It's our duty to tell them, before they hear it on the grapevine."

"Fair call. But after that I'm going to go and get very drunk."

"You bet. We'll make the next stop the Sea View Hotel."

Day drove them to the Sepoy Lines club where he knew that the two widowed women were camping out.

Tentatively, they climbed the stairs and poked their heads into the clubrooms.

"Can I help you, lads?" a mousey blonde woman with an Irish accent and a toddler clinging to her leg asked them.

"We're looking for Mrs Armstrong and Mrs Cole."

"Oh yes, that'll be the two APF women. I believe they walked over to the hospital to donate blood. Isn't that right Mrs Eversham?"

Mrs Eversham was an authoritative looking stout woman with pure white hair.

"That's right. And who shall I say was looking for them?"

"Ahh," Day stuttered and hesitated, while McGregor squirmed uncomfortably. "You could say that Crown Sergeant Day and Sergeant McGregor have a message for them."

"And what is the message," Mrs Eversham asked, looking at their lack of uniform in a pointed up and down manner.

"We'd rather tell them personally. It's a bit delicate, you see. Just say that we will come back later."

"As you wish. Good day gentlemen." Then Mrs Eversham indicated that they should leave by pointing to the door and they were glad to get away.

CHARLIE COLE

At about the time Day and McGregor had first arrived at the rendezvous point at the Causeway earlier, they had no way of knowing that Armstrong and Cole had just three properties left and were still going strong. A British major, seeing them pull out of a side road and turn against the tide of traffic, forced them to stop. Armstrong and Cole had been under strict orders not to carry any identifying paperwork and had therefore left their authorisations at the checkpoint. They did try to explain their mission, but there was no way of proving who they were and what they were doing, even had the young officer been in the mood to listen to them.

The major, verging on panic, had no time for their explanations. He required them to surrender their bike and return to Singapore on foot with the regular soldiers. He departed on the back of a 6x4 truck but not before he had ordered a nearby corporal to load an injured man currently on the back of the slow moving truck into the black painted sidecar and drive him at speed back to medical help in Singapore. As both the bike and the major's truck drove off, the two APF men began walking back to the causeway. However, as soon as the major was out of sight, they turned around and continued onto their objective by foot, thinking despondently that even if they walked directly to the causeway, they'd never get there before sunset.

The call of "Going the wrong way boys," continuously assailed them from the weary Australian soldiers. They braced themselves when a quarter hour later another high-ranking officer drove past them in the passenger seat of one of the new "jeeps". Sure enough, the vehicle slowed to a stop and then reversed back to their position.

"I say, is that you Armstrong?" the officer, a Lt Colonel, surprised them by asking. "Do you mind telling me what on earth you are doing out here?"

Blinking Giles Armstrong tried to place the Lt Colonel before he remembered that he had escorted him around the navy base a month or two earlier.

Quickly he explained their plight.

"Hmm, I doubt there'll be any civilians left around here. Not with all this racket going on. They'd need their head read to stay. Mind you we noticed several European families hunkering down on their estates further north. Damned fools couldn't be persuaded to budge."

"Just following orders Sir."

"Why are you dressed like that? In civvies I mean."

"In case we are captured, Sir. It is better that we are not connected to the navy. We are to say that we are prison guards."

"Well, I'd give you my car, but I'm already falling behind. Let's just see my lad. The next vehicle that comes along may suit your purpose. I'll requisition it for you if I can."

Armstrong took the opportunity to introduce Charlie Cole to the Colonel and the Colonel introduced his adjutant.

Several vehicles passed them and the wily Colonel made no attempt to flag any of them down.

"I'd have my man make us a pot of tea," he said after the 3rd armoured car passed them to the astonishment of the APF lads, "but it doesn't look good you know, to be sitting having tea, when the men all about us are struggling back to base."

"May we ask if we could have some water? We lost ours when the young major took our bike."

"Hmmm, did you happen to get his name? I'd like to have a word with that blighter later. No? Well, there's water in the canister I expect. Help yourself."

Armstrong poured a modest quantity of water into the offered cup and then did the same for Cole, who in return raised his eyebrows in a questioning manner over what the hold-up was. Armstrong shrugged ever so slightly and shook his head almost imperceptibly as if to say, "don't know."

"Oh look now, here's something. Here's something I say," the Colonel said behind them, whereupon he calmly stepped out onto the road and waved down an approaching motorbike. "I had a feeling that wasn't far behind us," he continued. "Not quite as nifty as your flash APF bikes, but I dare say it is a lot better suited to these dirt roads. Of course your man will have to ride pillion, but better than walking what?"

"Thank you Sir," Armstrong said.

Cole couldn't help notice the peeved look on the dislodged rider's face, but then the disgruntled lieutenant was mollified when the Colonel allowed him to ride in the rear of his jeep.

"Carry on," the imperturbable Colonel waved to all about him, almost as if he had an audience, before his adjutant drove off.

The two men turned into an empty tree lined lane. The only noise that accompanied them was the sound of the army issue motorcycle. The crowds of retreating troops may as well have disappeared. Turning a bend, they saw in the distance a small car, piled high with luggage, and standing around it was a man, woman and child. But no sooner had they spotted the family, the trio had disappeared from view. By the time the two men drew up alongside the parked vehicle there was still no sign of them.

"Hullo!" Armstrong called out.

Almost immediately, a man emerged from the tree line. "Weren't sure which side you were on," he called to them in a low Welsh accent, which became louder as he approached. "You couldn't give me a hand with this engine could you? She just puttered out. Can't understand it—she's usually reliable enough."

There was desperation in the man's voice, which surprised neither Armstrong nor Cole.

"We've got to help them," Armstrong murmured, to which Cole simply nodded. A million thoughts ran through Cole's mind, the first of which was "these blighters could cost them dearly." But he knew he couldn't leave a British woman and child out here.

The three men bent their heads over the engine and questions flew back and forth. Did they have petrol? Was the engine turning over? What tools did the man have? Did they have a torch?

The woman and child sat on the roadside, waiting patiently.

Rolling under the chassis, Cole smelt petrol and thought he knew what the problem was.

"I think you might have a split hose. Your fuel has leaked away."

Just as he was giving his opinion they heard distant gun shots. The front line was drawing closer. One pointed look from the mother to her husband, sent the girl into sobs of fear.

"Can you fix it though man?" the father asked.

Cole climbed back under the car. He needed time to think. There was no way he could fix it quickly. The fuel line was obstructed by the engine itself. It would be awkward to reach it, let alone to find a way to *jimmy* a patch. He was eager to get back to his own family. Thoughts of his daughter, helped him make up his mind.

"Not in the time we have with the tools we have. If I was you, I'd start walking. You are only a couple of hours away from the Causeway."

"Please," begged the woman. "Take our daughter. We'll be able to move faster without her and I'd be happier knowing she was safe."

"Can you give us an address to take her?" Armstrong asked.

The woman looked at her husband, the hope on her face visibly fading.

"We have no-one in Singapore."

"There was a family…" the woman began but didn't carry on.

"They left several weeks ago," the man finished for her.

"Couldn't you take her? Give us your address and we'll find you."

"But we are taking the first ship off the island. Don't you understand? We won't necessarily be there for you to find. We can't just abandon the girl on the streets of Singapore," Armstrong said helplessly.

"We could drop her off at the Salvation Army," Cole suggested. "Their headquarters are on Tank Road."

"Yes!" the man almost bit the words out of his mouth. "Her name is Gloria Davies."

Armstrong was already back on the bike and had it gunned into gear. Cole climbed into the narrow gap between the spare jerry can and his partner. The woman passed the confused child into his lap.

"But mummy, aren't you coming too?"

"No my darling, No…" she gulped down the tears

"Daddy wants you to be a good girl and do as these nice men say. Tonight you are going on a big adventure and you will go to bed when the nice people tell you to and we will see you when you wake up tomorrow morning. Be a good girl now."

"Here, take this," the father said separating a folded piece of paper from a group of papers in his coat pocket. "Some identification for her."

"We'd better make tracks," Armstrong said. "Keep your chin up and remember, Tank Road."

He turned the bike back into the centre of the road and began to speed up. The girl twisted in Cole's arms and cried out to her parents. Her voice took on a tone of terror, and she started to scream and scrabble her way back to them.

"I can't hold her," Cole yelled, but his voice was suppressed by the fabric of her thin dress, which was smothering him.

The girl scrabbled her way between Cole's lap and Armstrong's back. Cole grabbed hold of one of her legs, just in time, as she half fell, half leapt off the back of the back of the bike in her desperate attempt to get back to her parents. She screamed in pain, as her hand hit the hot exhaust.

"It's no use," Armstrong called back to her parents who were by now running to catch up to the bike.

"Don't leave me," the girl sobbed hysterically. "My hand is burning, Mummy please don't leave me. It h-h-hurts." Every word was interspersed with loud heaving sobs.

"It's no use," Armstrong repeated to the parents who having reached the bike were now comforting the girl.

"She's burnt her hand on the exhaust I think, Cole said examining her hand, while he ran his tongue gingerly over his own swelling lip where one of the girl's knees had bruised it severely.

"What'll we do?" the woman said in heaving sobs.

"Blast to hell," Cole said. He couldn't bear seeing women cry. "You're going to have to get that hand looked at urgently. You'll just have to take the bike yourself, if she won't come with us."

"I'll stay behind," the man offered. "My wife can't drive, but at least one of you could get away."

"No, if Cole is staying then so am I," Armstrong said. "It's best if you stick with your family. Leave the bike at the Sepoy Lines Golf Club. There's a group of women sheltering there. Give the bike to Mrs Armstrong or Mrs Cole. Tell them we will be back as soon as possible. But tell them, if we're not back before the ship leaves, then to go without us. Tell them, we'll send a message to Colombo when we can. Can you do that for us?"

Cole had already climbed off the bike and was removing the spare jerry can of petrol.

Armstrong handed the girl's papers back to the man and gave him a quick outline of the bike's controls.

A minute or two later when the putter of the bike had faded into the distance, the sounds of the jungle around them became more focused. Sporadic thumps from artillery guns and the occasional boom of grenades were worryingly discernible. Then, horrifically, the sound of far-off Japanese voices came to them through the jungle wall at the side of the road.

"Should we attempt to fix it, or should we just start running?" Armstrong asked.

9
SINGAPORE FEBRUARY 1942

RUTH COLE

At the Sepoy Lines Golf Club, just before the evening meal of rice curry was served, Victoria, Ruth and Jean returned from across the fairways, where Ruth had been able to donate blood. Mrs Armstrong had been turned down on account of her pregnancy.

Mrs Eversham passed on the message from Day and McGregor efficiently without affording any unnecessary information. The two APF women were left with many unanswered questions, to which Mrs Eversham had nothing further to add.

The following morning, Day and McGregor were much the worse for the wear after their evening drowning their sorrows and decided to postpone their dreadful task until they could present themselves more respectably. This was not to come to pass immediately though because their most pressing concern was to secure the motor launch they had earlier procured to take them to Batavia. It was currently sitting idle at the Changi Barracks wharf and they were worried it would be requisitioned if the soldiers they'd paid to keep an eye on it were moved out. It was an entirely likely scenario if nobody knew who it belonged to or why it was there. As it turned out, this was exactly what was about to happen, and only luck enabled the men to reach it before then.

They spent the next few days hiding the boat and planning. A perilous journey for such a small boat at the best of times, their plan was to cross the Strait of Malacca to the large island of Sumatra in the Dutch East Indies.

On the morning of the day that the Duchess of *Bedford* was due to leave, Armstrong and Cole had still not shown up at the Golf Course. Neither had

Day and McGregor nor any member of the Davies family. As far as Victoria and Ruth were aware, Armstrong and Cole were late.

They took a taxi down to Clifford Pier and arrived just before three in the afternoon finding themselves dismayed by the long queues of people. But after a moment, they realised that there was two queues: one for people with tickets and one without. They checked through, placing their luggage on a large trolley, but there was no customs or other formalities. They were directed to line up for the transfer out to the ship, which was laying at anchor in the roads and preparing to leave on the outgoing tide. The transfer launch or tender was expected within the hour. From their position under the shaded arches of the pier, they anxiously scanned the lines of people milling along the quay or waiting hopefully in the terminal. They could not sight their tardy husbands anywhere.

When the people with allocated tickets headed down the pier to the stone steps where they would begin boarding, Victoria and Ruth removed themselves to the back of the line, ever hopeful of a last minute rendezvous.

"They said not to go without them," Ruth told Victoria for the third time.

"We did say the *Clifford* Pier, didn't we?" Victoria responded.

"Of course we did, I distinctly remember."

"Well, what will we do if they don't come?" Victoria asked.

Ruth didn't answer immediately, but eventually she replied, ""I think it's clear they are not coming."

"Should we get on board?"

"I'm not leaving without him. He told us to wait for him and I trust his judgement. I just can't, I'm sorry, but I truly don't know what else to do."

"Well if you aren't going love, then neither shall I," Victoria said gently because she could see that Ruth was trying not to howl.

"Ladies, it's now or never. I can't wait around all day," the bosun called to them from the launch.

"I'm sorry, perhaps let somebody else take our places. We simply can't leave at present," Ruth's wobbly voice called back to him.

The bosun didn't even reply. He whistled towards the terminal and held up two fingers. The dock-guard looked towards the huge queue of people hoping for a passage and sent two ladies down to the ship's tender. These women gave Victoria and Ruth curious looks as they rushed passed them, no doubt wondering why on earth they would give up a chance to escape the island.

"What's happened then?" the ticket collector asked the APF wives once they had walked back to the terminal.

"Our husbands didn't turn up. They told us to wait for them. I just couldn't leave without them. Without giving my husband a chance to say goodbye to his only child."

"Well," the ticket collector scratched his head, wondering what to say. In his view this was the sort of silliness that one could only expect from women. Still, it was no skin off his neck whether they stayed or went, but he did think they owed it to the little 'un to get her to safety.

"I suggest you go back to P&O and put your name down for the next sailing."

"Yes, thank you. We really will get on the next suitable ship."

"Mind you're not too picky, ladies. There isn't much choice these days."

It was such an impertinent comment that Victoria looked up at him sharply. However, there was only concern in his face, and she nodded silently.

It seemed the best thing to do was to trudge back to the golf club via the P&O Office. There wasn't a taxi in sight and despite the odd drizzly rain, the day was sticky hot. After walking very slowly for a hundred yards or so, they were offered a lift by a solo driver who had just dropped his family off at the wharf. He did his best to cheer the two women up, which was a sharp contrast to the reception they got at P&O who were not sympathetic at all. Although they did revalidate their tickets again. The other ships in the convoy with the Duchess of Bedford were fully booked, so tickets or not, there was no passage available.

They went next door to Blue Funnel, where they were informed that the unfortunately named *Empress of Japan,* which was due to leave within hours, was fully booked and there were no other ships heading for Australia or any other destination there either. They put their names down for any available berth, but the list ahead of them was very long.

Back at the golf club, Ruth bent to squeeze Mack the dog tightly. He was pleased to see her, but none the wiser that he had nearly been abandoned. The remaining women gathered around the two exhausted friends. Some were sympathetic, but a few shook their heads in disbelief and wisely kept their thoughts to themselves.

The following day, they received unexpected visitors. It was a Mr and Mrs Davies, who looked very shabby in their well-worn travelling clothes. They had with them a little tear-stained girl called Gloria, who stood with one thumb firmly stuck in her mouth and the other, bandaged and clinging tightly to her mother's skirts.

They told of their adventure in Johore Bahru. How the men had offered them their bike to evacuate while they were following on foot behind. The men had asked them to bring the bike to the golf club, but unfortunately, the army had requisitioned it at the causeway. What with the curfew, the lack of public transport and their need to get their daughter's burned hand looked at in an overcrowded hospital, it had taken them a couple of days to find the golf club. They assumed that the men would no doubt be several hours behind them, if they had similar problems to deal with.

Despite holding a strong desire to throttle Mrs Davies, Ruth noticed that she was near on breaking point.

"Have you eaten?" she asked them kindly, blinking away her own worries.

"We got a tiffin yesterday from the hospital cafeteria, but I'm afraid, until we get to a bank, we have no money for much more than that. We need a bank and a place to stay and then we need to see about getting a passage out of here," Mr Davies said.

"Getting a passage is proving to be very difficult and even when you can, it's women and children only, I'm afraid," Victoria warned him bluntly. She was miffed that they appeared to be responsible for their husbands being stranded on the mainland.

"But I'm sure you can stay here. We're all evacuees ourselves. Isn't that right ladies?" She said *ladies,* but Ruth looked only towards Mrs Eversham, whom they had all come to treat as their leader, for confirmation.

"Good heavens, yes of course," Mrs Eversham said coming across to the little group at the door and taking in the exhausted nature of the arriving party. "By the looks of it, I'm sure you could all do with a good hot meal and a bath to boot. Fortunately, we've had several ladies leave and you are welcome to use their bedding. The only thing is that perhaps it would be advisable for Mr Davies to sleep on the porch, seeing as he is the only man here."

Ruth reached for the morning's paper and pulling Victoria aside, tapped an article which stated that fighting was still a good 20 miles north of Johore Bahru. Victoria said nothing. She had of course already read the report. Ruth lifted her eyes to meet Victoria's and no more was said. The look of disdain they shared said it all. They'd never been able to trust the newspapers, so why start now.

They were awakened very early the following morning by an almighty explosion. It was unusual in that it was not accompanied by the usual Alert sirens, so they went back to sleep. At breakfast, they were unnerved further by an unusually early Air Raid. Over the past several weeks they had become accustomed to the raids being carried out on a timetable of sorts, with the first being just after breakfast at about 9am. The new day brought more unconfirmed gossip which worried Ruth and Victoria further. Some were saying the enormous explosion during the night had been the British blowing a hole in the causeway. They knew this would only be a last ditch attempt to prevent the Japanese forces from taking the island. They forced themselves to believe that their husbands had already made it across.

Leaving Jean at the Golf Club in the care of Mrs Davies, they decided to drive up to the causeway to see if they could find them. Perhaps, like the Davies, they had no transport.

As it turned out, they didn't get far. A roadblock prevented them making it anywhere near Woodlands. They were advised that their husbands were at the Changi barracks. That was where all the APF men were apparently. But they were further advised not to attempt to drive to Changi, as there were similar roadblocks in place over there. The less civilian traffic on the roads the better, apparently. The armed soldier advised them to go back to their billet and wait for their husbands. He was sure they would contact them when they could. In the meantime, he said, they could make themselves useful by lending an injured Chinese couple, who were stranded at the roadblock, a lift into Tan Tock Seng Hospital in Moulmein Road.

When they reached the hospital, they were further put upon to take a Chinese businessman into Fullerton Square. Such was the lack of transport that people were stooping to commandeer ordinary citizens into becoming impromptu taxi drivers and they could hardly refuse. Ruth was eager to return to Jean and needed to stop and pick up some more supplies, including a pack of Klim milk powder for Jean's bottle. So it was late afternoon before they made it back to the Club and the futile daily telephone call to P&O. The paper had mentioned there were fares to be had to Calcutta. They phoned a number of the local agents, but were told that the advertised fares had been taken. They had no further vessels in their books.

A pattern began to take shape during the first three days of February. Victoria, Ruth and Jean would drive down to Collyer Quay to check into the shipping offices for news of any ships leaving for Colombo or India. In the afternoon, they would telephone around the agents to repeat the question. The answer was always the standard, "*No vessels departing today.*" By about the fourth day of this, it became too difficult to drive to the wharf. The debris and shell holes from bombings, fires, abandoned cars, furniture and luggage were starting to build up in drifts that often stretched across the roads. The women were finding it easier to walk, which took up most of each day.

Little Jean had become used to sleeping in her carriage and queues no longer terribly worried her, although she was often irritable at other times and hard to get to sleep at night.

Victoria was exhausted, what with all the walking, the heat, constant bad news, poor food and morning sickness. Ruth too was strung out, looking after Jean for the first time in her life completely by herself. The other women helped where they could, but often the two APF women were on their own at the Golf club, the others commandeered into helping at the hospitals, which were overflowing with injured. Local schools and even the very Cathedral that both women had been married in were commandeered as bases for the sick, misplaced and unclaimed dead. Victoria became unable to stomach the smell of cooking food, so she often took Jean outside to play, while Ruth struggled with cooking duties alone. Occasionally the women would dash out to the cold storage with a bundle of ration tickets or when that failed, any shop that was still open. Rationing was something that had finally caught up with the good people of Singapore, while Britain had been coping with it for the past two years.

Jean had become the only child at the Golf Club. Even the Davies had moved on—embarrassed perhaps at being the cause of their hosts' distress, they had luckily found accommodation at the Keppel Hotel.

One day Ruth rung through to P&O and found that they had given up their office at Collyer Quay, such was the difficulty of getting in to it. They had relocated to a private home a few miles away. It was opposite the Botanic Gardens in Cluny Road and for a few days they found it far easier to drive up there.

News came of the sinking of a large evacuee ship. There was some confusion over whether it was the *Empress of Japan* or the *Duchess of Bedford*, the ship she had meant to leave on. For the hundredth time she wondered if, she hadn't made a terrible mistake not leaving when she had the chance.

There was still no word from Charlie or Mr Armstrong. It had been nearly a week but Ruth refused to think the worst.

Victoria was very snappy and irritable these days. Mind you, the constant air raids and the living conditions were taking their toll on everybody. Some days and nights they seemed to spend more time outside in the soggy bomb shelters than inside the Golf Club. There had been several near misses and some of the ladies were accusing the Japs of deliberately targeting the General Hospital next door. But of course, Ruth thought that was silly. Nobody bombed hospitals on purpose.

The last few newspapers had consisted of only a single page and the rumour was that the printing was being done in temporary locations. Soon even these ceased.

The Malaysian-Broadcasting Corporation (MBC Radio) was still operating, but the upbeat bulletins felt manufactured and phoney to the women's ears. This coupled with regular urging all women to join the men in the war effort by helping with transport and taking over essential services and not just "rolling bandages" felt like badgering. More often than not, the radio was turned off by someone or other upset by it.

With trustworthy news reports hard to come by and gossip ripe, the rumour mill was saying that the Japanese had already landed on Singapore island. If that was the case, then where were they? The women agreed that you couldn't believe everything you heard, but it was strange that many soldiers were milling around Sepoy Lines looking lost. Some of course were merely walking wounded.

Victoria and Ruth found themselves again standing in the P&O offices at Collyer Quay. Apparently, the temporary P&O office on Cluny Road was too dangerous now since the Japanese aviators appeared to have cottoned on to the fact that many of the embassies were situated along that road. It was now considered safer back here on the waterfront.

They could clearly see many ships waiting in the roads or in front of the detached mole, but still the answer at P&O was "no vessels." They decided to trek down to the South Pier at Telok Ayer Basin and see just who exactly was embarking on the ships' lighters.

There were queues of women and children, both European and Chinese standing in the heat, desperately waiting to get onto ships. They randomly approached a few women to ask which steamer they were waiting for, and were surprised to hear that none seemed to have tickets. Then again, they had been waiting for hours.

At the head of the queue, wharf police guarded the entrance to the pier and they told Victoria and Ruth to move away or join the back of the queue.

Just as they were about to turn back, Ruth caught sight of a navy pilot boat moored just south of the South Pier and thought she saw Sergeant Sutton on board.

"Excuse me," she dared to ask the Wharf constable, "I know that man in that launch over there. How can I get his attention?"

"That's the Admiralty Anchorage, Mrs. Nothing to do with me. Probably waiting to ferry senior Navy bigwigs, here and there."

"But it is imperative that we speak to him," Victoria reiterated seeing what Ruth was driving at.

"Sorry, I can't let you onto the wharf without a ticket or a pass."

Victoria rushed off along the fence line to try to get closer to the anchored boat, while Ruth straggled behind with the pram.

"Yoohoo!" she called out waving her sola topee through the fence. "Sergeant Sutton! I say, Sergeant Sutton."

The sergeant heard his name and was peering up and down the shoreline trying to pick out where the voice was coming from. Eventually, he spotted a woman pushing a pram hurriedly towards, another woman. He was certain it was Captain Armstrong's distinctively tall, ash-blonde wife, which could only mean the smaller dark haired woman with the pram was Ruth Cole.

"Mrs Armstrong? What are you still doing here?" he called.

Victoria heard him yell something, but she couldn't quite make out what he was saying. It didn't matter, because he cast off and motored alongside the South Pier, tying up and coming ashore.

The women followed his progress back to the South Pier.

"I heard you had both left on the Duchess of Bedford," he said as soon as he reached the women.

"No, we are still waiting for our husbands to turn up."

Sergeant Sutton blinked twice, a shade of shock flashing across his face.

"Then you don't know?" he asked them in a choked voice before he could stop himself.

"Know what?" Ruth automatically responded, but even as she said it a chill clutched her chest.

"I don't know what to say. Really, you shouldn't have to hear it from me through a fence like this."

"Oh my ..." Victoria collapsed to the ground, and Ruth cried out in an agonised wail, causing young Jeanie to start crying.

A nearby Harbour Board policeman rushed to Victoria, attempting to assess her wellbeing, while Sergeant Sutton dashed through the gates to their side.

Ruth knelt beside Victoria just as she came to, and asked her if she felt any pain in her abdomen.

Victoria shook her head, seemingly unable to speak.

"How? When?" Ruth asked hoarsely when Sutton reached them.

"Oh, my dears, they were hit during an aerial bombardment on the 30th. It would have been very quick. They wouldn't have seen it coming."

"Over a week ago? Why weren't we told?"

"We all thought you'd left. We were informed you left on the Duchess of Bedford or the Wakefield or one of that convoy."

"Were you there? Did you actually see it happen?" Victoria had found her voice, but tears leaked down her face.

Sergeant Sutton crouched down and offered her a handkerchief.

"No I wasn't there. But I heard about it from Day and McGregor. They were there and saw it happen."

"Where are they now? Our husbands—where have they taken the bodies?" Victoria asked.

Sutton did not answer immediately, as he wondered how he could possibly answer that question sensitively.

"Please tell me," Victoria insisted shaking his forearm.

"There were no bodies," he replied quietly. "They were buried beneath a shell hole as far as anyone could tell. The army won't let us near there now. They are behind enemy lines."

"Oh my god! Oh my god! Oh my god!" Ruth wailed over and over, though no tears formed. Jean was crying enough for both of them. No doubt she could sense her mummy was deeply upset, and that was simply frightening to the little girl.

"Look, have you found a passage on an evacuation ship yet?"

Victoria shook her head, still sobbing, while Ruth continued to mutter things only she could hear.

"Leave it to me. I'll get you on somewhere. Go back to the golf club and I'll send word up to you." He gave each woman a stiff hug around the shoulders and strode back to his boat.

With tears staining her bright cheeks, Victoria blew her nose on her pocket hanky and noticed that Ruth seemed to be rocking in a state of shock.

"Come on old chook!" she managed to say. "Pull yourself together. I need you now more than ever and so does little Jeanie." She lifted Ruth's chin and caught her eye.

It seemed to have a steadying effect on Ruth who stopped muttering and glanced around. She felt surprised that the sun was still shining brightly whereas she could have sworn it had turned to night. The queues of people at the South Wharf were watching the scene curiously.

The police officer was still standing to one side, waiting to see if they needed further assistance.

Ruth quickly stood and reached to help Victoria stand up, the latter pressing down her hair and smoothing the hem of her knee-length spotted day dress. Then both women pasted flinty smiles on their faces and quickly made their way back to the Golf Club.

Sergeant Sutton had always been a good friend of Ruth and her husband. Indeed, he had acted as best man at their wedding. True to his word, he immediately set about ensuring the ladies' safety.

Victoria was lying down on her mattress and Ruth was absently rocking her daughter to sleep in her lap on the verandah when the Rear Admiral and his wife, Megan Spooner, pulled up at the Golf Club.

Warily, Ruth rose to greet them. She really wasn't in the mood for small talk or even being civil, but here was the most senior naval man on the island, and Ruth knew her duty was to give them the respect they deserved. After all, she had been lead to believe it was through Mrs Spooner's kindness that the ladies had been able to make use of the Golf Club rather than staying at one of the newly erected evacuee halls with all the displaced Chinese families and other government employees.

Admiral Spooner spoke the minute his feet reached the short stone steps.

"My deepest condolences Mrs Cole. Your husband was always a most trusted officer; a jolly good sort. I held him in very high esteem."

"You must be brave," Mrs Spooner added when Ruth's eyes began to water. "Your concern now is your little girl. We've come to offer our help if you'll allow us."

"But madam, we can't have any more silliness," the Admiral admonished her.

Ruth blinked in surprise.

"He simply means that he heard you turned down a spot on a ship last week." Mrs Spooner turned to admonish her husband. "Honestly dear, don't go on about it. It's hard to know what the right thing to do is sometimes. We don't blame you at all my dear," she said turning back to Ruth, "and we know what a big shock it must have been to you."

"Where is Mrs Armstrong? We have an offer for you both," the Admiral said.

When Victoria joined them on the verandah, he again offered his condolences to her.

"Of course, I knew both of your husbands personally and they aided me, my family and staff almost daily. I think it is only right that I repay their loyal service by ensuring their families reach safety. To that end, I've arranged another berth for each of you. There is a large convoy coming in overnight. We are expecting them any time after daybreak. The ship in question is called the *Empress of Asia*."

"Are you sure?" Ruth wanted to know.

"You have my word on it." He frowned at the silly question.

"We have tickets with P&O. Can we transfer them?" Victoria asked.

Just have your personal documents with you. I'm afraid we've passed the stage for needing tickets. The military is requisitioning every ship we can lay our hands on, but with that you need to understand it's not going to be a first class voyage. I'll be packing as many nurses and civilians on it as I can. Some may have to sleep on the decks. Food will be limited. I'll certainly request a cabin for the two of you, but it'll be up to the ship's purser to accommodate that request."

"But she is a lovely ship," his wife interrupted. "I'm sure you'll be comfortable enough. She is heading to Bombay via Colombo in the first instance."

"That would be perfect," Victoria breathed, to which Mrs Spooner's anxious face relaxed into a brilliant smile.

"I'll leave your name with the boarding officer. Just make yourself known to him on the South Wharf by fourteen hundred hours tomorrow. She'll be leaving in convoy at sunset, and boarding will be in the hours before then."

"Are you evacuating too?" Ruth asked Mrs Spooner.

"Not just yet dear. I will soon, but I still have much I can accomplish here. In fact, I'd very much like to have a look at how you are all getting here on at the Club. I've been meaning to find an excuse to come and look.

I also have a request for anyone with time on their hands. We urgently need socks knitted for the hospitals."

"I must get back to HQ, but I'll send the car back for you dear," the Admiral said to his wife. "Ladies, again, please accept my sincere condolences for your loss and may I just say, good luck."

With the night came a bombers' moon and true to its name, a sleepless night was had by all.

The next day, just before tiffin, Ruth and Victoria were saying their goodbyes to the few remaining women at the golf club when an unsigned note from the Rear Admiral was hand delivered.

"Hold your horses. Convoy under attack. Will do what I can. Stay at Sepoy Lines until further notice." The note was stamped: "Rear Admiral R. J. Spooner."

So they spent another day cooking, periodically ducking out to the bomb shelter and knitting. Although Victoria, who did not knit, watched over Jean while she toddled around outside. Her favourite game was to fill her absurd little wooden truck with sand from the bunker near the 5th fairway and drive it onto the softer "greens" to fill in the cups. It gave Victoria a perverse sort of pleasure to watch this little act of anarchy, all things considered. The Sepoy Lines Golf club was a competitor to her mother's club, the Royal Singapore. Besides, there wasn't much call for golf these days, so Victoria didn't suppose anyone would mind.

Thinking of her parents, who had evacuated to England a good six months earlier, put Victoria in a very morose mood which hung over her even after she returned to the clubhouse. She supposed she should write and inform her mother of the situation, but the only writing paper she had was the Sepoy Lines embossed paper they had discovered in the back room. It seemed irreligious to convey such important news on that and a telegram would only worry them. She resolved to telephone them from Colombo. Putting a trunk call through from Singapore all the way to England in the current situation was bound to be an exercise in futility.

Ruth, on the other hand, had been industrious with her time and had nearly finished one sock when Sergeant Sutton arrived the following day.

"Ladies, I'm afraid the *Empress of Asia* is sunk," was the news he brought them.

"Good heavens!" several of the women at the golf club exclaimed simultaneously.

Victoria motioned for him to take a seat on the verandah while she pulled a chair in closer to hear what he had to say.

"The remainder of the convoy has sustained some damage," he continued, "but the word is that they still plan to depart tomorrow at sunset. I can get you onto the *City of Canterbury* if she can be made seaworthy. She's not quite as glam as the *Empress*, but I should think you'll be comfortable enough."

"You'll not be wanting to go on that ship," an older Scottish voice drawled from the far end of the verandah. "I heard tell there was but a mutiny of her crew at Durban."

"Madam, she'll have a replenished crew. There will also be hordes of departing soldiers and airmen on board, so security won't be an issue. I don't know if you've heard, but the airbase was bombed yesterday at about the same time as this convoy was attacked. I've been told most of our aircraft are now grounded so I believe the Admiral is coordinating the redeployment of all unnecessary airmen. You'll be safe on board with plenty of officers to protect you," he reiterated.

"I can't thank you enough," Ruth told him, ignoring the pessimism from the older woman behind her.

"Yes, it was very good of you to come out to tell us. The admiral has been jolly kind as well," Victoria echoed.

"Ladies, I wish there was more I could do for you, but all I can offer is to be at your service tomorrow. The Admiral has given me leave to collect the three of you and deliver you to the appropriate wharf. I'll be here at fourteen hundred hours."

"How is it you are still working? I thought the APF had been disbanded." Ruth asked.

"I volunteered."

"And the other officers?"

"Well, some are helping the Harbour Board police, others have made plans to find their own way off the island and a few are crewing on ships. The City of Canterbury, for example needed new crew. I should mention, the Admiral thought it best you leave your car here for the other women. Driving is very difficult and we may have to walk some distance, but I'll try to get you a little closer. By the way ladies," Sutton lifted his voice to address all the remaining women at the Club, "the Admiral has ordered the evacuation of all women and elderly, whether you have children or not. So I recommend you all re-register yourselves."

"Be that as it may," one voice was heard over the ensuing din, "some of us wish to remain on the island."

Sutton ignored the comment and picked up Ruth's hand saying softly. "But *you* will get on that ship. That's an order, my dear." He waited until she nodded her agreement. "Until tomorrow then—cheerio!" he said firmly.

The following afternoon Ruth held Mac tight. Strangely, he had been clinging to her side all morning.

"I can't bear to leave him," she said to a young woman who was saying goodbye to Jean in the car.

"Have you ever thought of, you know, having him seen to," the woman asked. "I'm sure there are still vets around who will do it."

"No! I could never do that." Ruth sounded shocked. "Not when he still has a chance. Besides, after the war is over, I'll come back and find him. You never know, he might survive. Still, it breaks my heart to leave him. He has been with me through thick and thin."

Mac wagged his tail uncertainly and tried to lick his mistresses cheek. He made a long low whining sound.

"Oh, he knows. He knows I'm going to leave him. Look how strange he is acting."

"Give him to me. We'll look after him Mrs Cole. Promise we will."

"Goodbye my darling boy," Ruth said, planting a kiss on the dog's forehead and receiving a lick on the chin for her efforts.

As the small group drove away, Ruth could hear his howl carrying on the wind. She closed her eyes and tried to push the worry from her mind. She could feel her thumb in a tight little grip of her daughter's fist—yes there were more important things to worry about.

When she opened her eyes they were in the midst of Chinatown. In just the last two days, the altered state of affairs on the street shocked her further. Roads were now blocked by all manner of debris: bricks, iron, shop fittings, abandoned furniture and even abandoned luggage. Partially collapsed buildings surrounded them. Up ahead, she could see heavy suffocating smoke issuing from burning *godowns*. The few short streets they needed to traverse were nearly impossible to navigate. Driving was hopeless. In the end, Sutton turned the car around and went back via Outram Road to come at the wharf from the south.

Up ahead a fire truck blocked the road, while it manoeuvred back and forth. Looking out the rear window, Ruth saw a steady queue of cars forming behind them. From the front passenger seat, Victoria turned towards Ruth in the back. Her eyes were strained, her lips clamped shut and her complexion very peaky. Ruth was about to ask if she was feeling ill again, when Victoria spoke first.

"We'll be alright on the ship." Victoria said the words in a clipped manner as if she was trying not to regurgitate her lunch. It wasn't a very convincing statement, but who could blame her for being worried, Ruth wondered. With no air support, the ships were like sitting ducks. Nobody could guarantee safety.

"*You'll not be going on the City of Canterbury* if that is what is worrying you," Sutton said, placing his hand over Victoria's right hand on the seat between them.

Ruth saw Victoria draw herself up as if she was about to pull her hand back from his impertinence. But then her shoulders relaxed somewhat and she turned away towards the window, holding her left hand knuckles against her lips. Perhaps she realised he was just trying to comfort her.

Sutton continued chattily, unaware that he had very nearly overstepped the mark of propriety by touching the widow so. "We've got you onto the *Félix Roussel*. She's a free French ship essentially. Well, she was because now of course, she's a British troopship. I believe she has a British captain and officers, but most of the crew is French, so I hope your school-day lessons in that language are not altogether too rusty."

"Goodness, my French was always hopeless," Ruth said from the back.

"I'm sure I can speak for the both of us. I was always a straight A student," Victoria said.

"There's no boarding launch, you'll be able to embark directly from the wharf," Sutton said trying his best to be cheerful. He had replaced his hand on the steering wheel.

"Will we share a cabin, I wonder?" Ruth asked absently because she had become distracted by the people in the cars behind them who were just getting out and walking.

"I couldn't say," Sutton replied. "Look, I think we should park here and walk the rest of the way. Just let me pull over as far as I can. I'm going to need to reclaim the car later. I noticed yesterday the Harbour Board were bulldozing through the abandoned vehicles with their heavy machinery to clear the roads.

"Will you be able to accompany us on board? I'd feel a lot more secure if you could," Ruth asked as Sutton attempted to unfold the baby chair on the roadside.

"I should think they'll allow me that," Sutton smiled, as the contraption eventually snapped into place.

Ruth put her attaché case onto the hood of the chair and allowed Jean to climb in by herself. Sutton picked up the ladies' larger cases and Victoria carried her own small attaché case, umbrella and handbag.

The ensuing walk took them maybe 20 minutes to perhaps half an hour and during that time they saw no less than three aerial raids. Thankfully, these were too far off to cause much concern. Then, just as they approached the very long wharf simply named the East Wharf, a group of over 20 twin-engine bombers shot in over the Harbour Board's waterfront. Sutton pulled them in under the eaves of the wharf's main building. It wasn't the safest place to be, but with little or no warning, they'd had to make do. From here, they watched the bombers weave in and out of the ack ack flak often directly overhead. They seemed to be aiming for the wharf area and a woosh and whistle accompanied each malevolent host. By some miracle every bomb landed further east near the dry docks and coal sheds or into the sea. When it was over huge clouds of smoke smothered the area.

The small group hurried towards the far side of the wharf sheds. As they walked around the end, a line of white troopships could be seen sitting stern to bow with their thick hawsers securely attached to the wharf bollards. The ship closest was the Félix Roussel and at well over 500 ft in length she was a beauty, though still dwarfed by a larger ship in front of her. Her two funnels were distinctively square and squat instead of the usual tall round shape. She was slotted into the corner of the monstrous wharf and the gangplank was fitted to the lower of her three stern decks. It towered above the long queue of people of all races, which snaked to and fro down the length of the ship and back to the near corner of the wharf. The pandemonium of the last few minutes seemed to be subsiding and people who had run for cover, were now trying to reclaim their places in the line, while others had obviously taken advantage of the disturbance to promote themselves further up the ranks.

Far from only bringing one bag each, these people had all manner of household goods with them. There was even a piano. Children held onto pets and toys. Parents pushed barrows and handcarts full of kitchenware, books and precious ornaments. Soldiers were sifting through the queue, moving those with children forward, while single women and men were slowly being pushed back. This was creating no small amount of anxiety but, all things considered, the crowd was fairly well behaved.

"Jesus!" Sutton swore. "There'd be no hope for this lot if that air-raid had just centred up this way a fraction."

With Sutton wearing his official APF uniform the crowd parted to allow him to move through. The two young widows and Jean in her baby car kept close behind in his wake.

Now that Ruth was alongside the vessel, she could discern its dull white sides showed a few blemishes where shrapnel had dented it. Even as they approached, men were working on finishing repairs, and supplies were being both winched and rolled aboard.

True to his word, Sutton delivered the two women to the soldiers guarding the still closed gangway. They examined the paperwork provided by the Admiral and motioned for the women to wait behind the barrier with the other women and children, which fortuitously meant they were at the head of the line.

"Boarding will be any minute. We are just waiting on the last of the supplies to be wheeled aboard," one of the men said kindly.

"Where shall we put our suitcases?"

"You'll have to carry them aboard yourselves ladies. Perhaps the sergeant can help you carry the baby chair up the steps."

The soldier had barely finished his sentence when his attention was drawn away towards an entourage of women approaching the head of the line.

Turning to see what the commotion was, Ruth saw a senior woman, four adult daughters and two very well turned out Chinese servants trailing along behind. All, including the Chinese, seemed to be wearing several sets of expensive outfits and the matron appeared to be wearing her full wardrobe of jewellery. Otherwise, they had no luggage apart from an assortment of items piled onto one baby carriage, which actually did have a baby squeezed into it as well.

Ruth supposed that in lieu of luggage they had simply worn their wardrobes and possibly encouraged their Chinese servants to wear some gowns too. The result was seven women looking uncomfortably hot, bothered and quite ludicrous to boot. Stranger still, was the way the crowd grudgingly parted to allow the party to flounce towards the head of the queue. Ruth had no idea who this obviously wealthy matriarch was and was only slightly surprised when the woman nodded an almost imperceptible greeting to Victoria Armstrong as she arrived. The soldiers took her identity documents in the same impartial way they had Ruth and Victoria's and handed them back to the woman without saying much, merely indicating for the entourage to wait at the front of the line.

Ruth nudged Victoria discreetly and raised her eyebrows in question.

Victoria had an odd look on her face and speaking behind the back of her hand, said, "don't ask."

Intrigued, Ruth decided she most certainly would ask, but she'd wait until they couldn't be overheard.

"That's the last of it," called a naval rating just two minutes later. He seemed to be doing the job of a wharf coolie apparently due to the current lack of staff at the Harbour Board. The soldiers, holding back the line of hopeful passengers, lifted the barrier gates and began to allow the groups to embark up the stern gangplank one at a time. Soon the APF group had climbed to the lower deck and were directed by a purser up a companionway and along a passageway to their allotted cabin.

Everywhere Ruth looked there was evidence of the beauty of the ship. The luxurious fixtures and decorative panels were modern and exciting. But accompanying all the glamour were just a few incongruous anomalies. Ruth was sure that there would once have been crystal chandeliers, fresh flowers and porters to carry and unpack bags. These little details had obviously been stripped or forsaken. Halls were bare. A peep into a smoking room showed an empty bar, empty tables, no fernery in the large built-in pots and blackened out windows.

Sutton stopped in front of a cabin door. He opened it standing politely to one side with Jean, to allow the two widows in first. "This is it ladies. Looks like a first class cabin to me."

"Well I say, that is a stroke of luck," Ruth said.

"We were at the head of the queue. That's all there is to it," Victoria said.

"Well, I noticed your friend with all her finery is still on the deck below," Ruth said.

"Thank goodness for that. Being a first class brothel keeper doesn't earn a first class cabin here."

"She is never?"

"Yes, she most certainly is. Isn't she Sutton?"

"Well, I wouldn't know Mrs Armstrong," Sutton blustered. "A policeman doesn't, I mean to say that sort of activity is not.... Perhaps she has been allocated a deluxe cabin," he finally said changing tack.

"A deluxe cabin?" Ruth repeated. "You mean there are better cabins than this one?"

"Yes, I should think so," Sutton said. "They're probably reserved for the officers on board."

It was at that moment that Ruth began to have a good look around their new home. She noticed with regret that there were only two berths. Jean would have to bunk in with her. Of course, that might be safest anyway, she thought.

The berths were surrounded by metal safety rails and inserted in each was a neat mattress and pillow.

"There's no linen," Ruth blurted interrupting her mental appraisal.

"Oh dear god, were we meant to bring that?" Victoria asked no one in particular.

"You'll have to sort that out with the purser," Burrow said. "Normally, I'd say no of course not. But since this has been converted to a troop and supply ship, well I guess the troops would all have their own bedrolls."

Victoria had crossed to a built-in mirrored closet. This was completely empty except for a pair of life vests, which she pulled out briefly before stuffing them back in without comment.

Sutton rolled Jean's car into the room.

"Sheet!" said Jean, which made everyone laugh. She was slow in talking and while not her first word, sheet appeared to be a new addition to her vocab and one of the few words she'd ever uttered.

"Yes, we need sheets," Ruth said. "You know what we need, don't you my little lady."

"And probably towels and what have you," Victoria added.

"I won't presume to tell you ladies what to do, but if I had a wife, I'd advise her to sleep in her clothes with just a jacket over top for warmth. It won't be a long crossing and it'll be warm the whole way. Really and truly girls, I think you are doing well to have a cabin to yourselves. Don't be surprised if you are expected to share it later with women camping out on your floor."

Ruth and Victoria just stared at him, horrified, but then their combined attention was drawn to the passageway.

A uniformed crew member passed their open doorway. He escorted a woman with three children, all under ten, to the adjacent cabin. Only the small boy was not crying. He appeared to be attempting to comfort his mother and sisters.

"Father said I'm in charge now," Ruth could hear his little voice piping up as they passed. "And it'll not do to be carrying on this way. See here, this good man is showing us to a lovely cabin. Look mother, it has a balcony. That'll be dangerous for Lulu. We'll have to watch her with hawke eyes."

"Ah yes, about the balcony," the French accented crewman said. "You'll be told all the rules shortly, but possibly the most important one is that under no account is the balcony to be used. It is to remain locked with the blinds pulled down and all portholes are to remain closed for the duration of the voyage."

"But how will we receive fresh air?" the mother bemoaned.

"Same way as all the internal cabins do. Through the ventilation portals," he tapped something metal. Ruth's eyes fell upon a grille beside her own cabin door. Wandering out to the passageway she attempted to get a better glimpse of their neighbours, but only the crewman remained in the passage.

"Sorry it's captain's orders," he was saying. "And you can be sure that the naval vessels escorting us will be keeping a ... *hawke's eye* ... on any porthole that is opened. That is especially at night. The ship must remain in blackout in case there is any Japs floating around. They can tell exactly which cabin has flouted the rules from half a mile away and it'll be off to the brig if you are caught out. So little man, you need to make sure your sisters follow the rules. If you'll excuse me madam, petite monsieur, mademoiselles, I have other duties to attend to."

"Excuse me," Ruth caught his attention. "Were we to bring our own linen? Or will these be supplied soon?"

"Linen?" the crewman blinked in surprise. "Weren't you told to bring linen?"

"No! We were told to bring only one bag each. What shall we do?"

"I'm sorry madam, but we are all still finding our way to this new situation. The way the magnifique Félix Roussel has been defiled, it is tragic, no? First it is one thing and then it is another. I will speak to the commissaire, but sheets will not be high on his liste des priorités." With a shrug, he hurried back the way he had come.

"I have to get going as well ladies. She is due to sail soon after the sun sets but I have to report back to the Admiral."

"Well thank you Sergeant Sutton. You are one in a million to continue on working."

"Yes thank you ever so much," Ruth agreed and held out her hand to shake his.

Later that afternoon, the women carefully locked their cabin and pushed Jean out onto the promenade deck, where other passengers and a multitude of airmen and evacuating sailors from the *Prince of Wales* and *Repulse* were watching the scene below. The queue of people waiting to get onto the ship didn't seem to have reduced down much at all. A separate queue had formed for a large passenger cargo ship, *The City of Canterbury*, up ahead, and the result was the wharf side was awash with people, apart from a fenced clearway several feet wide running directly along the wharf edge.

They chatted with some of the men and discovered that the promenade deck was designed to be completely enclosed by glass panels, which could be screwed into place. These were missing and some of the men were guessing that these had been removed to reduce reflectiveness, though others thought they'd be put into place once the voyage got underway.

Ruth asked them how their accommodations were and was shocked to hear that many of them would make do with sleeping on the tennis court on the back deck. If that wasn't bad enough, she was even more shocked to hear that another troopship, the USS Wakefield, had drained the swimming bath and strung hammocks across it for troops. These men had already checked and indeed the Félix Roussel's pool was drained, but as yet no sign of anyone using it for quarters.

"Why would they drain it, unless they expected it to be used for a dormitory?" someone asked. "Mark my words; we'll be packed off down there."

"You're wrong mate. The less the ship weighs the faster it will go. That's why they drained it," someone else ventured.

"Anyone know where I can get some water for my daughter's bottle?" Ruth asked bravely.

"Already checked the kitchens and there'll be no food until we are underway."

"Don't listen to old Misery Guts over there Mrs. You might find some hot water in the 1st class dining room. Head to the top of the stairs and keep walking until you see two giant serpents."

"Serpents?"

"That's right. You can't miss them," the man smirked.

Ruth and Victoria began to negotiate the stairwell with Jean's carriage, causing Ruth to remark that she may in future simply carry her if they were to leave their deck.

Victoria wisely said nothing. Her pregnancy was beginning to show and lifting the carriage was a little awkward. Finally, a pair of servicemen came to their aid just as they were nearing the top.

Thus far, they had seen modern veneer clad cabins and passageways, and outdoor seating areas done up in an attractive pastel faux brick. Now as they came upon the luxurious top deck dining room two giant multi-headed bronze snakes guarded the entrance, signifying that they must be in the right place.

"Like, like," said Jean hiding her face behind her hands, and Ruth knew that in Jean's limited vocabulary the word like actually meant "don't like." Victoria pushed through the doors, and further exploration revealed eye-popping Angkor figures inlaid into the veneers covering the walls. This detailed marquetry was frightful in Ruth's opinion, but Victoria was captivated by the scenes.

While she was busy examining each in turn, Ruth set about looking for hot water and soon engaged a passing crewmember to help her.

An hour after the last rays of the sun disappeared, the ship finally threw off her lines. As far as they could tell, she was running late.

Watching from the second deck promenade, the two widows saw the ship's great search light play quickly over the wharf. They were dismayed to note that there was still perhaps hundreds of distressed people waiting with suitcases, apparently unsuccessful in their attempt to board. A pair of tugs pulled the Félix Roussel out of the basin towards the fabricated moles guarding the shoreline. Here she was allowed to make her own way towards the roads where she anchored again to wait for the rest of her convoy. The tugs returned to help the next ship.

On the horizon and around the docks fires raged uncontrolled. Now that it was night, the flames were discernible from the smoke. Even from this distance, the air had a coal smoke taste to it reminding her of the London convent on a frosty morning. Without warning, a lone plane swooped down from a great height. Its search light played across the waterfront area, but before the anti-aircraft guns could even have had it in their sights it was up and gone. It was just enough to frazzle the nerves even further and Ruth remembered Sutton's comment about the sitting ducks on the wharf. She hated to think what it must be like for the plethora of would-be passengers waiting on the wharves.

She was just contemplating the fact that the very ship she was on was just as much a sitting duck if not more, when a new and even more terrifying sound reached her ears. It was like an almighty clap of thunder or an explosion perhaps. The word canon fire formed in her mind without her knowing where that came from.

It was a completely different sound from either the ack-ack-ack of the anti-aircraft guns or the whiz and whistle of the aircraft bombers that she'd become used to over the past several weeks. This was a heavy thudding coming from the darkness beyond the city centre. Peering towards the hills, she could see nothing at first, and then suddenly the clouds lit up reflecting a quick flash of light. This was followed by another boom, so strong it really rattled her.

"Heavy artillery," a male voice murmured in awe behind her.

She swung around to the anonymous voice. "But what does that mean?"

"It means we are leaving just in time," he answered cryptically.

It took another couple of flashes, followed in quick succession by two more booms before Ruth caught on to his meaning.

"The Jap army is bombing the island," she finally said as the full meaning hit her. She knew the Japs had been doing aerial bombing for weeks. That was in itself devastating enough. But heavy artillery was an ominous sign. In order to get the big guns close enough to the island, it meant that the Japanese army was either on their doorstep or had already crossed the Johore Straits. Previous reports had placed small groups of Japanese scouts and infantry units racing down the Malay peninsula. But moving heavy artillery into the front line took time and infrastructure. It would seem that the Malaysian mainland must now be completely lost. How long could Singapore last on her own?

Apparently, the captain and accompanying ships didn't want to waste any more time before leaving, as very quickly afterward they heard the anchor being wound in and the flotilla began to move down the stream ready to negotiate the tricky path through the minefield. Ruth could barely see the minesweeper Bendigo leading the way. She thought they'd follow, but then the hurriedly re-floated Dominion Monarch crossed their bows. When the great ship had arrived last December, the papers had claimed that she'd be in the dry dock until April.

The Félix Roussel turned to starboard in readiness to follow, she supposed, and her view ahead was obscured. Off the port stern she could see the jagged outline of HMS Exeter, the lengthy cruiser equipped with six 8" guns, that would apparently accompany the convoy. As far as she could ascertain, their wake carried the City of Canterbury and another French Bibby Line ship the MV Devonshire, both requisitioned troopships, to complete the convoy.

On the land behind them, heavy bombing continued in the distance and the night air had become decidedly cooler with the smoke now forming thick smog. She felt a strange rumbling sensation beneath her and the ship followed a tight starboard arc. As it continued to turn, the glow off the stern from burning fires in the city, were obscured. It almost seemed as if the Félix Roussel had completed a full circle.

Sure enough, before long she glided back into her spot behind the mole and dropped anchor.

The passengers were buzzing with questions that nobody could answer and soon word was passed along instead that dinner was being served. They were all required to assemble in the dining rooms on the deck correlating to their cabins. Ruth found Victoria and together they went along to dinner.

Before anything edible was served, announcements were given regarding emergency procedures, rules and regulations. The reason for their return to the anchorage was also made clear. The Admiral had demanded they return and take on more passengers. This, they were told, would require them to be patient and accommodating. People may be required to sleep in the music room or even the smoking rooms. The passageways were to remain clear of sleeping bodies at all times. And sadly, the passengers must realise that the 24 lifeboats would not be sufficient for all the extra souls on board should something untoward happen. They were advised to wear their lifesaving-vests at all times.

It was outrageous, but Ruth and Victoria decided there was nothing to be done about it. There would be no point complaining to the Captain or anybody else. If the Rear Admiral had demanded the ship be filled, it was only because he needed to evacuate the Settlement as quickly as possible. Never would they utter a word against the good man.

At some point in the evening, there came a tap on their cabin door. Still dressed, as Sutton had suggested, Victoria went to open it. She was surprised to find Sutton himself grinning at the doorway.

"Guess you didn't expect to see me again quite so soon."

"Does this mean you are coming with us?" she exclaimed happily.

"Sadly no. But I have a gift for you both, from Mrs Spooner." Sutton said placing a large brown parcel into her arms.

"What on earth," Victoria cried, while Ruth dashed forward unable to contain her desire to see what was inside.

"Linen!" Ruth squealed as she tore open a corner of the parcel.

"Two blankets, four sheets, two pillow slips, three towels," Sutton said ticking each item off his fingers.

"Oh she is a dear," Ruth said throwing her arms up to her cheeks in delight. "What on earth did we do to deserve a friend in her? And you

Sergeant Sutton? You've been ever so kind to go to this trouble."

"You're more than welcome. Have you had any other problems?"

"No, not at all."

"Everything has been just fine."

"Well I cannot hang around any longer. I was given special permission to deliver this parcel and return immediately so I had better fly the coop before I'm trapped aboard. Take care both of you." With those final words and a salute, he disappeared off down the corridor.

"Oh, look it is all monogrammed too," Victoria said rummaging through the parcel. "Feel the quality. Aren't we a lucky pair."

The two widows set about making themselves more comfortable, but sleep was not forthcoming.

In the early hours before dawn on Monday February 9th, the ship finally departed Keppel Harbour with well over 1000 troops and civilian passengers aboard.

10
JAVA SEA FEBRUARY 1942

RUTH COLE

The sun rose and the passengers made various adjustments to their living arrangements as they settled in on board the Félix Roussel. The first leg of the trip was to be a short one, some 580 nautical miles across the Java Sea to Batavia. From there she would set out across the Indian Ocean to Ceylon and then on to Bombay. After that, the British captain would ordinarily have expected to receive his orders from the Royal Navy as to where the Félix Roussel was needed next. But for the time being, the Captain and his crew's only concern was getting across the Java Sea safely. Just because they had passed out of Keppel Harbour and safely made it through the allied-laid minefield, didn't mean they were out of danger.

The past few weeks had proven that the Java Sea was currently one of the most dangerous sea zones in the world. Well within aerial strike distance, the Japanese bombers and fighters had been patrolling the area daily causing havoc amongst shipping.

Once out past the Singapore Straits, there was a large area of small islands littering the seas. Should it prove necessary, these islands would provide plenty of inlets to hide in. As it turned out the widely spaced convoy was fortunate that their first day passed without event. Beyond these islands, the peril lay in a large stretch of open water that they would attempt to cross under the cover of darkness. It was not until one neared the southernmost tip of Sumatra, that some cover was again available in the form of Banka Island. The usual course was to sneak through the narrow gap between Sumatra and Banka. But this strait had been discovered by the Japanese to be a favoured Allied hiding place and because of their now regular reconnaissance there, it had recently earned the nickname Dive Bomb Alley.

At day break on the third day out, the convoy began their descent through the 110 nautical miles of Dive Bomb Alley. The accompanying naval ships had departed and just one camouflaged warship joined the diminished convoy. Not wanting to feel like helpless sitting ducks, the regular soldiers and airmen on board had spent the past two days mounting machine guns along the promenade decks. To their credit, they manned these day and night, though Victoria had voiced her opinion to Ruth that these would only really be useful against extremely low flying aircraft.

After Jean's morning nap, Ruth decided to take her for a walk or toddle as it were. They had been exploring the rear of the ship on the top deck when an alert was sounded. The passengers had been instructed that this meant they had to go inside for safety and stay away from large windows. Ruth lifted Jean, but had hardly had time to move when the drone of incoming aircraft could be heard and she knew it was not a drill. They were only just inside a portside door when she turned and saw between 15 and 20 green twin-engine aircraft heading directly towards their ship. The hustle of people behind her pushed her forward and she saw no more, but with one arm around Jean and her other hand gripping tightly to the handrail, she braced herself ready for anything. Several almighty explosions came from beneath them. Torpedoes? Ruth was not sure if there had been any direct hits or not, but something caused the vessel to roll & pitch violently.

Ruth lost her grip on the hand railing and she and Jean slid down the passageway. Then as the ship rolled back the other way, Jean slid out of her hands. Flinging out an arm she managed to grip the front of the frilly dress while her fingers bit into the child's shoulder cruelly. The ship continued to rock violently as it righted itself. Nobody could tell how badly they had been hit or whether there was worse to come. Shocked passengers were screaming and scrabbling this way and that. Pandemonium took hold of the ship. Ruth crawled to the wall and flattened herself against it, shielding the shrieking child with her body all the while wondering if Victoria was safe.

Then just as quickly as the screaming and rolling started, it stopped. The sound of the bombers was certainly receding. People took a grip on themselves and began to offer help to the wounded and distressed. Jean was crying, "like, like," and Ruth kissed her head and held her tight.

The quickest way back to her cabin would be by way of the rear stairway. She followed a group of others outside and was astonished at the mess. Everything was drenched in seawater. Soldiers' kitbags and accoutrements were sprayed around. Deck chairs were flattened and broken railings, lines and fittings littered the deck.

All the while, the ship was still making way and as Ruth passed through the debris on the deck, she caught sight of a disabled steamer of similar size

150 yards off the port deck. Its bow was perched on a submerged mass of rock in the centre of the straits and its stern was barely above water. Surely it hadn't been a victim of this attack? It had the look of a ship that had been abandoned for days or weeks. Its forlorn state brought home just how close they themselves had run to a similar fate ... and still might judging by the way the Félix Roussel was beginning to list slightly to one side. They steamed on by, until the ghost ship was behind them.

Ruth & Jean had just made the external companionway when the call to take cover came again. They almost slid down the stairs and tried to get across the slippery deck. At the side, a section of railing was missing and Ruth was horrified to note there was nothing to stop them sliding right into the sea if the ship were to lunge to the side again. Eventually Ruth scrabbled in behind one of the heavy pillars on a smoking terrace. She could see a port door tantalisingly close, but she dared not risk dashing across to it since the approaching aircraft sounded so near now. Peering out, she had a terrifying front row view of the Japs' craft flying in tight formation and getting closer by the second.

Ruth noticed the captain seemed to be running the Félix Roussel aground, he was driving her that close to shore. She hoped he hadn't been injured and was still in control on the bridge. Just as the Félix Roussel pulled into a little inlet, she hove-to. Perhaps the captain hoped to hide from the planes, but surely, a bird's eye view in the sky wouldn't be fooled so easily? Ruth decided it was more likely the captain sought shallow water in case it became necessary to abandon ship.

Now Ruth could see that the formation were not dive bombers, but a squadron of the infamous Betty Bombers with their distinctive glass noses. She knew these very planes were responsible for the aerial torpedo attack on the Prince of Wales and the Repulse last year. Were they carrying torpedoes or ordinary bombs? Or both?

The squadron zeroed in on their target and Ruth was astonished that as each payload came wheeling down, it sent up explosions in a haphazard circle around the wrecked ship. Eventually one of these warheads met its target. Then another. When the smoke cleared from the disabled vessel, Ruth got a last glimpse of it just before it sank beneath the turbid surface.

The enemy craft flew out as quickly as they had arrived, seemingly satisfied that they had added to their tally. How they had missed seeing the other troopship hiding only a few hundred yards away, nobody would ever know. Perhaps they had seen the cruiser rushing in to the troopship's aid or perhaps they had simply used up all their bombs. Either way, the passengers did not tempt fate by cheering or clapping their apparent survival. Each soul on board, allowed themselves only the economical luxury of breathing a little deeper before they got to work clearing the mess and repairing the damage. With the crew busy trying to keep afloat and get to their destination it became a case of all hands on deck.

The bombers did not return that day, but work parties continued until nightfall. Multiple holes in the hull from bomb fragments had to be plugged with cones of wood and the bilge pumps worked continuously. One of the Sulzer diesel engines must have suffered damage because it spluttered and coughed in a sick sounding way but the Captain did not allow it to rest. He prudently sought to put as much distance between himself and the area of attack as possible. Whereas previously they had only been aware of the accompanying cruiser at night, it now shadowed them so closely that they could clearly see the naval seamen aboard.

Ruth found Victoria in the doorway of their cabin wearing a life vest. She had been laying down when the "fun" had started and she was ever so pleased to see her friend return unharmed.

When they limped into Tanjung Priok the following day the crowds on the wharf cheered at their arrival. No doubt about it; the Félix Roussel looked to be in a frightfully bad state with her list and her sides shored up with a variety of emergency repair jobs. The rest of the convoy's evacuee ships had already arrived and those aboard the Félix Roussel saw that they had sustained various degrees of damage too.

The port of call was only long enough to effect slightly more substantial repairs. These included sending divers down to patch exterior holes, such as they could. The ship would need hauling out to effect proper repairs, but with the port of Tanjong Priok now practically on the front line, this wouldn't be possible here.

Nobody was given leave to exit the ship and the cramped conditions were made even worse by the necessity in moving people out of water damaged areas below.

For Ruth with a very young child, conditions were almost unbearable, but Victoria found the stability of being in port a lot better than the rolling out at sea. Whenever they found themselves struggling to keep positive, the two widows reminded themselves that at least they had a pleasant, albeit small, cabin in one of the nicer parts of the ship.

They went to their berths that night not realising that when they awoke the following morning they'd already be on their way. Strolling companionably along the promenade decks in the early light, the two women could see no sign of the coastline. Nor were their "sister" evacuee ships or their new escort in sight either. There was only the Indian Ocean in all directions.

11
CEYLON FEBRUARY 1942

RUTH COLE

Late on the 18th February, the Félix Roussel staggered into Colombo Harbour. They had suffered no further attacks and the captain could modestly claim to have achieved a steady 16 knots from the damaged engines.

The crowded seaport appeared to absorb their convoy while they pushed their way in to drop anchor behind the single mole. True to her word, Victoria seemed to be in a state of anxiety about their impending arrival at the stately home. Meanwhile Ruth was desperate to get ashore for supplies. Jean had consumed all of the milk powder, which she still needed to supplement her daily diet. Not that she had been able to digest much of the fare on offer. Ruth had resorted to filling her up with tiny spoonfuls of porridge, semolina soup, mashed potato, and pieces of mango.

The customs' officials boarded and made short work of passport examinations. The majority of the passengers and all of the troops were destined for Bombay and it was unlikely that they would be given permission to disembark in Colombo as the captain had announced that after refuelling he wished to make haste to the next port. Those disembarking were to assemble at a specific gangway amidships, where a launch would take them and their luggage ashore, twenty-four at a time.

Ruth, Jean and Victoria were joined at the gangway by their cabin neighbours whom they had gotten to know a little during the journey. As they waited for the launch to return for them all manner of sampans vied for a chance to get in close to the ship; some of these daring fellows even attempting to board with their wares. Ruth speculated they would probably do a roaring trade with many passengers desperate for supplies.

When the launch returned, the luggage, including Jeans' chair was loaded in the bow first. Those with children were seated on benches in the centre near the cockpit. Ruth, Jean and Victoria were seated amongst them all and were soon joined by their cabin neighbours—the family of four with the brave-hearted ten year old boy.

"Would you like to help me drive Sir?" the bosun asked the ten year old, before he set off.

"You bet your life! I used to drive father's car, so I expect I'll be up to the task."

"You never did," said his mother embarrassed.

"I did too. When I went with dad to the golf club on Saturdays, he always let me drive. He did the pedals and I did the wheel."

"Right then lad, come and stand here and hold this wheel. That's it."

The kindly man stood behind the boy and helped him turn the wheel, directing him left and right slowly through the throng.

"Do you know where the Earl of Rathbury's estate is?" Victoria asked the bosun. She had stood awkwardly and had to speak loudly to be heard over the din.

"I believe it's yonder," he replied pointing to a place that encroached right into the southernmost end of the port area.

Hearing snippets of the conversation, Ruth swung around, trying to gauge where the man was pointing. All she saw was several lengths of long walls in a state of disrepair. Large gaps in the stonework had long since been violated with merchant awnings and other clutter. Above all this rose a white washed long house with possibly a terracotta roof. It was impossible to tell whether the long house was just a single level building or if it had further lower levels behind the wall. A flagpole rose above, but there was no flag currently flying,

"And do you know if the family is in residence?" Victoria pressed.

"Sorry miss. I believe that's the place, but I don't know more than that."

Victoria thanked him and sat back down thoughtfully.

It wasn't long before the boatload were ashore testing out their shaky sea legs. The two widows though, lost no time in negotiating with a porter to take their luggage and find them a trishaw. The trio boarded the trishaw and the porter happily agreed to pull the luggage on his cart right alongside. No doubt, he would be back to the jetty before the next launch load arrived having made more money than usual for little extra work.

"Are you sure this place we are going is the Armstrong's palace?" Ruth asked delicately. She didn't want to offend Victoria, but in contrast to all the elegant colonial buildings springing up left and right as they passed through the streets, the long house had looked anything but palatial.

"Oh yes," it looks like the photograph Captain Armstrong showed me. Though that was taken from the front of the building rather than from the sea. "I do know it is a very old palace. It hasn't been used by a local king for 425 years. When the Portuguese took over, they built a better fort further inland. The first Earl of Rathbury purchased it some 50 years after that. They built their fortune on cinnamon spice you know."

"I see," said Ruth who had imagined a palace to be more along the lines of Kensington Palace than a medieval building like a Viking longhouse. Perhaps her voice sounded a little pinched because Victoria was quick to reassure her.

"Don't worry Mrs Cole. I am assured it is very pleasant inside with lovely cool high ceilings and latticed archways to bring in the sea and lake breezes. Mr Armstrong described it as a 'plain but delicious British dumpling floating in the centre of a hot curry.' I'm sure it will be the oasis we need to recover and collect ourselves."

Ruth thought about Armstrong's poetic description and managed to stifle a giggle, but one side-long glance at Victoria whose lips were also twitching, sent them both into fits of laughter. Jean laughed too and her comical guffaw kept them going. It was the first time they had all really laughed since they'd heard about the deaths of their husbands.

"Very funny ladies, we are here now," the wallah called pulling up in front of a set of rusted iron gates.

Immediately the women stopped laughing as their apprehension returned and they tried to glimpse the palace beyond the gates. Sitting on her lap, Jean's chubby fingers tried to twist her mother's lips back into a smile. She had liked the sound of her mother's happiness.

The porter arrived a half minute later. Victoria directed him through the gate, but after paying the trishaw wallah the two women preferred to walk to the entrance.

From this angle, they could see that the building was a pleasant two-storied affair. It had a Colonial style not too dissimilar to those found in Singapore. On the near side, it had been modernised and did in fact have two short wings extending out at each end, so that it was a U shape surrounding a hard packed earth courtyard dusted with dry leaves. Two tall and spindly cinnamon trees framed the scene, their exquisite perfume carrying across the courtyard to the approaching women.

There was no front door as such, but a wide set of concrete steps linked the courtyard to an arched portico with several latticed doors leading to various rooms. An elderly servant now hurried down towards them.

"My apologies Mrs Armstrong," he said by way of greeting, puffing slightly and looking first at Victoria and then Ruth. "I would have met you at the boat, but I did not know when you were coming in, madam."

Victoria spoke first. "You must be Baba. I am Mrs Armstrong."

"It is my honour to meet the beautiful young wife of the Earl's favourite grandson. I hope he is well."

A pain shot through Ruth's chest and she noticed Victoria stagger ever so slightly. It hadn't occurred to either of them before, but of course, nobody here would know that Giles Armstrong had been killed.

"Madam?" Baba enquired after a stunned silence.

But Victoria's mouth was dry and she could not speak of the matter.

"You'd better show us in," Ruth said, taking control. "If we could have a nice pot of tea and then we'll sit down with you to discuss the situation."

"As you wish," Baba said uncertainly. "Follow me please and I'll show you to your bed chambers. You will be the only family in residence, so you have the upstairs to yourselves."

They followed in his wake and Ruth noticed two young men coming along behind with their luggage. They were taken up an external set of stairs to the second floor arched-verandah of the main building. From here, many more doors led into a series of private bedchambers. Some of these rooms had obviously been renovated and enlarged with connecting walls removed. In all, despite there being ten doors, there were only six large bedrooms and one bathroom accessible from the verandah. Ruth's bedroom was an attractive high-ceilinged, airy space. The shutters were opened wide allowing a clear view across the harbour. The floors were tidily French polished but were bare, with no rugs. The minimal other furnishings consisted of a double bed and a dresser. Ruth noted that there was no bed for Jean and Baba explained that he had intended to put her in the nursery with her nanny. Since they had not brought a nanny, one would be sourced for them, he assured her. However, Ruth requested that they move Jean's bed in with her. She had become used to sleeping with the tot and she felt a deep urge within her to keep the child close.

She was thinking about this fresh need to keep Jean near to her as they traipsed back down to take tea. Ruth decided that it came from a general feeling of unease; that something was not right. But she couldn't put her finger on precisely what it was. The house was lovely. She was used to the climate. Baba seemed professional and she felt comfortable having native servants around. She decided perhaps, that it was just her nerves playing up after the tragedy and hullabaloo of the past few weeks.

She took her tea, flavoured with lemon with more mixed feelings. Why couldn't these people learn to make tea properly? With milk. She was too tired to make a fuss about it. After all, she didn't mind drinking tea without milk, it was just that it was never quite as fulfilling, and she had been looking forward to a nice hot cuppa. She sipped it silently waiting for her host to begin. The time had come to explain about Captain Armstrong and

Sergeant Cole's tragic deaths.

Victoria's news was received with obvious and immediate sorrow.

For a long while, Baba bowed his head to his hands silently, while the women sipped their tea. Finally he looked at Mrs Armstrong and asked about the funeral.

"Funeral?" Victoria questioned looking perplexed.

Neither women had even thought of holding a funeral. Nor had anyone suggested it. There were no bodies, no families and, well, there had been no time.

"Perhaps you could hold a memorial service when you return to England," Baba suggested. "Have you written to Lord and Lady Armstrong?

"England?" Ruth asked equally dumbstruck.

This time it was Baba's turn to look perplexed. "Yes, is it not your plan now to return to your families? Before the baby comes?"

"Baba, we had thought that with the blitz in London and whatnot that we were best to stay out here—that is, until the war is over. Captain Armstrong assured me that we both could live here. He said that there were western doctors available who could be contracted to deliver the baby."

"Mrs Armstrong, the Countess has also written to assure me that you are most welcome here. I am certainly not suggesting any different. However, the city is on high alert. We have learnt from the mistakes of Singapore."

"Mistakes?"

"Yes, madam. For you may not know, but Singapore has fallen to the Japanese."

"Fallen?" the two women kept repeating his words uselessly.

"Yes madams. Singapore is now a state of Japan. While the people of Singapore were having parties and engaging in all manner of frivolous activities, the wily Japanese have slipped in the back door unnoticed."

"Well, I'd hardly say that," Victoria began, while Ruth merely raised her eyebrows at the man's impertinence.

"This may be true, or it may not be true. But whether we believe it or not, it *is* what the Governor in Charge of Ceylon is saying. He says we will not be caught, erm, in the same way."

"What way?"

"That is with our trousers around our ankles. Madams."

Both women found themselves glancing down at the manservant's sarong-clad bare legs. Ruth choked back a near chuckle, despite the fact that her eyes were already blinking back a wave of tears. The worst had actually happened. As much as she had debated and discussed the very probability of Japan taking Singapore with the doubters (those that she could trust to discuss it with), she must, at her core, have always concluded that Britain would hold out. The revelation was definitely a shock. She sought to unravel the knot in the pit of her stomach and her mind raced with busy cognisance. She thought of Sutton and she thought of the Admiral. Her mind played over the safety of the ladies at the Golf Club. Mack! And all her belongings in her little bungalow, which now surely would be ransacked. Ruth sucked in her breath with each acknowledgement; her knuckle sought her mouth as though trying to deny the silent facts.

"I have to lie down," Victoria announced standing up. With that, she rushed from the room.

For a while, Ruth said nothing, merely staring at the fluffy head of the sleeping child in her lap.

Baba understood her shock. Bowing, he quietly told her, in his near perfect English, that he was at her service if she needed anything.

"Actually there is," Ruth responded looking up suddenly just before he left the room. She explained her need for milk powder for Jean's bottle.

"Milk is extraordinarily hard to come by. But I will send somebody out to search high and lower for you. Ah, careful, careful," he exclaimed racing towards two men who were attempting to carry a small bed up the stairwell at the far end of the long room.

After two days at the house, Ruth could not bear being cooped up any longer. The staff had not been able to find milk powder, though they did bring her some fresh goat's milk. She thanked them awkwardly, but there was no way she could risk giving her precious daughter raw milk from an unknown source. She'd lived long enough in the tropics to know that the only milk to be trusted was the powdered sort. She took the milk to the kitchen and heated it to a slow boil, before letting it cool again. Jean was very glad to have her bottle back, but she'd only take a few mouthfuls before stopping to grizzle. She obviously didn't like it.

Ruth had wanted to go and search for milk herself. She had seen plenty of markets on her short journey to the house from the port. There must also be department stores and cold storages, she thought. But Baba seemed disinclined to encourage any walking around the streets. He repeated his warning about it not being safe.

"The G.O.C. had shut down all the cinemas and dance halls, relocated the zoo, closed the sports fields and even restricted racing to one track," he droned on.

Ruth had no idea why Baba thought that limiting amusements such as those, made the city unsafe.

"There are many soldiers in the city. We may soon even find ourselves sitting under martial law."

Ruth scratched her head and crinkled her eyes. She felt like exclaiming, "*pff!*", but respectfully kept her mouth closed. He may be a servant, but he obviously had been entrusted with the upkeep of the entire household while the Armstrong's grandparents, the Earl and Countess, were away. That in itself said a lot to Ruth, but also Victoria had indicated that he had been with the family for many years and was well respected. As well as being in charge of the household, he had taken it upon himself to act as chaperone and father figure to the two widowed women.

His kindness extended to create a simple shrine on top of a sideboard, celebrating the life of Giles Armstrong. Ruth and Victoria hadn't known what to make of that at first, especially when on the first evening there was an almost constant vigil-like chanting going on in the background by one servant or another. This was continued the following morning but seemed to have stopped now. Giles had apparently visited his grandparents at the house many times in his youth, and Baba had seen him grow in leaps and bounds with each visit. Earlier, he had regaled them with tales of Mr Armstrong's expeditions into the city beyond the estate's walls until Victoria had been unable to stand it a moment longer. She had taken to her room for the afternoon.

"I'm going out," Ruth said firmly to Baba after walking around the property three times.

"But you will leave Miss Jean here with her nanny?" he said, referring to the new woman that had been employed.

"If that would please you then, yes, Baba."

"And you will take Maarten with you for protection?"

"If I must," Ruth said a little more churlishly than was polite.

"Where would you like to go Madam?" Maarten asked a while later, after she had collected her gloves, hat and handbag.

"I want to drive around the city until I see something I want to stop at."

"Oh, Madam would like to window-shop? I know the British ladies like to do this thing."

"We'll need a trishaw,"

"Yes madam. You wait here at the gates and I will get one for you."

With that, he ran off down the street returning a short while later, with an old-fashioned rickshaw in toe.

At a slow pace, Ruth rode through the streets. In Singapore, rickshaws had become little more than a novelty, since motorised vehicles had become common. But she remembered them from her youth in Hongkong. Here they still appeared to be the main form of transport in and out of the narrow alleys.

Maarten directed her straight to a large department store, House of Cargills, which happened to be just a couple of streets away. Here the rickshaw wallah was content to wait outside on a retainer, while Ruth went indoors. Maarten walked beside her, obviously well acquainted with the store's layout. He directed her to the fresh produce and dry goods sections where she enquired about powdered milk. The response was that certain products were hard to come by because of war restrictions. Milk powder was one of those and had been since before Christmas. Everybody wanted it for their tea, she was told. She was assured that if Cargills didn't carry it, nobody else would either.

Ruth wasn't going to give up quite that easily. She directed Maarten to drive on and soon they found an alleyway with market vendors lining both sides. But even with Maaten translating for her, she only received shrugs and disinterest. Maarten was on edge and this combined with the heat, the unfamiliarity of it all, the suspicious glances people were giving her and the constant negative responses had worn on her own nerves until finally she had snapped at Maarten to direct the rickshaw back to their residence.

She could hear Jean bawling before she even crossed the courtyard. The child had woken to find her mother missing and was clearly frightened. Surely, Victoria would have heard her crying? If she had, she'd made no attempt to leave her room to assist. Ruth felt let down and for the umpteenth time, she wondered what she was doing here in Ceylon.

"Battie" Jean began to cry, which meant she wanted her bottle. Ruth took her to the kitchens in search of something for her to suck on.

When Baba served dinner, Ruth was still out of sorts and didn't have much to say to Victoria.

Baba brought the evening paper in and sat it on the large brass table beside the staircase.

Ruth surreptitiously watched Victoria for a second to see if she would make a move to take it. Victoria seemed uninterested. In fact, the more Ruth looked at her, the more pale she realised she was. Ruth's anger subsided into concern.

"Do you want me to call for a doctor, Mrs Armstrong? You do look alarmingly pale today."

"I don't feel at all well. I suppose I ought to see someone, but tomorrow will do. No need to call a doctor out tonight."

Ruth reached across to the bell beside Victoria and gave it a ring. Baba came right in bringing a pot of tea with him.

"Thank you Baba, I might take my tea on the sofa. I wonder if you could send for a doctor to call on Mrs Armstrong tomorrow. Perhaps whichever doctor attends the Countess will be suitable."

Ruth rose and strode over to pick up the Ceylon Chronicle, taking it back to an easy chair. The headline news was the prediction that the Governor would call on the citizens to evacuate before long. The article recommended voluntary evacuation where possible.

Ruth dropped the paper to her lap while she considered what she had read.

"Well?" came the refined but blunt voice from the table. "Is there any news worth knowing about?"

"An official communiqué. They are suggesting all civilians evacuate to mainland India. The editor seems to think evacuation will be compulsory within days."

"India! I think not."

"Hmm, you know, if evacuation does become compulsory, it'll be like Singapore was when there were no berths to be had. I don't want to be here when that happens. It wasn't pleasant out on the streets today. Everyone glaring at everyone else. Maarten said it was because everyone is worried about spies."

"You could have asked me to accompany you today, Mrs Cole. I must say, I was rather put out when you went off on your own."

This came as a surprise to Ruth. "I thought you'd taken to your bed for the day. I didn't like to disturb you," she defended her actions. "Still, my point is, I think we ought to look into getting berths back to England. You could go to your parents. I could go to my aunts in Kent."

Victoria stood, but didn't come over to join Ruth immediately. Instead she wandered over to the window, looking out into the darkness.

Eventually she said, "By the time we get there, I'll be going on eight months' pregnant. I could have the baby early at sea. I could very well lose my last link to Mr Armstrong."

"No doubt, there will be a doctor on board and a stop in Cape Town. Or perhaps we ought to find a passage to Australia. That will certainly take no more than two weeks."

"There's nothing for me there, and then what happens when the Japs reach Australia and we have to evacuate again? No, I believe we should look into going by air. Supposedly the local airport is still fully operational."

"I can't afford that," Ruth said.

"Well, I can't afford not to," Victoria snapped. "I'm sorry, but unless I can get access to my bank account, I won't be able to pay for your tickets on top of my own. I'd like to, but well, you can see how I'm placed."

Ruth could see all too well. Her usefulness had passed and now she was on her own. She murmured her accord and continued to read the news. But she couldn't concentrate on any of the articles. Eventually, she bade

Victoria goodnight and left for bed.

The doctor duly arrived first thing the next morning. He considered the Earl and Countess to be amongst his most influential patients and he was eager to extend his services to their wealthy family members.

Victoria was mentally exhausted, he assessed. She needed rest and peaceful occupation. A tall order in this time of war, he admitted, but physically there was nothing of concern. The baby appeared to be growing normally with a strong heartbeat.

He had arrived in a motor car and so Victoria enquired if he could give the two women a lift to visit an air and shipping agent.

Around midday they found themselves walking through the door of Aitken Spence & Co, special agents of the Royal Netherlands Air Lines' various divisions. They were shown into the office of the travel adviser.

"I can get you on a flight to Durban," he offered, "at which point you'll need to switch carriers. You'll have to make your onward plans from Durban though. I would suggest you use BOAC and hopefully get on to Lisbon where you would be best to change to a sea passage."

"So, are there no direct flights to London?"

"Not currently Madam. It is just that most of our fleet has been requisitioned by the war office and flight paths are strictly limited and changing daily. We normally route via Suez or Lydda in Palestine, but are currently are not permitted to fly in that zone. The other thing I should warn you is when we do have a flight leaving, we are often required by the War Office to place officials in the seats whether or not we have already booked them to private citizens. But should that happen, of course, we will reimburse you. The plane in question has eight seats in total and is almost certainly going to leave on Thursday. The journey to Durban is two days, provided there aren't any hold-ups along the way and all hotels are included in the price. Durban to Lisbon will take you a further 3 days, I should expect, and I couldn't possibly say how long it will take to get to Southampton from there."

"I only have British sterling."

"That's no problem Madam. The trip to Durban will be, let's see, £80. May I have your travel documents please?"

Victoria placed her passport on the counter and began to fish inside her purse for the correct notes.

"Oh my dear madam, you have not had your passport validated."

"Excuse me?"

"On arrival in Colombo, you were obliged to present yourselves to the Immigration Officer within 24 hours. Really, they should have told you that when you booked your ticket out here. I can book you on the flight, but I won't be able to issue the ticket until you have done that."

Ruth and Victoria realised that it was going to be a very long afternoon—exactly the sort of extended activity the doctor had warned Victoria against.

"You look all in. I really think we'd better find somewhere to rest and have tiffin," Ruth suggested outside the travel agency. "I found a most agreeable department store yesterday. I suggest we go in there."

"I don't feel particularly inspired to eat. I think my appetite has deserted me."

"Well, even if you just have a nibble and a drink. Humour me."

Late in the afternoon, they finally were able to go about organising Ruth's voyage at a shipping agent and found that a local branch of the Orient Line was conveniently located.

"I'd like to book myself and my daughter on the next ship out to any country in the British Empire, but preferably Great Britain," Ruth requested of the booking clerk behind the counter.

"Well, we have daily sailings to Bombay and on to Karachi..."

"Except India," Ruth interrupted. It was far too close to Japan for her liking and her goal had been to leave the continent.

"Oh! Ah well let's see. We have a troopship going to Perth, Australia. She leaves day after tomorrow. You'd be in the Port of Fremantle in 5 days, all going well. Mind you, there are currently no other civilians booked on her; you'd be the only woman on board. If that is not a problem for you, I expect I'll be able to reserve a cabin for you."

"Anything going to the United Kingdom?"

"No madam, there is not. We have sailings to Durban planned but not confirmed as yet. If you wish to go to Canada, your best option is to get to Australia and rebook from there. The problem is, all our ships have been requisitioned by...."

"Yes, we know all that," Ruth snapped and then shocked by her own rudeness, she immediately apologised. "Look I appreciate you are just doing your job under trying circumstances but I've had very upsetting news lately and a desperate need to get home. Is there any point in my looking around at other agents? Not to be rude, but surely other nationalities have liners that haven't been requisitioned? What about S. A. L.? I believe they have ships in this part of the world these days."

"That is so, madam. But not surprisingly, those shipping lines are very coy as to which port they enter these days. They tend to avoid any port with a heavy military presence for fear of being confiscated, so we've seldom see them in here lately."

Ruth knew he was speaking the truth. That was indeed exactly what had happened in 1940 to the Free French ship Félix Roussel while it was in the process of traversing the Suez Canal.

"Would you like me to go ahead and book you on the RMS Orcades for Australia, Madam?"

"Yes, yes. You better had. Thank you."

12
SYONAN-TO FEBRUARY 1942

CHARLIE COLE

In the demoralising darkness, Charlie felt something nip his fingertips. His instinct was to jerk his bound hands away before the thing could touch him again. But he found himself unable to move. His befuddled mind couldn't grasp what was trying to nip him. Nor why he couldn't remove his hand to safety. Nor even why he should be worried about it. Then the touch came again, but this time it brought with it an unexpected warmth.

A welcome feeling, one that he knew he could trust, seeped into his fingertips before proceeding to wash throughout his body. It hadn't been a nip exactly, he realised. It was more like a grip, as though another set of fingers was squeezing the tips of his own. This benevolent energy flow coursed through his body feeding him with renewed vigour.

Still his mind felt empty. Answers and reason remained enshrouded in fog just out of reach. More time passed while his mind alternatively worked and rested until, eventually, snippets of cognisance helped him recognise what it was. Someone was trying to squeeze his hand, rubbing his fingertips. It was human touch. The fog cleared and he opened his eyes. Only dull shapes were discernible and for a moment a terrible grief engulfed him while he struggled with the thought that he had lost most of his vision. Even while his throbbing skull ached in despair, his eyes gradually managed to focus in the darkness, And then he remembered, with a rush.

He was in a wash-house. A wash-house on the back porch of an abandoned property in Johore Bahru. He and Captain Armstrong had been beaten, bound and locked in this tiny room for three days. They'd had no water during that entire time. No-one had come to check on them. It was as though they had been forgotten.

But now, Charlie was certain he could hear voices. Ugly Japanese voices. The closer and louder the voices became, the stronger Armstrong's grip grew on his fingers.

The door to the tiny room was flung open. Blinding hot sunlight poured across their filth encrusted bodies. Even as the two men battled with their vision, they were dragged and hauled out onto the porch. Their dry throats huskily begged for life saving water. Unintelligible voices answered their pleas with a sneer. Suddenly their heads were each dunked into a bucket of water. They weren't ready for it. The cold instantly brought them back to their senses. At the next dunking, Charlie took a mouthful. But he knew he wouldn't be able to swallow it without drowning until his head was lifted. He quickly sculled it down his swollen throat and managed to take a small breath of air before his head was dunked again. How he managed not to drown, could only have been by instinct. He was unaware of the spluttering and choking coming from Armstrong's bucket where his friend was attempting to do the same.

After a half dozen dunkings, their captors tired of the game and the next moment the two men found themselves hauled roughly onto the back of an open topped truck. This was driven from place to place, stopping occasionally to collect more captives. Each person was thrown onto the back like a side of beef, until the bodies overlapped as they lay where they landed. Some had rough-hewn bags tied over their heads. Others, like Charlie Cole and Giles Armstrong, had bare heads. Charlie was thankful that he was laying on his side, where his face was afforded some protection. He wondered what the intentions of these brutal captors was, but as long as he was alive, he knew there was a chance of escaping.

He was just deciding that if they were going to kill him, they would have done it already, when the truck stopped and the captives were pulled back off the truck one by one.

Being first on, the two APF men were amongst the last off and Charlie was astounded to find himself lined up with about 20 other people, who all appeared to be Chinese men. They were standing on the edge of the Johore Straits. Charlie took his bearings and could see that they were on the Malayan mainland, roughly opposite the Selatar Air Base on the Singapore side. Great pillars of oily smoke rose from areas around the base. He could see the island of Pulau Ubin to his left, but stretching his neck to look right he could not see around the bend to the causeway. Presumably, if things had gotten this bad, the British would have taken that link down.

Another truck pulled up and the process of removing prisoners began again. This time, the group was entirely Chinese, but amongst the men were a few women including a grandmother and presumably her granddaughter. The child was almost hysterical, whereas the adults around her appeared detached and compliant. The grandmother was attempting to give comfort to the small child, who must have been about ten years old give or take a few years, but with her hands bound behind her, all she could do was rub her chin on the child's head and mutter a gentle stream of words.

The guards seemed oblivious to both the child's hysteria and the grandmother's attempt to allay her fears.

A sharp stick poked cruelly into Charlie's back, causing him to stumble. Angry shouts from the guards and pokes with the sharp stick, a bayonet Charlie guessed, made it clear they wanted them all to walk forward. Into the water. He wondered if they going to make them swim across to Johore. With their hands bound, they would surely drown, as most of them would anyway, the distance being two to three miles at least, and the current generally strong at this point.

When the group was knee deep in water they were ordered to halt. It was amazing how quickly one learnt to understand the foreigner's guttural language when at the point of a bayonet.

They stood for several silent minutes looking out towards Singapore, no doubt each contemplating what was in store for them.

A vehicle drove up and Charlie imagined he could hear the crunching of footsteps crossing the sandy beach. There was a hushed conversation between the guards and this newcomer. New orders were barked out but none of the prisoners understood, so none reacted.

"Engrish!" Charlie thought he heard a voice yell. He dared to look across at his friend who was standing a few feet away in the knee deep water. A Jap Guard waded up behind Armstrong and cracked him across the shoulder with the stock of his rifle. Armstrong immediately dropped to his knees and struggled to keep upright. The guard grabbed him by the scruff of his dirty shirt and dragged him back to shore.

"Lekas! *Hurry!*" Charlie noticed the guards indicating him to follow, and he realised that they wanted the two English prisoners to leave the water. In a moment, they were kneeling in the dry scratchy sand, still facing Singapore, which was now obscured behind the rows of Chinese captives.

The next few minutes played out the most appalling spectacle Charlie had ever witnessed. The dozen or so guards walked into the water behind the ranks of Chinese prisoners and knocked each into the water. Bound at ankle and wrist, many with their heads still covered in sacks, the prisoners were unable to keep their heads above the water. The few that did manage to get to their knees were stomped on and knocked back under. The struggles went on and on. Horrifying spasms and jerks accompanied their last moments as the life drained from each of them. Although they were all strangers to Charlie, his tears made filthy tracks down his cheeks. He could not drag his eyes off the sight of the small child, just a few moments ago so full of health and fear. But now life-less and floating. The guards laughed and jeered and went amongst them cutting loose the bindings on their wrists and ankles, not caring if the sharp blades pierced or pricked the bodies. The lightweight rope fragments were left to float away on the currents or sink where they fell. The bodies were left to do the same.

A guard commander or officer marched to a stop in front of the two kneeling APF men and began to yell at them. On and on he went, sometimes stopping as if to wait for an answer. When all he got in return was confused shrugs, he just became angrier.

"We can't understand a jolly word you're saying," Armstrong finally said.

Taking a particularly long, silver handled swagger stick from his hip, the officer slashed it across Armstrong's face, swiftly cutting the flesh across his cheek. Armstrong cried out, but still managed to stay upright. The officer stormed back towards the road. Charlie could see his friend's face swiftly ballooning up, until his right eye closed over completely.

The two men were hustled back onto an open topped truck and driven further east along the coast.

The truck stopped and nothing happened for several minutes. Charlie's shoulders burned with the ache of being held awkwardly behind his back. His hands felt so numb, he had long ago given up trying to untie them. He thought that if they were to escape, now was probably the best time. Ever so slowly, he turned his battered body, so that he could prop himself up onto an elbow. He could just see over the low sides of the truck. There were several guards lounging around under the shade of trees and none seemed to be focused on the two men in the truck. Even so, Charlie realised that it would be nearly impossible for him to climb out of the truck unnoticed, hindered as he was by his bindings.

Escape seemed impossible in the broad daylight. Rolling over towards Armstrong he saw him open his one good eye.

"It's no use. There are guards everywhere," Charlie whispered.

The desire to just give up was very tempting, but he forced his mind to work, to explore any and every idea which could aid them.

Inching himself up towards the top of the truck, he managed to secure a sack between his teeth. This he slowly hauled back towards Armstrong. Even this movement brought a guard stomping over to peer into the back. Charlie froze, leaving the sack laying haphazardly beside him. Satisfied that nothing untoward was going on in the truck, the Jap guard wandered back out of view. When Charlie could no longer hear his footsteps, he again pulled the sack, until he had positioned it over Armstrong's injured head. At the very least it would afford him some protection from the sun.

"You're a good bloke," Charlie heard his friend say weakly.

Hours passed, and Charlie knew that he was both sun-burned and seriously dehydrated. His mind wandered and he lost track of time. Whenever reality came back to him, it was the pounding in his head and the convulsive dry retching that was his only concern.

At some stage during the long afternoon, Armstrong must have attempted to push the sack over Charlie's head because Charlie woke from his delirium to find the scratchy fabric being roughly pulled from him.

Soon he was dumped into the bottom of a punt like motor boat. Still later on, he became conscious again, to find himself in a familiar place. They were at the jetty beside the Kitchener Barracks in the eastern seaside village of Changi.

Dragged ashore, they had their bindings removed, but neither man was able to stand. Water was forced down their throats and Charlie gulped greedily. Unfortunately, he brought it all back up again. More water was dribbled into his mouth and Charlie knew that whatever else happened, he had to work at keeping the water down. It was all he could manage, and any thoughts of escaping were fractured by his pounding migraine. It almost seemed like they were finally being treated with something akin to compassion.

He tried to look at his captors. Perhaps they were British. Perhaps he had been rescued. But his eyes would not focus and his body shook with fever. Only disparate ideas floated in and out of his conscious mind.

The next thing he remembered was being dragged down a hallway and the cool darkness of the building was a welcome restorative. He became aware of the rough concrete floor tearing at his strangely belt-less civilian trousers.

They were pushed into a room housing a desk, behind which sat a man. It was a very familiar room, and his mind protested at the sight of the man sitting in the chair, but it took him a moment to realise why.

This was the very office from which he had occasionally worked, his own office. He knew he was inside Changi Gaol; a place which, as far as Charlie knew, was guarded by the Admiralty Police Force. But the man behind the desk was an impostor. He wore a white shirt open at the neck and a dark blue double breasted military jacket of sorts. He was undeniably a high ranking officer of the Japanese Imperial Army. Even as the two APF men were hauled to their unsteady feet, another Japanese soldier spoke to them in English.

"Who are you?"

Neither Armstrong, nor Charlie responded to his question immediately. When threatened with further violence though, Armstrong spoke up naming both of them by their first and last names. It crossed Charlie's mind that the plan had been to present themselves as civilians if they were ever captured. Being part of the police force, they were in fact civilians, so it wasn't exactly a lie. But convincing the Japanese of it, proved to be difficult.

They wanted to know why they were the only British men in the whole of Johore Bahru, other than captured soldiers. Why were they not wearing uniform? Were they spies? No? Then, what was their rank?

That was a trick question and Charlie recognised that Armstrong did not let him down with his answers, stating only that they were prison guards. In the end, a Punjabi prison guard was brought in to verify their statements. Both Charlie and Armstrong both instantly recognised the man. It was Lance Corporal Dalip Khaira, a man they both knew well.

To Dalip's credit, he gave only as much information as needed and no more.

When it was finally established that the two Europeans men were in fact prison guards for this very prison, the Japanese officer behind the desk thought the whole situation was very funny. He laughed so hard he could hardly breathe as he tried to explain to the soldier-translator what was so comical. Eventually, the translator began to chuckle as well, although Charlie thought he was only being polite. Dalip, the Punjabi prison guard, who was still in the room, did not laugh and neither did Charlie nor Armstrong.

It transpired that Dalip Khaira was being kept on to help the Japanese soldiers guard the prison. Charlie hadn't realised it yet, but one of the other Punjabi policemen helping the Japanese was Ude Singh, the very man who had been court marshalled on Charlie's evidence a few years ago. The man still held a very large grudge and once he learned who was now captive, he would have plenty of time to exact his revenge.

After the soldier had marched them to their prison cell in the main building, he gave Dalip more orders and left.

Prison Guard Dalip Khaira left as well, but was soon back with a half bucket of water, which he placed inside the men's cell.

Now was their chance to question their old subordinate.

"Hey thanks for not telling the Jap officer who we really are," Charlie whispered.

The man didn't answer, but merely frowned.

"I mean, about not mentioning the navy," Charlie insisted.

"That was not just for your sake, Sir. I mean Mr, ah, Prisoner Cole. None of us want them to know that we worked at the dockyard. We are all just prison guards now, not policemen. All the same rank."

"What of the British? Do they still control downtown Singapore?"

"No! They surrendered three days ago."

"So we've lost. Singapore is lost?"

"Yes it is so. The army and the people are being brought here to Changi. And just in case you think we Punjab's are lucky. Not so lucky for us. We also cannot leave Changi. We are camped in one of the barracks buildings. Yesterday, my cousin Arvinder was beaten severely after he refused to join the Indian National Army. He did not survive the night. It was a warning to us all. I had to sign my allegiance over to the INA so that I could work here. Otherwise I would be a collaborator. I had no choice. Not after what happened to Arvinder. It was a warning to us not to complain. Not to disobey."

"They got Arvinder eh? I'm sorry to hear that," Armstrong said.

"Hey, at least they will treat us all better as civilians, rather than captured soldiers. The Japs don't have any sympathy for POWs I've heard," Charlie said.

"Maybe. Maybe not," Dalip said oninously.

"What do you mean?"

"It's just that from what I've seen, you are locked inside a gaol. The POWs are camping in various army barracks around Changi. They are free to come and go, as they please so long as they stay within the boundaries. I know which I would prefer."

That statement stunned the men into silence, which was just as well. For at that moment, the Japanese soldier returned to find out what was going on.

Dalip cleared his throat pointedly. "Only half bucket of water per day per cell," he said loudly, so that his voice carried down the hall to the soldier. "Remain in cells, except during daily exercise and Tenko."

"Tenko?" Armstrong queried.

"It's the roll call. When you hear the siren in the morning, you must assemble near the door to your floor. Then you all march to the courtyard for the roll call," Dalip whispered.

"Prisoner will stop talking!" the soldier shouted as he approached. "Go!" he growled at Dalip before retreating back up the corridor.

The cell door was closed, but not locked they discovered.

Armstrong and Cole looked around the small space. They knew they weren't in one of the 24 cells usually reserved for European prisoners. Those had a slightly longer sleeping platform, slightly more total floor space and a pedestal water closet in the corner. This was a cell usually reserved for a single Asiatic prisoner with a squat loo in the corner. Now there were two, rather tall men to inhabit the space. One of them would have to sleep on the floor and Charlie's lip curled in disgust as he considered the idea of having his head near the reeking waste pan.

The cell was basic with no lighting and plain painted concrete walls which had seen better days. Above the sleeping platform there was a simple wall shelf and above that one of two windows. It was situated too high to look out of but it was in an exterior wall, so it emitted light and a little warmth. It was barred of course, but it was also covered in screen netting to keep out the mosquitoes. The other window was in the cell door. This too was barred and looked out onto the central corridor outside. It had no covering and so also emitted light when the electric hall lights were on.

"I could murder a hot curry right now," Armstrong said after helping himself to the bucket of water. There were no cups, so he simply drank from the filthy bucket.

"Hmm, I really feel like a tin of juicy sweet peaches. Or apricots. I'm not fussy."

"How many days is it since we've eaten? Four? Five?"

"I thought it was four. We were hiding in that last bungalow for two days weren't we? After they captured us, they put us in that laundry room. I really thought we weren't getting out of there alive."

"We wouldn't have been captured if I hadn't tried to steal that egg," Armstrong said. "Bloody chicken gave us away."

"Don't fret about it. They would have got us sooner or later. Especially since it appears that the god forsaken British Army have lost the whole of Malaya."

"Who'd have thought it eh? Seems almost like a dream."

"Funny dreams you have then," Charlie said, trying to lick away the dryness in his mouth. He considered the water bucket suspiciously, wondering how wise it would be to drink out of it. The last thing he needed was to get an infection. They'd need all their strength if they were to last the weeks until the British could realistically retake the island.

The conversation continued in this manner, until the sound of many voices could clearly be heard singing outside.

"That's English, I'm sure. What are they singing?" Charlie cried.

"Da-da da-doo, da-da da-doo ..." Armstrong hummed, until he suddenly realised he knew the words. *"Freedom remains, these are the chains, nothing can break."*

Giles Armstrong, winked at Charlie who joined in with the chorus to Vera Lynn's well known song.

"There'll always be an England, and England shall be free. If England means as much to you, as England means to me."

They had been joined by other equally croaky voices from neighbouring cells and for just a moment, their hearts swelled with hope.

Outside the song came to an end, but the sound of many feet, chattering voices and grizzling children could be heard.

Over the next half hour, the chattering outside gradually died down, but voices came and went up and down the corridor as new internees were deposited into cells.

At first, the two men made the mistake of standing in their doorway to watch the goings on, but a shout from a guard to close their door, soon sent them packing.

An hour before sunset, a bell rang and the prison guards rapped on each door on the floor, telling the men to come out into the hallway. It was time for the evening meal and they all walked in single file to another building within the prison walls. While Armstrong didn't get a nice hot curry, he did get a bowl of rice with two slices of vegetable, a cube of chicken and a scoop of broth. It was all he could manage anyway.

During these first few days, the meals were cooked by the Malaysian prison cooks and assisted by existing prisoners. These were the prisoners who hadn't been released, as obviously all the detained Japanese had. These remaining criminals had been moved to C Block where they could be kept together under the supervision of the Punjabi prison guards. After a few days, the native cooks disappeared. Whether they had all been sacked or perhaps run away, nobody knew and the criminal prisoners tried unsuccessfully to run the kitchens themselves.

Soon, a more organised approach came about, whereby the women internees worked shifts in the kitchen. The women and children were all housed in one of the two main Gaol blocks. Despite their best efforts, the food didn't get any better. The big oil ovens became useless as soon as the fuel ran out and the women resorted to using an open fire, which was hopelessly inadequate for the quantities required. Not that portion size was large. Oftentimes there was only one piece of vegetable and no meat. The quantity of rice also decreased gradually.

With the women running the kitchen, the men internees were not left idle, they were given cleaning jobs to do, depending on their Block, such as refilling water buckets. Armstrong and Cole were amongst the unluckiest, being told to clean the lavatory pans. It was a nasty job and they really didn't have the tools to do it properly, but at least it gave them the chance to get around the prison.

More and more groups of prisoners arrived during the first two weeks. The two men estimated that the prison, which they knew well enough was built for 600 inmates, now held three to four *thousand* prisoners. This was confirmed by Dalip who continued to visit Cole and Armstrong daily.

As crowded and cramped as it was, they soon heard that the entire contingent of captured armed forces were living in the air force and army Barrack buildings. These were meant to house 17,000 troops so were fairly extensive in nature, covering several blocks. Dalip estimated that at least 50,000 troops were crammed onto both sides of the Gully. Maybe even double that. Some men were being forced to sleep in the open, until better accommodation could be built or secured. Not that any building seemed apparent. Movement between barracks blocks was not permitted.

The following week another prisoner was shoved into their cell. They immediately recognised his clear American accent. It was Bernie Welcome, a radio presenter on the local radio station, WBC. He often did a late evening show from nine until the station closed each night at ten. He soon set them straight. Bernie Welcome was only a pseudonym. His real name was Frank Smedley.

"I know your work too," he then told Armstrong. "I've seen you on the stage a couple of times. I always planned to get you in to record a play with our little group."

"Well, I've never done just a voice before. Though I suppose it can't be much different than treading the boards. By Jove, I'd have been honoured," he said shaking Smedley's hand again for the second time.

"Well, maybe when all this is over …"

There was an awkward pause. Frank Smedley looked around the cell. Gee, there isn't much room for three is there," he observed.

"We've been take turns sleeping on the platform. The other has been sleeping on the floor over on that side," Armstrong said.

"I don't fancy being over near the john," Smedley said, observing the lavatory pan with distaste. Maybe it would be better if one lays down one side and one across the top here, see. Though it'll be mighty awkward if the door were to open suddenly."

"Yes, and that is provided we don't have to cram any more people in. If that's the case, we might have to have turns sleeping while the others sit up," Armstrong said.

"Are there many more civilians out there, do you know Smedley? We were captured before the surrender," Cole asked.

"Call me Frank."

"I think we should all use first names in here. It's going to get mighty cosy," Armstrong said.

"Well, we might as well face the fact that civilisation as we know it is over for the time being, so all righty, I'm up for that. What *is* your first name Captain Armstrong?" Charlie asked with a deadpan face.

"You jolly well know it is Giles," Giles responded.

Charlie grinned and repeated his earlier question to Frank about the situation in town.

"Well, there can't be too many more folks around to my way of thinking. I guess there might be the odd family from the outlying areas. There were orders, you see, for everyone to go to the Cricket Club Padang last week. They were to take ten days' worth of provisions with them. That's what we were instructed to broadcast at the station. Most of the radio announcers evacuated and the transmitters were destroyed, so we were only operating on a skeleton staff on a single transmitter. I volunteered to stay, see. The original plan was to transmit from a makeshift site in Batavia, but that didn't last too long. You know, I think the Japs have got in over there too. They've renamed the station Radio Shonan and it's all propaganda—left, right and centre. I got punished for refusing to read what they wanted me to read, so they sent me off here."

"Yes *punishment*. We've seen a lot of that. They're merciless. Still, lucky you weren't shot." Giles commented.

"So much for their bloody *bushido* nonsense. They don't operate on any code of honour that I recognise," Charlie whispered.

"Bloody agents of the devil more like," Giles agreed. "We watched them murder a child in cold blood."

"Well there's been a lot of that in town too. The Chinese are terrified, every last one of them. Too darned scared to even walk about. There are soldiers going from house to house, beheading them. The Chinese are being made to wear arm-bands. Those that are to be executed have stamped foreheads. It's dreadful."

"What about the Malays"

"They seem to be alright, though there aren't many of them about and those that are, are keeping their heads down. All Europeans are being incarcerated, but the Dutch are having an especially bad time of it."

Charlie thought briefly of the Ohlrichs and wondered if they had managed to get out. He didn't know any other Dutch residents.

"They've left a few men doing essential services, like electricity. And like myself at the radio. But from what I've seen they're under constant guard and are being forced to sleep at their place of work."

The men were silent while they digested all this information. They'd had very little new information in the past week or so, and their minds were reeling.

"The hospitals have all closed down," Frank added after a while.

"Where have all the patients gone?"

"Shot them!"

"What? Shot them all?" Giles asked astounded.

"Well, they went into the military hospital, you know Alexandra Hospital, and shot or bayonetted every doctor, nurse and patient. I haven't heard what is happening at the other hospitals."

"Things are a lot worse than we thought," Giles said.

"Oh, you don't know the half of it probably," Frank went on. "It's not just the radio station they've renamed. Singapore is now to be called Syonanto. The Singapore dollar was replaced almost overnight with some ridiculous currency that they appear to be just printing willy-nilly. And they've even changed the clock by an hour and a half."

"So that we coincide with Japan's time," Armstrong surmised.

"You betcha sweet mama!"

"I was wondering why tea is so early each night and why we have to get up so damnably early in the morning," Giles said.

"At least the women got away," Charlie said to him, meaning their wives. "I only hope they got safely to Ceylon."

"There was something about Ceylon, on the last news report I received. They wanted me to report that the Japanese had captured Sri Lanka and the whole of Southern India. But a radio engineer told me he was still receiving stations in India and there was no inkling of a takeover there. I thought it was just more propaganda. Sorry, to add to your worries," he said when he saw the shocked looks on the men's faces.

"Well, let's just hope that the girls had the good sense to get out of there if they could."

"Yes, they are probably half way to England by now," Giles agreed.

"As long as I know Jean and Ruth are safe, I can bear this. No matter how long it takes," Charlie said.

13
INDIAN OCEAN MARCH 1942

RUTH COLE

Ruth peered out of her cabin door to the passageway beyond. The way was all clear, so she slipped out. She was trying to avoid contact with the other passengers. When one of the ship's company had personally escorted her to her little cabin the evening before, she had been whistled at, jeered at, propositioned and even had her behind slapped by the troops aboard the ship. Noting the disturbance she was creating, the crewman had suggested she keep to her cabin as much as possible for her own safety.

This morning however, hunger had forced her to seek out a dining room. She had brought some supplies for Jean, but not enough for herself, and anyway the child had been restless and was grating on her nerves.

Not knowing exactly where the dining room was, nor whether she'd have to navigate the stairs of a companionway, she had decided against using the baby car. Instead Jean trotted along beside her, one hand stretched up to hers and the other sucking her thumb, like a little orang-utan. Hence her progress was slow.

Thankfully, unlike her last voyage, the signage on board was in English and she soon saw an arrow pointing the waywards a semi-automatic lift, or electric elevator as the American's called them. Soon she was in the central foyer and she followed the directions to the main dining room. Before she could get anywhere near the door a long queue of soldiers halted her progress. They were a noisy bunch and Ruth felt undeniably intimidated. She picked up Jean who hid her face against her neck.

"What've we got here?" one man announced seeing her approach.

"This here line's for soldiers only," another growled.

"Don't listen to him, I've got a spot for you right beside me," a third called out. She didn't like the lecherous look on his face at all.

She decided to pick Jean up and bypass the queue. It wasn't that she felt superior to the men, it was just that they were right—lining up amongst them wasn't a suitable place for a respectable woman.

"Excuse me, excuse me," she said over and over as she made her way alongside the queue. "Can I just get past please."

She was sure some of them pretended not to hear her on purpose and she couldn't understand why they were being so rude. She had lived amongst the armed services for several years now and had never come across this sort of behaviour before.

Eventually, she got in through the double doors to the dining room and with more space was able to high-tail it to the table where the stacks of bowls and plates were placed. She had heard something about how they did it on the troop ships. There were no waiters or menus to assist you at a properly set table on these ships. It would probably be just like the evacuee ship Félix Roussel where you took a plate and then filled it from a buffet table and then found a table to sit at. She reached out her hand to take a dixie type bowl for herself.

"What do you think you're doing missy? Where's your table card, eh? You can't just come in here and help yourself on our sitting," a burly soldier stated in a voice nearly loud enough to carry around the room.

She ignored him and waited until he had passed, before trying again. It wasn't easy with Jean on her hip and she felt her cheeks flaming as she looked over the line of soldiers to see if any of them appeared to be sympathetic to her predicament. But the line didn't seem to be progressing at all. In fact only a few soldiers were helping themselves and they each had a tray with a dozen dixies on it. She looked around at the various tables and noted that those men who weren't watching the sudden appearance of a woman and child in their midst were keeping an eye on the progress of these men with the trays. It seemed they did have waiters after all. Some of the men were also distracted by a fracas happening in one corner. An officer was reprimanding a soldier who was being forcibly held by the ship's Master At Arms. He had food spilt down his shirt and she wondered whether he had been involved in a fight, but she thought it best to pretend not to notice. She certainly didn't want the officer's wrath coming down on her.

Forgetting all about her dilemma for the moment, she surreptitiously watched the soldier's progress as he was frog marched out of the room by the Master At Arms. When a cool firm voice in her ear asked if she needed assistance, she nearly jumped out of her skin.

Spinning around to face the voice, she saw the same officer, looking at her sternly.

"I, ah …" she hesitated for a moment, while she glanced at the lapel on his uniform, noting the three pips which indicated she was speaking to a New Zealand Army captain. "I'm trying to get something to eat, but I seem to be doing it all wrong." Tears sprang unbidden to her eyes and she tried to blink them away. It wouldn't do to cry in front of these men.

"Only the mess orderlies are permitted to serve out the food in here. You have to be listed on their table. I'm surprised you weren't told all this. Follow me, miss," he commanded.

She trailed along behind in the captain's wake, as the men sprang out of his way, though few of them actually went to the effort to salute him, like she thought they probably all should.

He had traversed the length of the corridor and back to the foyer housing the lift and the grand staircase before he turned to continue his explanation.

"The officers eat in a different dining room and I suggest you stick to that one too. Those men back there haven't seen a British woman for a very long time and seem to have forgotten all sense of decorum. I wouldn't trust them as far as I could throw them. I know you'd think that they'd be keen to see a pretty woman, but amongst this lot are some of the very worst soldiers the army has ever produced. Many of them are on their way home to dishonourable discharge and prison. Others are simply walking wounded or retirees. Myself being one of the latter."

"Oh?" Although he appeared to be older than herself, he didn't seem old enough to retire.

He tapped his ear. "Deafness. I've been going deaf in one ear. Comes from spending so long with the heavy artillery."

He was silent for the rest of the way and Ruth had completely lost her nerve to speak.

Entering another dining room, the atmosphere was quite different. Here the captain brought her to a lieutenant properly attired in mess dress but with a bandaged head. He introduced him as Lieutenant Bradshaw. Instructing the young man to escort the lady and assist where necessary, he then explained that he had quartermaster duties which required his immediate attention. He wished her well and left them to it.

Lieutenant Bradshaw, another New Zealander, stuck to her side throughout the meal, even helping to hold Jean when Ruth needed both her hands to eat her eggs. The Lieutenant seemed to be a very cordial chap but severely tongue tied when it came to small talk. She quickly learnt to keep her conversation to necessities only although she did get the young man to divulge that other than the ship's company, the most senior military passenger on board was an Australian major who was heading home for retirement with command of the troops on board being his last duty.

When breakfast was done, the Lieutenant walked Ruth back to her cabin and promised to collect her again for luncheon. This routine, he told her, would continue for the duration of the voyage and Ruth found that she could take Jean in her baby car, seeing as there was a lift available.

After dinner that evening, Ruth asked Lieutenant Bradshaw if he would accompany her for a stroll along the promenade decks. She was going out of her mind sitting all day in her cabin, despite having begun work on a small smocking project, attempting to embellish one of her daughter's outfits a little.

They had only just begun their walk when the officer who had rescued her that morning approached and told the Lieutenant that he'd take over the escort duty from here.

"I never got your name before," Ruth asked him. She had calmed down considerably since their last meeting.

"Captain Whitlock," the man said.

"I'm, Mrs..."

"Ruth Cole," the captain finished. "Yes, I know who you are madam. May I be so forward as to ask if your husband is in His Majesty's service?"

"It's not forward. He is, was, in the Admiralty Police Force, in Singapore."

"Singapore? Oh dear. What has become of him? Surely not..."

"Yes. Yes, he is," Ruth stopped him. "He is ... dead." Ruth found herself gripping the hand railing in support as her knees flailed slightly. Not even with Baba had she actually spoken the word out loud in such a direct manner. She felt the constant crushing feeling in her chest compress just a fraction more.

"So much death, such a waste. All of it," the Captain was saying quietly. "I am sorry for your loss. And I am sorry for making you spell it out. I wouldn't have asked but with you not wearing mourning clothes, I naturally assumed that either your husband was still alive or, please forgive me, that you perhaps didn't have a husband and were just using the Mrs as a cover."

Ruth frowned at the suggestion.

"I know, I know, silly of me. But then it wouldn't be the first time a woman has done that."

"Well, we left Singapore in such a hurry there wasn't time for mourning clothes. When I was informed of his death I had already been evacuated from my home, and I hadn't thought to pack mourning clothes. I only packed two spare day dresses for myself as I had to save space for young Jean's things. Children need so much, what with all their napkins and such like."

"And I see that you intend on disembarking in Perth? Have you relatives there?"

"My husband's parents. Though they haven't shown much interest in my joining them. Still I haven't anywhere else to go. There's his sister in Sydney and my aunties in Bearsted."

"Bearsted?"

"Yes, it's a village near Maidstone, south of London."

"Oh, I see."

"My father, brother and another sister-in-law are in Hongkong. I've had no news on that front, but I expect they are being held by the Japanese. Anyway, what of you Captain," Ruth asked brightly, not wanting to discuss that subject any further. "Are you married and if so, where is home for you?"

"Me? No I'm not married. I was, but not anymore. Home for me is Auckland I suppose, though I've not lived there much. I also have two aunties. I daresay they are my closest living relatives nowadays. My father died shortly after I enlisted. My elder brother died at Gallipoli back in '15, and my sister died when she was eighteen." He noticed her interested look and explained further. "She had a fatal fall from a horse. Dreadful days those were. Then when Cyril died at the Great War, mother and father never truly recovered. I was the black sheep of the family, out at Norfolk Island in a disastrous marriage and never quite able to make up for their loss. My mother died while I was on the island." The Captain was staring out across the velvet depths, almost speaking to himself as if he had forgotten Ruth was there. "I guess I ran away to the army. Then as I said, my father died shortly after I volunteered, so there is only my aunties left; my mother's sisters. And now it's time to return. But to what, I don't know." He lapsed into silence and they began to walk again.

Over the next few days, while the ship's captain zig-zagged them towards Perth, Ruth's evening stroll with Captain Whitlock became part of her daily routine; and the one that she looked forward to most. It was such a human thing to do, to chat with another adult. Not having another woman to talk to, the Captain made a good substitute.

"Ruth, may I call you Ruth? I'm not used to calling civilians I know well Mrs this and Mr that."

"Goodness, even Mr Cole, didn't use my first name in public. In Singapore, everyone, even my closest friends, never resorted to using familiar names."

"Then why have first names? Honestly, those stuffy old rules belong to a different era. Look, if I can call you Ruth, you can call me Hunter. Although, in front of the other men, it might pay to call me Captain."

"Alright then. Hunter it is."

"Ruth! Nice to meet you," Hunter laughed.

Ruth looked at him coyly. She felt a little naked, as though by using her first name, he was stripping away her defensive armour. Mind you, she wouldn't mind if he did. Not at all. He was rather dishy in an older sort of way. She still couldn't figure his age and wondered if she could be bold enough to ask him outright. His body was as sinewy and bronzed as could be. He had regulation length dark brown hair which had receded at the front considerably, giving him an air of authority. His hazel eyes had a way of probing through her, always lingering just a moment longer than they should as if he was testing to see the truth in her every statement.

"How old are you Hunter?" There she had said it and she waited for the answer which didn't come immediately. She was just about to apologise for her impertinence when he finally replied.

"I'm 44. How old are you Ruth?" He empathised her name in a way that made the blood rush to her head.

"Twenty-five."

"And how old was your late husband?"

"He had just celebrated his 32nd birthday shortly before I last saw him."

"It must be so very hard for you," Hunter said kindly.

"It's all a nightmare really. I can hardly believe he has gone. But then again, so much has happened since, that I feel like, well I hardly know what I feel like. I feel like he's not really dead or like we were never really married in the first place. That sounds terrible, when I say that out loud. No, I just can't explain how I feel, because I'm not altogether sure. Sad, I suppose."

"Let's walk," Hunter suggested. His aim had been to keep the woman's spirits up, not bring her to tears again, and he appeared to be failing in that. "How has Lieutenant Bradshaw been treating you?"

"He's very good, although a bit on the reticent side. I do enjoy my chats with you, but I'm dreadfully bored in between, just sitting in my cabin. Too scared to walk around. Jean is very difficult to entertain in the cabin."

"I'm sure if you ask him, the Lieutenant will accompany you out of your cabin during the day. The men wouldn't dare approach you with an officer at your side. You are also welcome to use the officer's mess at any time or walk about the quarter deck."

"Couldn't you walk with me during the day?"

"Alas, I have duties on board during the day. I'm off duty in the evenings only I'm afraid." They continued their walk in companionable silence with just the odd remark or observation, until Captain Whitlock walked her back to her cabin door.

The following day, which was the fifth day of the voyage, the lieutenant escorted Ruth to breakfast and was very accommodating when afterwards she requested he take her about the ship. When she was tired of walking she asked to go back to the dining room, or Officer's Mess as Hunter had described it, but the ship's crew didn't seem to like them being in there while they were cleaning. So on the Lieutenant's suggestion, they went into the adjoining room, which was a lounging room for officers only.

The ship was so very modern. Unlike the Félix Roussel, which had been grand in a decorative way, this ship was comparatively simple. Yet her clean lines and smooth surfaces were refreshing and sumptuous. She also bore none of the damage that the French ship had and unlike that ship, the Orcades' mixed military and merchant marine crew were all British. That in itself was both familiar and comforting.

In the lounge-room, she finally met the major who approached for a brief chat.

"Captain Whitlock has told me a lot of nice things about you Mrs Cole. Oh, and please accept my condolences on the loss of your husband."

"Thank you. Wouldn't you say we must be getting close to Perth Major? How many days do you think we have left in the voyage?"

"Actually, we have just received new orders madam. We won't be berthing at Fremantle. We have been ordered on to Melbourne. So we'll be at sea another six or seven days I expect."

"Oh, I wonder how I'll manage to get to Perth," Ruth blurted unable to keep the disappointment out of her voice.

"I imagine you'll be able to take a train my dear. We'll not be stopping for long and our troops will not disembark until Port Jackson, but I'm sure the Lieutenant here will be willing to show you to the train station, won't you lad?"

"Yes Sir," the Lieutenant said, knowing that it was neither a request nor suggestion, but an order.

"Or perhaps Captain Whitlock might like to do the honours if he's not too busy," the major suddenly said. He watched closely for Ruth's reaction and was not surprised to see a blush creep onto her cheeks. "Yes, not to worry Lieutenant, I'll inform Whitlock that he is to accompany Mrs Cole to the Central Station. Enjoy the rest of your day madam." He left the room whistling a happy tune, no doubt feeling that had his wife witnessed his little action of matchmaking, she'd be proud of him.

The days passed slowly and one day Ruth was enjoying the sunshine and superbly calm water while pushing Jean's chair around the quarterdeck. Unexpectedly, the Lieutenant was ordered away on some errand or other.

"You'll be safe enough here, madam seeing as how enlisted men are not allowed up here. I'll come back to collect you as soon as I can or failing that I'll send another officer to fetch you."

"Go ahead, I'll be fine," Ruth laughed. Nothing untoward had happened to her since the first day and she was sure that the soldiers had gotten used to her presence by now. Besides, as Lieutenant Bradshaw had pointed out, the only men allowed on the quarterdeck were sailors and officers.

She sat down on a bit of wooden coaming, removing her light cardigan and shoes as there was no wind here. Her lightly tanned legs were bare today. She'd hung her only pair of stockings to dry in her little en-suite. She put a foot out to the chair to stop it from rolling, and then clutching one of its legs just above the wheels between her toes, she rolled the chair back and forth in an attempt to rock her daughter to sleep.

The warmth of the sun made Ruth drowsy and she allowed her mind to drift and day dream. Just two days ago, from a position not far from where she currently was, she had seen the men engaging in some fitness exercise on a deck below. Wearing just their shorts in the heat, it was hard to tell who belonged to which rank, but she had certainly recognised one of them as none other than her very own Captain Whitlock. *Her Captain Whitlock!* Really, she scolded herself. She mustn't think of him like that. He wasn't hers at all. But then, her mind drifted again, as she remembered his bronzed body, and long rippling muscles. He was in excellent condition for an old man of 44. Not that 44 was terribly old. She'd wished that she could watch him for longer, but at the time the prudish Lieutenant had not so subtly suggested they keep walking. What a pity that Hunter wasn't Australian. She felt almost sure he returned her interest and she would have liked to develop their friendship. As it was, there really wasn't much point. In just a handful of days, he'd be dropping her off to the central station and then that would be goodbye forever as he headed on with the ship to its final destination in Wellington, New Zealand.

As she was thinking these things and rocking the pram, cocooned in the sun's warming rays, she was unaware that the hem of her day dress had crept up well past her knees exposing a considerable amount of thigh.

A long shadow blocking the sun fell across her and looking up to see who it belonged to, she found Hunter's stern face looking down on her. At the same time, she realised how exposed she had allowed herself to be.

"The Lieutenant told me I would find you out here alone." His growly tone of voice immediately got Ruth's back up.

"Well, as alone as one can be," she replied indicating the sailors who were on watch.

"Yes, and a fine afternoon they must be having," he said pointedly. "Mrs Cole, might I give you some advice."

It wasn't a question. Ruth could tell by his tone that he intended to give her some advice whether she wanted it or not, but she replied haughtily. "My name is Ruth, Hunter. I thought we had established that."

His voice softened. "Sorry, Ruth. Look, how can I put this..." Since she had neither stood to greet him nor hear his advice, he crouched down to speak to her quietly. She had made no effort to cover her thighs and he had a tantalising glimpse of the soft white skin between them. Gently he reached out and tugged her hem down to her knees. This caused Ruth to raise her eyebrows at him.

"Blimey Hunter. There's no need to be that prudish. I'm sun bathing. Have you never seen a girl at the baths or the beach in a bathing suit?"

"You are not in your bathing suit and that is what I want to talk to you about."

"Well you are out of luck. I didn't bring one with me." Ruth was defensive and didn't want to give him a chance to say what she darn well knew he wanted to say.

He stumbled on ahead anyway. "I do care about your welfare. Probably more than anyone else on this ship."

"You are a dear. I enjoy our friendship too. And even though we have a considerable age difference, the thing I like about you most is you never treat me like a little girl and you never chide me."

Hunter coughed. "Well take this as a friendly warning then, rather than a telling off. If you carry on like this, displaying yourself to the sailors and any other man who happens by, then you can hardly expect myself or the young lieutenant to keep you safe. Some of these men have been court martialled for unbecoming behaviour towards native Greeks and Syrian women."

"Well, perhaps I'm just not used to the uncouth nature of the Antipodean armies," she said churlishly, standing up and taking the handle of Jean's chair.

"Every army had bad'uns. Some of the best soldiers I've seen have been in the New Zealand Infantry. But I've also seen some awful sights that I'm not prepared to detail. British soldiers are just as bad as any of them. God woman, it's all I can do to keep my own hands off you."

"Well perhaps you should go and report yourself to the Master At Arms," Ruth said sulkily stalking away.

She was not sure if Captain Whitlock had followed her or not. She dared not look behind. But nobody stopped her as she stormed back to her cabin and slammed the door, bolting it behind her.

She stewed on their argument all afternoon, until she came to regret her words. Truly he had only been trying to help her. He really was a gentleman. She was surprised when a knock at her door came half an hour before the Lieutenant was due to collect her for the evening meal. Perhaps it was Hunter, come to apologise, she thought peering through the peephole on her door. But it was just the Lieutenant. He held out a note for her and waited wordlessly.

Ruth flicked it open warily. There was but a few handwritten words.

"I'd be honoured if you'd accept my invitation to be my guest at the Captain's table this evening and hope you accept my apology for being so blunt this afternoon. Yours truly, Captain Hunter Whitlock."

Well, she didn't give the apology a second thought. She had already forgiven him. But her mind immediately flew to the immediate pickle. She had but half an hour to prepare herself. Not that she had much to do. None of her three frocks were suitable for a cocktail party much less a formal dinner. She could run a brush through her hair but there'd be no time to curl it. Other than that, she could apply a bit of colour to her lips.

Meanwhile all the officers would be wearing their dress uniforms no doubt.

Since the Lieutenant seemed to be waiting for a reply, she quickly scribbled one out.

"I'd be delighted Captain, but please understand that I have nothing formal to wear." She handed the note to the Lieutenant who turned on the spot and left as wordlessly as he had come.

Ten minutes before she expected his return, another knock sounded on her door. This time she could see Bradshaw standing there with a brown paper parcel in his arms.

"Compliments of the captain," he said unable to contain himself this time. "It's a dress Mrs."

"Good heavens, is it really? Where on earth did Captain Whitlock find a dress. He's not that way inclined is he?" she asked half mockingly.

"No madam," he grinned back. "It is not from our Captain. This is from the actual Ship's Captain. He says he hopes it is your size."

Ruth shook the dress out and exclaimed happily. "Well I never. It's rather posh. What do you think?" She held it up against herself.

Lieutenant Bradshaw blushed and mumbled something like, "I think you'd look lovely in anything, madam." Then he said more clearly, "I'll be back for you in fifteen minutes. Will that be enough time madam?"

"Oh, it should be. Well, it will have to be won't it. Thank you Lieutenant."

The dress was a floor sweeping emerald green satin with a deeply scooped back and modest V-neck. It fit her curvaceous figure like a second skin with a double row of green covered buttons running down the low rear waist of the smooth bodice. Removing her slip, brasserie and the only good pair of shoes she had, a pair of black slippers, she carefully stepped into the dress and pulled it up over her shoulders, looking at herself in the mirror on the back of the en-suite door. "Typical men", she muttered, realising they'd have no idea that a dress of this kind required special under garments and a maid to help do it up. She twisted this way and that, but it was no use; she couldn't even get one of the little pearl-shaped buttons done up. With no other women on board, there was nothing else for it. She would simply have to ask Lieutenant Bradshaw to help her. She harrumphed to herself as she thought of the terror this was likely to create for the young man. Still, he had been ordered to assist her in any way necessary and she was hardly a young maiden anymore. She checked again, and felt that she was fairly well covered. Although she wasn't able to wear her only slip under a backless dress such as this, her half girdle covered her skin in the area. It wouldn't be that immodest and she felt sure the trustworthy young man would not go blabbing about the ship.

She checked herself in the mirror again and was thankful for her mother's set of pearls which, while they may not have been the most ideal necklace for the neck line, were certainly better than nothing. It was as she was considering her reflection that she noticed she was twisting her wedding band. She weighed whether to move it to her right hand or take it off altogether. What was the right thing to do in this sort of situation? In the end, she decided to leave it where it was.

At the allotted time, the knock came at the door again and expecting the Lieutenant, Ruth flung it open without checking through the peep hole first as she usually did.

Lieutenant Bradshaw and Captain Whitlock both stood in the corridor and both men bowed in formal greeting.

"You look stunning, Mrs Cole," Hunter said.

"Thank you Captain Whitlock," Ruth replied equally formally, guessing he preferred to use her proper title in front of others. "But I do have a bit of a problem. I need a maid to do me up at the back." Ruth caught two sets of eyes widen in unison. "Would you mind awfully giving a girl a hand?" Without waiting for an answer she turned on the spot, presenting her back to the two men.

Without a word, the two men took a side of buttons each and began to work. The Captain was just finishing his second button by the time the Lieutenant had finished his entire row and took over from the Captain.

"You seem to be an expert at buttons Lieutenant," the Captain teased him.

"Three nieces. Triplets," Lieutenant Bradshaw said in his usual laconic way.

"Well surely you didn't help them into their evening gowns...did you?" Ruth asked.

"They are only young tykes, just starting school when I left. My sister died shortly after she birthed them you see, and I've helped my ma plenty in getting them dressed and just well, looking after them."

"Well, sorry to hear that lad."

"Gosh yes, that's terrible. But no wonder you are so good with Jean."

"Actually, the Lieutenant proposes that he will stay here and look after Jean for you tonight."

"But she needs to eat too."

"Well, I'm sure he can rustle up something for her. Bradshaw?"

"Yes sir. Come on sweetheart." He took Jean's hand and led her away. Jean had gotten very used to Lieutenant Bradshaw over the past week and Ruth was reassured to see she was chirpy and excited to be in his company.

"She looks like a baby chimpanzee holding the hand of the Lieutenant," Hunter remarked as they watched them disappear down the corridor. "I mean in a charming sort of fashion."

Ruth smiled, because her thoughts had run more or less along the same lines.

The rest of the evening progressed happily enough. If Ruth was to be less than gracious she would have said the evening was slightly stilted and odd at times being the only female amongst a room full of male guests at a formal dinner party. But the Ship's Captain and the Major were delightful company as was Captain Whitlock who was never far from her side, and usually slightly behind her staring at her bare back, if she interpreted correctly.

There was dance music put on, but nobody danced. Ruth was itching to get onto the dance floor with Captain Whitlock, or any of the officers for that matter, and she did whisper the idea to Hunter. But despite the music, dancing was apparently not on the cards. He whispered back that it wouldn't be fair to the others if he was to dance with her. On reflection, she thought that perhaps it might look a bit vulgar to be dancing so soon after being widowed. Although who knew if those sorts of rules still applied in a situation like this.

The talk of the evening was the latest war news that had come over the ship's long range receiver. Colombo had been attacked by the Japanese. Yet again, it seemed that fortune had been smiling upon Ruth allowing her to get out just in time.

At night's end, Hunter escorted her back to her cabin. Initially they were accompanied by a group of several officers all heading the same way. Each member of the party peeled off as they reached their respective cabins and the number had dwindled to just four by the time they arrived at the corridor to Ruth's cabin.

"Perhaps a stroll down the promenade, Mrs Cole," Hunter murmured into her ear with his trembling hand lightly placed at the small of her back.

Feeling a knot of excitement, she readily nodded her agreement.

"Evening, gentlemen," Hunter said to the pair of lieutenants, whilst turning Ruth towards the nearest companionway. Before the others could even reply, he had whisked her away.

The promenade deck was full of men lounging about, and an odd wolf whistle floated across to them, causing Hunter to say aloud that perhaps it wasn't a good idea to come out here after all.

"Oh no, please don't lets go back just yet," Ruth pleaded. "I just love being out here at night."

"You like the sea?"

"Oh yes, voyaging is something I've done a lot of. I never tire of it. Maybe it's in the blood with my father being a navy man. Though of course I much prefer a voyage during peacetime."

"Have you ever been aboard a small sailing yacht?"

"Once or twice in Hongkong I sailed with father and my brother Jeffrey. It was pleasant out on the deck, but I dare say it would not have been pleasant sleeping aboard. The bunks were squeezed into nooks and crannies below decks. It reminded me of the time Father showed me inside a submarine. It all felt a bit close. I didn't like it terribly much."

"But you don't appear to suffer from seasickness?"

"No, indeed. I've never had that misfortune."

The wolf whistles had turned into a menacing hum of whispers and crude comments.

"I really must insist we head back," Hunter said.

They turned into another hatchway and wound their way back in the direction of the row of cabins where Ruth was situated.

"Where is your cabin, Hunter?" Ruth asked sweetly.

"Oh no! Don't even suggest it, you wicked, wicked siren. You'll have me spellbound before long," Hunter said swiftly. She could tell he was in jest, but his breathing had become noticeably heavier.

"Suggest what?" Ruth asked innocently, playing along.

"I think we'd better head back to your daughter and the Lieutenant." And just like that Hunter's tone and posture had affected the no-nonsense officer's mask that he hid behind.

Ruth said nothing. Turning back into her corridor, where just minutes before they had said good night to the other officers, they found the length of it was empty. Hunter stopped and turned to Ruth.

"I do appreciate your company this evening. I've been the luckiest man on the ship tonight. You look a million dollars in that dress."

"It was awfully kind of the captain to allow me to keep it, wasn't it?" Ruth said. "He never did explain how he came to have it."

"No, he kept beginning the story, but then he always got side-tracked onto other tangents. Though I expect it was simply a case of lost property that the ship's purser has held onto."

There was an awkward silence where Ruth did not reply to his comment. Truth be told neither of them were thinking about dresses. Ever so slowly, Hunter leaned in towards Ruth. His clear hazel eyes had become murky and cryptic, but even so Ruth recognised that brief moment before a man was about to kiss a girl. Ruth was mesmerised. She could feel herself burning under his intense simmering gaze.

"Ruth, I want desperately to …"

And then the moment was gone. Interrupted by a group of voices about to turn into the corridor. Hunter couldn't have stepped away from Ruth faster if she had prodded him with his own ceremonial sword. He held out his arm for her to take and despite the fact that each of their hearts was racing, they walked quietly towards her cabin. For a short stretch of time she had felt that she was living in a world full of possibilities, but now it was time to return to her loathsome reality. A world where Ruth was a widow with a child in a war-zone with no security and no future at all to speak of.

Bradshore was anxiously waiting for their return.

"I think she needs her napkin changed, Mrs Cole," he greeted them. Sure enough the smell was proof that he was right. I would have done it, but I don't like to go searching through your cupboards.

"Well, that's my cue to leave you to it, Mrs Cole. Good evening," Hunter said bemusedly and the two men escaped quickly.

After that evening, the remainder of the voyage passed without much of note happening other than a bit of nasty weather as they crossed the Australian bight. There were no attacks from enemy ships and no more parties. Captain Whitlock continued to take Ruth for her evening stroll, but he never crossed the line between friendship and courting again. Their conversation remained neutral. On the plus side, they covered many topics and really got to know each other.

Lieutenant Bradshaw relaxed a little around Ruth and she occasionally got a few superfluous sentences out of him. Jean had really taken to the young officer and cried whenever he left, so the Lieutenant visited more often. Sometimes he took Jean off on a tour of inspection, "to make sure everything was ship-shape," which of course was not one of the Lieutenant's responsibilities, so Ruth really didn't know what they got up to together. But "ship-ship" became a part of Jean's vocabulary. Ruth learnt to trust him not to let the toddler slip overboard and the child always came back exhausted which suited her perfectly.

The day finally came when they steamed into the calmer waters of a massive bay known as Port Phillip Bay. As the pilot arrived to take them in to the Melbourne docks Ruth had already said her goodbyes to both the Major and the Captain of the ship and to many of the other officers whom she had met. Her bags were packed and left by the cabin door to be collected. She propped the door open and sat waiting on her bed until they were ready for her to depart. Eventually the Lieutenant arrived.

"Oh," said Ruth, unable to hide the disappointment in her voice. "I thought Captain Whitlock was going to take me to the station."

"Don't worry Mrs Cole. He will be waiting for you at the gangway. But first you just need to complete your quarantine procedures. There is an immigration officer waiting for you in the first class dining room, if you'll only accompany me up there now."

Before long the ship had berthed at a wharf and with her paperwork all in order, Hunter arrived to escort her.

When they were finally standing on the wharf Jean had them in stitches exaggerating the feeling of being unsteady on her feet after the voyage. Kneeling down to the toddler, the Lieutenant ruffled her hair and told her to be good for her ma. Then he shook Ruth's hand and shot back up the gangplank.

As they looked about for a wharf trolley, a woman holding a clipboard rushed up to them.

"Gosh, it looks like I nearly missed you. You see it was only at the last minute that I heard there were any civilians on board this ship. Sorry, I haven't even introduced myself," she said hurriedly after noticing Ruth and Hunter's confused looks. "Miss Coates. I'm from the Department of Labour and Public Health. It's my job to see that evacuees are housed and cared for."

"Oh, hello," said Ruth. "But I'm not staying in Melbourne. I'm taking a train to Perth, where I have family."

"Well that's excellent. You'll do so much better with the support of family. Can I just give you these pamphlets. They are designed to help those that will be staying within the jurisdiction of the Victorian Government, but I expect Western Australia has similar practices in place. For starters, your train fare will be paid for by the Government. Now, let me get a trolley for your luggage. Do you know the way to the station?"

The woman chatted away while a porter pushed the trolley just ahead of the group. They crossed an area set aside for parking cars and engaged a taxi. Here Miss Coates wished her luck and said goodbye. Sitting in the back seat with Jean in between them, Ruth had so many things she needed to say to Hunter before it was too late. But it was Jean who spoke first.

"Little Brad come?"

"Little what darling?" Ruth asked distracted.

"If I'm not mistaken I think she is trying to ask if Lieutenant Bradshaw is coming with us," Hunter interpreted correctly. "No he's not coming darling."

Ruth stifled a giggle and soon both Hunter and Ruth dissolved into peals of laughter.

"What a great name," Hunter said. "He'll never live it down when I tell the boys. Little Brad, he's the very opposite of little."

And they continued laughing, even though it wasn't that funny. Perhaps it was just what they needed to relax and blow off a bit of pressure. Ruth finally calmed down enough to wipe the tears from her eyes.

When she opened them again, it was to find Hunter's mouth on hers. It all happened so fast. One minute she was giggling, the next he was kissing her with a desperation that left her gasping when he pulled away. Ruth wasn't going to let him go that easily. She put her hand behind his head and pulled him back to her. This time when he claimed her lips, she responded just as eagerly.

After losing herself for a moment, Ruth realised the lengthy kiss was outré. Forcing herself to pull back, she instead pressed her forehead to his and breathed in his masculine scent, wishing the moment never to end. But eventually, they each leaned back in their seats feeling a little embarrassed considering both the taxi driver and Jean were in the car. Although Jean sitting beneath their embrace was sucking her thumb obliviously and the driver was humming a tune and pretending that he hadn't noticed their improper behaviour.

"Hunter, the best thing that has come out of all this has been meeting you. If only it was another time and place, I would have very much enjoyed developing our friendship."

"Ruth my darling, I think you know how fond I am of you."

At that moment the taxi came to a stop in front of the large station building.

"This is the place, I believe," Hunter told her before asking the driver to wait for his return.

Soon they were standing in front of a large board displaying the timetable.

Trans Australian Express to Adelaide and Perth dep 1545 hours.

"That looks like your train. You'll only have to wait a few hours. Book your baggage in first and then you'll have plenty of time for lunch. Have you got enough money for meals and a taxi at the other end?" Hunter asked.

"Oh yes, thank you. That is presuming they'll allow me to change my Pounds Sterling here."

"It's a major station. I don't expect that will be a problem."

"There's so much more I want to say to you Hunter."

"I know, but as much as I'd like to stay and keep you company my orders were to take you safely to the station and return immediately to the ship. I don't want to risk being written up for AWOL. It wouldn't be a good example to set for the enlisted men." He laughed humourlessly. "Even though there are always rumours on these troopships that one officer or another is being court martialled," he said. "I don't want to make it true."

Ruth wasn't interested in his prattling conversation. "But we haven't even exchanged addresses. Would you like me to write to you perhaps?"

"I'd like that very much."

Ruth fished in her handbag for her address book and Hunter wrote in the address and phone number of his two aunties who lived in a bay on Auckland's north shore. In return, Ruth tore out a sheet and wrote down the address of Charlie's parents in Perth. "Do be a bit delicate if you write. After all, they may not approve of me having a gentleman friend so soon after Charlie's death. I've only met them the once."

"Are you sure going to Perth is the right thing to do?" he asked her.

"Actually, I'm dreading the reception I might get there. But I have to think of Jean. Charlie would want me to go to his family, for her sake. Besides, until I can get Charlie's pension sorted out, I'll have no income."

Hunter pocketed the address and then at a loss for words, he embraced her into a tight hug.

"Take care Hunter," Ruth said against the wool of his uniform.

After a moment, they stepped apart. "Good bye Ruth. Good bye Jeanie. God bless." Hunter sauntered towards the door.

Ruth stood amongst her belongings. Her trunk, attaché case, handbag, plus the carpetbag she had purchased in Colombo which now contained Mrs Spooner's linen and the paper wrapped evening gown, and the baby carriage in which her toddler was valiantly trying to climb out of. In all it was just too much for one woman to deal with on her own. Especially an emotionally charged woman who genuinely felt as though she had just been widowed the second time. Her lips were still tender from his demanding kiss, but her heart was grinding away so erratically it hurt.

She stared down at the little address book which she still clutched in her hand and flicked through to W to read the address. As well as his contact details, he had written, *"You have touched my heart in a way that no other woman ever has. Love Hunter."*

Her eyes immediately sought him before he left the building, hoping he would turn and wave. Sure enough he was already standing by the door watching her. He had seen that she had read his words and he blew her a cheeky kiss before ducking out the door.

She closed her eyes tightly, trying to hold onto that last impression of him. She knew it was unlikely she'd ever see him again.

How different her rushed romance with Hunter was from her conventional courtship with Charlie. It had been a slow waltz with Charlie, whereas it was love at first sight with Hunter. *Love?* Was that how she truly felt? She wasn't sure she could call it love. And anyway it was over now. Over before it had really begun. But that kiss! So full of need. So passionate. She still felt giddy about it.

After a moment she opened her eyes and looked back down at the words he'd written. That's when her eyes caught sight of another name: *Muriel & Robert Wallace*—Charlie's youngest sister and her husband.

At that moment the direction forward couldn't have been clearer if there had been an arrow pointing the way. Ruth decided she'd go north to Sydney instead of all the way across the continent to Western Australia. She knew Charlie would probably approve of that idea just as much or even in preference to Perth. After all, the original idea had been to go to his sister—before the whole fiasco of Colombo.

Ruth also knew that Hunter's ship was dropping about half its passengers off at Sydney. Of course, that had nothing to do with her decision she told herself.

14
SYDNEY MARCH 1942

RUTH COLE

The *Spirit of Progress* Express to Sydney wasn't a direct train. Ruth found it necessary to change trains several times because of some ridiculous anomaly in the track widths between Victoria and New South Wales. She didn't fully understand it all even though a strongly accented man who sat opposite her in her second class carriage had delighted in explaining it to her. It was all she could do just to keep up with his vernacular. In fact he had flapped his tongue on the subject for so long that Ruth's head hurt. She knew she would have to lose him on the next platform or she'd be stuck with him for the whole journey.

The first change of trains came when they left the Melbourne metropolitan area to connect with the state railway. Ruth took the opportunity to use the ladies conveniences on the platform which were easier to manage than the on-board lavatories. While she was at the hand basin, she struck up a conversation with another mother with a small child. Sympathetic to Ruth's dilemma with the irritating passenger, she invited Ruth to sit with her and introduced herself as Gladys.

The man appeared to be most put out when he finally found Ruth. He almost looked like he was going to climb across to the window seat beside Ruth. Recognising his intention, both women promptly put their children on the seats beside them. The man cast around and found a seat across the aisle from Ruth. Ruth gave Gladys a dismayed look, and fortunately her new friend came to her rescue again.

"Not in the army then Mr?" Gladys called over to him, just as he was about to plonk his bottom onto the vinyl. "My husband is in Europe doing *his* bit," she added pointedly so that he could be under no illusion as to what she was getting at.

The man had nearly parked himself into the seat, but on hearing her question, he swiftly swung back up again. "There's some of us do, and some of us better placed elsewhere," he replied vaguely before hightailing it through to the next carriage.

"Just as I thought. He's a ruddy shirker," Gladys said after the man left. "Mind you my husband isn't in Europe either, I made that part up. He *is* in the RAAF, but he is based just up the tracks in Wagga Wagga. I suppose your husband's doing his bit then miss?" she asked Ruth carefully.

Ruth began to tell her tale and the two women wiled away the miles in deep conversation until the train stopped again. Both women looked around them in surprise as they seemed to have stopped between stations. The view out the windows showed a fire-blackened lunar landscape where scorched earth and charred tree stumps dominated as far as the eyes could see. Ruth was both fascinated and horrified, while her new companion explained that a bush fire had run riot through the area the previous year despite the Railways' policy of maintaining fire breaks along the length of the tracks.

Dotted amongst the apparent wasteland, haggard trees prevailed, still showing signs of life despite everything they'd endured. In fact the longer Ruth looked, the more signs of life she saw. Here and there bold tufts of grass and fronds of bracken had begun to re-emerge. In the distance, a flock of beasts too small to distinguish which species were gradually moving up a scorched hillside. It appeared as if mother nature was reclaiming what the wildfire had stolen from her.

While the train rested on her tracks, Ruth was glad of the air conditioning to keep them cool, but it was well into the evening before the carriage began to move again. Already the cabin lights had been dimmed to facilitate sleeping and they tried to make the best of it in their upright seats.

It was nearly dawn when the train pulled into Albury station near the border between the two states. They were now way behind schedule. Here they were required to change to another train. Shortly before lunch they reached Wagga Wagga Station where Ruth bid farewell to her female companion. There was another long unexplained wait here, although Ruth overheard someone suggesting that it had been necessary to take on extra supplies to supplement the journey.

Just before sunset the train finally arrived into Sydney's Central Station, a full six hours late.

Ruth was nearly dead on her feet and Jean was bored and grizzly. Ruth struggled into a taxi and gave her sister-in-law's city address to the driver.

"Glebe it is then," the man said conversationally, as he pulled out of the taxi rank.

"You wouldn't happen to know if the Orcades is in port would you?"

she asked him hopefully.

"Yes as a matter of fact she was here at midday," he said. "I took a number of jobs to and from Garden Island. That's where all the troopships are coming in, if you didn't know, and there's been a few of those in the past couple of weeks. They are bringing our soldiers back home, now that the war has reached our doorstep. The Orcades, well I reckon she won't be in for long, judging by the comments I got from those disembarking. Did you know somebody on her? Your husband perhaps?"

"I was on her. I got off at Melbourne."

"Well that's a puzzle. And then you took a train to Sydney, when the ship was coming here anyway. Were you seasick?"

"No, nothing like that. I had expected to take a train to Perth, but then I changed my mind at the station."

"Well, my wife's a bit like that. Last week she went into the butcher supposedly to get a nice leg of mutton for my Sunday dinner and she just changed her mind at the counter and came out with a piece of pork for boiling instead. I says to her, I does, that I had been looking forward to me bit of roast mutton, and she says she wasn't of a mind to cook it. Come in from Colombo did you?"

"Yes, and before that Singapore."

"Heavens Mrs. You weren't caught up in all that mess up there were you? I've just been reading about that."

"Well yes, if you mean did I escape from the peninsular with the Japs on my heels then the answer is yes. We only just got away with our lives if the truth be known," she said embellishing the story a little seeing as how the man seemed to be lapping it up. "It was awful, the harbour was going up in flames behind us as we pulled out. The jap planes were often so low that you could see the pilots and our guns following them with trails of flak. Then our ship was torpedoed, but in the end we made it safely. My husband wasn't so fortunate. He didn't make it."

Despite the bravado, the tears which began to leak from her eyes were real. Her tired mind momentarily played over the death of her husband. With hardly time to devote to mourning, she'd largely been coping the last few weeks by purposely not thinking about him in any measure of depth at all. Her fleeting romance with Hunter had helped keep her mind busy. But now the news that she had probably missed his ship in port topped by a reminder of her husband was almost too much to maintain her stoic demeanour.

She noticed the taxi driver glance at her in the rear view mirror.

"Look luvee, I'm sorry to hear about that. And here's me prattling on about my wife and all. I'd be honoured if I could drop you off to your destination without payment."

"Oh that would be kind of you. Thank you awfully."

"A relative, is it? The address I'm taking you to?"

"Yes. My sister-in-law. I was going to go to Perth to my husband's parents but then I decided to go to his sister's instead. I just hope it works out."

"Well, I don't want to be the bringer of more bad news dear, but I read in the papers this morning that the train between Adelaide and Perth is about to be suspended, possibly for the duration of the war. So I hope you don't regret your decision to come here. And here we are. Hmmm. Are you sure this is the place?"

Ruth peered out of her side window. The building she was parked in front of was in a miserable row of tiny two level brick flats on a back street. Each unit appeared to be one room wide with its own front door and a single ground floor window covered in blackout material. Plucking up the courage, she stepped out onto the pavement and a moment later, thanked the driver for helping her through the front gate with all her luggage. As she stood looking about her and contemplating life in these shabby little abodes, she wondered if she should ask him to wait, but it was too late. He was already pulling back into the street.

She was about to knock on the door with an iron number "7" on it, when a woman from several doors down called out to her. "You there! What do you want?"

"Oh, hello. I'm looking for Muriel Wallace. She lives here I believe." Ruth lifted her hand again to knock, but was beginning to doubt anyone lived here. It had an empty feel about it.

"There's no point knocking on that door. The Wallaces packed up and left before Christmas."

"What? Why? Where have they gone?" Ruth exclaimed conflicted as to whether or not she should trust the woman or keep knocking. In the end, she went towards the woman.

"Mr Wallace found building work. It was some government project I believe out at Broken Hill. I was sorry to see them go, truth be known. They were good tenants."

"Broken Hill, did you say? Oh, I wish I hadn't let that taxi go."

"Taxi? My dear you're not from around here, I can see that. You'll need more than a taxi to get you to Broken Hill. The distance must be nearly 800 miles or more. Besides I have no forwarding address."

"800 miles?" Ruth gasped. "But I am so tired. I've come all the way from Singapore."

"Well, I can offer you a roof over your head."

"Really? That's so very kind of you."

"Not at all. The rent will be 4 shillings a night or 20/6d for the week. You'll not find a better deal than that. Payable in advance, no exceptions."

"Oh, I see!" Ruth exhaled in disappointment. She had thought the woman was kindly offering her a free bed.

"Linen is not included and it'll be an extra 2/6- if you want hot water. No gentlemen callers, no late nights and no nonsense from the child."

"Nonsense?"

"That's right. I have my other tenants to think of. You're to keep it quiet and not running around, interferin' in other people's business."

"Well, I guess I could pay for the one night and then I'll see tomorrow, if my daughter Jean is not too bothersome to the other tenants I might extend that to a week or more."

"Right-o, this way when you're ready!" the woman said sharply, unsure if Ruth was giving her cheek. "You'll see the flats aren't large, but they are furnished and happen that's what you'll need by the looks of you. There's a bedroom upstairs, and downstairs there's a kitchenette and an indoor water closet. But if you've a mind to bathe you'll have to do it out on the back verandah. Mrs Wallace had rigged up a curtain for her purposes, which is still there, but be warned it might just need a brush down for spiders. Not squeamish on that score are you?"

Here she paused to look at Ruth for a response, before continuing. "Given the time of evening, I might manage a little supper for you, but ordinarily you'll keep your own house and you'll keep it tidy and air it out regularly, keeping in mind the blackout regulations from sun down to sun rise. I don't want no ARP men tap-tapping on my window."

Ruth waited silently while the woman opened the door to the same flat as the Wallaces had rented.

"Haven't been able to rent this one out on a regular basis since they left. My name is Nora Watts. You can use my first name no worries. Here's your key, keep the place locked. I don't want them squatters getting in. I'll be back shortly with some supper, if you could have the rent ready by then. Oh, and no hanging washing out the front. There's a line out back for that."

Ruth looked around the self-contained flat. Just like it had appeared from the curb, it was shabby inside, but surprisingly clean enough. It would do for the night she thought. In the morning, she'd go and see if the Orcades was still in port, but she was just too worn out to go now. Anyway, she reasoned, it wasn't likely that they'd let her on board at this time of the evening.

The following day, she discovered that a tram line ran right down the middle of Glebe Point Road at the end of her street. A kindly matron showed her how to hop on and off and told her which station would get her closest to the naval base. Soon she was on her way all the way to St James Station near the Botanic Gardens. It was while she was trying to establish how to get to Garden Island from there that she was informed that HMS Orcades had indeed departed.

"Oh well," she said to Jean. "That's that then."

She had more immediate problems anyway. For starters, she had to get in groceries. Then there was extra supplies for Jean, writing paper, stamps, a newspaper and extra clothing. The weather currently was very pleasant if only slightly cooler than Singapore, but she knew winter was on its way and she had no idea how cold it might get in the weeks ahead. Besides Jean was growing daily. The clothes she had left with were already short on her arms and legs.

The thought of shopping lifted Ruth's spirits considerably. She was right on the edge of the bustling modern business precinct where there were bound to be a multitude of shops to explore. Ruth's preference was to shop in department stores, where she could drift between counters and find everything she needed without fuss. The only department store she had ever heard of in Sydney was the world famous Anthony Horderns. She knew by its reputation that it would carry everything she needed. She figured the giant store must be somewhere in the main shopping area so she set out to search for it.

As she pushed Jean deeper into the business district, the 19th century buildings rose up around her. Every block appeared to be made of the same straw-yellow stone and she began to feel uncomfortably enveloped inside the grid like web of streets. Soon she had lost all sense of direction. While the crowds of people were nothing in comparison to Singapore, everyone seemed to be in a greater hurry and unwilling to make eye contact, so Ruth was unable to ask for directions. Finding a particularly ornate building she realised it could only be the General Post Office. She hauled Jean's chair up the steps and left her at the door, while she nipped in to purchase a book of postage stamps.

The clerk at the counter told her that Anthony Horderns was a long walk down the street, but right across the road from the GPO was another department store that he recommended as just as good. On emerging back out into the strong sunlight she spotted the recommended place. It was a large multi-level store called David Jones and was situated on the opposite corner of George street leading around to Barrack Street. Ruth negotiated her way across the tram lines and stepped into the old fashioned interior.

Despite the layout, the selection inside seemed to be every bit as good as Robinsons in Singapore. The prices, however, were exorbitant in comparison. If she was to buy everything on her list, she realised she wouldn't have enough left for rent. It was obviously imperative that she'd need her husband's pension, but she had no idea how to go about that or even who to ask. First things first, she told herself, deciding to move onto another shop.

As she was making her way down the stairs to the street she came across a Red Cross booth, right inside the store, which seemed like providence considering their involvement in evacuees and repatriations. However, after briefly explaining her predicament to a sympathetic girl at the counter, she was told that they were American Red Cross and couldn't help directly. They were merely there to package David Jones care parcels being sent off to soldiers and POWs around the world. The girl did give her a Red Cross leaflet, which had a useful map on it with directions to the Australian Red Cross Society who were handling all evacuee affairs for British citizens. On the map, the friendly girl circled the building Ruth needed to find in Jamison Street. It looked simple. Just head out to the street and go north for three blocks.

Still completely disorientated, Ruth walked out on the street and turned south by mistake. After walking quite a way, she didn't find Jamison Street, but she did eventually came across a store called McCathies which had the most reasonable prices she'd seen yet. She purchased a few new undergarments and a dressing gown for herself, a cotton frock, vest & bloomers for Jean plus a suitable bag for carrying shopping. She also found a navy crepe dress for herself which was more in keeping with the local styles and which had been marked down to 29/11-. More than a week's rent she thought ruefully, before returning it to the rack.

Jean was getting tetchy so she headed back on the tram towards the western suburb of Glebe where her rented room was. On the way she made the decision to pay for the whole week's rent, since she had no other options at present.

She had passed a grocer that morning whose premises looked decent enough, so after she got off the tram she called in there before returning to the flat.

Unlike Singapore, rationing hadn't officially come in yet and coupons weren't necessary, although grocers were already restricting a few key items. Generally the produce was fresh and plentiful, even if the brands and choices were more limited than she was used to. Ruth's cooking repertoire was fairly basic anyway as was her kitchenette so it didn't matter to her particularly. In the end the only things she couldn't find at all were suitable spices and coconut milk for a good old Malayan curry. The items that were restricted were tea and sugar of which she was only allowed 2 oz and 2 lb respectively—more than she wanted anyway. Matches were more of a concern. The grocer would only sell Ruth three boxes of those.

Jean welcomed her bottle which she was finally able to make up and fell fast asleep, her tummy bulging. Ruth took the opportunity to go and find her landlady offering to pay the whole week's rent. She was horrified when the officious woman asked her to stop for a cup of tea. Ruth didn't dare turn the offer down.

Nora soon dragged Ruth's whole tragic story out of her. She was shocked to learn that Ruth was in mourning.

"But you can't go around dressed like that when you are mourning your husband. What will people think? All I can say is thank the lord your husband's sister was *not* here."

"I don't really have a choice as I've only got three day dresses with me and frankly packing mourning clothes was pretty much the last thing on my mind ... Nora." Ruth had to force herself to use the woman's first name. It felt very disrespectful, especially considering she didn't even like the woman. She'd never use another woman's first name back in Singapore. "If you must know, I had a look at frocks in town this morning. I saw a nice navy crepe, which I would have liked but I couldn't risk purchasing it. Not when I don't know how long it will be before I can access my widow's pension."

"Hmmph! Navy is hardly what I had in mind. Might I suggest you scoot around the corner to St Johns Church. They are running a thrift store for the needy and collecting for the Children's Clothing Fund. It's a new idea where people can donate clothing that they don't need and those who are in need can make use of it. You would have passed right by the church this morning, if only you'd come to me first. And talking of scooting, they have toys for children too. As for your pension, well I can't help you with that. I've no idea how you go about it, but perhaps Reverend Dryland will be able to help you. Might I also suggest you look for work."

"But I'm not qualified for anything."

"Look girlie, if there's one thing I can't stand it's people who can't or rather won't pull their weight in this world. My husband died seventeen years ago, but I don't go around moping in self-pity. No, I've got up and made a place for myself. Everybody is capable of doing something in my opinion. It's just a matter of wanting to. Cleaning for instance. Surely you know how to cook and clean?"

"Well, I did learn the basics at the convent school. But you know in Singapore you are expected to take a maid ... several maids. It helps the local community."

"Did you not do your own cooking? What about breakfast?"

"Well occasionally I prepared something myself. There was one time when Cookie, er that's the native woman who cooked for us, ah Cookie was poorly, and..." Ruth's voice trailed off as she took in the expression of disdain her landlady had clearly written across her face.

"Gardening?"

"Yes, I had quite a collection of orchids and other hanging plants. I was quite proud of them, although, well I guess our house boy did most of the work. But I did water them regularly and er, look at them."

"I was thinking more along the lines of potatoes and carrots," Nora said dryly. "That's the type of gardening they do around here. I don't think there is much call for orchids. In fact I can honestly say that I've never seen an orchid, nor would I know what to do with one if I did. What about sewing?

I expect you had a personal tailoress and all?"

"No, of course not. Actually, I'm rather a dab hand at needlework, if I do say so myself. Especially cross-stitch and smocking."

Nora just stared at her blankly.

"And knitting," Ruth added meekly.

"Well that's a start. There'll be wool at the Thrift Store and if you can get your hands on a pair of needles, you could knit your winter wardrobe. You could try to take in some mending jobs. Mind you, it'll take time to build up a clientele, get a name for yourself and such."

"I think I could do cleaning, if worst came to worst."

"Worst has come to worst. For you anyway. Go and get a paper and see if you can't sort something out. Mind I have a telephone for emergencies only. I'm not looking to be running back and forth up the street running messages for my tenants at all hours. If you have to phone for a job, you'll have to use the public booth at the post office on Glebe Point Road. You would have passed that this morning and all."

Nora got up to clear away the cups and Ruth took this as her cue to leave.

Returning to her sleeping toddler, she spent the next half hour writing some well overdue letters. She had already begun one letter to her aunties while she was in Colombo. This she now finished, and she also wrote to Charlie's parents. She had thought she would be telling them the sad news in person, but a letter would have to suffice. She carefully blackened the edge of the paper to mark that it contained distressing news of the worst kind before sealing the envelope. Finally, she wrote a brief note to Hunter in New Zealand advising him of her new address in Sydney. She didn't have much else to say to him, so she promised she'd write again tomorrow or the following day. Presumably his ship would get in before her letter, but either way, he'd get the letter sooner or later.

She waited until Jean woke up and then left the flat. Leaving the chair behind, she took her little hand and made her way slowly to the local post office and then across to the church where she managed to pick up several items from the sympathetic vestry woman who was volunteering there.

Jean did some shopping of her own. She picked out a set of wooden stackable blocks and a *Pop-Eye the Sailor Man* bead doll, which she promptly named Little Brad. The wooden beads were attached to a central piece of rope, which Ruth later discovered she could conveniently tie onto the baby chair so that Jean could take the doll with her when they went out without fear of dropping it onto the pavement.

This proved very useful the following day when Ruth decided to try to find Jamison Street again. By mid-morning, she succeeded and spent the next two hours filling out forms and meeting with the Red Cross representatives. Jean happily played with Little Brad in between naps and the Red Cross volunteers even heated her midday bottle.

Ruth managed to achieve several things in the Red Cross office. She registered her current address and reiterated her need to find her father and brother in Hongkong. She advised them of the date of death of her husband.

There currently was no official compilation of missing civilian persons, but the Australian Red Cross had knowledge of dozens of people suspected missing and they thought that this number could run to the thousands. They didn't even have lists of military persons missing in Singapore and this was their priority over civilians, although the Red Cross in Geneva was beginning to receive jumbled uncollated prisoner lists out of Hongkong.

What Ruth really needed at this stage was financial assistance and to this end, the Red Cross couldn't give her any immediate hope. They helped her fill out the application for her Police Widow's Pension. These forms needed to be sent to UK's Ministry of Pensions Office in London and the Red Cross could do this on her behalf. No pension could be issued without a death certificate, so the Red Cross could also assist in ascertaining her husband's status, but couldn't guarantee how long that would take even with the information provided by Ruth. It all had to be verified. If successful, she would be eligible for 27 shillings per week.

"But in the meantime, shouldn't I be able to draw on his wages? I mean if I can't prove that he is dead then he must be still alive. Either way, there should be wages owing, shouldn't there?"

"It should be that simple," that woman sympathised, "but in practice it may not be. Why, just last week I had a similar case of the wife of a merchant navy sailor who can't access her entitlements until they know whether he has been captured or whether he sunk with his ship. Unfortunately, the Japanese have not responded to any enquiries in Singapore. We were in irregular contact with the Singapore Red Cross up until approximately five days after the surrender. But communications with not only the Straits Settlement but the whole of Malaya is no longer functioning. We simply do not know what has happened to the likes of the telegraph operators, let alone the Red Cross volunteers, let alone the general populace. We do know that all soldiers have been interned by the Japanese and we suspect that the civilians may have been too or possibly are under house arrest. The best case scenario is that they will put the civilians onto ships and repatriate them to Australia since we are closest. There's no chance of that with the military of course."

"So, how am I to pay rent and put food on the table?"

"Well, first let's establish if you have any bank savings and which bank are they with?"

"Charlie moved our savings, such as they are, to the Post Office Savings Bank two years ago. We were with HSBC, but we thought our money would be safer at the Colonial Post Office bank. Is there are branch here in Sydney?"

"I think there might be inside Anthony Horderns, but I'm not entirely sure," the girl said.

When Ruth left the Red Cross building, only one thing was clear to her: there was a need for the British government to set up an organisation which had the authority to co-ordinate information received about missing persons and assist evacuated British and Dominion civilians. At the moment, no such organisation existed and in the void, the Red Cross volunteers were doing their best with few resources.

Back onto George Street, Ruth caught a tram down past the town hall until she finally came to the vast acreage of Anthony Horderns Emporium. It was impossible to miss, being the size and colour of a grand palace. Not to mention, the massive letters running the height and length of the sixth floor declaring it to be the famous store. At the street level, gay banners, empire flags & awnings stretched out along the street frontage. The doorman helped her up the entrance stairs and directed her to a bank of lifts which could take her to any of the six stories. Ruth decided to eat first and found a most elegant cafeteria. Before long, a floor walker approached her and suggested that she may like to take Jean to the children's play area, which was currently decorated in the Easter theme evident throughout the shop.

Indeed she found a large area set aside for children with a giant Easter bunny and little ride-on trains, seesaws and bouncers, etc. The only problem was that Jean, who had never seen such delights in her short tragedy-filled life, didn't want to leave. She wailed and gripped hold of the side of the train so hard that Ruth found herself unable to pull her free for fear of pulling the arms from her sockets. Eventually, a nursery aide suggested she leave the child in her care while Ruth finished her shopping.

Unfortunately, the kiosk for the Dominion Post Office Savings Bank was unable to allow her to withdraw any money, despite the clerk consulting with the manager. While she was assured that her savings would be safe—apparently the majority of the company's wealth was invested in British bonds and very little would fall into Japanese hands, there was still the necessity to verify her savings book against the records they held centrally and all Singapore accounts were temporarily frozen. Who was to say, for instance, that her husband hadn't withdrawn funds since she had left Singapore? Ruth tried to tell them that her husband had been killed before she left, but to no avail. They needed proof of his death.

Again, it was all coming down to the need to get a death certificate for her husband. It was as if her own life was on hold until she had that piece of paper.

During the remainder of the week, Ruth spent her time applying for positions that had been advertised in the papers. By Thursday she had secured a cleaning job for a woman who lived in Kings Cross, an affluent suburb on the easternmost side of the business district. The entire interview had transpired over the telephone, and so Ruth hadn't mentioned Jean to the woman. In fact, she had hardly given thought to what she'd do with her while she was working.

She was due to start the following Monday, and all equipment would be supplied. So wearing one of her newly acquired outfits and taking an appliqued apron to put over the top, she took the tram into central station where she transferred to Kings Cross. Then using her Red Cross map, she found her way to the very smart address.

The front door was opened by another maid presumably, who looked her up and down and frowned briefly. Ruth didn't miss the unimpressed look the woman had given her before her face resumed a pleasant expression. She was taken into the kitchen and asked to wait. On the way through the halls and passing several open doorways, Ruth perceived that the owner or someone in the household was a watercolourist with an aptitude for very modern works. Half-finished boards were stacked in piles here and there, many of them portraits of a kind. The furnishings, on the other hand, were old fashioned and had seen better days; curtains were faded and rugs were frayed.

"Heavens!" exclaimed a woman's voice behind Ruth. "Well, I didn't expect two of you."

Ruth turned to see a woman wearing a pair of baggy woollen trousers and an old paint stained shirt with the sleeves rolled up to the elbows, staring at her.

"This won't do, no not at all." She didn't pause to introduce herself nor even to establish who Ruth was. "What do you propose to do with the child while you are working? I can't have it running around here, messing with my work, creating distractions. The place is not suited to that. She'll be messing the place up faster than you can clean it."

"But...."

"No, I'm sorry, but the job offer was for a single woman. Not a woman and a child. Mrs Keane, will you see her to the door please." With that, she turned and strode from the room.

"I thought there'd been a mistake, when I saw you at the door," said Mrs Keane, the maid who had shown her in. "Now it's going to be another week before I can get some help around here," she finished reproachfully, before walking back to the front door and indicating that Ruth was to leave.

Ruth went back to her newspapers and endless telephone calls. She asked the nice woman at the church for advice, but all she could offer was a crèche during the Sunday morning sermons. They did not run any other child care service.

Nora was equally unhelpful. "Looking after children is not my business. Never had any of my own and don't intend to take in those of others."

Ruth wrote a depressing letter to Hunter, telling him her news. She paid for another week's rent and determined to go back to the Red Cross on Monday. According to the pamphlets they had given her, there was emergency accommodation available at the YWCA. At this rate, she'd need it.

The Australian Red Cross volunteer put her name down for a billet. Families across the city were hosting billets, but the majority of these wanted soldiers on leave, not women and children. Hosting a soldier was looked upon as helping the war effort. Hosting women and children didn't have the same prestige. There was therefore quite a waiting list, as several boat loads of evacuees had come in during the past few weeks. The majority of those waiting for billets were paying for hotel accommodation in and around the Bondi district. Nevertheless, the YWCA was always an option. The ARC volunteer recommended she stay where she was, if she could still afford it. Ruth reckoned she could last one more week and reiterated how urgently she needed a billet.

She left the office still without any news of her relatives in Hongkong and no official death notice for her husband.

Ruth started looking further afield for jobs. She went door to door at the local shops, asking for counter work. But nobody would permit her to bring in a child. She heard that Anthony Horderns ran a crèche for the children of working mothers. She went in to see about any possible work and was told that they'd only just awarded a position in the hat department earlier that week. They put her name down for future positions.

By the following Friday, she returned home feeling dejected and almost reconciled to the idea of moving into the YWCA. She was also thinking about the possibility of taking a train out to Broken Hill. This could be risky if things didn't work out, as it was even less likely she'd find work in a provincial town. She could write again to her in-laws and ask if they had Muriel's address, but as yet they had not responded to her first letter.

She was looking forward to a hot cup of tea, but that awful landlady was calling to her.

"Yoo-hoo! I say, Yoo-hoo. Ruth! I need a word with you."

"What have I done wrong now," Ruth muttered remembering the telling off she had received for using all the space on the clothes line with Jean's flannelette squares. Nora had been very snappy with Ruth ever since she had explained that she wouldn't be able to pay for a third week.

"The telegraph man came by while you were out. I have it here. Right here, I tell you."

Ruth dashed across to Nora's front door. The telegram was from New Zealand. She ripped open the envelope, expecting it to be from Hunter.

"It's from New Zealand," Ruth told Nora who was standing waiting to see what could be so urgent as to require a telegram.

"And?"

"It's from a friend. Oh heck! That's good of him. He's offering to pay for a passage by steamer to Auckland in New Zealand."

"What sort of friend? What'll he want in return?"

"Oh, it's not that sort of thing," Ruth brushed off her criticism. "I'm sure he is being very kind. I'm to stay with his elderly aunts when I get there. He wants me to confirm a booking at P&O as soon as I get this telegram. The name of the ship is blacked out for censorship I suppose and no dates. Oh, its all very hush hush, but this could be exactly what I need."

15
SYONAN-TO MAY 1942

CHARLIE COLE

Daily life for the internees quickly established itself into an oppressive routine. This was no detention centre merely aimed at restricting movement of enemy citizens. The civilian internees at Changi Gaol were being held as though they were ordinary prisoners. Furthermore, the quality of life was significantly lower than that which had been experienced by the Gaol's previous criminal and political prisoners.

Cells were overcrowded, bedding uncommon, nutrition inadequate, exercise restricted, hygiene deplorable and basic medical provisions were non-existent. The only thing in plentiful supply was physical brutality which was wreaked upon the men, women, children, and invalids daily.

On top of all this, the Imperial Army were unable (or perhaps purposely hindering efforts) to furnish the Red Cross database in Switzerland with lists of prisoners.

In three years' time, after Victory Over Japan Day, the world would discover that the primitive and cruel injustices inflicted on the people of Singapore were only the tip of the iceberg compared to the way the Japanese were treating Chinese and Europeans throughout many other parts of South East Asia.

But our heroes in B-3-2, (that is Charlie, Giles and Frank), had no idea about any of that. Nor did they have any idea how long their incarceration would last. Each day seemed intolerably long and the desire to find out reliable information on the state of the war was immensely tempting.

Radios were contraband—not just in the Gaol but also in the Changi barracks. Somehow though, somewhere, there was at least one set and possibly more, which were feeding the rumour mills. And it wasn't good news that reached the prisoners.

The Allies seemed to be losing on every front and the men began to realise that there would be no quick end to their internment.

Many of the Indian & Punjab turncoats were now cruel masters. Perhaps more correctly termed "sub-masters" because no matter how hard they tried to align themselves to the Japanese, they were still considered inferior even to the lowest ranking Japanese infantryman. During these early days, they seemed to have free reign to reap terror amongst the civilian and POW populations in Changi. The Japanese soldiers appeared only to be interested in guarding the perimeters. Day to day guarding of the gaol prisoners was left to these INA soldiers.

Conversely, there were many Indian and Punjab military or police who had no love for the Japanese and who had good intentions towards their old masters. For these men, signing themselves over to the INA had been a matter of survival and many remained secretly loyal to their Colonial principals. Week by week, life under the Japanese was becoming worse than it had been under the British and Dutch and many British Indian Army men silently lamented the Indian National Army.

Dalip remained one such person, and because he regularly travelled between camps, he became a great source of information. It was also though Dalip, that the men in Cell B32 were able to barter for mattresses and blankets quite early in their incarceration. Contact with locals was limited, but still possible in those first weeks and if they had something to barter with, they could get in limited supplies from Singapore. Occasionally, small groups of incarcerated prisoners were even allowed to drive into Singapore for supplies. Though none of the three men in B32 were ever given this privilege and before long, the vehicles were taken and the practice was prohibited.

The routine in the gaol began at 7:00 am each day with the Tenko or roll call. This of course was really 6:00 am in *pre-capitulation* time. The internees soon came to know and fear Tenko.

The routine never differed except if there were to be punishments dished out. It would start with lining up in rows facing North-East, towards Tokyo. Soldiers would then walk amongst the rows as they counted each prisoner. Inevitably they would lose count and have to start all over again. Then, when the prison's commandant arrived, (a position held at first by Tominaga and later Susuki), they would be told to bow, "Kerei!" Always the orders given in an angry shout. The Commandant might bark out a short speech which would be translated line by line by an interpreter. The interpreter at Changi Gaol was a Eurasian prisoner.

"You are now all prisoners of the Shōwa Emperor Hirohito. You have dishonour upon your shoulders and disgrace written on your faces. You have been abandoned by your families in England. They are disgusted with you for your surrender. You are no longer British masters. You are no longer wealthy Dutchmen. You are not worthy of my time. You are not worthy to look upon my face or the faces of any Nippon soldier. Your lives are worthless. Even a dog has more value to us. But we are an honourable people. We will continue to feed you until the Emperor decides your fate. You will work and you will be satisfied."

Sometimes he would spell out changes to their routine or inform them of new rules and recently outlawed contraband. He would remind them that they must stop and bow whenever they passed a Nippon soldier. At first they were expected to bow to the Punjab guards too, but months later the Japanese decided that the Punjab guards were overstating their rank and this obligation was revoked.

Until the Commandant arrived, they would be forced to stand in their lines. The Commandant was apparently a busy man, because they often had to wait for lengthy periods. Occasionally, someone would collapse in the heat, or faint from extended periods of bowing where the blood would collect in their heads. These people were sometimes left on the ground but at other times they were beaten until they stood again. A few of these unfortunates died in the process. Sometimes the soldiers would allow the prisoners on either side to help them to their feet. Other times they would not and unconscious person lay on the ground until Tenko was over.

There were many children housed in the prison in the women's quarters. Although the Japanese were generally benevolent to children, during Tenko they too required to stay in strict lines. Those that were too young to reason with, would often cry or even scream during the longest tenkos. Mother's would desperately try to comfort & quieten them in their arms. The Japanese considered any mother who could not control her children ought to be punished. Exhausted from standing so long and near fainting, it was not unheard of for an infant to slip from its mother's arms onto the ground.

Fortunately, most tenkos only lasted a quarter hour or so, after which prisoners would go about their business. There were no work parties in those early weeks, but general duties around the Gaol were done by roster.

Kitchen staff would get to work cooking their first meal of the day, which might be served just before midday. This generally consisted of a few spoonfuls of rice porridge or even an oat porridge. When stores of oats in Singapore ran out, the rice porridge or kunji became the breakfast staple.

In the Gaol, there were shower facilities but no running water. So the bucket allowance of water had to be carried to the shower room and carefully doled out. None of the men in B32 had toothbrushes, so they would gargle water and then be sure to swallow it. One of the prisoners on Floor-3 hid a bar of soap under a sink and it was commonly understood that it was there to be shared, sparingly. The men would each use it every other day on underarms or groins until it ran out. Then they would work together to smuggle in a replacement, using code-words to advise of its arrival. Although there were no explicit instructions forbidding soap in the camp, the men soon discovered that any luxury could be taken from them as punishment. Examples of tooth pastes and powders, shaving soap and Brylcreem being taken away from other parts of the Gaol was common knowledge, so the men felt it better not to let on that they had it in the first place. It was a testament to the comradeship of the internees, that as the months wore on, no prisoner on Floor 3 was selfish enough to steal the soap for themselves. However, there were often weeks when after running out, a replacement took a while to source and eventually, when supplies of this sort became unobtainable in Singapore, they had to make do without. Small beard scissors and cut throat razors were also secreted items that were generally thought of as contraband. While the PoWs in the Changi barracks took great pride in keeping up their shaven appearance, the civilian population were not so disciplined. Beards became commonplace and tearing beard hair out by hand was a common punishment. The problem eventually all but resolved itself, as nutritional intake became smaller and smaller, body hair stopped growing for most. Even children's head hair grew thin.

After Tenko and again after the midday meal the children would be allowed to run around outside, but within the prison compound. Cleaning parties of adults would do their best to clean the kitchen and bowls. Cutlery, other than spoons, had been confiscated. The prison kitchens did not have adequate supplies of bowls or plates for the swollen prison population so the inmates made use of a variety of other objects, such as half tin cans to eat from and invariably used their fingers to eat with, native style.

Other cleaning parties went off to attend to other duties around the various gaol buildings. For the large part they were kept under supervision by the regular prison guards. As the months wore on, the regular Indian guards were often replaced by Koreans. In these days of War, one's race was one's identity. So-called "half caste's", or those with mixed parentage, were not treated any better by the Japanese, and oftentimes were worse off. The exception was interpreters who were generally treated well by the Japanese and tolerated by the prison population.

Unlike in some of the POW camps around Changi and other parts of Singapore, there were no gardens to grow fresh vegetables in the Gaol, nor was there any place to keep chickens. Everything, therefore, had to be brought in. At first, relatively normal supplies continued to come into the prison each day, but as the weeks wore on, and the Japanese insisted on paying for these supplies with Banana money (the nickname for the new currency), supplies began to dry up. The Imperial Army confiscated warehouses and cold storages, but it was obvious these stores wouldn't last forever. Food was soon severely rationed. There was no sign of any Red Cross food parcels, but while the prisoners got skinnier and skinnier, and the guards got hungrier and meaner, the soldiers seemed as plump and fresh as though there was no war going on. They always had freshly pressed uniforms, though there was a great variety of these especially amongst the officer class. Sometimes they could be seen eating chocolate bars or drinking coffee.

For the internees, the evening meal, served at about 4pm, consisted of a vegetable soup or even a fried hash. It was not very exciting but it was nutritious enough. But after several weeks, the vegetable content in the soup dwindled to just a few leaves and the hash stopped altogether. Tea was drunk without milk, until eventually tea supplies ran out as well.

In the evening, each floor of each block were allowed free time in one of the four high walled block yards or even had a turn at walking around the exterior perimeter of the prison for exercise. This was when contact with locals was possible. A large majority of the Malay people were horrified to see the way the internees were being treated. Many a faithful servant risked the wrath of the Japanese to check on their old employers and plenty of canny entrepreneurs made a living from bartering with the internees.

For the large part, in the beginning, the Japanese turned a blind eye to this system. Essentials like supplementary food, medicines, pencils, blankets and even mattresses were dragged into the gaol and surrounding camps. For currency, prisoners used black market Singapore dollars, watches, jewellery, handbags, photo frames. Even wedding bands were exchanged. In fact, anything that they had brought in with them, which wasn't a necessity for daily living was eventually sold by desperate owners. What was an engagement ring to a mother when her son desperately needed the protein an egg could give him? If the necessity was great enough, prisoners even bartered amongst themselves. A pair of shorts in exchange for some Horlicks Malted Milk Tablets, for example.

Although he was sure Ruth and Jean had left Singapore long before the city fell to the Japanese, Charlie took to asking after her every chance he got—every time he met someone new who might have seen her in those last days.

One stifling hot evening, Dalip was eager to impart news to Cole and Armstrong but Ude Singh, the ex-police guard whom Charlie had arrested and charged, was loitering around Floor 3 of Block B. He had singled

Charlie out and was intent on revenge, making Charlie's life as miserable as possible. Dalip did not like or support Ude, but to show Charlie and Giles any kind of preferential treatment while Ude was watching would certainly end in corporal punishment of one kind or another. As it was, Charlie was already sporting a suspected cracked rib, broken tooth and bruised jaw.

So it was not until just before lights out, that Dalip whispered his news. He had found a staff member from Rear Admiral Spooner's office in one of the camps. The man was 100% certain that the two APF wives had gotten out the day after the Japanese had invaded the island and six days before the official surrender.

For Charlie, it was enough reassurance to keep his chin up. Wherever she was, wherever his darling baby girl was, at least he now knew they weren't here in this hell hole.

16
AUCKLAND JULY 1942

HUNTER WHITLOCK

In New Zealand, Auckland's east coast was a boater's paradise with its beautiful coastline comprising multiple deep water bays, uninhabited islands and picturesque coves. Boats of all kinds had long been Captain Hunter Whitlock's passion. It was befitting then that now he was about to be released from the army, he had come full circle back to the place he had been born, Auckland, the twin-harboured city of sailors.

Hunter lost no time in looking up his old contacts, but few of them were sailing. Most had either enlisted or were too busy making up for the shortfall in the local work force. Added to that was the lack of funds for frivolities, the fact that access to some of Auckland's waterfront was restricted including the Royal Akarana Yacht Club building at Mechanics Bay, and not least the fact that it was the middle of winter meant that sailing opportunities were few and far between. Nevertheless Hunter joined the Royal New Zealand Yacht Squadron with a crew membership and took every opportunity he could to get out on the water.

He took a stop-gap job in the office of a busy menswear shop on Karangahape Road. The tenants that the family lawyers had installed in his father's townhouse were given notice to vacate and the Mount St John house was placed on the market. Meanwhile he took up residence at the family farmhouse on Orchard Road in Western Springs. When he wasn't busy, he sorted through his brother's 24-foot boathouse at St George's Bay. It now belonged to him and he thought it might come in useful if he was ever to return to boat-building.

One bright and promising morning Hunter was ambling around the marina adjacent to the Yacht Squadron looking for any yachts that might be advertised for sale. He hadn't been at it long when he was approached by a skipper who was keen to take his 38 foot B-class keeler out for the day but hadn't been able to collect sufficient crew numbers to really give her a good run. Seeing as it was Hunter's day off work he happily accepted the last minute position.

The winter's morning was very warm with only a gentle NW breeze when they cast off. Hunter shared bow duties with one other and it wasn't long before they were approaching the harbour's limit. From here they were about to enter the danger zone where, as it was war time, there were restrictions on where and when they could sail. Of particular concern was a rectangular area between Rangitoto island and the Eastern Suburbs which extended right out to the Navy Base on Motuihe Island—known to all as HMNZS Tamaki. Just traversing this area meant registration and reporting in to the patrol boats who were stationed at the three channel entrances. Of course the other channel beneath Browns Island was an absolute no-go zone. Then there was a much wider area from the north-easternmost tip of Waiheke right up to Kawau Island where fishing and anchoring were prohibited. On top of all that, they would have to be back in the harbour by sunset. Not adhering to these rules would result in being fired upon by the heavy guns on the surrounding cliffs.

These were the worries of the skipper, which was not Hunter's job this day. Once out on the Hauraki Gulf, with the inevitable lift in breeze, Hunter was able to sync his mind on the finer points of sailing, concentrating his reduced hearing on nothing more than the skipper's voice and the light banter between the crew. Out here, he could put the horror of war behind him and simply live.

They headed on a slightly north heading of 70 degrees taking them directly towards Motuihe Channel. As they passed the patrol boat, they waved—they'd only have to report in on the way back. Then they turned due north to arrive at Motutapu Island in the sheltered anchorage of Home Bay.

It was a popular bay with sailors and one of the few places, since the restrictions were enforced, where pleasure craft could anchor overnight; provided of course permission had been sought first. But their plans were to merely stop for lunch and then return.

"The water is so clear here. Look how the sunlight is reflecting off the shells on the bottom. It reminds me of the sea around Crete," Hunter said somewhat whimsically to his companions.

"But the sea would not be so cold there as it is here," the skipper guessed.

"No, indeed. I'm almost tempted to take a dip, but you're right of course. It will be far too cold."

"Deceptively cold," someone else agreed, shivering despite the sun's warm winter rays.

"What was it like in Crete?" Jimmy, the youngest crew member, asked.

"Oh, you know. It had its moments," Hunter said non-committedly. He wasn't quite ready to speak of the brutalities he had witnessed to someone who hadn't been there, who couldn't possibly comprehend. Hunter knew he didn't have enough words in his vocabulary to describe it.

The little group lapsed into silent contemplation. From that moment, the magic of the day was lost. With something akin to new sight, Hunter looked around him and found that even out in the middle of the Gulf there were reminders of war everywhere. He suddenly didn't have the ability to keep the tormenting memories at bay. It was not just the mention of Crete that brought it all back, but a mere two miles south across open water was HMNZS Tamaki with its barracks blocks taunting him in their neatly laid out rows atop the cliffs of Motuihe. Tiny figures marched back and forth and snatches of a military band wafted across the channel making his cheeks burn with thoughts that he was out here enjoying himself, while the rest of his battalion was still in the northern hemisphere.

Idle chatter resumed around Hunter whilst he battled with his memories. Thoughts of his brother floated into his minds-eye unprompted. His brother Cecil, older by eight years, had lived and breathed sailing, only to die at ANZAC Cove way back in August 1915. Now that Hunter had been to war, he knew first-hand what his brother's last hours might have been like while he lay on the Turkish beach waiting for a longboat to take him out to a hospital ship. He could envisage, the terrifying sounds of war, the smell of death, the painful heat, the loneliness, regret and the inevitable helplessness that would have been his brother's lot while he was still conscious. War was not glorious. Hunter almost regretted his decision to sign up so early. Life would never be innocent again. Life at the front was far worse than being married to Hester had ever been.

"What are you scowling about?" the skipper asked him.

"The ex-wife," Hunter replied abruptly, but it was explanation enough to the skipper who was divorced himself.

"They bleed you dry alright," Hunter heard him say. "Best way to get over them is to find a new love. For me it's this beauty," he claimed, patting the long polished tiller, "but for you it might be a new woman. Someone kind…"

"Yes kind," a red-headed crewman interrupted, "but the real test of a good woman is in the measure of her sponge cake skills."

"I didn't realise you were so partial to cake," Jimmy said, causing the other men to guffaw loudly. The boy's innocent remark even brought a brief smile to Hunter's face.

"What did I say?" Jimmy asked.

"All right, leave the lad alone," the skipper said. "No, you can't expect the perfect woman. If she's kind to you, that's all a good man can aspire to."

Hunter thought of Ruth and his scowl reappeared.

He had believed Ruth was as much in love with him as he was with her. That's why he brought her out to New Zealand in the first place. Even little Jean seemed to like him. But the biggest problem they had was finding time to be together.

Just as he had promised her, his two elderly aunts had warmly invited her to share their large but simple cliff top home. A widow and a spinster, Millicent and Margaret enjoyed Ruth's youthful company. Both were unfortunately childless and they therefore doted on her daughter. Indeed the arrangement had worked out well, except Hunter had been expressly forbidden to stay at the house while Ruth was there. They had indicated that his constant presence was unseemly and he was expected to pre-arrange visits as if he wasn't family.

Millicent and Margaret didn't approve of any romantic liaisons between the two and he knew why. But confound it all, she was his friend first. And come to that it was none of their darned business what he and Ruth decided to do.

The aunties had a busy social schedule into which they had slotted Ruth as naturally as if she was a key in a cabinet. Ruth found herself accepted by all the ladies in their circle. Being a "bona fides" war widow, left with a child, she had everyone's sympathy.

Twice a week there was mahjong tournaments to compete in at the Milford tennis pavilion. Tennis itself was not currently popular because tennis balls were no longer being manufactured due to the world shortage of rubber. Club members instead utilised their new clubrooms by holding mahjong parties.

With mahjong being ubiquitous in Singapore, Ruth was already a dab hand at the Chinese game. She was quick at the draw and a popular choice to fill a fourth seat. In fact, in the two short months since she had arrived in the city, she had already adjusted to the slightly altered rules that the locals played to, and was the second best player in the Milford club. Only Beulah Greensway was able to best her and even then not every time. Needless to say, Beulah was the one person who treated Ruth like an interloper.

Over dinner just a few days ago, the ladies had reported to Hunter how unkind Mrs Greensway was with all the little snipes and put-downs that she regularly aimed at Ruth. He was proud to hear that the aunties thought she handled these well with decorum and grace, and he was pleased that she had found a place amongst the social set. But he couldn't help feeling that they were being kept apart by the constant rounds of mahjong, whist and social visiting. Not to mention both the voluntary war work Ruth had signed up to of making camouflage nets, and the early-to-bed evenings that were routine in the auntie's household. Where did he fit into that schedule? And why was Ruth content to be ordered about by the aunties? Why wasn't she fighting for him?

Hunter wasn't the slightest bit interested in cards or mahjong, but he desperately wanted to share his love for getting out on the water with her. He wanted her to feel the euphoria of dolphins riding the bow wave just an arm length or two away. He wanted to show her the unspoilt isolated landscapes that he loved to explore. She had coped with shipboard life well, without any sign of seasickness, but he remembered her saying that she would not like to sleep aboard a small yacht. She thought it would be too confining. That would be a deal breaker, Hunter realised. He knew that most yachts had berths added in as after-thoughts wherever space allowed. Even those with double berth in the bow, still didn't have room to stand, or wardrobes to hang clothes in. He hoped Ruth was not too refined to adapt.

Hunter's reverie was interrupted by the Skipper ordering the anchor to be hauled in. For the trip home he was swapped into the cockpit and kept so busy trimming the sheets, that he didn't have time to think of anything but the technicalities of sailing.

After helping the skipper to pack up the yacht, he accepted an invitation to stay on at the yacht club for a meal. They were joined by an impromptu party of fellow bachelors. During pre-dinner drinks, Hunter made enquiries after yachts which might be for sale.

"I'm not looking for a racer," he said. "I'm thinking more along the lines of something which is suitable for family cruising around the Gulf. Something which I can manage on my own or with just one extra crew member, but large enough to sleep aboard. Perhaps a small project. I've built a yacht before and I'm keen to get my hands dirty on another one."

"Well there's plenty of boats around that need new owners, but we can't sell them without their owner's permission, as much as we might like to," one man said. "I think many of the boys went off to war thinking they'd be back in a month or two. Now that it seems to be dragging on, some of the yachts are getting into dreadfully sorry states. You just can't leave a boat in the water for months on end with no maintenance."

There was a general murmuring of agreement and then a man called Ted, took the opportunity to speak up. "If you are open to something a little, let's just say, out of the ordinary, I know of a ketch for sale which might suit your purposes—with a bit of work," he added with a wry look on his face.

"Well, there's nothing wrong with a ketch. What's the catch?"

"There's nothing *wrong* with it. It's just that she's not a keeler, she's not, how shall I put it? She's not a pleasure craft."

"Well, spit it out man. What is she?"

"She's a workhorse essentially. A scow, used for carting scoria. Probably the smallest hold-scow ever built in fact. But don't let that worry you. She's a real beauty at a little over 56 foot. She's too small for the owners, their fleet is getting larger. But they've not had much luck selling her. Sailing scows are a bit old-fashioned these days."

Most of the men at the table scoffed at the idea of it. It wasn't a gentleman's sailing yacht. It wouldn't have the beautiful lines of a harbour racer. This was an out and out ship. A small ship to be sure, but a ship none the less and an ugly flat bottomed one at that.

"But surely I'd not be able to manage her on my own," Hunter asked, surprising the other men by his serious tone. "She'd take a hefty crew, wouldn't she? How much sail does she run?" He did not want to hear a negative answer, so he rattled out a series of questions without waiting for the response, exactly as if he was thinking aloud. Then he stopped involuntarily while his diaphragm sucked in some much needed oxygen. This gave Ted a chance to respond.

"Well, I'm very familiar with her, having owned a similar vessel myself. I think you'll find that she is very adaptable. With a little work you could add a cabin. Crew you ask? That depends. She's had a fairly new diesel engine added; 10 horse power I believe, so you'd only have to sail her if you wanted. Look, why don't you go on up to look at her. She's moored at Warkworth, about two hours north. I've got a number here," he said scrabbling in his wallet for a bit of paper. He copied the details down. "And here's what the owners, two brothers, are asking for her. I think you'll agree it's a steal at that price."

Hunter looked down at the note. "SS Pahiki," he read, sounding the name out. thoughtfully. It had a happy ring to it, he decided.

They arranged a time to meet the following day, Ted having agreed to act as the go-between. Now that the men at the table understood that Hunter was seriously thinking about the idea, they took it more seriously themselves. During the meal and throughout the evening, Hunter's possible purchase of the little scow became the main topic of conversation. Advice and suggestions as to how to improve her were tossed back and forth. Before he knew it, a group of five men had invited themselves to come along to the inspection.

Hunter let the conversation flow around him. He was never one for heeding other people's advice, being more of a lone wolf. He contemplated whether he should ask Ruth to accompany him to look at the scow. After all, if she was not happy with it then there'd be no point in purchasing it. After a moment's deliberation, he decided against the idea. For starters, how would he explain her presence to the other men. Then there was the likelihood that the remodelled ship which he was envisaging in his mind's-eye would not match its current state of repair. He had a fair idea of what he'd find, having been accustomed to seeing scows plying the coastline all his life, but she may be shocked. He couldn't take the risk that she'd feel negatively about the idea before it had come to fruition.

Within the week, the deal was done. Hunter was not disappointed in his find. She was a real gem. Rather than being a negative factor, he could see that her flat bottom would mean that the number of remote island coves they could anchor in would be double that which they could reach with a keeled boat. He immediately set about his plans to add a deckhouse where Ruth and her child could sleep in a pair of comfortable cabins.

He realised it would be closer to Christmas before he could finally unveil the project to Ruth. Therefore he decided to make it his Christmas present for her. It would give him a goal to work towards.

The Pahiki would be their very own little love nest, where they could get away from prying eyes and judgemental nosey-parkers.

17
AUCKLAND DECEMBER 1942

RUTH COLE

Christmas Day was a glorious affair. The aunties invited Hunter to join them for lunch and while roasted turkey was not on the menu, they at least hadn't resorted to roasting a rabbit. They did in fact tuck in to a nice roast chook with a trifle for afters. Though there was of course no cream on top nor strawberries, for at 9/- a chip, Ruth had agreed you'd have to be "barking" to justify that expense.

There was much to remind Ruth about Christmas dinners spent with her own aunties in England not to forget the emulative hotel roast dinners in British Singapore. However, there were also a lot of peculiarities. The importance of strawberries for one thing; the aunties had seemed overly upset about missing out. Then there was their love of roasted pumpkin. She'd always considered the pumpkin to be pig-food. She had also noticed that they called it Christmas lunch here. Dinner seemed to be a term reserved for the evening meal.

That being said, it was not the food that made the day memorable. It was the way in which they had sat down at the table like a family. There were none of the usual pointed frowns or icy comments which followed every time Hunter accidentally, or perhaps purposely, brushed Ruth's hand or attempted to speak to her privately.

Ruth had seen that Hunter was as confused by the relaxed atmosphere as she was. She wondered if the aunties had finally relented on their stance or whether they were just making an exception for the special day.

Having just celebrated her second birthday, Jean seemed able to comprehend that today was another special day with a present to open and a special pudding. Also, her favourite person, Hunter, was going to spend the whole day with them. There was something about Hunter that the child liked and trusted. He never forced himself into her world of play, but was always receptive whenever she engaged with him. Jean responded positively whenever she saw mummy smiling—something which happened more often whenever Hunter was around.

Ruth was overwhelmed by Hunter's generosity. Not only had he brought along a present for each and every one of them, but they were such lovely, thoughtful presents too. For Jean, he had chosen a bright yellow metal sand bucket and spade. For herself, he had picked out an attractive honeycombed woollen sea suit for bathing. She could tell immediately that it would be a good fit and it was exactly what she both needed and wanted.

In no time at all, Hunter had told Jean all about making sand castles and from then on the aunties had no say in the matter—there would have to be an expedition down the cliff to the adjacent beach so that she could try out her new sandcastle set. Ruth was also keen to try her swim suit. She had missed the exercise that swimming brought her.

The aunties needed to rest by the time they arrived at the wide swathe of sand. Hunter erected a sun shade for them while Ruth preferred to take a sun nap. Jean promptly set to work with her spade and bucket and soon had drafted Hunter to help her. He directed her to carve out a magnificent palace and then he showed her how to decorate it with shells and seaweed.

With Jean satisfied, Hunter and Ruth left her in the care of the aunties and slipped into the sea for a bathe. Keeping a respectable distance from each other, they were nevertheless close enough to carry on the first truly private conversation they'd had since Ruth had arrived in the country several months earlier.

"I've got another Christmas present for you," Hunter said with a grin.

"Oh really Hunter, you needn't have. You've already been very generous. I feel like the scarf I knitted you pales in comparison."

"I shall treasure that scarf, I'm telling you. And I know you haven't the funds of your own to buy expensive gifts."

"No, I still can't access my bank account. But I was thinking that if either Margaret or Millicent would agree to look after Jean, I could at least get a job in a shop, like you."

"Well, let's worry about that in the new year. In the meantime, I have planned a little holiday for the both of us, and Jean of course. That's what the gift is for and if my aunties are willing, we can all go and have it look at it tomorrow."

"Goodness! Now you've got my curiosity going."

On Boxing Day, Jean, Ruth and the aunties accompanied Hunter in his car for the long drive around the harbour to St Georges Bay near Parnell.

All along the eastern edge of the bay were little boat sheds, and as Hunter pulled his motor car up outside one of them, he explained that he had inherited it from his late-brother Cyril. Watching him pull open the shed door, Ruth was expecting the surprise to materialise. But there didn't seem to be anything particularly exciting inside. Just tools hanging above the bench on one side. Ruth looked at Hunter, knowing that this was all part of his teasing, but unsure where he was going with it.

Hunter strode to the hinged doors at the far end of the shed and pulled them open. Moored to the front of the shed was a large boat. The aunties caught on to the idea well before Ruth did. Ruth thought perhaps they were going for a ride on the boat. The aunties realised that Hunter must have purchased it himself.

"Well I never," Millicent said, while her sister mirrored the exclamation by asking, "You never?"

"I most certainly did," Hunter said feeling very pleased with himself and beaming from ear to ear.

Ruth was hesitantly smiling, and feeling a little bewildered. What was so extraordinary, she wondered.

"Would you like to step aboard?" Hunter asked.

"All right," Ruth agreed while Hunter tugged on a thick line which secured the boat to the boat shed. Soon he had it pulled in so close that Ruth could simply step aboard without climbing over anything or needing to jump a gap.

Margaret passed Jean over and Hunter helped her aboard and before long they were all standing next to a gleaming coach house.

"Well, what do you think?" Hunter asked delighting in Ruth's obvious confusion.

"What do I think about what?" Ruth asked. "Surely, you haven't bought a boat … have you?" The idea had finally begun to make traction in her mind. Suddenly, she realised by his glowing expression and the wry expressions on the auntie's faces that was exactly what he had done.

"She's all mine. Ours. She's called the Pahiki. We shall be able to sail her or motor anywhere in the Gulf and even further once the war is over. Look, there are two cabins aunts. One for Ruth and Jean and a completely separate one for me." He was gesticulating in a very animated way.

"I've remodelled downstairs and I'll show you there is a lovely saloon with a small wood heater for cold nights. There's also a darling galley that you'll love Ruth. Just think, your very own kitchen!"

That comment brought smiles to the aunties faces, who knew that

Ruth's cooking skills were very limited.

"She looked nothing like this when I bought her, I tell you," Hunter said, looking for Ruth's approval.

"So this is what you have been busy doing all these months. And here I thought you'd lost interest in me," Ruth said.

This comment brought Hunter up sharp making him wonder if she was making fun of him. Surely, she realised it was she who had been avoiding him, not the other way around. He noticed the look on her face was guileless.

"Hunter dear, surely you realise that it would be most unseemly to take Ruth away with you. She has her reputation to think about," Millicent interrupted his scrutiny.

"Unless there is a bedroom for one of us as well," Margaret added. "We could chaperone, I suppose. Though I'm not much of a sailor."

"No aunties. I'm sick of worrying about what people think. And it's time you realised that you can't keep me away from Ruth forever."

"Well, no, not forever. We do hope that in time you will be able to freely court her. She is a lovely young lady and I'm sure she would make a lovely wife, if that is going to be your intention," Margaret replied.

"This war will be over soon, and then I'll officially be declared a widow," Ruth told the aunties. "But in the meantime, I'd very much like for Hunter to take me out on occasion. I'd love to go away on holiday with him on the Pahiki."

There was a pointed silence, which almost unnerved Ruth. Finally, Millicent said, "holiday?"

"Yes a holiday auntie. I've told Ruth, that this summer we are going on holiday and this is how I intend to take them. I'll ask some friends to help me sail her up to Warkworth where I've sorted out a mooring for her. Then I'll drive the three of us up there and we will motor her across the short distance to Kawau Island. Nobody who knows you will see us. Nobody will think anything other than we are a married couple on holiday with our child. Ruth needs this and I need this. By god I need it."

When Millicent appeared to be about to voice her concerns further, Hunter added, "and that will be the end of the matter."

On New Year's Eve Hunter called on Ruth. She was to accompany him to the Auckland Motor Yacht Club's Great Hawaiian Night dance at Westhaven, while the aunties had agreed to look after Jean.

Ever since Boxing Day, they had stopped voicing their concerns over Hunter courting the young widow. Unbeknownst to Ruth, Hunter had pulled the two women aside and told them that if they continued to interfere, he would take Ruth away to live with him at his Western Springs farmhouse. They knew that letting him carry on an affair with the woman was a far better option than encouraging him to live in sin with her.

After being offered and accepting a sherry in the living room, Hunter waited impatiently for Ruth to come downstairs. Given Ruth's lack of wardrobe, they had agreed to go in black tie rather than the optional fancy dress. He knew she would be wearing the emerald evening gown she had been given aboard the troopship Orcades and on the advice of the aunties, he had brought along a single white orchid corsage. Being a retired army officer, he was entitled to wear the dress uniform, but instead he opted to hire a formal suit.

Despite knowing what she would wear, he was still dazzled when she came to greet him. Done up properly this time, the effect was quite different. Millicent had lent her a pair of black lace gloves and a black stole to cover her bare back. While Margaret had lent Ruth her sequined evening bag with its silver bugle beads and chased silver top. Ruth had also borrowed a daring pair of Cuban heeled black velvet and silver court shoes from a friend at the tennis club. Her hair was done up in a flattering style with cascading mahogany curls set with a tortoiseshell comb. The whole effect, together with lipstick and face powder looked very glamorous.

Hunter always appreciated Ruth's beauty, but when he saw her now, he had to fight the stirring feeling that threatened to expose him as the blood rushed to his extremities.

A tear stained Jean, who had only recently discovered that she would not be accompanying her mother, refused to look at Hunter. For the first time, he was taking her mother away. But ever resourceful, Hunter had come prepared with a gift for Jean too.

From a bag he produced a chip of the finest looking strawberries Ruth had ever seen. Jean was unimpressed, never having tasted them before, but her curiosity soon got the better of her, when Ruth tasted one of the delights. Tentatively, Jean tried the sweet bright red treat and quickly it was all gone. She reached out for a second portion, but Hunter was purposely holding the chip just slightly out of her reach.

"You may have the rest of the strawberries once we have gone my dear. But you must let Auntie Margaret get you ready for bed and say goodnight to mummy now. Mummy will be home by lunchtime tomorrow because the drive is far too long to come home tonight and besides you will be fast asleep anyway."

Jean wasn't listening to a word, her sole intent was to have another delectable strawberry.

The night passed gloriously. Ruth danced to the sound of Gus Lindsay and his Hawaiian Island band until her feet could not carry on. She had no idea that Hunter detested dancing; that he was only accommodating her to make her happy. Ruth was relieved to find that most of the other guests had also opted for evening dress rather than fancy dress. Nobody appeared to think it strange or inappropriate for the two to be romantically involved. Nobody knew either of their pasts exactly. Hunter simply introduced Ruth as a war widow and consequently spent much of his time ensuring that she was not whisked off to dance with someone else.

Despite having both a house and a house-boat to spend the night after the party, Hunter had decided to book a room in a hotel for them. He was not quite ready to allow Ruth into his old life at the farmhouse where who knows what she might find if she were to go snooping around. Besides there was his neighbour's house within viewing distance of his front door and he really didn't want any gossip despite what he had told the aunties. They thought he'd spend the night aboard the Pahiki, but he didn't think the small ship was quite ready for an evening gown, not to mention the Cuban heels.

They checked in to the respectable private hotel, Glenalvon, as Mr and Mrs Whitlock. Ruth thought the whole ruse was a hoot and despite not having tasted a single alcoholic drink the whole evening, she was intoxicated with excitement. They may have just come from a New Year's Eve party rather than their wedding breakfast but the night was undoubtedly going to be the honeymoon they would have shared if it had been.

A butler showed them to their room. He deposited their small overnight bags onto the bag rack, switched on the lamps and pulled closed the curtains. All the while, Ruth and Hunter stood in the centre of the small room, eyeing each other with silly grins.

The second, the door of their bedroom closed behind them, their lips met. Ruth wrapped her arms around his neck, her mouth desperate to taste all of the past year's longing and hopes. Hunter pulled her body in closer than ever until she was left in no doubt about his desire. The moment had come to validate their passion and bind their hearts together.

Ruth could feel Hunter sliding her hem up until his hands pressed against her bare thighs. On they travelled, up over her silk clad derrière and under the lower bodice. Her lips paused while she waited eagerly, wondering what he was going to do to her. Hot expectant shivers engulfed her, sending darts of ecstasy to her heaving bosom. His strong calloused hands gripped her hips lifting her clear off the ground. She gave a restrained squeal in surprise and delight as he carried her to the dresser, setting her atop it. From here, he removed first one shoe and then another, carefully setting them aside. Then he pulled the tortoiseshell comb from her hair and again, and to her amusement and delight, carefully put that aside.

He really was a gentleman, Ruth reflected before being shocked as he reached beneath her skirts again and unclasped and tugged down her stockings, throwing first one silk piece over his shoulder, closely followed by the next. This was followed by more kisses in which Ruth closed her eyes, losing herself again, almost unaware that his busy hands had unclipped her suspender belt. She felt him lift her slightly and it was only a second afterwards that she realised he had slid her panties down and over her knees, allowing them to drop to the floor. She opened her eyes in time to recognised the intensity of sexual desire etched across his taut face in the dull lamp light. But before she even had time to smile in encouragement, he picked her up again and as if she weighed no more than a sprite, he flipped her face down onto the bed.

It hadn't hurt at all, but Ruth felt a little flustered at this unseemly manhandling. Where had her gentleman gone? The one who had just moments earlier so carefully placed her comb on the table, but now tossed her onto the bed like a sack of potatoes. She pushed the palms of her hands against the bed and made as if to sit up.

"Oh no you don't. I've got two rows of buttons to attend to," he growled and she felt his body straddle her, with a knee to either side.

"Hunter," she gulped huskily, then paused because she wasn't sure whether to protest or whether she was in fact very much enjoying this. Her only other carnal experience had been with her late husband. The contrast between them was so different as to be eerie. Charlie had been big and burly, tough at work, but cultured and sweetly romantic, considerate even, in the bedroom. Hunter was almost as tall but with wiry muscles rather than bulky ones and sun bronzed skin. He was undoubtedly a gentleman outside of the bedroom, if a little unsophisticated at times. But his rough kisses and the way he almost tried to own her here in the bedroom was domineering. Yes domineering was the right word.

She gave a little giggle as she imagined him struggling over the buttons. "Can you manage?" she eventually asked.

"Nearly there, these blasted things, if only the light was a little better. Don't want to pull the little blighters off. Almost done."

He slipped the straps off her shoulders and slid the dress right away as if he was peeling a mushroom. Gentle but firm.

"I've been wanting to take that dress off you ever since I saw you in it this afternoon."

Ruth went to sit up again.

"No don't," he implored her. "I want you like this." She felt him lay down on top of her back.

"But don't you want me to, you know...." It had taken a long time for her to find the courage to name and speak of the acts of sex with her husband, and even then she barely dared to. She certainly wasn't up to it with Hunter yet."

"No. I don't want you to do anything. Anyway I'm ready for you. I've been ready for a while now."

His lovemaking was vigorous and vocal and left her giddy and exhausted almost to the point of delirium. She was thankful in the end that she was laying down as her legs were spent and her made-up face lost in perspiration. When his final stroke exploded through her body in a crescendo of hot pulse like waves, she simultaneously released her clenched muscles. But while he seemed to relax like a deflated weather sock, her body continued to thrum sweetly like a guitar string which has been pulled and then left to pulsate softly.

Pulling back the bed covers, he rolled her onto the crisp white hotel sheets. Then he quickly swaddled them both in a cocoon of bedding. She kissed him warmly and he responded gently.

"I love you so much," she whispered in his ear. She'd never experienced such overwhelming lovemaking as that before, and although it had always been wonderful with Charlie, she had seldom been so aroused. She felt rapturously content and totally infatuated in him. They lay for a while in their own little world of satisfied silence, until she couldn't resist breaking the magic by speaking.

"Hunter that was, well words can't describe it. It was exhilarating, I am sure. But I must say, oughtn't you have taken precaution. I mean, aren't you worried I might be impregnated."

He kissed her forehead then. "There's something you should know, my darling. And I hope you won't love me any less for it. But I might as well tell you now before, well before…"

"What? Just say it darling."

"I'm incapable of fathering children," He blurted quickly before barging on with his explanation. "I wasn't able to impregnate my ex-wife. That's one of the reasons it didn't work out. I thought… I thought perhaps, since you already had a child, you might be agreeable to not having any more."

There was a long silence while Ruth sorted through her feelings.

"Is it so very important to you that we have children?" he asked her eventually when she still hadn't replied. His tone of voice sounded hurt.

"No, I don't suppose it is. Charlie and I had always planned to have a large family, but I guess that has all changed now. I don't know how I feel about it, really I don't. I only brought it up because I don't want to have a child now. I mean to say without first being properly married."

"Well, you don't have to worry about that. We could make love morning, noon and night, and you'd be safe. In fact I hope that we do."

"What was your ex-wife like?"

"How do I answer that? What do you want to know?"

"Well, I don't know. What was her name for starters?"

"Hester."

"Hester and Hunter. That has a nice ring to it."

"It's a hateful name for a hateful woman. She was very cruel, taunting me, despising me and eventually ignoring me. I prefer not to talk about her. But she has made me determined to find a wife who is kind and caring. Someone who is about 5'6", with thick dark wavy brown hair. Someone with deep brown eyes and curves like this." He ran his hand lightly up and down the arc of her hips."

"Go on with you. I could read that as a marriage proposal."

"I'd like you to," he whispered.

"What? She sat up suddenly, so that the sheets fell away from her leaving her mature breasts fully exposed."

He sucked in his breath and tore his eyes back to her face.

"Will you marry me?" he asked. "I know you have to wait until the death notice comes through. But after the war, will you marry me?"

"Only if you'll take care of me, and love me like you just did, brutally often," she laughed.

"Well then. We'll be secretly engaged until we can officially get married. Probably best not to announce it to the world yet, my darling."

"But we can tell the aunties, can't we?"

"Well, if you must. But I don't think we should mention it to little Jean yet. She won't be able to keep a secret."

He reached up to stroke her cheek. Then his hand dropped to her bare breast and he traced her areole of her nipple softly. In return, she reached beneath the covers to discover his manhood for herself. He jerked away from her before she had the chance.

"Don't!" he said quietly. "I'm not ready for that yet." He pulled her into his embrace and switching off the lamp, pulled the covers around them. "Goodnight my darling," he whispered into her neck.

"Good…night," Ruth replied. She was very confused. Why wouldn't he let her touch him or even look at him while he made love to her? She knew something was wrong, but couldn't work out what. For hours, she lay awake thinking. Was he hiding something? Was he so damaged from this Hester that he couldn't bear another woman to look at him? Had she just made a terrible mistake agreeing to marry him?

She dozed intermittently but was unable to drop into a deep sleep. At first light, she was wide awake but irrationally tired. Hunter still breathed deeply beside her. Pulling on her nightie and house-gown, she let herself out into the hallway to find the bathroom. When she returned she had made up her mind. Hunter still appeared to be asleep, so he'd never know if she slipped back the covers to slide in beside him. If she happened to accidentally get a glance at his body, then she'd be able to either discover or rule out a war wound or skin infliction that he might be hiding.

She had heard the term "brazen hussy" and that was exactly what she felt like as her eyes raked his taut frame. At first nothing seemed untoward, but then it slowly dawned on her. Yes, there was something mismatched about his testes. She couldn't help the confused look which must have been plastered across her as she glanced back at his face. This turned quickly to shock and then flamed in embarrassment when she discovered that he was awake and watching her silently.

"Yes, I'm a monorchid. Have been all my life."

"A ... sorry, what?" she stumbled over her words.

"You know, like Hitler. Less than a full man," and he began to quietly sing the tune to the *Colonel Bogey March*.

"Hitler has only got one ball, Göring has two but they're small, Himmler's are..." his voice died out as Ruth simply stared at him, speechless.

"Are you so very repulsed?" his voice trembled.

"Repulsed? No, of course not. Not at all." Ruth wondered what she was supposed to say. "For goodness sake, is this all you've been worried about? I realised there was something you were hiding, when you wouldn't let me look at you or touch you last night. But my darling, you are beautiful, just the way you are. And as for being half a man, well that is simply rot. You are all the man I need and could ever want."

"But just now, you seemed so shocked."

"Well, I have just never come across this before. I mean what does one say? And then I was embarrassed that you had caught me looking."

"You were embarrassed? I'm the one who should be embarrassed."

"Oh my darling, your little secret could have been so much worse. I'm relieved it is something and nothing. Certainly nothing for me to worry about." Ruth snuggled back in beside him and soon he made good his promise to make love regularly. But this time, he was not afraid. While last night had been almost animal like, this morning he was gentle and wonderful. At times, Ruth thought she caught a glimpse of tears in his eyes, and afterwards he could not stop embracing her even long after they had left the hotel.

18
AUCKLAND JUNE 1943

RUTH COLE

The blissful harmony experienced by the intimate couple continued for several concupiscent months.

Initially, the little family spent nearly every weekend aboard the Pahiki, travelling all the way up the Mahurangi River and out over to Kawau Island. That soon got tiresome at the Pahiki's slow speed and they'd found a more convenient mooring at The Sandspit, which was near a popular camping ground in Lower Matakana. It was also from here, that Messrs Gubb's ferry service to Kawau commenced aboard a 45ft diesel powered launch called the Nancibel.

While the Nancibel was limited to sidling alongside the long wharves of island residents, the Pahiki was able to traverse right up into all the nooks and crannies of the coastline. The new family unit (Hunter, Ruth and Jean), spent many weekends searching for the perfect hideaway. They had determined it needed to be approachable in all tides, deserted, sheltered and sandy.

They finally found their Shangri-la in a long narrow cove just north of the busy Bon Accord Harbour. Now that they had found it, they motored directly to this secret spot every time they came out.

Jean learnt to float and became so proficient in the water that she no longer needed Hunter to hold her hand. Together they fished and rock pooled and even climbed to the top of the hill above their secluded beach. The only building, an old fisherman's hut just above the high tide mark, became her play house.

"What do you suppose the owner of that hut would think if he saw young madam rearranging its contents in such a fashion," Ruth idly asked

Hunter one day. They had always assumed the hut belonged to a man judging by the meagre contents.

"The fact that we've never seen him, makes me think that he is away at war. There's a stack of old newspapers dating up to 1940 and then they stop. I shouldn't worry yourself my love. It's not like she is doing any harm besides."

"Hmm," Ruth said non-committedly. She had noticed that Hunter doted on the independent youngster. The child could do no wrong in his eyes.

Thoughts of war, very rarely entered Ruth's head. All of those feelings were tucked into a discrete corner of her conscience. It was as if her memories were packed into an old sea trunk under lock and key and she had no desire to examine the contents. She had a new life now and a man whom she was so head over heels in love with that she could barely remember her old life. Singapore seemed like a distant memory. All that business of servants and bustle. Life had become so much simpler, and happier.

As the weather cooled, so did Ruth's enjoyment in sailing. Despite the cosy wood burning stove on the Pahiki, she found the stormy weather difficult to manage when there was a small child cooped up inside.

Occasionally, when the weather was behaving particularly beastly, Hunter would invite Ruth away on a road trip to Rotorua, Hamilton or Waitomo. It was because they were away on one of these road trips that they completely missed both Auckland newspapers on the very day when the NZ High Commission published a list of POWs in Changi, Singapore.

Three weeks later an advert in the personal columns advised a Mrs R M Cole, wife of Sgt C Cole to contact the P.O.W. office urgently. Ruth didn't see that notice either, but somebody else did. The little advert was gleefully spotted by that busy-body Beaulah Greensway from the mahjong club and she lost no time in making a big scene about it during Tuesday night practice.

"Oh my dear Mrs Cole," she began, emphasising the word Mrs. Have you seen this? She waved the newspaper clipping at Ruth, who took it from her and blanched noticeably.

"What do you suppose that they want?" Beaulah asked Ruth after informing the other ladies what the contents of the advert was.

"Well," Ruth gave a shrug and felt herself withering under the woman's gaze. "I suppose they have my husband's death notice in hand."

At that, there was an outpouring of renewed sympathy for Ruth and Beaulah Greensway was left forgotten at the back of the crowd.

The following morning, Ruth caught the bus to Devonport and crossed by ferry to the POW office in Swanson Street, where she was escorted to a private office.

"It can't be possible," she said when it was explained to her that her husband had been officially listed as a POW in Changi, Singapore.

"Well, certainly there can always be mistakes made. But in this case, I think it is far more likely that you are mistaken that he had died," the official tried to suggest gently. "Did anyone actually witness his death, did you bury the body?"

"Yes! They did! Two of his colleagues actually saw him being killed. His body was blown apart. There was nothing left of him. I'm afraid these records must be wrong. Or perhaps someone else is using his identity, to protect their own, in the camps."

"Well," the official drawled slowly, while his mind ticked over the likelihood. "I suppose that's a possible explanation. These lists are everything but reliable. Although whoever the chap was at the London Commission that put these names together, certainly would have done so in good faith from information given to them by Switzerland. We do agree that the Japanese have been very slow in providing a concise manifest of prisoners. In fact it would be true to say they have been doing everything in their power to hinder the process."

Ruth didn't answer immediately. Her mind was reeling.

"There's also the matter of your father and brother," he went on. "It seems that they, too, are prisoners in Hongkong. Apparently still alive too, unless you know anything to the contrary?"

"No, that's the first I've heard of them since the siege began in that settlement."

"Well, that's something to cling on to, isn't it?" the man said kindly.

"Yes, but I'd rather hoped that you would give me the death certificate. You see, I'm engaged to be married. It's unofficial of course, until I'm legally widowed."

"Oh!" the man did a kind of constipated half leap out of his chair. "Well, my congratulations, I suppose. Though I'd have to advise you, under the circumstances, to well… If I may take the place of your father for a minute, I'm sure he would advise you not to be too hasty. Especially now, with this latest intelligence."

The man was clearly feeling uncomfortable and this in turn was making Ruth feel much the same. He suddenly seemed unable to look Ruth in the eye, and muttering told her that he'd let her know if the situation changed.

Before Ruth knew it, she had been ushered back out into the street, her chest pounding an erratic beat. It seemed as if that old sea trunk in her heart had sprung open. Unwanted thoughts and ideas were popping into her head. She needed to put the lid back on it. *Indefinitely!*

Ruth began the long walk up the hill to Karangahape Road, where she had arranged to meet up with Hunter. He worked as a clerk at Leo O'Malley's corner menswear store and planned to drive her home.

Hunter agreed with Ruth that the Red Cross must have got it wrong. He asked her how she had spent her afternoon while she'd been waiting for him to finish work and the conversation continued on in that way, with small talk. No more was mentioned about the unsettling news, until they arrived back at the aunties. Jean launched herself into Ruth's arms and while Ruth was occupied, Hunter gave the aunties a brief rundown on Ruth's meeting. Perhaps wisely, neither woman offered an immediate opinion.

The long disappointing day had left Ruth particularly tired. Her overactive mind inhibited deep sleep and she awoke feeling washed out. Over the next few weeks, the aunties became increasingly worried about her. She seemed to be languishing. Her skin was pale and clammy and she had frequently left her meals uneaten, citing queasiness.

When she finally decided to make an appointment with the doctor, the aunties were relieved and offered to watch Jean, so that Ruth could go alone.

The seed of an idea had been growing in Ruth's mind. From being an almost laughable concept, she had over the past two weeks run the gamut of denial, shock, feeling sick about the idea, to coming to know and accept it. By the time of her doctor's appointment, she was convinced that she was pregnant. When the doctor confirmed the fact, Ruth privately welcomed the budding prospect.

Even so, it was nonetheless shocking news. Despite these being modern times with the Victorian bourgeois morality far behind them, a widow still did not openly flout a pregnancy. There was the aunties to consider too. The scandal would touch them detrimentally. Their suitability as chaperones would be called to account; their moral boundaries questioned. Ruth realised that her newfound quiet life was beginning to unravel.

Before she confessed to the aunties, she would have to deal with an even bigger obstacle: Hunter's reaction. Would he be pleased that he had fathered a child? Ruth liked to think he would. But the little voice in the back of her head, caused her chest to tighten and her heart to flutter in anxiety. Perhaps he would think poorly of her. She argued against herself on this point, thinking that he was as much to blame—more so— for if he had not insisted that he was unable to father a child, she would have been more careful. *"What if he does not believe that he is the father?"* the little nag in her mind suggested.

Privately, the aunties did not believe that the doctor's appointment had helped poor Ruth much. She continued to decline, her mood darkening further. She seemed to hold no interest in conversation nor her daughter's various trivialities. Indeed they wished the weekend would hurry along, so that they could consult with Hunter.

19
SINGAPORE OCTOBER 1943

CHARLIE COLE

The morning's Tenko stretched on for much longer than usual. They had bowed for the arrival of the commandant but he had stormed past without stopping. Now they were standing at attention while they waited. Charlie's stomach growled furiously, but missing breakfast was the least of his concerns. As the day grew hotter, he began to suspect that they mightn't eat at all this day. There was no water handed out and here and there amongst the tired lines, people were periodically keeling over from heat exhaustion.

Older folk collapsed when their knee and hip joints could no longer carry their weight. Some of these were prodded until they stood again, others were simply ignored. The prisoners were forbidden to give aid. There was no let-up for toilet breaks and many people had obviously wet themselves or, judging by the smell, worse. They stood in their numbered rows within the main yard, unsure what they were waiting for.

From time to time, numbers were called out. Each prisoner knew his own number in Japanese and had come to know that when their number was called out they were to step forward, head bowed to await their fate. This was something that they all feared, as in the past to be singled out meant punishment more often than not. But this morning, large numbers were called out together and these prisoners were marched off to the various block yards enclosed by the prison walls. It seemed that after 20 months of imprisonment at Changi, the prisoners were being sorted somehow. Charlie would like to have held onto the hope that perhaps the war was over and they were to be repatriated, but he knew from snippets of news that he'd heard handed down from those with smuggled radios that the war was far from over. Still one never knew what to expect next. His mind was so confused these days, from months of deficient nutrition, lack of stimulation, the constant brow beatings and diminishing hope.

The sun passed over its zenith and still they waited. Charlie had developed a pain in his kidney and his feet were numb. His back ached and his swollen tongue filled his mouth. He spent the hours feeling for each part of his anatomy. Analysing and collating the various aches and pains. At the very least it was a way to keep his mind occupied. His earlier prediction that they may not eat at all began to look probable if the cooks weren't to be allowed to start preparations for the evening meal soon.

Occasionally he would remember his friend standing beside him and when the guards weren't looking his way, he would turn his head ever so slightly to the left and swing his eyes right over so that he could see Giles. They communicated with their eyes, facial twitches and the briefest of nods. Giles seemed to be pointing out the military police who had mysteriously arrived in camp that morning. The Kempeitai they were called but they were more like Gestapo than ordinary MPs. They had been barking out orders all day and an awful lot of furious shouts could be heard while ordinary Japanese soldiers were rushing in and out of dormitories to comply with these unintelligible commands. The Indian prison guards were not involved. They were standing in their own rows in another yard, under guard themselves.

The prisoners had only seen the military police come into the prison a few times before and never in such numbers. Something out of the ordinary was up and Charlie felt the pit in his stomach churning from more than just lack of food. Although it seemed that their anger was directed at the soldiers rather than the prisoners, Charlie knew that this would result in recriminations the following day, once the feared Kempeitai had gone.

He jerked himself into alertness as he heard the number of his cellmate, Frank, called out. He was unable to see Frank from where he was standing. Frank had arrived at Changi several days later than Giles and himself so his number was higher and he stood several rows behind.

Then Charlie thought he heard his own name being called out and next Giles'. He felt Giles move beside him and then in his disassociated state, he was surprised to find his own swollen feet walking forward. Ten other numbers were called out and they limped slowly behind the black uniformed Kempeitai officer, while a pair of Japanese soldiers in mismatched khaki's pushed and prodded them on with their bayonetted rifles.

They found themselves in Yard 2 with another 20 or so European prisoners who must have been called earlier.

Lined up in rows again, they continued to wait. From this angle, they could better see the activity coming in and out of one of the prison dormitory blocks. A variety of rubble: mattresses, chairs, books, etc, was gradually building up in small hillocks as soldiers dragged the meagre possessions of the prisoners out of the multi-storied buildings.

Charlie, Giles and Frank, who was now standing beside his cellmates, could see that a prison-wide raid was going on. They had suffered events like this before, but never on this scale. From time to time, whole floors were ransacked and looted by the guards under the guise of looking for illicit belongings. But it was never to the point of removing mattresses and the odd bit of paltry furniture that some of the prisoners had garnered. It appeared that even the ordinary prison guards were under suspicion and Charlie wondered why he had been segregated with this odd assortment of twenty or thirty people in lines around him.

As the sun began to relax its grip over the barren complex, the number of prisoners in the yard with Charlie swelled until there were nearly 40 of them all together. Only one was a woman, Charlie noticed. There were all European apart from a couple of Indian prison guards, including their friend Dalip Khaira. There were no children amongst the group.

In the dim light of dusk, through the wire fence, they could see lines of weary prisoners returning to the cell blocks. Their own mini-group stayed put.

As the noise around them quietened, their fears grew. Finally they discovered that they were leaving the camp on lorries. The rough treatment they received as they were bundled onto the vehicles, left them in no doubt that being amongst the "chosen" ones was not a good thing. With the tarps down on the sides, they could not see where they were going, but Charlie and Giles both recognised the Central Police Station when they arrived. They soon realised the building, which contained four small jail cells, and one larger holding cell, had been taken over by the Kempei for their headquarters.

The prisoners were put haphazardly into the cells with no regards as to race or gender. There were a dozen people in with Charlie in a cell built for one. Laying down was not allowed, even if there had been room. An even more pressing concern was how to juggle themselves when someone needed to use the water closet. Despite having had no water to drink all day, their bodies still betrayed them by making urine, seemingly wasting the valuable resource.

Charlie and another man unknown to him, noticed the single woman in the cell was doubled over in pain. They tried to establish the cause of her malady and eventually realised she needed to use the lavatory. But how was she to do so with all the men about? Soon they set about organising the men to turn about face, so that she could relieve herself the best she could. This would become an ongoing problem.

They were given no food or water, but having gone all day without either, all but one of the prisoners resorted to drinking from the toilet cistern. Even Charlie risked disease. His gums and nasal passages were so dry that he knew his body needed water urgently. The cistern was slow to refill. The prisoners groaned at the wait and shuffled around to allow those at the back to get a turn.

The following morning the man who had refused to drink from the cistern was only semi-conscious. They urged the guards to give him water, but nothing was forthcoming. Eventually, they forcibly poured cistern water down the man's throat. It was enough to revive him, but he was still very weak.

Throughout the day, a few people were randomly removed from the cells. Horrendous sounds of pain echoed throughout the building but when these unfortunates returned, they were generally unable to speak. Their bodies spoke for them, with the signs of torture—bruises, macerated skin from whippings, cigarette burns and nailings—all too obvious.

On the second day, Charlie, Giles and Frank were moved to the YMCA building which had been converted into a military prison. Tiny cells held not just the uplifted Changi prisoners, but also disobedient Japanese soldiers and locals. Here they were kept generally three to four per cell, but still with no regard as to race or gender. From eight in the morning until ten at night, they were required to sit with their knees upright and without leaning against walls. They were only allowed to move around the cell if they needed the toilet and a ten minute walk after dinner. Talking was not allowed. Nevertheless there were occasional times when a whispered word or two could be shared and the prisoners became adept at their own form of sign language.

Charlie, Giles and Frank had been split into different areas the night they had arrived, but over the course of time, they were occasionally moved in and out of each other's cells, so that they could share a modicum of knowledge.

The days of Changi Gaol seemed luxurious in comparison to this. Yet if Charlie had known what was to come, he would have been more grateful for his ten minute walk and latrine water.

There were the regular prisoners in the military prison, and while the group from Changi Gaol were not segregated, it seemed as though they were invisibly marked somehow. Certainly everyone knew whether they were part of the group or not. Originally, the group consisted of the original 40 odd people who had been arrested at Changi. But as the days passed more civilians were arrested at Changi and brought in for interrogation. Including amongst them were two more women, one of these women was a European doctor who Charlie knew had been at Changi. As well, several Chinese and local Malays and even Bishop Wilson of St Andrews was arrested from Singapore town. In all there were 57 people held for interrogation at three Kempei locations: the Central Station, the Smith

Street Station and the YMCA.

Although they were never officially charged, they soon realised through the consistent lines of interrogation that the allegation against each one of them was that of spying and harbouring a radio transmitter inside the camps. Some of the locals were also being accused of being informants and smuggling money into the camps. Every one of them denied all of the charges, despite the brutalities inflicted. At first the prisoners couldn't help but deny any wrongdoing, since they didn't know what it was they were being charged with. Eventually though, as time wore them down, both small and large admissions were made here and there, if only to stop the pain. They counted the hours that one man held out—fifty five in total. Finally his ordeal fell silent, but he never returned to the cells. The body count grew slowly, as the days turned into weeks with no let up.

During that initial period while Charlie waited for his turn to be interrogated and inevitably tortured, he was given no water apart from the occasional tiny cup of tea with a meal. The water closet cistern turned out to be all they had for their every need. The Japanese prisoners alone received water in buckets and they were not allowed to share even if they had been inclined to, which they generally weren't. Once a day the prisoners received a meagre food ration: 200 grams of rice and occasional slice of radish. It was less than half what they needed to survive and their already emaciated bodies soon became skeletal. It was becoming harder than ever for the prisoners to withstand the torture.

Their efforts to shield the women amongst them from total loss of dignity were generally in vain, as the cruel Kempei forced them to watch the women relieve themselves. The three women were made to do the most disgusting sordid tasks in the cells.

One of the women was sexually violated in front of the prison bars. When the men went berserk, a shot rang out and a single prisoner dropped inside the cell, not dead, but with a smashed knee. No medical help was given, and despite the best efforts of the prisoners, the poor man died a couple of weeks later from blood poisoning, but not before he was further interrogated.

Frank seemed to be of special interest to the Kempei. Perhaps this was because of his previous association with radio. One day Frank was dropped unconscious into the cell with Charlie. He later relayed his encounter with the Kempei interrogators. He had been tied with his hands behind his back and laid on the concrete floor. A piece of cheese cloth had been draped across his face. Then the usual questioning began. He knew by now that it was no use to explain that he was simply a radio presenter rather than a radio engineer. So he stayed silent. He felt the uncomfortable sensation of water being poured over the cloth. Unable to breathe through his nose for fear of drowning, he tried to breathe through his mouth. The water came faster now, and he gulped it down in huge quantities to keep it out of his lungs. Then the water stopped and even as he sucked in urgently needed oxygen an immense pain buckled his water filled stomach, causing him to simultaneously vomit and scream in pain. The cloth over his face accidentally slipped to the ground and he saw that one of the Kempeitai had jumped on him with both his booted feet.

This water torture went on for an hour, each time ending in being jumped on, or as the quantity of vomit and blood increased, they resorted to using a metal bar. Eventually, he was too far gone to answer their questions. He told Charlie later that at that point he no longer cared for this life. He simply gave up and let himself drown. The Kempei were perhaps refining this method of torture, because surely the subject should not be allowed to die. The next thing Frank remembered was waking up in the cell with his head in Charlie's lap and his exhausted body being held by several other prisoners.

As the days wore on, Charlie found himself increasingly anxious. Waiting for his turn at interrogation was a sort of torture in itself. Some of the arrested prisoners, had been in for several turns before Charlie was taken out for his first go.

They led him through the rabbit warren of hallways and into a brightly lit room. After weeks of semi-darkness, his eyes took a while to adjust and when they did he nearly closed them again in shock.

In an instant he took in the dreadful sight. One of the arrested women, the Chinese one, was topless and kneeling on two sharp edged pieces of wood. Her hands were bound behind her and a rope connected her wrists to her ankles. Several sharp sticks were inserted between her calf muscles and the backs of her knees. With her shoulders twisted back and her ankles tied in the way they were, she was unable to loosen her grip on the sharp sticks. She could only sink down into them. To her right the man Charlie knew to be her husband, was suspended by a rope tied around his wrists. His tear stained eyes met Charlie's briefly before jerking back to his wife's ordeal. He uttered a continuous stream of cries and pleadings. Charlie had only been in the room a moment when the man's cries went up a notch in pitch and desperation. Charlie did not expect what was to come next, but suddenly the woman's body jerked convulsively and she let out a single harrowing scream. A trail of blood ran down the backs of her legs. Even as she regained her composure, such as it was, he realised that she had just been given an electric shock. He hadn't even noticed the wires before. Falling silent again, she gave her husband a brave half smile before retraining her eyes to the floor.

Before her questioning could begin again, Charlie was moved out of the room. He realised that the only point of taking him in to witness that whole episode was to frighten him. And it worked! His knees were weak, he was trembling uncontrollably and his bowels evacuated, a wet slimey mess running down his legs. He had never seen a woman, of any race, being so degraded. He was more than sick. His mind even doubted whether he had actually witnessed such a thing. Perhaps his mind was playing tricks. Yes, he decided he had just imagined it. Then, as he was dragged into an interrogation room of his own, stripped and hosed down, he heard her involuntary scream again accompanied by the heart-breaking howling from her husband. The water against his irritated skin felt like sandpaper and brought him back to his senses. He knew he hadn't imagined it.

He was tied naked to a chair in the centre of the room. Right then he decided that whatever they accused him of, he would admit to it. If he was lucky, he would receive imprisonment. If unlucky, death. But either way, he didn't know if in his current unhealthy state, his body could handle the sort of torture he had just witnessed that courageous woman silently taking, while her tormented husband was forced to watch. He knew he could never be that brave.

While he sat and waited he counted another three screams from the woman. He was unaware of any further noise and shortly thereafter several Kempei marched ominously into his room. The most senior, with three stars on his collar, Lt Colonel Sumida sat in a chair in one corner and commenced to chain smoke an endless cigarette. Perhaps he was nervous, Charlie thought hopefully, stealing a glance at him. The middle aged officer smiled at him briefly with an almost angelic look contrasting starkly with the smoke that he periodically released out of his nostrils. Charlie returned his eyes to the floor.

Counting himself, there were five men in the large room. Oddly, especially since Charlie was still naked and bound, they began with formal introductions. Sgt Major Terada Takao seemed to be in charge, despite the presence of the officer Sumida in the room. Slightly lower in rank, but older in age, was Sergeant Nozawa Toichiro. The two sergeants also had two and three silver stars on their collars, but Charlie knew the red background of the insignia, rather than yellow, denoted the enlisted ranks. Finally, the interpreter introduced himself, as Nigo Masayoshi sama. He did not wear any insignia, despite being dressed in what looked like the black Kempeitai uniform. But after a snigger from Sumida and a snappish word from Terada, he said, "You will call me Nigo-san." Charlie noted that he spoke near perfect English with an American accent. Yet he looked as Japanese as the others.

The questions started slowly and quietly. He felt as if the Kempei were coiled and ready to strike like poisonous snakes.

Charlie's plan to admit everything was doomed to fail. Unbeknownst to any of the prisoners, an act of sabotage had happened in Singapore Harbour which had destroyed seven Japanese naval vessels. It was a perfectly executed raid by an Australian special forces unit. So undetected did they engage, destroy and retreat that the Japanese had no idea that enemy forces had ever infiltrated the harbour. Japanese authorities assumed that the raid had been carried out by locals. Acting on instructions from the Chief of Kempeitai Col Kojimo, Lt Col Sumida had been ordered to round up those responsible, starting with the civilians in Changi Gaol. The considerable sum of $400,000 had been found hidden in a mattress inside the Gaol. Kojimo was determined that the masterminds of the harbour raid were civilians inside the Gaol who had bankrolled the locals using those who still lived relatively freely in Singapore, such as the Bishop, European doctors and those locals who traded with the prisoners or who had worked in Government positions.

In fact there *was* one spy who lived like a ghost, moving up and down the peninsular. Previously an employee of the Malayan Department of Information, his name Chrysostom was whispered amongst the prisoners as a source of underground radio news. But if the Kempei were aware of his name, they did appear to realise his significance. Certainly his name had not come up in the questioning.

If only Charlie had thought to mention Mr Chrysostom. The first questions had nothing to do with radio. They had to do with making diver's magnet mines. Charlie had read something a few years ago, about a new invention, Limpet mines. He only had a vague memory of how they worked, but squeezing a few drops of creativity from his tired mind he supplied the Kempeitei sergeant with what he thought was a plausible recipe. The Sgt-Major tested the truth of his testimony by laying traps. Soon Charlie was admitting to things that had not even happened. Disgusted, the Sgt-Major hurled abuse at him, getting into his face with a torrent of Japanese words.

Charlie could not work out why they did not want his admissions. What did they want, he wondered. The translator, Nigo Masayoshi, probed on and on in his perfect English. At times Charlie suspected he went far beyond the questions that had been tasked to translate.

Within half an hour, the questions had increased in ferocity. Suddenly the Lt Colonel leaped from his chair in the corner and drove his cigarette butt into Charlie's Adam's apple. "You think me fool!" he shouted in English, as Charlie's skin blistered and he bucked in the chair. The intense pain of the burn was all Charlie could think of. For several minutes he was unable to answer any question while he both felt and smelt his flesh burning.

When he regained his senses, the Lt Colonel had returned to the window with his back to Charlie. Sgt-Major Terada, changed tacks.

"When the radio is on, where do you run the aerial?"

The word aerial ran circles around Charlies mind. Aerial? What was an aerial again? He knew that word, but it was so hard to concentrate. He needed to give a believable answer. *I'm such a coward,* he thought. *Why not just deny it all?* But the intense heat from the burn on his throat made him weak. *I know the answer!* he thought in a Eureka moment. He smiled slightly as he gathered his thoughts.

Sgt-Major Terada misinterpreted the smile as defiance. "We'll try the hose on him!" he barked out.

Sumida turned from the window, and as Charlie felt the chair being slipped out from under him, he saw that dreadful smile beaming from Sumida's face. Now he was laying on his back on the damp concrete floor, with his arms still tied behind him. His shoulders were beyond aching and he shivered with both cold and fear.

Forcing his mouth open, the sergeant and the sgt-major pushed a short rubber hose down his throat.

Charlie gagged and nearly drowned on his own bile. For a while he choked involuntarily. His brain was disconnected and time had no meaning. It was just a struggle to exist in that moment. His head bounced off the concrete floor like a jack hammer with every convulsion. Finally he was able to relax enough to use his nose to breathe.

Tereda wasted no time. As soon as Charlie stopped convulsing, he put a peg on his nose and holding the rubber hose up, indicated for Sergeant Nozawa to fill it with water.

Charlie was forced to swallow and he felt his stomach distend painfully.

"That's enough!" Tereda must have barked. The rubber hose yanked painfully out if his throat.

"Tell us about the aerial!" the interpreter Nigo shouted over Charlie's head.

"Pointed ...out ... window," Charlie said. Charlie had very little technical knowledge of these things. On an ordinary day in his homely little bungalow, he had struggled to even tune in the news.

"You lie!" Tereda said in English.

Next thing Charlie knew, Nozawa had jumped onto his stomach, boots and all.

Charlie lost control of his body completely. Foul smelling liquid streamed from his mouth, nose, anus and penis. He was aware of the Kempei quickly stepping back out of the mess before his eyes rolled back in his head.

He was not unconscious exactly, but was certainly close to it. He was placed back on the chair and he felt his bare bottom slide in his own filth.

"Perhaps we have not perfected that method of interrogation yet," Nigo began. "Please answer our questions truthfully, or we will have to practice it some more on you."

"Please Nigo-san I just want this to stop. I'll say whatever you want," Charlie began weakly. "But I don't know anything. I really don't know anything about bombs. I know nothing about radios. I was just an ordinary prison guard before the war."

There was a period while the Kempei had a discussion in Japanese. Sumida continued to sit in his chair at the back of the room. Listening but not taking a direct part in the discussion. Suddenly he cut through the discussion with one heated sentence. Then he left the room.

Charlie saw the other three Kempeitai turn slowly towards him wearing nothing but menace across their faces. The snake was about to bite.

At some stage later that day, or perhaps the next day, Charlie awoke. He did not comprehend where he was, but he remembered having been beaten senseless. Gingerly testing his swollen eyes, he looked around. He seemed to be laying on lengths of bamboo. A sticky, smelly substance filled the two inch spaces between them. It reminded him of dried up dog vomit. Immediately in front of him were more bamboo poles to which further bamboo lengths were tied crosswise. In fact, he appeared to be lying in the foetal position in a bamboo cage. His bent knees had sticky blood plastered across them. His feet were pressed against the far end of the cage and his swollen right ear lay squashed beneath the weight of his aching head. At least his hands were no longer tied together, but they were awkwardly stuck behind him.

He moved as if to stand up. Then he realised that the bamboo bars of the cage were pressing down on top of him. The cage was only 2 foot tall by about 3 foot wide.

Gradually his eyes adjusted to the semi-darkness and he realised that he was still at the YMCA station. He could see the shadowy figures of prisoners behind the bars of an regular cell across a hallway. A Kempeitai sergeant, accompanied by a different interpreter, was ordering them to sit up. *It must be about eight in the morning*, Charlie thought as he recognised the day's routine beginning. A surge of sea sickness rolled through him before he recognised that he was moving.

The grunts of three small Chinese guards found their way to his ears as they man-handled his cage upright.

Now Charlie felt himself standing on the bamboo bars. His knees pressed against what had been the roof and his bottom sunk as far as it could go towards his ankles. His back seemed to be stuck to what had moments before been the floor of his cage and was now a wall. He wriggled his shoulders to free his back causing a painful tearing as semi-healed scabs bled anew. Ever so slowly, he manoeuvred his arms free. His stiffened joints and slashed muscles responding sluggishly in protest.

For three more days and nights he was left in the cage. The only variation was being laid down at night and lifted into crouching position during the day. He became desperate to straighten out his legs. He would have given just about anything to do that.

During those long days he was given no food nor water. He would have welcomed water, even latrine water, despite the memory of the water torture and his painful throat and stomach which was empty now and churning with gastric acids from the vomiting. He told himself to be thankful that he was being held here in the semi darkness, and not out in the heat of the sun. As his need for water became paramount to his survival, he began to float back in and out of feverish delirium. He imagined that flies were attacking his wounds and their maggots were burying their way through his skin. He imagined himself slapping them away and picking the eggs out of his flesh, crying out in disgust. When he periodically came out of his hallucinations, he realised that he was not covered in flies and while he may have been scratching his skin, he was not digging holes through his flesh. His throat was so parched, that he even doubted that he had been crying out.

Charlie practiced the Lord's Prayer in his head. Over and over he repeated the mantra until he never knew where it finished and began again. His mind wandered to his wife who he imagined tenderly caring for him. Sometimes she softly pressed a cool cloth to his forehead. Other times she gently washed and bound his wounds. He could smell her rose perfume and occasionally he caught glimpses of her full bow lips and milky white chest as she concentrated on his ministrations. Inevitably his mind sought out his daughter, even though he tried not to go there. The ache of knowing that she was growing up without him, that he was missing out in her daily doings, hurt far more than any beating could. He imagined her in Colombo, with servants attending her every need. Or perhaps she was back in England with Ruth's aunties.

One day Charlie had been asleep, but was just coming out of another thick brain-fog. The image of Terada materialised in front of him. He was sitting on a box, sipping a whiskey and soda.

He held it out to Charlie to take through the bars.

"Yes, Cole-dono," Terada encouraged, as Charlie was slow to take him up on the offer.

Still he teased him with the cool drink until finally Charlie felt confident that he was for real. Charlie reached out his hand to the bar. Just as his fingertips touched the crystal glass, Terada pulled it back out of reach. Then he laughed. A loud belly laugh.

Then he sat on his box and sipped his drink, making exaggerated noises of satisfaction all the while.

Charlie let his eyelids flop closed. He didn't want to look.

Slap! Charlie jumped in fright. He hadn't noticed a Kempeitai interpreter standing to his left, until he had wacked the cage with his cane. "Eyes open!" the man said.

Terada finished his drink and eyed Charlie.

"You want drink. You will answer Sgt-Major Terada's questions," the interpreter said.

The cage was lifted onto a wheeled trolley and Charlie found himself being rolled back into an interrogation room. Here the same Kempei men as before were gathered, other than the fact that there was a Chinese interpreter this time.

The questioning began again and this time Charlie answered truthfully. Occasionally he was rewarded with a water soaked sponge to suck. He was told that if he gave them the answers they wanted, he would get an ice cold glass of soda. But Charlie didn't have the answers they wanted.

After four hours it became clear that Charlie knew nothing about radios. That he had never seen Frank operate a radio in his Changi cell. That he knew even less about limpet mines and nothing about the sinking of any ship. They also discerned that, as a prison guard (he still did not let on that he was in fact a police sergeant himself), his wages were insufficient for him to ever be in possession of sufficient funds to pay for the operation.

Unbeknownst to Charlie, Sumida angrily pronounced him a waste of space. A non-event. He had confirmed every word of Frank's interrogation. Similarly, Armstrong had been questioned during Charlie's incarceration in the cage. Despite being flogged until the skin hang from his back in strips, Armstrong had not shown any knowledge of any of the events.

Charlie looked over at Sumida. He may not have understood a word he had just said, but he felt the finality of his tone of voice. He knew Sumida had given up.

Sumida turned and caught Charlie watching him. He gave another one of his seraphic smiles and then strode towards the door. It was only a second later, that Charlie realised he had stopped behind the cage, whereupon he ground the stub of his hot cigarette in between Charlies buttocks and left it there before storming out of the room, slamming the door behind him.

Charlie reached around and flicked the butt away, grinding his teeth together to stop himself from crying out.

For the next hour or so, he was left in the room by himself. Eventually, the Chinese interpreter came back and rolled his cage back to the cells. The lid to his cage was opened and after a little push he fell onto the other prisoners crouching in their day-time position. Perhaps the Kempei felt some sympathy for him, because they rolled the cage away, leaving the prisoners to gather him up and massage his aching joints without reprimand. Still naked and with no spare items of clothing to put back on, the prisoners could only give him latrine water, cautioning him not to drink too much.

Shortly after that, they were given their rice ration and today it was accompanied by a piece of carrot and a cup of tea. Frank and Armstrong were not currently in sight, but looking around him, Cole could see that some of the others were in a worse state than he was.

The prisoners were allowed their ten minute walk around the cells, and this they did in an orderly fashion. Three of them marching around the perimeter. One man, whose ankles were smashed up stayed put in the centre. His moans were commendably quiet. Charlie asked if doctor had been called. They said he had been told that he wasn't sick enough for a doctor. Nobody said it out loud, but they could both see and smell the gangrene and in these conditions that essentially meant that the poor man was dying.

Their slight reprieve by the guards allowing whispered conversation, their dinner and the walk around the cell was over. It was the daily luxury. Now the guards returned and told them to sleep. This meant they could lay down, but must remain silent until morning. Charlie stretched out his legs and arms, and tried not to think about the filth on the floor infecting his wounds.

None of the men in Charlie's cell were questioned again. But within three weeks, all of the cell had contracted dysentery. All except the man with the smashed ankles who had long since died. It had been an agonisingly painful death which they'd all had to watch unable to help at all. Now desperately sick themselves they were unable to do more than nibble their rice ration and drink their tea. The floor around the latrine was a slimy mess. The wound between Charlie's buttocks became ulcerated, as had several wounds on the other two men. Soon, they knew that if they didn't get help, they'd suffer an equally painful death as their cell mate. But on about the third week since Charlie had been liberated from the cage, the prisoners were taken out to a lorry. The bright sunlight, made it impossible to do anything other than squint. Almost blinded in this way, they were several miles away before Charlie even realised that Giles Armstrong was on the lorry too. He had been laying on his stomach because the ulcerated welts on his back were too painful to lay on, and he was too sick to sit. Frank, he learned later, had died. Nobody knew why, but it was possibly heart failure. He had spent days at the hands of the interrogators. The final time he was returned to the cells with hardly a new scratch on him, but later that afternoon, he had apparently just keeled over, dead.

The seven mile journey came to an end and those of the prisoners who were still sensible to the world around them were astonished to find that they had arrived at the old RAF camp at Sime Road.

In a dusty old hut, with a crumbling roof, the prisoners were ordered to find a place to lay down and rest. Some were simply dragged in and dumped. All were far too emaciated and ill to run away, though there was barely enough guards to prevent them had they the strength to do so.

They lay all night, unattended and forgotten.

Early the following morning a European doctor and a nurse bustled in.

In his semi-coherent state, Charlie recognised the doctor as being a fellow prisoner in his block at Changi.

"Are we at Changi?" he asked him, when he was being checked over.

"No, we're at Sime Road. The prisoners at Changi have all been relocated here. You are fortunate that one of the Nippon guards is a kind man who implored the Commandant to allow me to attend you all. You'll be alright now, once we get a bit of food into you."

"Not so good for my mate," Charlie said nodding his head towards the prisoner on the floor beside him. Charlie was holding his dead hand.

"He died just before you came in, I think."

"Oh dear," the doctor scooted around to the man to check his vital signs. "What was his name?"

"I never knew it," Charlie answered. "He was prisoner 3124. That's all I know."

One by one the doctor triaged them into *Urgents* and *Not-So-Urgents*. Charlie and Giles were both categorised as urgent, but those that did not have dysentery or any other infectious disease were moved to another hut. So Giles, who had yet to succumb to the deadly illness was taken away.

The brief conversation was the last Charlie was to have with the doctor. Despite the vastly improved housing, food and basic nursing care Charlie slipped into a fevered state. The dysentery raged through his frail skeletal body.

The doctor and his helpers had seen some terrible sights during their incarceration, but the state of those that returned from what was now known as the Double Tenth Incident, because it began on the 10 October, were beyond comprehension. They did not need to be told that they had all endured horrific injuries. On the whole they were too traumatised to speak, but the doctor learned snippets here and there. The more he learnt, the more angered he became. He didn't believe that even a scavenging dog could be more abused. Several men, Charlie Cole amongst them, were touch and go. He had resorted to feeding those poor souls the water that the rice had cooked in, rather than the rice itself. It was the only nutrition their digestive tracts could handle.

20
KAWAU ISLAND FEBRUARY 1944

HUNTER WHITLOCK

The news that Ruth was pregnant had rocked Hunter's world in a manner analogous to the wake created by Messrs Gubb's ferry as it raced past his great lumbering flat bottomed scow moored at The Sandspit.

At first he had indulged in doubts as to her fidelity to him. Subsequently, a clandestine visit to his old family doctor put paid to those suspicions. Looking over his notes, the doctor reminded Hunter that his position had never been that he couldn't father a child. Rather he had only indicated that it might be difficult.

"Did you not consider that it might well be your wife, er Hester, who could not conceive?"

"No. Well naturally, with my disability, we both assumed that it was me at fault."

"My dear boy, in science, we never assume the obvious. Besides, I have a theory that it's not a matter of fault, more a matter of practice and precision."

"What do you mean?" Hunter wasn't sure if the doctor had been giving advice or merely thinking aloud.

"Oh nothing, nothing. Don't mind me."

In his heart, Hunter hadn't needed the doctor's confirmation. He knew that Ruth hadn't been unfaithful. He was also under no doubt that she was keen to legitimise their relationship. This was creating quite a strain to his mind.

Hunter decided to rent a small flat for Ruth in Takapuna. She would be close enough to the aunties, if she needed help with Jean. But she would also be independent of them and their neighbours. Ruth dropped out of the mahjong club and the ladies circle which volunteered their time to make camouflage-nets for the war effort. She stopped attending afternoon teas. To a large extent, she dropped out of society entirely, spending her days doing her needlepoint.

As the weather warmed up, they increased their little sojourns out to Kawau Island. But just like night cannot exist without day, Hunter wondered when the yin would catch up with their carefree happy yang. He suspected that the baby would be the turning point. Marrying her was out of the question, but the current state of unwedded bliss could not continue past the birth either.

Hunter edged his great boat in to their idyllic beach slowly until he felt it touch the sand. The forward momentum stopped his inner musings abruptly.

"We're here! Mummy we're at our secret beach," Jean squealed down the hatch, unable to contain her excitement. "Can I go ashore daddy?"

Hunter smiled indulgently. "Aye, ye lily livered land-lubber. If ye must. But mind you don't let the crocodiles get ye."

"Crockdials! There are no crockdials daddy. Are you jesting with me?" Jean had become a proper little chatterbox with a decidedly squeaky voice.

"The whales then. Mind you don't get swallowed up by a great … big … whale."

"But Daddy, whales can't come to our little beach." She had already climbed over the rails and was getting ready to drop into the shallow water like a lithe little monkey and Hunter could hear her shrill voice floating back to him. "They're too big."

This was followed by a splash and he stopped what he was doing to take a precautionary peek over the side. He knew she could get the few feet to shore by herself, but even so she was only three and he liked to reassure himself that she was coping. She dog paddled for a moment until she was able to stand and wade ashore.

This was their private little harbour which they had discovered months ago. Hunter and Ruth called it their secret beach, and Jean truly thought it belonged to them. As yet they had not seen another soul or boat in it. Much of the cove was inaccessible with swamp coming right down to meet the sea and there were only a couple of nice sandy beaches, along the right hand side as you entered. The water depth was too shallow for most vessels but the Pahiki had no trouble reaching the sandy spot. These were the conditions that these flat bottomed scows were built for.

By the time Hunter had dropped the steps over the side, Ruth had struggled up the companionway with a picnic basket.

"I won't be able to do this for much longer," she said.

Hunter did not reply. Her words mirrored his own dark thoughts.

"I'm getting bigger by the day. I must be nearly seven months gone now. I think this might perhaps be the last time we can come here together until after the birth."

They began their wade towards the beach, Hunter holding Ruth's arm so she didn't slip. Flopping down on the sand, with their toes in the water, Hunter eventually spoke.

"Any new thoughts on names my darling?"

Ruth grinned at him. She enjoyed their battles over names. He teasing her with preposterous labels that she could never consent to saddling a baby with. She suggesting the most effeminate boys names and masculine girls names she could think of. Every so often, Jean would float by and add in her own idea of baby names, such as Silky and Fluffy. Her only experience in naming babies was the chicks that had hatched in the auntie's back yard a few months previously.

"What about Cecil if it's a boy and Christina if it's a girl," Hunter finally surprised Ruth with his two sensible alternatives.

"I like both of those," Ruth said after testing them out loud. "And what about for second names Henry or Mary. That way the baby will have your family names for the first name and mine for the second."

"Henry and Mary? They're both a bit kingly for my liking, but alright, if it pleases you."

"What would please me, is if we knew what his or her surname might be."

"I would want it to have my name, of course. Nobody else need know."

"Beulah will pounce on that like a cat on a mouse."

"Who?"

"Beulah Greensway. You know, the woman at mahjong who enjoys ridiculing me."

Hunter merely frowned and scrunched his shoulders up.

"Really Hunter, your aunties and I speak about her all the time. Surely you remember. She's a nasty piece of work. She has already started turning the gossip mill about my pregnancy. She's the reason the aunties don't go to the Tennis Club anymore. That woman is determined to find out who the father is."

"Oh!" Hunter said. But he felt the blood drain from his face and knew he must look blanched. "I'm going to take Jean swimming before lunch." His instinct was to end the conversation, which was leading down a dangerous path; leading to questions he did not want to answer.

21
AUCKLAND JUNE 1944

RUTH COLE

It was a cold dark morning with heavy clouds and fat drops of rain leaking here and there. Ruth put the hood up on the perambulator and parked it outside the butcher's shop. She held no concern about leaving Christina outside the shop, other than her getting wet should the drops turn to real rain. But with one last look at the ominous sky, she figured she only needed to dash in for a few minutes—just long enough to purchase four mutton chops which the aunties had requested for a communal dinner that evening.

The chief butcher had a fondness for small children and he hovered his giant fork over the counter towards Jean with a choice piece of baked ham on the end. This she took with a pleased smile. It was a little ritual that the child had come to expect from this store.

Meanwhile, as Ruth fumbled in her purse for the correct coins, her peripheral vision caught sight of a woman bending over the pram. She turned to stare, wondering who on earth the woman was.

"Mrs?" the junior behind the counter reminded her that he was waiting for her payment so that he could help the next person in the queue.

She quickly made the transaction and rushed outside. The strange woman had already crossed the street and was turning into a laneway. Ruth checked on Christina, who was still asleep. What was it about the woman that made the hairs on the back of her neck stand on end? Ruth wondered if it was her oddly black clothing. Not that wearing black was uncommon in this day when so many people were in mourning, but this woman had an almost witchy appearance to her that would have suited the previous century. Yet she had only appeared to be slightly older than Ruth was herself.

It wasn't the first time, she had seen the woman either. Several times in the past six months, she had felt she was being followed. She had caught sight of a similarly dressed woman in each of these occasions, but always upon being detected the woman would disappear around a corner or into a shop.

This time, Ruth was determined to find out what her game was. Dashing between the few vehicles on the road, she was about to follow the woman down the laneway, when the sky opened up. The downpour forced her to seek refuge under a shop awning.

Shivering, she hoped her new daughter wasn't too cold. It was only the second time she had taken her out since her confinement. Ruth shook out her raincoat and put it on, instructing Jean to do the same. Then she opened her umbrella and placed it over the pram. As soon as there was a break in the rain she would dash along the street to the flat.

For some unknown reason, the aunties had listened to her story about the woman in black with more attention than she'd have expected them to. They followed up with a plethora of questions. When was the first time she had noticed her? What was her shawl like? How did she wear her hair?

"We'll have to phone Hunter," was their ultimate decision.

"If you like, but it wasn't that serious. I'm simply saying it was odd, that is all," Ruth said frowning at having caused them such distress.

Hunter was similarly worried. Ruth could tell by the answers Millicent was giving him over the telephone line.

"Need it come to that?" Ruth heard Millicent say.

"I still think she would be safer back with us than out there alone," she said after another long pause.

"We'll see you for dinner then. Mind we only have four chops and one of them is a small one for Jean. Yes that would be nice dear. Bye bye."

Ruth joined Margaret at the kitchen table to hear what Hunter had said to Millicent.

"He wants to come for dinner," Millicent said.

"He's coming all the way up here, just because a woman looked at my baby?"

"We'll have to have a late dinner. He'll never make it by five," Margaret exclaimed.

"We're to eat ours when we're ready. He will bring an extra chop for himself and cook it when he gets here. I suppose we'll just keep his potatoes warm on the range."

"Never mind the dinner. What is it you two aren't telling me?" Ruth demanded impatiently.

The aunties just pursed their lips and went about their business. In Ruth's opinion they were bordering on rude by ignoring her question, and their tight lipped secrecy only served to increase her suspicion that there was something the three of them were not telling her.

When Hunter arrived, Millicent took charge of the kitchen and set about frying his chop. It would be a bit tough she announced and Hunter reassured her it would probably be better than his own bachelor cooking.

Margaret brought out the sherry. "I thought we might need a bit of fortification," she said. "Now mind, that the children are just in the next room. I don't want any shouting or to-do. You're both similarly at fault, in my opinion."

"Whatever do you mean?" Ruth asked taken aback.

"Ruth," Hunter began. "This woman in black. From the description, it sounds like it's Hester, my wife."

"Well it might be your ex-wife, I suppose. I hadn't thought of that. You did say she wasn't quite right in the head, didn't you." It wasn't a question. Ruth was simply speaking her mind.

"No Ruth, now listen," Hunter said. "I didn't want to ever tell you this, but Hester is not my ex-wife. She is my legal-wife. I have been trying to divorce her for years. But the blasted woman won't sign the papers."

"She's your…." Words failed Ruth and she promptly drained her sherry.

"I tried to divorce her on the basis of insanity, but I discovered that she would have to be incarcerated for that to be a legal reason for divorce."

"Incarcerated?"

"Yes, hospitalised in an asylum. Her father supports our divorce, but he won't agree to having her committed. He doesn't think she is that bad and she has improved recently, I believe."

"You believe? You mean you are still in contact? Does she live with you? Is that why you won't let me live with you? Of course, no wonder you don't want to marry me. That would make you a bigamist."

"Come now dear," Margaret tried to placate her. "Hunter can no more marry you, than you him. You are still legally married as well."

"Legally may-be. But my husband is dead. Dead! Not scurrying around back alleys trying to steal babies."

"We don't know what she was doing," Hunter said. "She might have been thinking of abducting Christina. Or perhaps she just wanted to look at the infant."

"Oh my Lord. What have I gotten into. I won't be able to leave her for a second. We should phone the police. But then again, how can we? I've been carrying on with a married man. I'm no better than a common adulterer. My mother would turn in her grave." Tears started slipping down Ruth's face and she felt herself losing her grip on reality. She suddenly felt as though she was looking in on someone else's private life, instead of her own. The darkness grabbed her and she noticeably swooned, causing Hunter to rush to her side in concern.

Margaret passed the smelling salts under Ruth's nose and touched her hair. "Please don't be angry with Hunter. He really does care for you, not her. Don't you dear? And we have grown to love you too. You are family in all the ways that are meaningful. I am sure that God is sympathetic in these abnormal days of war."

"But you both knew. All this time, and you never said," Ruth accused them.

"Well, it's not quite that simple dear, you see..." Millicent began but was interrupted by Margaret.

"Yes it is that simple. We did know and for that we are sorry. We had no right to keep this from you. I see that now."

"Where will I go? What will I do? How will I support myself with two babies?"

"You are going to come and live with me," Hunter said. "That's why I've driven up here tonight?"

"Live with you? Have you lost your senses? Do you think so little of me, that you believe I'd stoop that low? I could never trust you again?"

"You'll have to trust me Ruth. We don't know what Hester is capable of. I have to protect Christina from her. And like you said, where else would you go?"

"It might be for the best Ruth," Margaret said. "But stay the night Hunter. You can pack in the morning."

"I'd rather leave now. She could be watching the flat by day."

"Well my dear nephew, you know her best," Millicent said, causing Ruth to crumple in tears and Hunter to comment wryly:

"How strange then that the one I've known the longest is the one I understand the least."

Ruth had a tendency towards dramatic tearful displays during times of high stress. Yet she was not the kind of person to be crushed by despair nor to wallow in self-pity for long. She was a practical and optimistic woman who had an inexhaustible bank of mettle from which she could withdraw equal measures of gumption and prudence to light a foggy course. Her instinctive judgement grasped just when it was time to *cut and run* or whether it was better to *back and fill*.

In the weeks that followed that awful admission from her illicit fiancé, Ruth tried hard to glue their broken bonds back together. For the large part it worked. She moved into the farmhouse out at Western Springs, Avondale in Auckland's western districts where she found the semi-isolation to be comforting. It wasn't as though Hester could just wander up their lane and stand watching her from the roadside without being seen. There was only one other house in the vicinity and foot traffic was rare.

Despite the apparent peace in the household, there was something missing from their relationship. The realities of life created emotional barriers. The aphrodisia they had shared, as young lovers hiding away from the war, no longer carried them. Nurturing the baby, rather than lust, became their mutual driving force, and it seemed that they each navigated their respective helms with their internal compasses set to differing deviations.

Christina was never going to be an infant forever. By September she was crawling and despite Ruth's intention to watch over her constantly, it wasn't long before she was out and about. Much to Hunter's chagrin, Jean delighted in leading her baby sister through the commercial citrus orchard which surrounded the rear of the property. From time to time, people worked the rows. The government leased this citrus farm from the Whitlock estate, and Hunter had no say in who worked there or when.

Ruth was still struggling to reconcile the fact that Hunter was a married man. At first she pushed Hunter to secure a release from his marriage, even if it meant admitting to adultery. It was a scandal that she felt they would have to face and forge through. People would eventually forget. Besides she had very little social network, so she didn't really care.

Hunter did not approve of that idea at all. He had recently applied for the position of truancy officer for the Education Board and he was under no illusions that being an officially published adulterer would preclude him from getting any position from the fusty Board members. Niggling arguments, such as this, continued to gnaw away at their relationship.

And then a bombshell hit. A letter for Ruth had arrived at the auntie's house. It was from Charlie's parents. Of course they didn't dare open it, but they put a call through to the Western Springs farmhouse and waited until Hunter could drive Ruth up to collect it on the weekend.

22
SIME ROAD CAMP 1944

CHARLIE COLE

The days had taken on a sameness for the internees at Sime Road Camp. In particular, those who had suffered the Double Tenth and survived, found a robotic rhythm where they simply existed rather than lived. It was hard to rustle up any enthusiasm for the dull highlights of prison life when measured against the extreme fear and pain they had experienced in the hellholes of the three Kempei prisons.

Even so, the Sime Road camp was idyllic compared to the cramped cells at Changi Gaol. Rough attap huts, scattered amongst 470 acres of rubber trees provided the rude prison accommodation. The healthiest amongst the prisoners had eventually repaired the huts and had even begun growing vegetables with random success and failures. The women and children, separated from the men by fences, had their own compound within the perimeter. Over the months more and more prisoners poured into Sime Road and it wasn't long before the camp became overcrowded again. Each prisoner being allotted a tiny floor space.

Charlie had lost track of the days and weeks, but he knew that another Christmas must be closing in on them when he heard the sounds of carols floating in through the windows. Many prisoners kept calendars of sorts, but Charlie did not care enough to bother. He was still battling with extreme emaciation and confined to the hospital hut, having suffered one illness after the other. Currently, he was dealing with another bout of malaria.

If there was a highlight in his week, it would be receiving a visit from his old friend Giles, whose shredded back had eventually healed. Giles had even left the hospital hut and occasionally helped arrange camp concerts.

Although since the Double Tenth incident, the Japanese had curtailed merry-making and large gatherings, so that these mini-concerts were limited to small groups during religious services. They had constructed a mini-church for this purpose within the wire fence of the prison perimeter.

The International Red Cross had until this time, been unable to directly access the civilian internees in Singapore, but they'd succeeded in making some positive influence, such as convincing the Japanese to add rice *polishings* to their diet. This helped to combat beriberi, a devastating and often deadly illness.

Then one day, Red Cross parcels were handed out. As well as the welcome luxuries that each parcel contained, such as sewing thread and needles, soap, cigarettes and maggoty chocolate (maggoty because some of the parcels had been sitting for over twenty months to be delivered), permission was also given to allow the prisoners to send home a postcard. For this particular group of prisoners, it was the first letters home they'd been allowed.

Giles made sure he was at the hospital hut in time to help Charlie fill out his card.

The simple correspondence, consisted of a short series of impersonal multi-choice sentences and each prisoner could tick the declarations that applied to them. These were along the lines of: "I am in good health" or "I am receiving medical help for an illness", or "I am currently occupied with useful employment." There was space to write one personal sentence along the bottom and Charlie asked Giles to write for him, "Give my love to Ruth and Jean in Colombo."

Actually, what Giles wrote was, "Charlie gives his love to Ruth and Jean in Colombo," hoping that by using the third person, they would read between the lines that he was gravely ill. Together they decided to address the card to Charlie's parents in Australia, as they was not sure whether Ruth would still be in Colombo or not.

"I almost dread to think what my parents will feel when they get this blunt note," Charlie whispered to Giles. He was too weak to speak with much volume.

"We all feel the same, my dear fellow," Giles assured him. "But you can't not send it. This is the first chance we've had to let everyone know that we are still alive."

"It'll be a cruel shock," Charlie replied still not convinced. He let his eyes relax and drifted back into his own world, no longer aware that Giles was still sitting beside him with the card in his hands.

The machinations of the International Red Cross whirled into action like the workings of a complicated Omega time-piece.

The brief cards to be posted home were first sent to neutral Switzerland and then flown out to Spain. From there, they were shipped to London and then the various Colonial Red Cross branches. It took many weeks before Charlie's letter reached his parents and then, for reasons known only to themselves, they hesitated before contacting Ruth.

23
AUCKLAND FEBRUARY 1945

HUNTER WHITLOCK

Sitting at the auntie's familiar kitchen table, Ruth opened the letter with trembling fingers. Hunter, leaning against the enamel sink, watched her darkly. *What did these people want from her after all this time?* They'd sent no financial aid despite Ruth having written to them to advise of her dire situation. He didn't have to wait long. Ruth had barely begun before she had finished reading. She placed it onto the table in front of her and carefully smoothed it out. Apparently she was bidding for time, keeping her thoughts to herself. Hunter could see that the words did not even fill a whole page.

"It doesn't say much," Ruth began eventually. Her voice sounded clipped, and Hunter wished she would look up so he could read her face. He was aware that the aunties were leaning forward, as anxious as he was.

"He's alive."

Nobody said anything in response. For Hunter's part, his mind was slow in ticking the two words over.

"They have, apparently, received a letter of sorts, from inside the Japanese prison of war camp." She looked around at the blank faces staring back at her. "Charlie doesn't seem to be dead after all." Her voice had risen to a little girl's squeak.

Auntie Margaret was first to recover from the shock. "Well, that is er, *good* news, isn't it?"

"How can it be good news, silly woman. It's a pickle that's what it is," Millicent said.

Hunter's face was approaching beetroot.

Millicent stood up. "Come sister, we'll take the girls for a stroll around the garden."

"May I?" Hunter asked once they had departed, indicating the letter.

As he perused the contents, pacing back and forth, Ruth covered her face in her hands.

"Talk to me Ruth. Tell me what you are thinking."

"Truth?" Ruth replied unnecessarily. "Happy, panicked, sickened, saddened. I feel like I'm in a magician's Box of Mystery after a dozen magician's swords have been thrust into it. Why didn't they enclose the actual letter?"

"Do you still love him?"

"I love the memory of him. Of course I love him."

"But are you still *in love* with him?"

"I honestly don't know. I haven't allowed myself to think of him in that way for so long. It's you I love."

"Then the way forward is clear."

Ruth was picking at a knot on the wooden table.

"Isn't it Ruth? If you love me then you must know what you must do."

"But I have a child with him."

"You have a child with me," Hunter reminded her exasperated.

"But I am *married* to him."

"I'm married to Hester."

"Oh stop it Hunter. You know it's not the same."

"Isn't it?"

"Your marriage is failed. Your wife abandoned you years before your marriage collapsed. My husband is at this very moment suffering at the hands of the Japanese." She shivered at the thought. "He must—oh god—he must, believe, that I'm waiting for him."

"By all accounts, life isn't too bad for those that are interned. Good food, tropical climate—they'll not be cold."

"Oh Hunter! How could you be so naive."

"Well! I mean what am I supposed to think? I don't want to lose you, but I'm not going to beg. Besides I already know what you've decided. I can see it in your eyes."

"How can you know Hunter, when I have no idea myself."

Late the following afternoon, Hunter returned to the farmhouse to find Ruth sitting on the front porch. The children, oblivious to her distressed countenance, were playing with dolls in the garden, enjoying the balmy summer weather.

"I know you think I've got a choice. But really I don't," Ruth began the moment Hunter stepped onto the porch.

Hunter gritted his teeth.

"I been thinking about it all day. There really is only one thing I can do. I have to find a place of my own. Find a position somewhere—perhaps behind a counter somewhere. I need to return to England as soon as possible. By all accounts, it looks like the Japs are beaten. The war in Europe is largely over. It shouldn't be that hard to get a passage now."

"So who will look after the children while you are working in a shop?"

"Well Jean is old enough for kindergarten…"

"And Christina?"

"If only there were nursery schools in Auckland. Other cities in New Zealand have places for babies and toddlers."

"So, you're back to square one. It's up to you to look after her. I have a full-time job."

"I've decided to find someone to board her. At least for Monday to Friday and possibly full-time once I go to England."

"No child of mind is going to be adopted out."

"It's not adoption Hunter. Although that's a possibility we ought to examine. She's an illegitimate…"

Hunter interrupted. "Christ Ruth! She's a child, not a sucker to be pruned off the main plant."

"Don't be ridiculous. Just think on. What future will there be for her in England, even if Charlie was willing to take her in as a ward. Is that what you want for her? To be a second-rate citizen?"

"But I've treated Jean as if she is my own. Why wouldn't he do the same for Christina."

"Society in England is different…"

"Blast England!"

"I want to go back, Hunter. Once I'm there I'll stay with my own aunties, where I'll wait for Charlie to be released. They are saying this war with Japan is nearly over—the Nips are losing on all fronts. I don't know what state he'll be in or whether he will want to continue with our marriage. But I ought to give him a chance. I owe him that much. If he doesn't want me, I'll come back."

"So I'm to be your second choice."

"Once he is over the shock, I'll tell him about Christina and send for her."

"She's a toddler. You can't just send for her like a mail order."

"Well, you know what I mean. I'll come back for her. No doubt Charlie will want to return to Singapore. After all, that is where he works. I'll skip across to New Zealand and pick her up on the way home."

"So you've decided then."

"Yes. And I've decided that I should start by moving out from here. It isn't right, my staying here a moment longer. I've already found a flat in Herne Bay and I've phoned the Ponsonby Kindergarten. It's within walking distance of the flat. I was wondering if you would put up the money for my rent—just until I get work and my first pay packet."

"Oh swell! So I'm losing my own flesh and blood—probably the only child I'll ever have—and I have to jolly well pay for the privilege too. You know Ruth, you really take the cake, don't you." Hunter stormed inside the house. He felt powerless to stop this wild train ride of a situation which was charging full steam ahead, despite the tricky corners and doubtful bridges that he foresaw. Pulling himself up sharp, he discovered that Ruth had already packed. The hallway was full of an assortment of luggage.

In a rage, Hunter picked up each piece of luggage and loaded them wordlessly onto the car.

Ruth hovered anxiously on the edge of his angry activity. "Ah, I'd arranged to move in tomorrow Hunter," she offered timidly.

Hunter ignored her and continued loading the car.

"But I, ah, suppose I can go today. The landlord lives next door apparently."

"You coming then? Let's not put this off any longer," Hunter growled.

"Just let me put a call through to the landlord to expect us."

Fifteen minutes later, they had unloaded the car again in front of a small wooden cottage.

"Get the key Ruth."

Ruth ran next door, looking red in the face.

Hunter looked at the drab single story building in front of him. There was no front garden and only a narrow alley ran between the similarly sized cottages to each side.

She soon returned. "There is no key. The man said I could go right in. He'd be over shortly for the deposit."

Hunter lifted the boxes and bags into the front room and inspected the property. There wasn't much to it. It was sparsely furnished with five rooms including a converted bathroom on the back porch. It was older and in far poorer condition that the flat he had rented for her in Takapuna. He slapped a fiver onto the kitchen table and giving each of his daughters a bear hug, for he felt that Jean was as much his as Christina, he left without a second glance at Ruth.

Then he hit the road, his vision blurred by tear drops that kept forming in the creases. At first he had no idea where he was driving to, but soon he recognised the well-trodden road around the harbour to his aunties' house. They were the only people he could confide in.

"You can't bring up a young girl by yourself dearie," Millicent said after hearing his news, "and we just aren't young enough to cope full-time ourselves."

"I could hire a maid to help."

"But what kind of life would that be for the child. A life without a mother. No, you leave it to us, we might have a solution that will suit everyone," Margaret said with a pointed look at Millicent. Her sister nodded, seeming to understand what Margaret was thinking.

Within a couple of days, they telephoned their nephew with their promised solution. There was a cousin whose husband had a nephew, Duncan, who was married to a lovely young Christian girl. The couple had been unable to conceive a child despite being married nearly ten years. The aunties had only been lunching with this cousin, the day before Hunter had approached the aunties with his problem. She had told them all about her husband's nephew's predicament. The couple had been advertising for a small child without success for the past few months. When told about Christina, they had jumped at the chance to board a small child for several months or as long as necessary.

Hunter and Ruth agonised over the decision. Yet, it made sense all round. Ruth had already found a position in a small stationery shop. She urgently needed to confirm if she was able to take it.

"It's a better choice than just strangers out of the personal column," Hunter eventually conceded. "Though I'm not entirely happy about it."

"Just know this then Hunter Whitlock; I'm not happy either. I wasn't happy to find that you were still married. I was especially unhappy to find that you'd lied about it all along. I'm not right pleased that I was misinformed about my husband's death. I'm certainly not happy that he has been a prisoner all this time. And I'm not happy that I'm stuck in New Zealand, about as far away from any of my family as I can get, with two children under five, each with different fathers. This is not the life I imagined for myself. I'm not happy either. Not by a long shot."

RUTH COLE

The couple lived in a small town some 30 miles to the south of Auckland. They did not know Auckland city well, and so had thought it would be easier to meet in a public place. They agreed on the Auckland Domain Wintergardens' carpark.

Meanwhile, Ruth packed Christina's meagre possessions into the carpet bag she'd purchased in Ceylon. She did not allow her mind to examine what she was about to do, but fixed it firmly on trivial things, such as the price of pumpkins at the local store which was 1½d less than the current ceiling price. She had become rather fond of pumpkin since she had been living in New Zealand and she supposed Christina might quite like a pumpkin mash for her dinner. Too late the realisation that she wouldn't be cooking Christina's meals anymore stole through her heart before she could stop it. She took a deep breath and examined a little pair of Jean's socks that had found their way in amongst Christina's clothing. They needed darning. She set them aside.

A toot on the road made her look up and she saw Hunter's aunties had arrived to watch Jean. They were very kind Ruth thought, when really they had every right to be angry with her. Instead they seemed to understand and support her. She hoped so anyway. They gave her some last minute details about the fostering couple whom Ruth and Hunter were going to meet in about an hour's time. That is if Hunter ever turned up. The aunties assured Ruth that they would keep in close contact with the people.

Despite the cool overcast day, there happened to be a lot of activity to watch in the Domain when Hunter parked the car with the three of them in it. The United States temporary Naval Barracks was being removed building by building and the place was full of workers and lorries. In contrast, the area surrounding the Wintergardens' duck pond with its temperate glasshouse at one end and the tropical glasshouse at the other, appeared relatively quiet. They waited in their car until eventually an elegant Singer 9 saloon pulled up alongside.

Ruth sat with Christina on her knee and watched warily. The first to leap from the car was the driver, a smiling man in his mid-30s that could well be Duncan. He was dressed extremely smartly in a tweed sports coat and carefully pressed trousers, shirt and tie. Rather incongruously, he wore a green marled Scottish bonnet on his head.

"That's them, I think," Hunter said getting out of the car.

Ruth stayed put and clung to her daughter.

The driver opened the passenger doors and helped out first a woman who was equally fashionable. Her smooth H-line skirt had a contrasting jacket with severe pleats dropping from a belted waist. She wore a long set of beads, heels and gloves but no hat. Her trim figure and immaculately set strawberry blonde hair made Ruth, in her cotton sun dress and sensible shoes, feel undeniably frumpy.

Ruth watched the woman smoothing down her pleats as if that mattered, while the man was simultaneously greeting Hunter and opening the rear doors for two elderly women. The mother's no doubt.

Soon they had all shook hands and as a single unit they turned to look at Ruth and the baby. There was nothing for it, Ruth would have to get out of the car.

"This is Ruth and Christina," Hunter announced, opening the door for them.

"Funny name for a Presbyterian child," the sternest of the two elderly women stated.

"Mother," Duncan warned. "Hello Ruth, we're so very sorry to hear of your predicament."

"Hello Ruth dear," his glamorous wife said. "I'm Betty. We're very thankful for the chance to be foster-parents. Aren't we Duncan?"

"Absolutely, my dear"

"You are aware it will only be board for six months or so," Ruth said. "Are you sure you know how to look after a child?" Ruth regretted her words as soon as they slipped out. She saw Betty's face fall visibly.

"Well really!" The sterner of the two older women turned heel and returned to the vehicle in a huff.

"I'm sure they'll manage, and we'll be there to help," the other elderly woman said kindly.

"We understand how hard this is for you. I know you wanted to have her back in the weekends, but it's a very long drive and we just feel it would be very unsettling," Duncan said.

"Yes, we've discussed that and we want whatever's best," Hunter agreed. "But I'd like to receive progress reports occasionally. Even once Ruth has left for England, I'd like to be able to visit."

"Of course you can," Duncan said. "And we don't mind posting an occasional letter and snapshot to England, if you'll give us an address Ruth."

"No!" Ruth was alarmed. "Absolutely not, you mustn't contact me. They won't write to me in England, will they Hunter?"

"It would be very awkward for Ruth to receive letters from New Zealand. Her husband doesn't even know she has been here," Hunter explained to the startled couple.

"Oh?" Betty sniffed. "As you wish. Well we shall wait until either Hunter or yourself want to contact us. Presumably we'll hear from you when the time comes for your return?"

"Yes. I'll wire Hunter's aunties and they will contact everyone," Ruth said.

"Well then…" Betty held out her arms.

Ruth froze.

"Come on Ruth. This is what *you* wanted, remember?" Hunter said. Ruth was under no illusions. She knew he still held out hope that she'd change her mind at the last minute.

"This is not what I want. But I feel like I've been dealt a very bad hand. Just give me a minute, please. I'll just walk through the Wintergardens and say my goodbye in private."

Worried looks passed between the three who wanted to take the child. They began to wonder if Ruth was about to change her mind.

Hunter was worried too. He was still holding onto hope that Ruth would change her mind. Now he was realising that she was really prepared to go through with it. For the umpteenth time he wondered how she could live with herself.

Ruth pulled open the door to the Temperate House and walked through to the duck pond, pointing out the koi that swum in it.

"Darling girl. It's just like boarding school. I'll see you for your first birthday in a few weeks' time, but then I'm going to sail on a big boat. You have to understand it takes me a long time to sail on a big boat, so you have to be patient. And those very nice people will look after you. And daddy will visit whenever he can. Just remember mummy loves you and Jean loves you and I'll be thinking about you every single day until we see you again." She meant every word.

"Daddy's boat?" Christina asked.

"No, not daddy's boat. Mummy has to go on a great big ship."

"Kwisina go too?"

"No my darling. You are going to have a lovely holiday with that pretty lady. And daddy will visit you sometimes."

She paused as she realised that she had already walked full circuit. She stood in front of the glasshouse door and saw them all staring back in her direction. Waiting. Watching. Judging. Full of their own thoughts. *This is it,* Ruth decided. *Be brave.*

"Who loves you sweetie-pie?"

"Ma-ma."

"That's right. Mummy loves you. Kiss? Now be a good girl for mummy. Big smiles."

Christina's smile only faltered for a second as Betty gratefully took her into her arms. It soon returned, after she was handed a biscuit to suck.

Hunter and Ruth took the chance to dash back to their car. Ruth wound down the window to wave, just in time to hear Christina begin to scream in panic as she fully realised that her parents were leaving without her.

In mid-July, a steamer arrived into Auckland and Ruth had secured a cabin on it. The Themistocles was due to leave the following day and Ruth could not put off the inevitable any longer.

Just three people stood on the wharf to wave good bye to Ruth and Jean. From the deck above, Jean waved her white handkerchief. Ruth caught Hunter's eyes and saw the seething look of disbelief and anger in them. She had hoped he would understand, would let her leave in peace with his support. Evidently, he was unable to do that. Auntie Margaret was crying and Auntie Millicent was alternately waving back at Jean and blowing her nose.

24
SINGAPORE AUGUST 1945

CHARLIE COLE

On the 26 August 1945, morning Tenko began the day at the Sime Road Internee and PoW camp as usual. There was however a few differences between this Tenko and the 470 odd other morning tenkos the prisoners had endured since they had been moved from Changi to Sime Road Camp. The first was that as the prisoners stood waiting for the command to bow, there was an insistent buzzing of whispers floating up and down the lines. Usually silence was insisted upon. But today none of the guards said a word. The rumour mill had been particularly active in the past few weeks. Rumours had come and gone many times over the past three years and six-odd months of incarceration, but for the past few days they refused to be muted.

The second difference was that Charlie was present at this Tenko. He was still very ill, but was capable of walking and the team of medical prisoners knew from past experience that only those patients who were near death were excused from the daily roll call.

The third major difference was that Mr Collinge, the latest camp leader that the male prisoners had elected to represent their needs, and his assistant were standing beside the Commandant's translator.

Eventually the camp commandant, Captain Susuki, stepped up onto his wooden footstep, and paused while he focused his red rimmed eyes at the interpreter standing beside him.

The interpreter gave the command "Naore" for the prisoners to stop bowing. As one, they lifted their shoulders, but still kept their eyes trained on the ground. This was something they had all learned to do when in the presence of a Japanese soldier, especially a high ranking one. To appear to be staring at the ground, while in reality keeping an eye on the person who was addressing them, was a vital skill to master if one wanted to avoid punishment.

And then something unheard of happened. The Commandant bowed to the prisoners. It was so outlandish, so unexpected, so frighteningly worrisome that they had no idea how to react.

One or two internees even twisted slightly to see if there was a more senior Japanese officer, such as General Saito, standing behind them. The whispering increased by a notch.

The Commandant issued a loud order in Japanese and many prisoners jerked their eyes towards the interpreter to hear his version. But the interpreter stayed silent. Instead, all the other Japanese soldiers, lay down their rifles and bowed to the prisoners.

By now, the whispers had developed into low chatter.

"Is it over? Is this it?"

"It's a trick. Don't fall for it. We'll be standing here all day."

"Maybe the Emperor himself is here. He might be having another birthday."

"Why have they laid down their arms? Why are they allowing all this chatter?"

Charlie kept his dull eyes on the ground. He could hear the voices, but he did not attempt to join in. His only thoughts were of keeping on his feet. Keeping alive. Getting back to his sleeping mat.

After a long pause, the Commandant stood upright and watched the chattering prisoners for a moment longer. Then he uttered a single sentence in halting English.

"The wrar is ovrar!"

There was a stunned silence, and none of the prisoners made a sound. They needed more than these four words. Who had won, for example. They looked to the translator hopefully.

The translator looked to the Commandant for instructions, but the senior man merely stepped down from his wooden box and walked towards the women's compound. The other soldiers melted away in the same direction.

"Yasume!" the translator gave the word for the prisoners to be dismissed. Then picking up the commandant's step-box, he too hurried after Susuki.

All that remained were the camp leaders. The two of them walked towards the hospital hut and made their way to the top of the steps. The prisoners, broke ranks and followed them like a gang of ragtag dogs, surrounding the hospital hut in a wide semi-circle.

Charlie also made his way to the hospital hut. His head was spinning from the activity and excited hum all around him. He wanted to get in to his bed, but the kindly camp leader stopped him.

"Sit here, Cole," he said indicating the bottom step. "You'll want to hear this."

"People! Hush now. People, do you want to hear me out or not?"

There were shushes from the crowd.

"Captain Susuki has informed us that Japan surrendered to the Allies about 10 days ago."

His speech was interrupted by wild cheering and semi-naked skeletal figures doing little jigs. All around men began hugging each other. Tears traced dirty paths down hollow cheeks. The few that had woven themselves native style hats tossed these into the air as though school was out.

"Alright boys, alright! Quiet!"

It took a while for the men to settle down.

"We've been informed that the Commandant and his men are from this moment no longer in charge of the camp. Again hoots and hollers sounded.

"However! Shoosh, yes, yes, yes. However, as we have nowhere to go from here, because there may still be Japanese soldiers outside these gates who do not accept the surrender and because we do not know how the natives will react, we are to stay inside this camp until the Allies come to relieve us."

These last words were largely lost in the boos and angry voices. The prisoners had had enough. Just as liberation seemed likely, Collinge was seemingly betraying them by saying they had to stay in this hell hole longer than necessary.

"Alright, I understand your frustration. People listen. The Japanese guards will be guarding the perimeter fence against any marauding groups. Their job will be to keep people out, not to keep you in. There'll be no more punishments. From what I've been told, the general populace out there is very unsettled. It might be best if we take their offer."

"What about our families?" a lone voice called out.

"The women will be able to come and go between the camps. Families can be reunited. There will even be opportunities for small groups of armed people to go into Singapore for supplies. But, as I say, please be patient. Await for the official surrender. Let's wait for the Red Cross to come and help us."

The rest of his speech was drowned out as the crowd dispersed into little groups to discuss the situation.

Before long, the hated Japanese flag was torn down from the flag pole and burned in the compound. Then from through the trees, women and children came tearing into camp. Names were called out as hundreds of desperate families tried to locate each other.

"Has anyone seen Benjamin Farrell?"

"Fraser Wilcox?"

"You'll find Tom Jackson in the hospital hut, over there."

Women who had stayed brave to the last, collapsed in distress at hearing their husbands had died in captivity.

Men were reunited with orphaned children, who may as well have been strangers.

Boys as young as ten, shyly greeted their mothers, unsure if they could cling to her legs in joy or if they needed to remain staunch, the single trait that had ensured their survival amongst the adult men.

Nobody noticed Charlie slip away to his bed. In his heart he *was* pleased but he didn't have the energy to demonstrate his elation yet. He knew he had to remain patient for a while longer. It would take a few weeks for his wife to come from Colombo or Australia, if that was where she was. He needed to save his energy for his reunion.

In fact, it didn't take long before the camps in Singapore were relieved. British troops arrived on 5th September and by the 10th the first 100 civilian internees had boarded hospital ships for Colombo. In the following days over 1,500 people had left for home either on repatriation leave or permanently.

"All I want to know, is why isn't my wife here yet?" Charlie exploded for the fourth time in as many hours to the dismayed young woman in front of him.

"Mr Cole…"

"Sergeant Cole. I'm a god-be-damned police officer in His Majesty's god-be-damned service."

"Sergeant Cole then. It is completely out of the question for your wife to come here. Singapore does not have resources for women and children to reunite here. Shipping is difficult besides anything else. Every bed in town is full. There's hardly enough food to feed all the troops and internees not to mention the locals."

"But you're here. You're a woman."

"Yes, but I'm a RAPWI staff member. Ordinary citizens are not allowed in except for essential services."

"RAPWI! What does that stand for eh? *Retain-All-Prisoners-Of-War-*

Indefinitely? That's what I heard! That's what I think!"

"Well I'm glad you've still got a sense of humour."

"Why can't I go home yet?" Charlie ignored her. He was beginning to bellow. "Others are leaving all the time. Armstrong was flown out last week."

"Well I don't know who Armstrong is. But you are not well enough to go anywhere. There's no point in nagging like a child. I'm afraid you'll just have to be patient."

"I've been a patient for the past year and a half. I've had a guts full," he said, using the new slang term that he had heard his fellow prisoner's utilise many times.

"Have you received a telegram from your wife yet? That's the first step."

"No. I bloody well haven't. I don't even know if she's alive. I sent a telegram to my folks in Australia and they replied that she had never turned up. Last they heard she was in New Zealand, god knows why." Here he fell into a fit of choking tears that overwhelmed his ravaged body.

The inexperienced young volunteer awkwardly tried to comfort him. "Many evacuees were sent to New Zealand, I believe. I'll get a Red Cross volunteer up here and see if they can locate her." When she had rocked him to silence, she leaned him back to his pillow to rest.

Charlie withdrew into himself a little more. He knew these people were trying to help, but they just didn't understand. He was fast learning that displays of emotion didn't help his cause at all. They just embarrassed everyone.

He also knew that he was supposed to consider himself relatively lucky for being housed at the Raffles Hotel in his own bedroom wearing his new pale blue and white striped pyjamas. The majority of the other internees were still at Sime Road Camp in a scarecrow assortment of rags. But because he was dangerously underweight, they had moved him and a few of his fellow internees into these better accommodations where, he felt, they could be watched like goldfish in a glass bowl.

Charlie hated his pillows and his soft mattress. The food was too rich and the looks of annoyance he received when he only picked at his meal were only eclipsed by the looks of shock that crossed every single one of the faces that came to view him for the first time. Weighing less than 6 ½ stone, they seemed to marvel that he could be so skeletal and yet survive. Charlie was certainly one of the skinniest survivors, possibly due to his continual sickness. Although his predilection to sickness could equally be attributed to his lack of decent nutrition. The Japanese had a policy of refusing food rations to those who weren't able to do a minimum of four hours work a day.

"Animals have to work for their food, and so do you," was the common refrain from their captors, who showed no mercy for those who weren't able to work due to illness. The other prisoners of course divvied up their rations between everyone in the camps, but obviously, if you were laying in the hospital, you got less than those who weren't. And less of not much, amounted to insufficient nutrition.

Charlie looked at the plump bodies of his rescuers and felt sickened in return. He had become accustomed to his own body and everyone else around him in camp had looked only degrees better or worse. Even the Japanese guards had lost a lot of weight in the last year, as the grip of war had affected their supplies.

He was beginning to think of himself as nothing more than a walking skeleton; a rattling collection of worthless bones.

There was one delegation in particular, that made him feel useless. A man and a women had been trying to interview him, asking questions about his time in the Kempei prisons. Charlie wanted to exact revenge on those evil perpetrators, but he wasn't yet ready to explore the depths of those hateful days.

Whenever he did attempt to describe something, like his time in the bamboo cage for instance, the necessary words would fail him. His body trembled at the first onslaught of memories and then it shook with the frustration of not being able to find the suitable descriptions. It annoyed him to inadequately label his experiences. Just when he had composed himself, a face would pop into his mind of someone who had died, a woman who had been defiled, a dead child bobbing about in the waves. The resulting spasms of pain would render the interview at an end for another day. He sometimes thought they'd keep him in this once-luxurious hotel until he managed to give the evidence they were looking for. They had a certain amount of urgency in their requests because of the mounting war crimes trials and they wanted to document the crimes while they were still fresh. Whereas Charlie felt he had buried those days already. The pressure on his already burdened shoulders was too heavy. So they'd leave him alone for hours. Then with the space to think he would find himself ready to say something worthwhile, only there was nobody around to hear him. Just four white walls, enclosing him in a gilded cage of sorts.

He wanted desperately to go home. Back to his little bungalow at Sembawang. When he asked about the possibility, he was informed that there was little left of the naval base. What hadn't been destroyed by the retreating naval force, had been looted and destroyed by the Japanese and even the desperate locals had resorted to ransacking properties in their attempt to stay alive during the long war years. Whatever was left was being requisitioned and was unavailable at present.

He asked about his personal possessions and was told they would look into it. Always the same non-committal answers. It seemed to Charlie that they wanted answers from him, but weren't prepared to return the same courtesy.

Always at the back of his mind was a vexation that he couldn't quite resolve. The letter he had received from his parents for one thing. It hadn't said much. But it was what it didn't say, rather than what it did, that worried him. Their choice of words had a negative ring. He couldn't dismiss the nagging feeling that his wife had done something or moved on perhaps. There had been no letters from her in camp. None at all. Whereas there had been a round of mail that arrived a good six months before the Nips surrendered. Most of the other fellows had received something. Some had got a whole pile of belated letters.

He was feeling very let down by everyone, including Armstrong who Charlie felt had abandoned him. Such was Charlie's inward-looking frame of mind.

And yet bit by bit the good food and hygiene were beginning to have a positive effect on him. He had already put on about $1/12^{th}$ his body weight. His eyes had recovered to the point that he was now able to make sense of newspapers.

Prisoners from all parts of the Far East were flooding into Singapore. Some of these had suffered dreadfully, especially those in outlying islands from the Philippines to Borneo. In comparison they were saying that Sime Road had been almost comfortable. *How lucky I was*, he thought sarcastically. Every week they were finding new secret camps of prisoners that local commandants had not even registered with Tokio High Command.

The business of repatriation was apparently a massive operation. Repatriation ships were packed so tightly with civilians returning to England, that they were often only a fraction better than the slave ships of old. Charlie's rheumy eyes read with interest a group of internees who had walked off one ship in disgust at the lack of sanitation, food, accommodations and limited air circulation that they'd be expected to endure during the long passage up through the Red Sea on their way "home." These would-be passengers had returned to what was now known as the "Sime Road Holiday and Transit Centre" in protest. Still, it seemed the majority of people were only too keen to take any transport off the settlement as quickly as possible.

Those that had lived in Malaya all their lives, were attempting to find jobs and reclaim some of what they'd left behind. They found themselves saddled with the requirement of paying back their camp loans incurred during their incarceration and worse their recuperation costs afterwards. The government's offer to assist in any way possible seemed to be £1 each, the equivalent of about five Singaporean dollars, and only if they remained in camp until they were officially released and processed. It was a minuscule amount considering the exorbitant rise in prices. Charlie almost felt guilty because, as a government employee, he was expecting to receive full pay for the entire three and a half years internment and he had worked out that it would amount to nearly £500. As well, his recuperation was being fully funded by the British government as would his repatriation leave. He still felt incredibly angry, but bit by bit, as he read the other letters to the editors of the various papers, he began to come out of his shell.

About a week after his last outburst, a RAPWI (Recovery of Allied Prisoners of War and Internees) representative visited with the news that he was well enough to leave in the morning on the ship *Nieuw Holland* bound for Liverpool.

"You'll be home in time for Christmas," the man said expecting a joyous response.

"Where's home? My home is here in Malaya." Charlie sounded disinterested.

"Well on that score, I also have a telegram for you, from your wife." He placed a thin yellow sheet onto Charlie's lap. There was no envelope, it was simply folded in half with the address details written on the back.

Charlie dropped his eyes to the page. With trembling hands, he picked it up and read the handwritten message out loud, unable to contain a patina of sarcasm encrusting the words.

> "SO GLAD TO HEAR YOU ARE ALIVE AFTERALL STOP JEAN AND I ARE WELL STOP STAYING WITH MY AUNTIES IN BEARSTED STOP LET ME KNOW YOUR MOVEMENTS STOP LOVE RUTH"

"What's all this *STOP* business?"

"Oh that?" the man sounded surprised. "It simply replaces the punctuation for the period. Since the war started, the government has ordered its use. Surely you remember in the last year or so before The Fall?"

"No I don't. Everything has changed," Charlie said angrily. "Do I have to wear these pyjamas down to the wharf?"

"Well, I can see if any spare clothing can be rustled up. Happen, it's one of the things we are short of." Noting Charlie's irritated expression, he tried to be cheerful. "Try to keep your tail up chum. I can jot down your reply and send it down to the post office for you now if you like."

"No need to bother yourself."

"You ought to let her know your arrangements."

"I said no!"

The *Nieuw Holland* arrived at Port Aden ahead of schedule. During refuelling, Charlie was encouraged to walk around the lido deck and sit beside the swimming pool. He hardly recognised anyone on board. He barely even recognised the ship, despite having travelled on it twice pre-War. In those days, it had taken 150 paying passengers. Now there were over 1,000 grateful souls on board, not counting the crew.

Hobbling towards the pool, he came upon a drinks table. These offered tea, coffee or slightly warm water and a plain sweet biscuit. The mess rooms were unable to serve morning and afternoon teas because the lengthy meal sessions caused them to be in almost continual use. As a work around, drink stations had been set up in areas around the deck. Charlie took a proffered cup of coffee and continued his painfully slow walk towards the pool, passing rows of occupied deck chairs. As luck would have it, one of these was vacated at the precise moment he passed, and he managed to slide into it before anybody else could.

Laying in the sunshine, in his new pair of shorts and army issued shirt and hair-cut, he almost felt human again. As he sipped his coffee he began to think about life back home. For the hundredth time he wondered what his wife meant when she said in her telegram, 'Glad to hear you are alive—after-all.'

"After-all?" he sounded the word out on his tongue.

"What was that son?" an elderly man beside him asked.

"Don't mind me, talking to myself," Charlie muttered.

"We've all done a bit of that these past few years, I say we've all done a bit of that. Gorgeous weather what? I almost feel like dipping my toes into the…"

The ongoing conversation in Charlie's head drowned the man's words out. *After-all!* I'm pleased to hear you are alive. After! All! It was a strange thing to say. Most people would say something along the lines of 'Pleased to hear you are alive and well.' A slight difference maybe, but reading between the lines, he was sure he could hear a subtle hidden meaning in there. Had she thought him dead? The reasonable side of his brain tried to convince him he was being paranoid. But the other side of his brain could not ignore the tone of resentment in the words, as if she wanted him dead.

He supposed she had been living the high-life while he was incarcerated. What would she look like? Would she be horrified by the sight of him? Probably. He imagined he'd be able to tell if his scarecrow looks repulsed her, the moment she saw him. He'd have to watch her reaction closely before she could disguise it. Before she plastered a fake smile on her face, just like the horrified RAPWI and Red Cross workers who had taken him from the hospital at Sime Road camp.

Tears began to tug at the corners of his eyes. He blinked them closed, trying to hold down the lump that was building in his chest.

Perhaps he fell asleep, because when he opened his eyes, the ship was moving up the stream towards the Suez Canal. Pulling his stiff joints to the ship's rails, he leaned out to watch. The distant shoreline slid past, untouched and unexplored by those on board. The last three years of his life was just like that shoreline, he reflected. There had to have been a reason for his personal sacrifice, for the years he lost. He had to believe that his family were waiting for him back home. That after everything he'd been through, he'd have a happy-ever-after ending. By tomorrow the ship would be back in Europe, a mere ten days from Liverpool.

"Will the nightmare be over or will it just be beginning?" he whispered to himself.

Several days later the *Nieuw Holland* anchored in Liverpool Bay. The following morning, she was due to berth at the Prince's Landing Stage. But as it happened, thick fog kept them out—the pilot unwilling to risk the journey across the Mersey bar.

News on board was that the local dockers were out on strike. Apparently 200 soldiers were trying to pick up the slack and the word was it wouldn't affect the off-loading of passengers.

The Officer Commanding the Ship, used the extra time to reiterate the disembarkation instructions to those aboard. Different instructions were given depending on which regiment they belonged to or whether they were Commonwealth citizens or ordinary British civilians. Charlie was to be looked after by the navy. He'd be free to leave the special disembarkation camp within a day or two.

After repeating these lengthy instructions, the OC warned them all not to speak about the atrocities inflicted upon them by their Japanese captors. He reminded them that the sons, husbands and fathers of many families would not be coming home. It would only add to their suffering to hear the horrific details of their loved ones' deaths. He also painted the story of one soldier on an earlier repatriation ship who had given the press his name and parent's address.

"The following week the soldier's family were inundated with people telephoning, writing and turning up at all hours, trying to ask if he had met their family member from the same camp; wanting to know if they had any information on how they had died, etc. The poor fellow could never get a moment's peace. In the end the family resorted to shutting up house and going away to the seaside. So I am warning all of you," the OC said, "don't make the same mistake as that poor chap. Put a soft pedal on the horrors you've seen."

The ship was finally guided in at about midday. All along the river, the repatriates were greeted with a fanfare of ship's horns, hoots and cheers. Charlie was not expecting to see anyone he knew. So still in a funk of sorts, he stood at the back of the less crowded 01 level, feeling a bit out of it all. The excited bunch of people in front of him were moving around, some jumping up onto the life-boat struts to see better. As the fluid group tried to get the best view, Charlie unintentionally found himself at the front. He gripped the smooth wooden rail for support and watched, mesmerised by the interest the mercy ship had created. There were ferries and small craft ringing bells and hooting their fog horns whilst criss-crossing the river or simply milling about.

As they came alongside, he could see literally hundreds of people waiting in the cold to welcome them in. Many were waving hankies and gloves. Banners and naval flags were dripping from every structure right across the Pier Head. Before they had even docked, Charlie could see a brass band start to play. Possibly of the South Lancashire Regiment by the looks of them. The familiar notes of *Long Way to Tipperary* floated across to him. This was followed by a rousing *Take me Back to Dear Old Blighty* as they came in close.

After those two choruses, while the ship was being made secure, the band gave a full rendition of *Land of Hope and Glory*, during which a respectful silence fell upon the crowd. This led naturally into an official welcome from the Mayor of Liverpool speaking into microphones. The formalities passed quickly and suddenly the passengers began disembarking with their army issue kitbags full of new uniform, or in the case of civilians, donated clothing that they had been allocated while stopped in Alexandria. Beyond the gangway, tables were set up laden full of cigarettes and chocolate free for the taking as they filed past. All the while the band played *Down at the Old Bull and Bush*.

"I suppose the band will play *Pack Up Your Troubles In Your Old Kit Bag* next," Charlie said grumpily to a young navy-man behind him.

"I hope they do. They've been wonderful," the fellow gushed unabashedly as they moved off the landing platform up onto the pier. A moment later two women rushed towards the man, his sisters Charlie guessed. The crowd parted again to allow an older woman, presumably his mother, to get to him. She enveloped him in her ursine arms. Pausing to watch the touching reunion, Charlie could see that she was overjoyed, her sodden handkerchief dabbing at her eyes and nose was proof enough.

A sudden chill gripped his shoulders. Why hadn't he sent word to his own wife to meet him? He wanted a reunion like that. Then he realised that she wouldn't have come all the way up to Liverpool anyway, because of course, it would make more sense to meet him in London off the train.

The queue of disembarking passengers pushed Charlie forward and he lost sight of the unknown man who had found his family already. Within 10 minutes, Charlie found himself on an army lorry being driven to a nearby camp.

25
WATERLOO STATION OCTOBER 1945

RUTH COLE

Ruth pulled the telegram back out of her purse to read it for the umpteenth time.

ARRIVED IN LIVERPOOL YESTERDAY STOP MEET ME AT EUSTON STATION MONDAY AFTERNOON STOP CHARLIE

It was very abrupt, she reflected. The only date on it was the Telegraph Office stamp. So presumably he was talking about this particular Monday. She chewed her top lip, taking off the coating of new red lipstick that she had applied especially. She stuck out her neck continually, straining to catch a first glimpse of any approaching trains.

"When is daddy coming?" Jean asked her mother, jiggling her legs impatiently.

Ruth looked at her sharply. She had explained that her *real* father was coming home from war today, but the way she was referring to him as *daddy* made her wonder if she really understood.

She was about to remind her again not to talk about her New Zealand daddy, but Jean took to sneezing.

"My throat is dusty," she explained adding a few extra sneezes for effect.

It was true, Ruth could see in the shafts of light that streamed through the rafters that the air was laden with dust. They had been waiting for ages and several trains had come in from the north-west, but none of them held PoWs.

Ruth had read that all of the PoW ships were coming into either Liverpool or Southampton and inevitably many of these soldiers would arrive in London by trains put on especially for them. From here they simply needed to embark on a forwarding train. Just like the telegram service to and from repatriated PoWs was free, so was the transport to take them home.

The platform was becoming dangerously crowded. Ruth was of a mind to hold onto her daughter's shoulders for fear of losing her. She saw a refreshment trolley edging onto the platform a bit further along and decided a cold drink and piece of cake could be just what Jean needed to keep her going and clear her throat. With the volume of people, it was doubtful that the trolley would be pushed along the platform for any distance and Ruth expected it to be sold out before long anyway. She'd have to get there quickly, so holding Jean's hand, she pulled her through to a space under one of the large archways. As she had suspected, by the time she got there the man had run out of nearly everything.

"There's a tea room just around the corner," he suggested to Ruth.

With one last look down the tracks and seeing no sign of a train, Ruth decided to take a break from the platform and go in search of food. Twenty minutes later, they both needed the ladies room, which took some finding.

When they headed back to the platform, they could see the crowd had thinned significantly.

Ruth shyly approached a happy little group, which included a uniformed man with a kitbag over his shoulder, to ask if the Special from Liverpool had come in.

"Yes it did, quite a quarter hour ago," was the response from one of the young women.

Ruth and Jean walked the length of the platform, but there was no sign of Charlie. Now she didn't know what to do. He might be on a later train, she thought. Or he might be wandering around the train station looking for her. She decided to check the concourse. Enquiring at the ticket office, she was told that the only PoW train expected today had come and gone. She began to head down to the lower platforms which linked the station to London's Underground network.

"Ruth?"

The man's voice barely carried over the general din, but it made her heart hammer out a double beat in recognition. She spun around, searching for its source. It could only have come from a stooped man standing several yards away beside the arrivals' board. She squinted her eyes against the bright light coming through the roof windows. It could be him. She found herself walking towards him and only checked herself when Jean's tiny hand still clasped inside her own pulled taut. She stopped, uncertain, but as every half second ticked away it was becoming more apparent that it was him. He was expressionless, but his eyes held hers tightly in surveillance.

"Charlie?" Ruth questioned.

"Ruth! You're running late I take it?"

"No, I um... By god Charlie, is that really you?"

"Well yes, erm yes. Of course it is. Have you forgotten me already?"

"You look, so—thin—so tired." She was standing in front of him now and she reached out to touch his drawn cheek bone.

He automatically pulled his head away from her touch and she let her hand drop into the space between them.

She only remembered Jean hiding behind her skirt, when he dropped stiffly to his knees and held out his arms for the child. Ruth could feel Jean clinging to her leg and when she looked down, she saw her peeping out from behind.

"I suspect you don't remember me, but I remember you precious," Charlie said.

His voice was all wrong, Ruth thought. You can't talk to a child like that and expect a result. But she said nothing, standing frozen in tumult, while Ruth watched the scene play out with both dread and morbid fascination. Charlie was ploughing on ahead, apparently oblivious to the child's distress.

"It's daddy. I'm home. Come and give me a hug. Come on little Lovie."

Eventually, he looked up at Ruth. "What's wrong with her?"

"Ah..." Ruth had no idea how to answer that, but she was interrupted by Jean.

"You're not my daddy. My daddy is in New Zealand with our baby."

Ruth felt her feet and hands instantly become clammy with perspiration. She wasn't aware of much else at that moment, except that it took Charlie a long time to regain his feet and look at her with an accusatory look of question.

It wasn't that Ruth wanted to hide the fact from him forever. It was just that she had ideally thought she'd like him to settle in first. Or at least to be at home. She didn't want to do this here. Not in the middle of a public railway station.

She took a deep breath and lied.

"Oh, she's just talking about the nice neighbour we had, and his little girl. He often took Jean off my hands for a few hours so I could earn some money." Ruth dared to glance down at Jean, only to find her disconcertingly glaring at Charlie. "Give her time Charlie."

Ruth could hardly bare to look at her husband, but when he didn't give a verbal reply, she found herself needing to re-check his countenance. His eyes seemed to have almost withdrawn into the deeply recessed sockets. He was a closed shop, giving no clue as to his thoughts. Was this cold man, who hadn't even given her a hug, really her loving husband? Yes she recognised him, despite his twisted, jaundiced appearance. But what had happened to him, to them?

"Come on, we've got to take the tube to Victoria." She attempted to link arms with him and, surprisingly, he allowed this. Gradually, the tightness in her shoulders relaxed and later on the train he even allowed her to rest her head on his shoulder. She began to believe that everything would be OK.

The days following went by in a blur. There was so much that Charlie had missed out on. He knew very little about the war and he knew nothing about the privations that the population had suffered. Ruth on the other hand, had spent the past two months living with her aunties who had regaled her with the miseries they had put up with, so she was well versed in life in south-east England.

Ruth tried to ask him about the origins of his many scars and he told her little snippets here and there. He often began to tell her, but then left her hanging with unanswered questions. It sounded absolutely dreadful and she wanted—needed rather—to know more.

They only ate a light supper at the kitchen table that first evening, but the following night the aunties prepared a sumptuous dinner in the dining room. Charlie's appetite had largely returned, but he was still only able to manage small portions in his shrunken stomach. He soon recognised the irritation written across the aunties faces when he served himself a very small serving and refused second helpings.

Ruth asked Charlie to tell the aunties about some of his experiences that she had discussed with him that morning, hoping he would expand on his explanations with a larger audience. But he had hardly even scratched the surface of his tales when the aunties told him that it wasn't suitable dinner time talk and for that matter it wasn't the sort of thing ladies should hear about at any time. They even insisted that he wouldn't burden their niece with these disturbing images that no young lady should possess in her mind.

Ruth gave Charlie a look, which she hoped he would read to mean that they'd talk later. For one reason or another, they found little time to discuss anything of any great importance. Charlie had shopping to do in Maidstone. He required a suit for church on Sunday and a decent pair of shoes. His brand new ration book was immediately depleted and he realised how fortunate he had been to have been set up with most of the clothing he'd need in Colombo and Port Said.

Jean had started school shortly after arriving in England but was taking time in settling in. Ruth was called in to help in the "babies" room as they called the five year olds. So she was often occupied. After walking her to school, Charlie explored the village and frequented the White Horse pub. He wasn't much of a drinker and he was never there of an evening. Rather he visited during its quiet times when he could sit by himself and think. Ruth supposed it was more pleasant than being at the aunties' beck and call all day. She knew that they were want to spend their mornings in their extensive cottage garden which almost grew wild and they had no end of jobs for Charlie to help with. They seemed to think the fresh air and lifting would build up his strength again.

Quite the contrary, Ruth knew it often sapped his strength, so she never harangued Charlie for his time away from the family. In fact, some days in those first few weeks, he seemed to spend the entire day away. Knowing that the local pubs did not open early in the morning, she often wondered where he went.

On about the second or third week after his arrival, Charlie received a letter from his solicitor in Maidstone.

"I didn't know we had a solicitor in Maidstone," Ruth remarked after reading the letter.

"Yes, yes we do," Charlie replied blandly. "I approached them to look into our various interests. You know our property in Singapore and such."

"Oh! Well I guess that makes sense," Ruth said. "And so they want to see us on Friday? I guess they have news then?"

"Possibly. I suggest we catch the train in immediately after dropping Jean at school."

A couple of days later, Ruth and Charlie were shown into the slightly shabby boardroom of their new lawyers' rooms. Ruth was directed to sit in a club chair positioned along one length of the table. The chair was an awkward shape, low to the ground and she felt like she could barely move her arms. Charlie on the other hand, was put on a wooden dining chair, at the head of the table. Two solicitors, presumably, sat directly across from Ruth, both in matching carver chairs. It was an odd set-up and Ruth's intuition was screaming warnings to her.

The moment the secretary left the room, one of the solicitors slapped a folder onto the table in front of Ruth, without even welcoming the couple or introducing themselves.

She was so taken aback that she looked at Charlie in astonishment. He did not seem to share her shock, but instead was looking intently at the folder. Ruth was unable to catch his eye.

"Open the folder and tell me what you see," one solicitor said.

"Who me?" she asked.

"Yes, Mrs Cole. Just as I said. Would you please do as you are told."

With her hands shaking, completely unsure of whether the folder contained good news or something awful, she flipped over the cover of the folder. The first thing she saw was a British passport. She knew, without looking inside, that it was hers and contained stamps going to and from New Zealand. Sliding it to the side with the barest touch, she saw a small framed photograph of Jean and Christina together. It was a proper portrait which Hunter had arranged at a studio in Auckland. She knew the back contained the inscription, "to my love, from Hunter." Underneath the framed picture were a tiny bundle of snapshots. She didn't need to untie the ribbon to know that they were holiday shots, mostly taken by Hunter of her and Jean at Kawau Island, on the Pahiki and Christmas at Campbell's Bay. There were baby photos, one of Margaret and Millicent standing in their garden and photos of their holidays in the Waikato.

Ruth picked up the bundle and put them on her lap. *How dare they steal these things from her,* she thought. She felt cornered. Anger began bubbling up inside her. The last item in the folder was Christina's birth certificate. With both the mother and father listed.

Feeling like she was about to cry and being determined not to, Ruth blinked to hold back tears, but found her eyes were dry and gritty. She opened her mouth to speak, but nothing came out. There was a painful lump at the back of her throat and she shut her mouth again like a fish gulping air.

Keeping her trembling head facing the folder in front of her, she slid her eyes towards Charlie on her right. The bland face that she had become accustomed to these past few weeks now held a look of triumph. The bastard! He had planned this. Obviously. He had wheeled her in and she had been caught on the end of his line and now she hang there dangling. Darn it all, she wasn't going to speak first.

"We asked you a simple question. What do you see?" the solicitor asked coldly.

"I see some of my personal items, which have been taken from my aunties home without my, or their, permission," Ruth said as evenly as she could.

"So you don't deny these are yours then?" the solicitor asked.

"Of course I don't."

"So you don't deny that you have been caught in an adulterous affair?"

"Yes I do."

"Come now, Mrs Cole. Even a woman of your, er … lack of education, must realise that you can't possibly deny it."

"I was told that he was dead. Dead!" she screamed at her husband. "I was left in India with no money—none whatsoever—a small child I couldn't feed—and war threatening the borders at any hour. I took the first allied ship to Australia, planning on asking your sister for help."

"But instead you shacked up with the first man you met?" the solicitor asked.

"No, it wasn't like that. Your sister wasn't there," Ruth said angrily, ignoring the solicitor and speaking directly to Charlie. "She had moved away with no forwarding address. I wrote to your parents but they never replied. I was a pauper. Unable to work because I had a child. Unable to access our bank account. Unable to access any pension because they hadn't issued your death certificate."

"But surely you must have realised that if they hadn't issued a death certificate there was a reason for that. That perhaps there was still reasonable doubt about his hypothetical death. That perhaps you could have at least given him the benefit of doubt. At the very least waited until the end of the war before you began to see other men. Isn't that so, Mrs Cole?"

"No. You have no idea what it was like."

"Are you saying you had it worse than your husband? A man who was suffering at the hands of the Japanese, while you were playing the field?"

"I'm saying that there were witnesses to his death. They saw his motorcycle being blown apart. These were people who knew him well. How was I supposed to know that they'd made a mistake?"

"So why did you not tell your husband the truth when you reunited? Come now Mrs Cole, you've had almost three weeks."

"I was planning on telling you. But you haven't been well. We've barely had any time together. We haven't been intimate at all. I just wanted to wait until the time was right." Ruth was still feeling like she was on the back foot, losing a battle.

"Mr Cole has instructed us to inform you that under the circumstances he is willing to forgive and forget all of this. That is to say, everything in this folder. He is willing to continue to live with you as any normal husband and wife. Do you want this marriage to continue?"

"Of course I do. As soon as I heard he was alive, I made plans to return to England."

"Mr Cole has instructed us to inform you that he has a few conditions that must be met first."

"Then why doesn't Mr Cole speak to me himself?"

"Now, now Mrs Cole. There's no need to become hysterical. Let's try to keep this meeting cordial. Condition number one is easy. It's something that you probably will want yourself. You are to never speak of this *affair* again. To anybody. Am I clear?"

Ruth nodded. Inwardly she was fuming.

"Two: you are to surrender all rights to this illegitimate child. We can help there by organising an official adoption if that hasn't already been done..."

"No, I can't do that."

"Three, please don't interrupt. Three, everything in this folder and anything else you may have in your possession relating to your time in New Zealand is to be handed to us for destruction.

"And finally—four, you are never to contact or accept any contact from this fellow, what did you say his name was?"

"Mr Whitlock."

"Do you agree to those terms Mrs Cole?"

"No."

"No?"

"No, I don't. I refuse to give my daughter up for adoption. That's just inhumane and I do not give you permission to destroy the photographs. The other things I will assent to."

"This is not up for negotiation. Either you comply with all four criteria or we will apply for divorce on the grounds of adultery. But be aware, Mrs Cole, that should you choose to do that, you will lose all access to your eldest daughter, ah Jean Daisy Cole, on the grounds of desertion due to adultery."

"I'll get my own lawyer."

"With what monies, Mrs Cole? Your husband does not permit you to use his account book to conduct business with another lawyer."

"So I either have to give up one daughter or I give up the other? What sort of a choice is that?"

"It was your choice, when you chose to have an affair with another man, Mrs Cole."

"How much time do I have to decide?"

"We'd like you to decide now. You would hardly expect your husband to go on home with you, unsure whether you are living a double life or not, would you?"

"I want to keep at least one photograph of my baby."

"No Mrs Cole. The deal is you keep nothing. Think of it as a fresh start. A *clean* slate to re-start your married life upon."

"Can I at least send the photographs back to New Zealand. I won't send them to him. I'll send them to a couple of female friends of mine. People who knew me. The birth certificate and passport will need to go back anyway."

"Yes, that would be acceptable to our client. But we will arrange this for you. There is to be no communication, except from ourselves. If you'd be so kind as to write down an address for us of this man here and also the female person you'd like to send the photographs to. Then I'd like you to sign here, and here. We will advise your husband when the adoption is completed."

"I'd like to know…"

"That will be up to your husband, should he decide to share that information with you. Mrs Cole? The photographs please."

Ruth placed the stack of snapshots onto the table.

"That concludes our business today. We hope we can be of assistance to you in the future."

Ruth wanted to run from the place back to the solace of her aunties' house and ask for their help. Of course, she knew she couldn't. Her two elderly aunts would almost certainly side with Charlie. They would never ever understand. Neither would her father who had been extricated to Australia where he was stuck for the time being. She desperately wished that Margaret and Millicent lived nearby.

"I have some more news," Charlie said on the train in a voice that belied that he had ever just done what he had. "I've got a new job."

Ruth looked at him, but said nothing.

"Ruth, I demand that as my wife, you show some enthusiasm. Did you not just hear me?"

She nodded glumly.

"I've got a job at the Camp 40. It's a POW camp over in Tonbridge. I don't know how long it'll last before they send the Jerrys and I-ties home. But it is unlikely that my position will be reinstated in Singapore in the short term. They are doing something called restructuring. Yes that's what they called it I believe. They are restructuring the whole—well the whole structure of the naval base I guess."

He chatted on in a better mood than he had been since Ruth had reunited with him.

Ruth looked out the window of the train, but instead of seeing the scenery, she only saw an image in her mind's eye of her little girl crawling through an orchard after her four year old sister. The endless straight rows of citrus creating a road leading away from her heart.

26
EPILOGUE

Charlie struggled with ill health and malaria for the rest of his life. He suffered from mood-swings and his marriage was alternately stormy and happy. He did return with his family to Singapore to live and work, but did not stay long. He hated everything Japanese to the point of refusing to buy any Japanese imported car. Eventually though, I believe he came to terms with Japan, even visiting the country in later life.

Jean lived with the unsettling memory of a little sister that didn't quite add up in her mind, but she instinctively knew never to ask about it. She grew up, married happily and had children of her own.

Christina's foster parents eventually formally adopted her and she lived a happy, fun-filled life until her adopted father was diagnosed with lung cancer. He died when she was 14 after a long illness and only then did she discover that she was adopted. The secrecy continued with her questions remaining unanswered until the New Zealand adoption laws changed in 1985 and she was able to access her original birth certificate. She spent several years searching for her birth parents.

Hunter received occasional updates about his daughter, but remained aloof, respecting the adopting couple's desire not to complicate her life. Christina remembers when she was 11 years old being called into the principal's office. Thinking she was in trouble, she was confused when told the truancy officer wanted to look through all her school books. She had no idea that he was her father. He eventually received a divorce from his first wife and married a woman named Olive. They spent many happy years at Kawau Island together, where he purchased and expanded the fisherman's hut and planted an orchard. He died in 1966, just a year after Christina was married. The Pahiki was inherited by Olive, but sadly it was abandoned and sunk at Waiheke Island in Auckland's Hauraki Gulf and has now completely broken up and disappeared under the sands. Olive met with Christina and handed over some of the photographs that had been returned to Hunter in 1946.

Ruth stayed true to her promise to her husband not to contact her illegitimate daughter. She never spoke of it again, but thought about her most days. She went on to have more children and spent a lot of time travelling with her husband. The month after Charlie died in the late 1980s, she received a letter from Christina. She admitted that had it arrived just a few weeks earlier, she would not have answered it. They met a few times and corresponded regularly, until she passed away aged 95. She never saw Hunter again.

ABOUT THE AUTHOR

Ally McCormick lives in and grew up in rural Auckland, New Zealand. She has two daughters and coincidentally looks out at Kawau Island every day from her living room windows.
She works in public relations, where she writes copy for social media and occasionally printed media. Ally is a committed hobby-genealogist. She loves history and finds research to be liberating. She believes that the only way forward is to learn from the world's collective past. To that end, Ally is constantly discovering new things and taking lessons from the *University of Life*. This is her first published novel. You can find her on the Internet at: allymccormick.com.

2017 will mark the 75th anniversary since the Fall of Singapore.

The British Prime Minister, Winston Churchill, described the Fall of Singapore to the Japanese to be *"the worst disaster in British history."*

An estimated 61 million people were killed (on all sides) in WW2 and 10 million of them were Chinese civilians.

In Singapore, 160,000 Chinese were rounded up and stamped on their face, arms or clothing with either a square or a triangle denoting whether they were to be executed or not.

Between 18 February and 4 March 1942 alone, an estimated 70,000 Chinese in Singapore and mainland Malaya were executed by the Japanese in batches, including entire villages. Many were simply buried alive.

After capturing Singapore, the Japanese stormed Alexandra Hospital and murdered every patient, nurse, doctor and other personnel that they could find.

It is estimated there were between 250 - 500 POW/Civilian camps in the Japanese-held Far East.

The Tokyo Tribunal published the death rate of Western Prisoners held by the Japanese to be 27.1%

4,500 European civilians were released from their 3 year 8 month internment in 1945 in Singapore alone. Records do not tell how many died during their captivity.

The Tokyo Tribunal convicted Japanese military for the worst known instances of torture, medical experiments, starvation, rape, mass graves, mass executions, beheadings, death ships, death marches, genocide and cannibalism. Lesser crimes largely went unpunished.

Before Japan entered the war, they had signed the Hague Convention but not ratified it.

When Japan entered the war, Japanese civilians living in Allied countries were ostracised, rounded up, incarcerated in accordance with the Hague Convention and in many cases sent home on repatriation ships.

To date, Japan has never officially apologised to Commonwealth citizens, and neither admitted that it's treatment of British civilians was wrong, nor made reparation for looted personal property.

Printed in Poland
by Amazon Fulfillment
Poland Sp. z o.o., Wrocław